JAMES JOYCE: THE CRITICAL HERITAGE
VOLUME 1, 1907–27

THE CRITICAL HERITAGE SERIES

General Editor: B. C. Southam

The Critical Heritage series collects together a large body of criticism on major figures in literature. Each volume presents the contemporary responses to a particular writer, enabling the student to follow the formation of critical attitudes to the writer's work and its place within a literary tradition.

The carefully selected sources range from landmark essays in the history of criticism to fragments of contemporary opinion and little published documentary material, such as letters and diaries.

Significant pieces of criticism from later periods are also included in order to demonstrate fluctuations in reputation following the writer's death.

JAMES JOYCE
VOLUME 1, 1907–27

THE CRITICAL HERITAGE

Edited by

ROBERT H. DEMING

London and New York

First published in 1970
Reprinted in 1997 by Routledge

2 Park Square, Milton Park,
Abingdon, Oxon, OX14 4RN
&
270 Madison Ave,
New York NY 10016

Transferred to Digital Printing 2009

British Library Cataloguing in Publication Data

ISBN 0-415-15920-2 (set)
ISBN10: 0–415–15918–0 (hbk)
ISBN10: 0–415–48750–1(pbk)

ISBN13: 978–0–415–15918–0 (hbk)
ISBN13: 978–0–415–48750–4 (pbk)

Publisher's Note

The publisher has gone to great lengths to ensure the quality of this reprint but points out that some imperfections in the original may be apparent.

General Editor's Preface

The reception given to a writer by his contemporaries and near-contemporaries is evidence of considerable value to the student of literature. On one side we learn a great deal about the state of criticism at large and in particular about the development of critical attitudes towards a single writer; at the same time, through private comments in letters, journals or marginalia, we gain an insight upon the tastes and literary thought of individual readers of the period. Evidence of this kind helps us to understand the writer's historical situation, the nature of his immediate reading-public, and his response to these pressures.

The separate volumes in the *Critical Heritage Series* present a record of this early criticism. Clearly, for many of the highly productive and lengthily reviewed nineteenth- and twentieth-century writers, there exists an enormous body of material; and in these cases the volume editors have made a selection of the most important views, significant for their intrinsic critical worth or for their representative quality—perhaps even registering incomprehension!

For earlier writers, notably pre-eighteenth century, the materials are much scarcer and the historical period has been extended, sometimes far beyond the writer's lifetime, in order to show the inception and growth of critical views which were initially slow to appear.

In each volume the documents are headed by an Introduction, discussing the material assembled and relating the early stages of the author's reception to what we have come to identify as the critical tradition. The volumes will make available much material which would otherwise be difficult of access and it is hoped that the modern reader will be thereby helped towards an informed understanding of the ways in which literature has been read and judged.

B.C.S.

General Editor's Preface

Contents

CONTENTS

CONTENTS

NOTES ON THE TEXT

Lengthy extracts from the writings of James Joyce have been omitted whenever they are quoted merely to illustrate the work in question. These omissions are clearly indicated in the text. References to chapters and pages are to the following editions: for *Chamber Music, Pomes Penyeach* and *Ecce Puer* to *The Collected Poems*, New York, 1937; *Dubliners*, New York, 1954; *A Portrait of the Artist as a Young Man*, corrected by Chester G. Anderson, edited by Richard Ellmann, New York, 1964; *Ulysses*, New York 1934, 1961 [page references to *Ulysses* are given by episode to the 1934 and 1961 editions respectively (i.e. the Sirens episode, p. 254, p. 258)]; *Finnegans Wake*, New York, 1939 [page references to 'Work in Progress' are given to the pages in *Finnegans Wake*].

The order of the contents is chronological. Reviews and notices published within a year or two of a book's appearance are grouped under the book's title. Reviews of the American and the English editions of *Ulysses* are grouped after the 1922 reviews. Reviews of the French translation of *Ulysses* will be found in 1929 (Nos. 211, 213, 215, 216, 218, 249). After 1922, the first part of a year's work on Joyce is given over to general works, the second part to studies of *Ulysses*, the third part to 'Work in Progress'. A footnote reference to later criticism will be found under the heading for *A Portrait, Dubliners* and *Ulysses*. When a conjectural date can be set for material which appeared after 1941, the material is placed with its contemporary documents. In the absence of an original dating, these items are placed at the end of the volume. When only the relevant Joyce portion of a long article is included, the first page reference in the headnote is to the actual page or pages used, and the bracketed pages are the entire article (i.e. pp. 28–29 [23–31]). The use of 'n.p.' in the headnote indicates that the exact pages of the item are unknown. Many items in this volume survive only in untraceable press clippings found in the files of the Universities of Buffalo and Kansas.

Introduction

I

If the materials in this volume do not immediately lead to an understanding of how Joyce's life and art are 'interwoven in the same fabric', it is not that the selection of materials is an arbitrary one, but that the materials themselves do not offer that understanding. Joyce's greatest influence has been upon other writers, not upon his critics. And this influence has been absorbed in later writers in terms of two characteristics of Joyce's work—his vision and his style. The first is a moral, cognitive, orderly and encyclopedic phenomenon. The second is an artistic, musical, linguistic and substantive difficultness. Joyce is, after all, a modern writer not so much because of the impact of the first quality upon writers and readers, but because the 'intellectual machinery' so characteristic of the second is also so integral a part of the first. The criticism and commentary and opinion presented in this volume are concerned, by and large, with Joyce's 'machinery' and only rarely with Joyce's vision. To a certain extent, Joyce has himself limited critical apprehension of that vision, his true genius, by his own plan, stated at the end of *A Portrait of the Artist* in terms of 'silence, exile and cunning'.

Silently Joyce unfolded his world view in each successive work. Only his brother Stanislaus, at first, and his closest friends, later, were allowed to penetrate into his intentions, aims and methods. Perhaps none of them—not Stanislaus, or Harriet Shaw Weaver, or Frank Budgen, or Eugene Jolas, or Paul Léon—ever truly knew Joyce's vision. But they, at least, shared partially in its light. The critical world was, however, kept completely in the dark night Joyce seemed to weave in his works. Yet his artistic silence actually provoked critical volumes. Further, his exile from the social and political and artistic worlds while in Italy, Switzerland and France seemed merely to enhance the exile from literary traditions that his readers and critics experienced upon reading his works. From the first work, *Chamber Music* in 1907, through the earlier prose works, *Dubliners* and *A Portrait of the Artist,* and up to *Ulysses* in 1922, no keys or explanations or aids to frustrated readers were provided, nor were they until much, much later. Throughout this same quarter of a century Joyce wrote and revised, and wrote and revised again. And as each work appeared he cunningly wrote advance notices, translated foreign reviews (No. 56), directed the writing of some reviews (particularly those on *Ulysses* and 'Work in Progress'), and thereby laid the foundations for later criticism. In this sense, the artistic programme of 'silence, exile and cunning' did not prevent Joyce the detached artist from planning his own critical reputation.

The present array of critical commentary, limited as it is to the period 1902 to 1941, admirably illustrates Herbert McLuhan's comment in a survey of Joyce criticism from the 1940s, that Joyce's critics are intimidated, that they 'approach their subject in an awkward and diffident spirit'.[1] Criticism after the 1940s is equally diffident. It reflects the strain Joyce puts upon his attentive readers, and lacks Joyce's own sense of a lively artistic world. This is by no means a fresh comment to make upon current Joyce studies, but the need for re-appraisal as well as for the endless numbers of catalogues, word and check lists, and exegeses, is greater now than it was in 1941 or any time earlier.

It is evident enough from a perusal of this book that the quantity of critical material is overwhelming. Before the manuscript was reduced to its present size, the volume of material which might have been included was over 700 items and almost a million words. Some will no doubt feel that a collection of the fifty or so most important articles is still a desideratum and will find this book fragmented. Others will no doubt agree that the present large sampling of articles, some extracted and some in full texts, is desirable, but will find the selection too arbitrary and subjective. Still others will find fault with the 1941 terminus date. To anticipate the first two objections, it can be said that as Joyce's method was accretive so also should this collection be, and from as many divergent points of view as possible. This will provide as complete as possible a spectrum of the contemporary response. As to the third objection, there are literally hundreds of articles and books about Joyce after 1941. A selection of these up to the present time would be extremely difficult to make and subjective to be sure. If a Joyce cult existed before 1941, a Joyce 'industry' now flourishes. While this industry produces much that is manufactured and therefore dangerous to Joyce's works, the best products of this organized and automated 'funferall' are eminently useful. The 1941 terminus is, then, more than a matter of convenience; it is a silent act of industrial cunning.

Because the quantity of material on Joyce before 1941 is so great, much of the material in this volume is excerpted. The use of ellipses indicates omitted material. Whenever the omitted material is of such length that an ellipsis would be deceptive or misleading, a bracketed summary has been inserted in the text. Only key notices, reviews and articles are reprinted in full. Unrevised or minimally revised articles which are reprinted in books are presented here in their original form; where extensive revision has been made, the later text is used and is so indicated. Book-length studies (such as Frank Budgen, *James Joyce and the Making of Ulysses*) and articles of such length (for example the Joyce section of Edmund Wilson, *Axel's Castle*) that judicious excerpting is not possible are placed in Appendix C. Collections of articles (such as *Our Exagmination* and Louis Gillet's *Claybook*) are also listed in Appendix C. It would be desirable to have these in the volume, particularly Gillet's early article on *Ulysses*, but the unwillingness of some publishers to have a competing volume with the same essays, the unwillingness of some critics to allow any extracts to be taken from their works, and the length of this volume, all argue against their inclusion here. The exclusion of these kinds of items does not mean that they are unimportant—indeed, Gillet's change in attitude towards Joyce is a microcosm of the change in attitude generally—but only that they are available elsewhere, and *should* be read in those other volumes. Finally, reviews and critical studies which are omitted for reasons of limitation are listed in Appendix D. The text of this volume and the list in Appendix D, which do not by any means exhaust all the reviews of Joyce's works, provide a supplement to the existing bibliographies of secondary criticism listed in Appendix B.

II

Even before the first published criticism of Joyce's writings, his brother Stanislaus, a constant critic and the financial support of Joyce's family for many of the troubled years between 1904 and 1917, forecasted that Joyce was 'no student' (later Joyce would be called too learned for his or anyone else's own good). Stanislaus was at least partially incorrect when, in a comment in his *Diary* in 1903, he wrote, 'Whether he will ever build up anything broad—a drama, an esthetic treatise—I cannot say. His genius is not literary and he will probably run through many of the smaller forms of literary artistic expression' (No. 3). Joyce did build up something broad, the play *Exiles* and the aesthetic theory of *A Portrait of the Artist*. In the next year Stanislaus commented 'He may be a genius—it seems to be very possible' (No. 5), and the proving or disproving of this point nourished later criticism. What Stanislaus already knew in 1904 became the course that Joyce's reputation took and an outline guide to Joyce's new art as it unfolded in one book after another until it culminated in *Finnegans Wake* in 1939.

JOYCE'S POETRY: *Chamber Music, Pomes Penyeach, Collected Poems*

The critical reception that *Chamber Music* received upon its appearance in 1907 is epitomized in a comment from Arthur Symon's review, 'I have little hope that the rare quality of these songs will captivate many readers' (No. 9). Traditional as Elizabethan lyrics in rhythm, image and meaning, some of the poems had, as William Butler Yeats wrote to Joyce in 1902, 'more subject, more magical phrases, more passion' than some others. Yeats's comment is significant in its generosity, for Yeats and Joyce were at opposite ends of the poetic spectrum. Joyce's cynical disregard for the principles and programmes of the Irish Literary movement, of which Yeats was the leader, did not, however, prevent Yeats from being a lifelong advocate of Joyce—even if he never did finish *Ulysses*. Yeats was singularly responsible for bringing Joyce to the attention of Ezra Pound, thus passing Joyce on to someone who was more sympathetic to what Joyce was trying to do after he ceased writing the kind of poetry found in *Chamber Music*.

Though later he had critical notices of *Chamber Music* printed up to circulate with press copies of *Dubliners*, Joyce was quite sure of the significance of the slim volume of poems. To Herbert Gorman, his early biographer, he said, 'I wrote *Chamber Music* as a protest against myself'.[2] Yet, to his brother Stanislaus he wrote just before the publication of the volume that 'a page of "A Little Cloud" [one of the short stories in *Dubliners*] gives me more pleasure than all my verses'.[3] And later to his brother, Joyce unknowingly corrected many of the reviews of the book, 'I don't like the book but wish it were published and be damned to it. However, it is a young man's book.[4] I felt like that. It is not a book of love-verses at all, I perceive . . . Besides they are not pretentious and have a certain grace' (Ellmann, *Letters*, II, p. 219). The reviews assembled in this volume grant the 'grace' of *Chamber Music*, but the praise is slight.

Joyce the bard who believed his songs were 'pretty enough to be put to music' was gratified that their musical qualities were so quickly recognized. He wrote to G. Molyneux Palmer (19 July 1909), 'I hope that you may set all of *Chamber Music* in time. This was indeed partly my idea in writing it. The book is in fact a suite of songs and if I were a musician I suppose I should have set them to music myself.'[5] In the same letter he provides the structure of the suite, Poems I and III are preludes, XXXV and XXXVI are tailpieces, and XIV is the central song. But few reviewers, apart from Padraic Colum (and his comment only from the perspective of the later works), perceived that the poems in *Chamber Music* were not just 'recreations of Elizabethan and Jacobean song', that there was 'drama' in the lyrics, and that, read in the light of *A Portrait of the Artist, Chamber Music* is the lyric complement to *Stephen Hero* (the first draft version of *A Portrait* not published until 1944 and 1955) and to *A Portrait* in theme, mood and emotion (see No. 81).

Although Yeats commented on the thinness of the thought in *Chamber Music*, the relatively unknown study by John Kaestlin in 1933 cautions against a facile surface reading because the poems, though lacking depth of content, 'achieve a rare union of "harmonic purity and rhythmic freedom" '.[6] After the publication of *Dubliners* and *A Portrait*, a reviewer in the *Egoist* (possibly Harriet Shaw Weaver, a lifelong benefactor and amanuensis) would remark on the 'great deal of thought beneath fine workmanship' (No. 12). Still another review, of the New York 1918 edition, would remark that Joyce was 'in verse a shadow of himself and others, a dilettante playing a safe and pleasant game' (No. 13), but the same reviewer, no doubt illuminated by Joyce's statement of his artistic credo in *A Portrait*—silence, exile and cunning—added that the author of *Chamber Music* was 'a mere disembodied third person, aloof, detached'.

Morton D. Zabel, reviewing both *Chamber Music* and *Pomes Penyeach* (1927) in 1930, sensed the 'creative impulses' that guided Joyce's mind in the twenty years intervening between the two poetic volumes. *Chamber Music* lacked the 'finality of single intention' and was artificially elegant, Zabel wrote, but in *Pomes Penyeach* 'Joyce achieved . . . his own poetic character for the first time'. Yet a neo-classical sense of decorum only rarely allows a strict form and emotional content to diffuse Joyce's lyric temper (No. 14). Louis Golding, echoing Rebecca West's essay 'The Strange Necessity' (No. 199), remarked on the tastelessness of the poems and on Joyce's and Stephen Dedalus's desire to exercise the subconscious mind in poetry as well as in prose (No. 15). To a very great extent, Joyce's intention in publishing *Pomes Penyeach* when he did (at the time the first fragments of *Finnegans Wake*—known until 1939 as 'Work in Progress'—were appearing) was touched upon by Miss West. Joyce remarked in a letter to Miss Weaver (20 September 1928) that Miss West was quite delighted by the 'blowing up [of] some bogus personality' (Gilbert, *Letters*, I, p. 268).

Joyce's intention in presenting *Pomes Penyeach* in 1927 was not, moreover, only to show that he could write grammatically and recognizably. *Pomes Penyeach*, like *Chamber Music* before it, is a part of a consistent and unified artistic plan. Joyce's preoccupation with words, with linguistic experimentation, and tonal unity are foreshadowed in *Chamber Music* and continued in *Pomes Penyeach*. But his 'cloacal obsession' (to use H. G. Wells's famous phrase describing *A Portrait*, see No. 41) did suggest the tastelessness observed by Miss West and Golding and may be responsible for the essentially scatological reading —the 'chamber pot' obsession—of William York Tindall's edition of *Chamber Music* in 1954. Even with this obsession, Tindall's insistence upon the unity of all of Joyce's work, beginning with *Chamber Music* and leading to *Finnegans Wake*, upon the thematic cohesiveness of *Chamber Music* (the 'disease of love'), and upon the multi-levelled symbolism has been the main stream of later criticism of Joyce's poetry, what little criticism there has been. Perhaps the single most significant critical study of Joyce's poetry after Tindall's is still Irene Hendry's essay 'Joyce's Alter Ego' published in 1938, one year after the *Collected Poems* appeared (No. 291).

But, *Chamber Music* is, as Herbert Howarth has observed in the latest review of its place in Joyce criticism, 'at once first, last, and nowhere. Chronologically, it is first. It is last for most critics. It is nowhere for most readers, who ignore it or read it too rapidly to gather what it can give.'[7] Whatever the final place of Joyce's poetry is to be in the critical firmament, it is not as a poet *per se* that Joyce will be remembered by most.

Dubliners

The original twelve stories of *Dubliners* were submitted to the London publisher Grant Richards in 1905 and were accepted for publication on 17 February 1906. Yet it was not until 15 June 1914 that *Dubliners*, by then expanded by three more stories, was published. The publishing difficulties during these eight years are described in great detail in Herbert Gorman's biography published (with Joyce's blessing) in 1924 and, of course, in Richard Ellmann's 'definitive' biography in 1959. Only the highlights and low points need discussion here.

When Richards wrote on 23 April 1906 that his printer would not set the story 'Two Gallants' because of some 'objectionable passages', Joyce obdurately replied, 'I have written my book with considerable care, in spite of a hundred difficulties and in accordance with what I understand to be the classical tradition of my art. You must therefore allow me to say that your printer's opinion of it does not interest me in the least' (Gilbert, *Letters*, I, p. 60). Shortly thereafter, to Richards's continued objections, Joyce stated that his 'intention was to write a chapter of the moral history' of Ireland, focusing on Dublin because it seemed 'the centre of paralysis'. Emboldened, he continued, 'I have written it for the most part in a style of scrupulous meanness and with the conviction that he is a very bold man who dares to alter in the presentment, still more to deform, whatever he has seen and heard', and 'I have come to the conclusion that I cannot write without offending people' (Ellmann, *Letters*, II, p. 134). Richards was offended by passages using the word 'bloody', by a reference to 'a man with two establishments to keep up', and by references to a woman who 'continued to cast bold glances . . . and changed the position of her legs often'. Having deleted some of the offensive passages, Joyce foolishly raised the question as to why the story 'Counterparts' was objected to but 'An Encounter' was not. Richards quickly objected to that story as well. While Joyce yielded, as he says in a letter to Richards on 20 May, on 'the points which rivet the book together', the chapter of the moral history of Ireland was marred. Joyce was, furthermore, adamant about deleting some passages because in writing *Dubliners* he felt he had begun the 'spiritual liberation' of his country. And he was frequently blunt, 'It is not my fault that the odour of ashpits and old weeds and offal hangs round my stories. I seriously believe that you will retard the course of civilization in Ireland by preventing the Irish people from having one good look at themselves in my nicely polished looking-glass.'

Joyce was, moreover, aware of what critics were later to acknowledge, that the stories in *Dubliners* are indisputably well done. They are organized around the plan of presenting the entire life of the self from childhood ('The Sisters', 'An Encounter', 'Araby'), through adolescence ('The Boarding House', 'After the Race', 'Eveline'), to mature life ('Clay', 'Counterparts', 'A Painful Case'), and to stories of Dublin public life ('Ivy Day in the Committee Room', 'The Mother', 'Grace'). The three last stories, 'Two Gallants', 'A Little Cloud' and 'The Dead' were added before 1914 (Elhmann, *Letters*, II, p. 92; Ellmann, *James Joyce*, pp. 215–16).

Grant Richards rejected the book in September and other publishers followed suit until April 1909, when the Dublin publishers Maunsel & Company accepted it, printed it, but then, aroused by objections which Joyce believed were made by his 'enemies', burned the entire edition except one copy which Joyce retained. Afterwards, Joyce wrote 'Gas from a Burner', a broadside which scathingly attacked Maunsel and Dublin and publishers in general. Finally, in 1913, Richards re-accepted the book and published it in 1914. A gruelling ordeal for Joyce, and yet never have so many difficulties engendered such dismal and sparse critical fruit.

Dubliners received scarcely any attention in the reviews. Gerald Gould's review in the *New Statesman* hailed Joyce as a 'man of genius'. The stories had, Gould felt, originality, maturity, 'individual poise and force', yet it was a pity that Joyce had insisted upon 'aspects of life which are ordinarily not mentioned' (No. 22). The anonymous reviewer in the *Irish Book Lover* also wished that, while the prototypes of some of Joyce's characters did exist, Joyce had 'directed his undoubted talents in other and pleasanter directions' (No. 26). Joyce had anticipated this kind of Irish reaction as early as July 1905. In a letter to his brother at that time he wrote: 'The Dublin papers will object to my stories as to a caricature of Dublin life' (Ellmann, *Letters*, II, p. 99). Finally, the *Academy* reviewer called for a novel and compared Joyce to George Moore, as did the *Athenæum* reviewer (see Nos. 21, 24).

None of these reviewers took the time or the trouble to examine the realistic tradition that Joyce was working in, the tradition of Flaubert, Zola and George Moore, though the last influence was, indeed, mentioned, to Joyce's detriment. Only Ezra Pound was to point out, as he later did with *Ulysses*, the strong bent toward Flaubert, the 'clear hard prose' in the stories, the rigorous selection of detail and the symbolic content (No. 25). Later critics, particularly the French critics reviewing the 1926 translation of *Dubliners*, were much more conscious of the artistic and narrative mastery in the stories than were their English counterparts (Nos. 27–30). Yet even among the French, who were always Joyce's first champions in the critical field, agreement was not unanimous, and very early a note of regret that was later to become a chorus was raised because Joyce had stopped writing short stories.

Later critics have had little to say about *Dubliners*, with the exception of commentary on the last story of the collection, 'The Dead', which elicited comment primarily because it is so unlike the other stories (rather than because it is a typical story) in the collection. Certainly the objectivity, the aims and techniques, the realism, and the 'backgrounds to *Dubliners*' (perhaps the most worth while of Stanislaus Joyce's contributions to criticism of the stories) have been frequent sources for critical essays. But textual studies of *Ulysses* and *Finnegans Wake* have made *Dubliners* seem simple by comparison. Marxian critics have tended almost totally to ignore *Dubliners* in favour of what they consider the more obscure 'degenerate product' of a capitalistic society, *Finnegans Wake*. Two Joyces—the Joyce who wrote *Dubliners* and *A Portrait*, and the Joyce who wrote *Ulysses* and *Finnegans Wake*—have emerged. Perhaps not enough attention has been paid to Joyce's own comment that he was writing a 'series of epicleti' (Gilbert, *Letters*, I, p. 55), or to his remark, reported by the not always infallible Stanislaus, that there is a 'certain resemblance between the mystery of the Mass' and the stories in *Dubliners*.[8]

The concerns of the first readers of *Dubliners*—that the stories were without plot, that the style was flat and uninteresting, and that there were no 'truths' to be found—are no longer the concerns of the Joyceans. The pattern of the collection, the variety of techniques, the relation of the parts to the whole—these are the concerns today, because they provide some insights into the later works, particularly *Ulysses* and *Finnegans Wake*. After *Chamber Music* and *Pomes Penyeach*, *Dubliners* is the next most neglected part of an evolving fabric of artistic expression.

A Portrait of the Artist as a Young Man

Joyce's difficulties in getting published did not cease with the publication of *Dubliners*. By 1913, however, he had a new ally in Ezra Pound. Yeats had introduced Joyce's work to Pound, an American expatriate, contributor to numerous 'little magazines' and a member of the editorial boards of H. L. Mencken's *Smart Set* and Harriet Monroe's *Poetry*. Wyndham Lewis, who with Pound produced an English 'little magazine', *Blast*, has suggested that, without Pound, Joyce 'might never have emerged from his central European exile' and that it was Pound who 'sold' the idea of serializing *A Portrait of the Artist* to Harriet Shaw Weaver's review, the *Egoist*.[9] The novel was sent in parts to Pound, who passed them on to Miss Weaver for the *Egoist*, where they appeared from February 1914 to September 1915. And, when no English printer would set the most promising novel of the period, it was Miss Weaver who suggested that the *Egoist* turn publisher and produce the book. Unfortunately, even with Miss Weaver's reputation behind it, the book could not be set up in England and eventually had to be printed in the United States and shipped back to England.

Pound was drawn to *A Portrait* by its prose style. He wrote to Joyce (17–19 January 1914), 'I'm not supposed to know much about prose but I think your novel is damn fine stuff' (Ellmann, *Letters*, II, p. 327). When Pound, Yeats and George Moore were trying to get a Civil List grant for Joyce in 1915, Pound wrote, '. . . still it gives me a certain satisfaction to state that I consider Joyce a good poet, and *without exception* the best of the younger prose writers . . . His style has the hard clarity of a Stendhal or a Flaubert . . . He has also the richness of erudition which differentiates him from certain able and vigorous but rather overloaded impressionist writers' (Ellmann, *Letters*, II, p. 359). (Yeats's and George Moore's letters are found in the text, Nos. 35, 36, 37.) On 7 September 1915, after reading the final chapter of *A Portrait*, Pound again wrote to Joyce, 'Anyhow I think the book hard, perfect stuff. . . I think the book is permanent like Flaubert and Stendhal. Not so squarish as Stendhal, certainly not so varnished as Flaubert. In English I think you join on to Hardy and Henry James' (Ellmann, *Letters*, II, pp. 364–5). At the same time Yeats wrote to Pound commenting that the novel is 'a very great book—I am absorbed in it' (*Letters*, II, p. 388), and to Edward Marsh that Joyce is a 'possible man of genius' (No. 36). Thus, the genius of *A Portrait* was recognized by important men of letters even before its complete appearance.

When the complete novel finally appeared in book form late in December 1916, published by B. W. Huebsch in New York, the editors of the *Egoist* classified the reviews under such headings as Drains, Opportunities of Dublin, Wisdom, Advantages of Irish Education, etc. Attacks were numerous and of a kind. They ranged widely throughout the field of condemnation, from inartistic composition, 'His story is lacking in incident, and the little that happens is so indefinitely treated, so swamped with vague discussion, that the result cannot be other than hazy and ineffective' (Italo Svevo had made somewhat the same comment in 1909 on the unimportance of the events and the aridity of observation in the first chapter, see No. 17); to 'another Irishman, in short, with a bit of genius and a mission'; to charges of dullness induced by 'sleeping through a series of confused and rather unpleasant dreams'.[10] Characteristically, Stephen Dedalus's loss of faith was identified with Joyce's supposed own loss of faith. This began what soon grew to be almost a school of autobiographial Joyce criticism. Again, and again, reviewers were faced with the insurmountable problems of reconciling the sincerity, the mastery of style, and the enigmatic quality of the novel, with the fact that the book was 'unpleasant', 'nasty', 'futuristic', 'a negligible treatment of Irish politics, society and religion'.

Joyce had, indeed, anticipated most of these criticisms. With his uncompromising clarity of vision, he confided to his brother as early as 1908 that *A Portrait* would never be published, 'What I write with the most lugubrious intentions would probably be prosecuted in England as pornographical' (Ellmann, *James Joyce*, p. 274).

To balance such early criticism that Joyce was a 'clever novelist, but . . . he would be really at his best in a treatise on drains' (No. 40), there were a number of early perceptive reviews, notably those by H. G. Wells (No. 41), 'Solomon Eagle' (No. 48), John Macy (No. 52), Ezra Pound (No. 39), and John Quinn (No. 50). Also, Francis Hackett sought to place Joyce as part of, or apart from, the Irish literary background which, as a first-hand savant of Irish life, he knew so well. Hackett concludes his review with a typically Irish statement, 'Many people will furiously resent his candor, whether about religion or nationalism or sex', but then very untypically adds that 'candor is a nobility in this instance' (No. 45). An anonymous review in the *English Review* remarks that 'once more Ireland has given us a writer, a man of a soul and what seems to be a talent original and elusively stimulating, with a fine Irish veracity.' American reaction to the novel seems, in retrospect, more generous, as exemplified by the reviews of James Huneker, Francis Hackett, and H. L. Mencken. Mencken's pronouncement was remarkably prophetic that 'a Joyce cult now threatens'.[11]

If this spectrum of various critical light seems a bit bewildering to the contemporary reader, he must realize that *A Portrait of the Artist* seemed very bold and enigmatic in 1917–18. The generation of critics which greeted the novel was not prepared for a realistic-impressionistic novel which had an artist-hero who was so personally cathartic, whose mind recorded significant as well as insignificant details and impressions in a combination of the symbolic and the realistic and in a form so candidly personal. It would be many years before the theories and novels of Conrad, Forster and Ford presented Joyce's significant patterns of meaning to that same generation of critics. Joyce was, even at this early date, a writer's writer.

By 1923, a year after the publication of *Ulysses*, *A Portrait of the Artist* was virtually forgotten and sales had virtually ceased. By 1930 the critics, no doubt baffled by 'Work in Progress' and somewhat overcome by the astonishing intricacies and wealth of information in Frank

Budgen, *James Joyce and the Making of Ulysses*, and Stuart Gilbert, *James Joyce's Ulysses, A Study*, and by *Ulysses* itself, turned back to *A Portrait* and began constructing such a critical apparatus around the novel that one recent critic is forced to admit that 'almost nothing can be said about *The Portrait* which is not trite'.[12] The same kind of symbol and source probing that was being concentrated on *Ulysses* and 'Work in Progress' was turned on *A Portrait*. Finally, Harry Levin's 1941 study, *James Joyce: A Critical Introduction*, related the confessional-autobiographical *Portrait* to the European tradition of realism symbolism in Mann, Proust and Gide, thus assuring the novel's 'place' in literature.

This is surely not the place to rehearse the exigencies of *A Portrait* during the forties and fifties, except to note that symbol and source hunting continued, Stephen's aesthetic theory was debated, structure and cosmic pattern were analysed, and Wyndham Lewis and Hugh Kenner founded the 'Stephen-hating school' wherein Stephen Dedalus's callowness and sentimentality, as well as Joyce's irony, were established. *A Portrait* was well on its way to being a 'popular modern classic' primarily because so few people were reading or were able to read *Ulysses*. One of the main criteria Joyce envisioned for himself as a writer, and explicitly one of Stephen Dedalus's artistic tenets, was that of the unity of the artistic endeavour; it had clearly been overlooked. Each of Joyce's works presumes familiarity with every other work.

At least a word in passing should be said about *Stephen Hero*, the first draft version of *A Portrait*, edited by Theodore Spencer and published in 1945. Nearly everyone will concede that *A Portrait* is the economical final version of the embryonic *Stephen Hero*. Stephen Dedalus's character is essentially the same in both versions; the relationship between him and the author is changed. Joyce often reports, though he never comments or makes generalizations as he does in *Stephen Hero*. Furthermore, the difference between the two works is indicated by the way in which Joyce in the later work used symbolic allusiveness to evoke feelings directly. The use of this technique in *A Portrait* presents Stephen's life as a complete harmonious image. Edmund Wilson remarked in his review of *Stephen Hero* that 'Joyce's intellectual maturity, his singleness of purpose, his clarity of vision, are absolutely astounding in this "schoolboy's production", as he called it, written in his early twenties. Joyce was not a great artist yet, but he knew what it meant to be one and that was what he wanted to be.'[13] In observing the difference of the language between the two versions, we become more aware of Joyce's consciousness of language. This was, after all, the feature that attracted the attention of Pound and Yeats to *A Portrait*, and it was the element that was subordinated after Joyce's death. This 'magnetization of style and vocabulary', in Richard Ellmann's phrase (*James Joyce*, p. 151), was the surest key to the language of *Ulysses* and what appeared to be the excessively conscious manipulation of style and language in *Finnegans Wake*.

If Stephen Dedalus has become not a particular young man, or an artist, but 'Every-boy' as Marvin Magalaner has suggested, perhaps it is owing to the 'hot-house' environment of Joycean experts. Certainly, *A Portrait* is not being accepted in the terms that Joycean criticism has so laboriously and exhaustingly presented it in. It is a 'modern' book which speaks to a 'modern' audience, albeit a younger modern audience than heretofore. It represents to today's readers the portrait of man, even of a particular man, James Joyce, and this in spite of fifty years of critical commentary.

Exiles

Joyce's early play, *A Brilliant Career*, has not survived, and little can be said about his dramatic theory, particularly its aesthetic adumbrations as he applied them to the writing of *Exiles*. Many critics have suggested that Joyce hypothesized his aesthetic theory in *A Portrait*, experimented with it in *Exiles*, and then applied it to its fullest limits in *Ulysses* and *Finnegans Wake*. For, as in the two novels, adultery, homosexuality, the life of the artist, the union of the artist with those who love him, and Ibsenite women, are motifs in *Exiles*. The play found its first critic in Ezra Pound, who wrote to Joyce in September of 1915 that the play was 'exciting. But even to read it takes very close concentration of attention. I don't believe an audience could follow it to take it in, even if some damd impractical manager were to stage it. . . . Roughly speaking, it takes about all the brains I've got to take in [the] thing' (Ellmann, *Letters*, II, p. 365). Yeats two years later commented in a letter to Joyce that he thought the play 'sincere and interesting', but not as good as *A Portrait* (Ellmann, *Letters*, II, p. 405). And Stefan Zweig, after reading the published version, exclaimed that he thought the play 'a great artistic revelation' (Ellmann, *Letters*, II, p. 420). Although the play was published in May 1918, in both London and New York, it was owing to Zweig's influence that it received its first production in German translation in Munich on 7 August 1918 and was, in Joyce's own words upon reading a telegram describing the performance, 'a fiasco!' Ellmann, *James Joyce*, p. 476).

The reviews of the published play were, however, very favourable. Pound, commenting on the play even before its publication, in the *Drama* for February 1916, took the occasion to scourge the modern stage, dramatic agents and managers, and to use the play as a 'very solid basis' for his 'arraignment of the contemporary theatre'. He found the play 'unfit for the stage' not because it deals with adultery, or because it carries the mark of Ibsen, but because Joyce 'is not *playing* with the subject of adultery' and is dramatizing the 'age-long question of the relative rights of intellect, and emotion, and sensation, and sentiment' (No. 68). Desmond MacCarthy found the play 'remarkable' because it caused him to wonder and ponder over its characters and, outside the drama of Ibsen, such contemplation was rare (No. 71). Padraic Colum sensed that narrative rather than drama was Joyce's 'peculiar domain', but recognized the 'real and distinctive' character of Bertha (No. 72). Francis Hackett emphasized Joyce's 'intuitive and occult' gift and his 'genius for idiom and idiosyncrasy', but faulted the play for its unreality (No. 73).

Not all the reviews, by any means, were as favourable as these. W. P. Eaton, reviewing for the *Bookman*, found 'sewer gas' in the play. The reviewer for the *Freeman's Journal* complained that though Joyce obviously borrowed from Ibsen, he borrowed the wrong things—Joyce lacked the 'dramatic reality' found in Ibsen (No. 69). A. Clutton-Brock noted that the play was an 'unacted problem play', but that it had 'resources of spiritual passion and constructive power' which, with experience 'in the use of words and the management of scenes', might make a dramatist of Joyce. At the end of the review he calls upon the Stage Society or the Pioneers to produce the play (No. 70). The former's consideration of the play, with George Bernard Shaw as villain or hero depending upon which critic one reads, is indicative of the fluctuations of Joyce's reputation. Some time between 27 January and 11 July 1916 the Stage Society voted on accepting *Exiles*. The results of the Reading Committee's balloting are summarized by William White (Nos. 66, 67); at the bottom of the ballot in Shaw's hand is the statement 'Just the thing for the S. S.'.

The *Little Review*, which was publishing a serialized version of *Ulysses* at the time, contained a symposium on *Exiles* in its January 1919 issue (No. 74). And when the Neighborhood Playhouse in New York produced the play in March of 1925, Robert Benchley summarized his dissatisfaction with the play in these words, 'We now understand why Mr. Joyce wrote *Ulysses* in the incoherent style that he did. When he puts his words together so that they make sense, as he has done in *Exiles*, they sound just like ordinary writing. Very, very ordinary writing.'[14] Joseph Wood Krutch's review of the same performance is much more perceptive. The characters, he said, 'stand on the threshold of contemporary thought', but they 'seem to have had so much intelligence and so little wisdom'.[15] Not until 1932 did *Exiles* receive an extensive critical commentary, that of Francis Fergusson in *Hound & Horn* (No. 76). Fergusson analysed the influence of Ibsen, particularly Ibsen's *When We Dead Awaken*, and showed how Joyce went a step beyond Ibsen in freeing himself from typically Ibsenite dramatic conventions. Demonstrating the dramatic 'circling of the mind around a fixed, compelling thought, which is the Stephen-Rowan-Joyce thought of himself', Fergusson suggested that the 'Joycean cycle will doubtless not be understandable till long after it is completed'. Until then, the play is the 'most terrible and beautiful of modern plays'. The contrary view was expressed by Bernard Bandler the following year in *Hound & Horn* (No. 77). Since that time Joyce's only play has not received adequate attention because the critics very soon became absorbed first by *Ulysses* and then by the imponderables of *Finnegans Wake*.

1918 TO 1922: YEARS OF PROMISE AND PRODUCTIVITY

The four years from the publication of *Exiles* to the publication of *Ulysses* in 1922 were marked by three events in Joyce's life. The gift of a large sum of money by Harriet Shaw Weaver enabled Joyce to write for the first time relatively unencumbered by financial pressures (though these by no means ceased with Miss Weaver's generosity, which was extended a number of other times in the future). This gift allowed Joyce time for the writing of *Ulysses*, which appeared in a serialized version in the *Little Review* from March 1918 until the *Review* was suppressed after the September–December 1920 issue. And, finally, Joyce and his family arrived in Paris in July 1920, with Pound's help, encouragement, and advance publicity.

Joyce's wartime exile in Zürich was enriched by what Richard Ellmann has labelled 'a great exfoliation of Joyce's creative powers' (*Letters*, II, p. 346). During this period he was writing *Ulysses* and corresponding regularly with Pound, Miss Weaver and Frank Budgen, whose book, *James Joyce and the Making of Ulysses*, is a far more adequate and detailed account of Joyce's writing than any other work. Since Miss Weaver's gift had been given anonymously, Joyce was curious about the identity of his benefactor. He wrote to her solicitors, Monro Saw &

Company, inquiring about her and received this reply: '. . . Briefly, the qualities in your work that most interest her are your searching piercing spirit, your scorching truth, the power and startling penetration of your "intense instant of imagination" ' (Ellmann, *Letters*, II, p. 445). This was not unusual praise at this time, for with the appearance of *Ulysses* in the *Little Review*, Joyce began to receive something like 'comprehensive' treatment in the literary journals.

Pound's influence and reputation brought Joyce to the attention of Margaret Anderson and Jane Heap, the editors of the *Little Review*, who heroically began publishing *Ulysses*. Pound received the chapters from Joyce, often deleted lines, and then sent them on to New York. Joyce was aware of Pound's dissatisfaction with parts of the new novel. In a letter to Miss Weaver in July 1919, he wrote, 'Mr. Pound wrote to me rather hastily in disapproval but I think that his disapproval is based on grounds which are not legitimate and is due chiefly to the varied interests of his admirable and energetic artistic life' (Gilbert, *Letters*, I, p. 218). Yeats was also following the course of the Irish comet; in a letter to John Quinn, a New York lawyer, Joyce benefactor and later buyer of Joyce manuscripts (at prices Joyce considered too low), Yeats waxed enthusiastic: '. . . his new story in the *Little Review* looks like becoming the best work he has done. It is an entirely new thing—neither what the eye sees nor the ear hears, but what the rambling mind thinks and imagines from moment to moment. He has certainly surpassed in intensity any novelist of our time' (No. 84). Padraic Colum, a contemporary of Joyce in Dublin, wrote one of the earliest articles on him. It is filled with reminiscences, praise for *Chamber Music* and the now rather curious judgement that *A Portrait* gives a 'glimpse into a new life—into the life that has been shaped by Catholic culture and Catholic tradition' (No. 81). One critical touchstone had been scratched. Another was exposed in Colum's story that in his youth Joyce had said to Yeats, 'We have met too late: you are too old to be influenced by me.'

A new edition of *A Portrait* in May 1918 prompted a summary of criticism and some new comments from Ezra Pound in the *Future* (No. 82). Pound noted a 'finer volume of praise for this novel than for any that I can remember', but also much 'impotent spitting and objurgation'. Praising the novel as 'literature', Pound commented on Joyce's 'swift alternation of subjective beauty and external shabbiness, squalor, and sordidness'. He also found *Chamber Music* 'an excellent antidote for those who find Mr. Joyce's prose "disagreeable" and who at once fly . . . to conclusions about Mr. Joyce's "cloacal obsessions" '.

Silvio Benco, writing in the Triestine journal *Umana* (No. 83) in July 1918, remarked on the 'precision and extreme lucidity of the draughtsmanship' of *A Portrait.* And in a very long and detailed criticism in the *Dial*, Scofield Thayer (No. 85) attempted to comment on all the works published up to that time (1918), though he chose to comment on *Ulysses* in terms of the similarity of style between the first chapters and *A Portrait.* He considered *Dubliners* Joyce's finest work and *A Portrait* a 'cross-section of contemporary Irish middle-class life'.

Jane Heap was Joyce's most outspoken advocate in America, and her replies to letters to the editor of the *Little Review* (and her letters themselves) are a gauge of American reaction to Joyce. According to Miss Heap, and here again we find a foretaste of later critical concerns, Joyce is not concerned with audiences and their demands. He is not obscene, for he is 'too religious about life' and, because he is aware of 'cerebral irraditations' he 'conceives and records'.[16] T. S. Eliot, reviewing W. B. Yeats's *The Cutting of an Agate* in the *Athenæum* for July 1919, took the occasion to compare Yeats's 'crudity and egoism' with the 'exploitation to the point of greatness' of these qualities in the later work of Joyce:

> Mr. Joyce's mind is subtle, erudite, even massive; but it is not like Stendhal's, an instrument continually tempering and purifying emotion; it operates within the medium, the superb current, of his feeling. The basis is pure feelings, and if the feelings of Mr. Yeats's were equally powerful, it would also justify his thought.[17]

Pound also compared Yeats and Joyce, finding in Joyce a 'concentration and absorption passing Yeats'—Yeats has never taken on anything requiring the condensation of *Ulysses* (No. 86). And Virginia Woolf quite generously suggests that in *A Portrait* we have the 'proper stuff for fiction', that it comes 'closer to life' and preserves 'more sincerely and exactly what interests and moves' writers 'by discarding most of the conventions which are commonly observed by the novelists' (No. 63). In *A Portrait* and in *Ulysses*, she finds a distinct sincerity.

As the previous paragraph indicates, this period witnessed a great exfoliation of Joyce's reputation. Joyce was discussed and hailed by many: by Evelyn Scott in the *Dial* (No. 87), by Ford Madox Ford (No. 65) and others. Richard Aldington, on the other hand, remarked that the achievement of *Ulysses* was remarkable, but the influence would be 'deplorable': 'From the manner of Mr. Joyce to Dadaisme is but a step, and from Dadaisme to imbecility is hardly that' (No. 93). Joyce's reputation among men of letters was greatly increased by the suppression of the *Little Review* for publishing *Ulysses*. John S. Sumner, secretary of the New York Society for the Prevention of Vice, lodged a complaint against the *Little Review* and its editors, Margaret Anderson and Jane Heap, for the publication of the 'Nausicaa' episode in the July–August 1920 issue. The *Review*'s lawyer, John Quinn, had, with Ezra Pound, urged Joyce to wait until the entire book was finished before publication, so that isolated passages would not be condemned as obscene. But the outcome of the trial was never in doubt in spite of the favourable testimony of such critics of stature as Scofield Thayer and John Cowper Powys. When the ultimate suppression occurred in 1921, Burton Rascoe in the *New Age* hoped that 'some reputable English publisher' would produce the book (No. 92). Such would not be the 'notable triumph for the Empire over America', as Rascoe suggested, for the book appeared in Paris in 1922, in America in 1934 and not in England until two years later.

But by the time the suppression trial started Joyce had arrived in Paris heralded by Pound (and by himself). Copies of his works were placed in 'strategic hands' and press notices were distributed. Offers to translate his works appeared, along with beds, free flats and an overcoat. Soon he met Sylvia Beach, the proprietress of the Paris bookshop, Shakespeare and Company, and the now famous agreement was made to publish *Ulysses* under her imprint. The campaign for the publication of *Ulysses* was unlike that waged for any other novel in history. Even help from Valéry Larbaud, distinguished *homme de lettres*, was enlisted, and in his often-quoted letter to Sylvia Beach in February 1921 we have the fountain-head of all *Ulysses* comment, 'I am *raving mad* over *Ulysses*' (No. 91). On 7 December 1921, two months before the publication of *Ulysses*, at Adrienne Monnier's bookshop—La Maison des Amis des Livres—the first full criticism of *Ulysses* and of all the previous works was presented to an enchanted (and, we note, carefully entrapped) audience (No. 118).

Ulysses

When the large, square, blue-covered and white-lettered *Ulysses* appeared in February 1922, it was an immediate sensation. The critics were, however, first bewildered by its lack of any apparent plan. The plan was a carefully withheld secret until Stuart Gilbert's *James Joyce's Ulysses* appeared in 1930. Even then, the scheme was not complete. None the less, Joyce allowed portions of the scheme to be 'leaked out', though as part of his publicity strategy, and he later admitted to Samuel

Beckett that he may have 'over-systematized *Ulysses*' (Ellmann, *James Joyce*, p. 715). At the time of the writing of the book, however, Joyce seems to have had a very clear, general plan, he states:

> It is an epic of two races (Israelite-Irish) and at the same time the cycle of the human body as well as a little story of a day (life) . . . It is also a sort of encyclopaedia. My intention is to transpose the myth *sub specie temporis nostri*. Each adventure (that is, every hour, every organ, every art being interconnected and interrelated in the structural scheme of the whole) should not only condition but even create its own technique (Gilbert, *Letters*, I, pp. 146–7).

How far short the reviewers fell from an understanding of these intentions is a key to Joyce's reputation in February 1922.

The sin of 'boredom' was raised by the *Pink 'Un* reviewer, boredom in the decent *and* the indecent passages (No. 96). James Douglas in the *Sunday Express* labelled Joyce 'a rebel against the social morality of Europe, which is based upon the Christian religion',[18] a judgment for which he was attacked by Joyce 'advocates', Sisley Huddleston, Middleton Murry and Arnold Bennett. A reviewer for the *Evening News* suggested that the book was being purchased as an investment, which indeed it was, and that it had limited general appeal (No. 97), while the anonymous cry of the *Dublin Review* was '*écrasez l'infâme!*' (No. 100). Shane Leslie in the respected *Quarterly Review* found the book impossible to read, undesirable to quote, 'opposed to all ideas of good taste and morality', and a gigantic effort 'made to fool the world of readers' (No. 102). Joyce's reaction to this was that 'as a criticism or even an attack Mr. Leslie's article is rather ineffective but as a leading article . . . in the most authoritative review in the English-speaking world it is very effective in a way in which the writer did not at all intend' (Gilbert, *Letters*, I, p. 185). The exaggeration and the sensationalism of the reviewers can, however, be overemphasized.

The first favourable English review was Sisley Huddleston's in the *Observer*. He found Joyce a genius, but maintained that he would remain 'caviare to the general'. He emphasized the psychological advances Joyce had made and stressed that sex did not play such a vital part in the book (No. 104). The *Observer* review was a stimulus to sales, for the day after it appeared 145 letters came into Sylvia Beach's bookshop asking for prospectuses. Joyce's reaction to the review was, however, a cool one: 'I do not count the *Observer*,' he said, 'which was merely preparing the way' (Gilbert, *Letters*, I, p. 183). Misquoting (as Ernest Boyd was later to do also) Valéry Larbaud's statement that 'With this book Ireland makes a sensational re-entrance into high European literature', J. Middleton Murry sought to disprove this assertion. For, if a European work is an 'artistic acknowledgment of and submission to the social tradition of Europe', then Joyce's work is none of these things (No. 98). The reviews which most pleased Joyce were those by Edmund Wilson in the *New Republic*, Mary Colum in the *Freeman*, and Gilbert Seldes in the *Nation*. Wilson chose to argue to Ezra Pound's contention that Joyce is like Flaubert (No. 119), though he devoted most of his review to a discussion of the Homeric parallels, to the scale and microscopic fidelity of the chief characters and to the humour (No. 108). Mary Colum placed *Ulysses* in the 'Confession Class of Literature'—an autobiographical work which is also the life of a man (No. 109). She is supported to some extent by a letter from Stanislaus to James, written in August 1924, which concludes: 'It [*Ulysses*] is undoubtedly Catholic in temperament. This brooding on the lower order of natural facts, this re-evocation and exaggeration of detail by detail and the spiritual dejection which accompanies them are purely in the spirit of the confessional. . . .'[19] Gilbert Seldes made the significant point that in *Ulysses* Joyce wears the dual mask (in Yeats's sense) of Bloom and Stephen, and acknowledges Joyce as 'possibly the most interesting and most formidable writer of our time' (No. 110).

In the *Outlook* and the *Bookman*, Arnold Bennett presented the middlebrow point of view. He showed that he had read Joyce's earlier works, had read Valéry Larbaud's article in the *Nouvelle Revue Française* (an expanded version of his lecture of 7 December 1921), and had even read *Ulysses*. The suspicion always lingers that Joyce's reviewers did not read his books. Bennet found 'pervading difficult dulness' along with a 'mean, hostile, and uncharitable' vision of the world and its inhabitants. His final comment, however, is that 'in the finest passages it [*Ulysses*] is in my opinion justified' (No. 106). Joyce feared that the review would not help because Bennett had not mentioned the name and address of the publisher.

Valéry Larbaud's long article in the *Nouvelle Revue Française* in April 1922, lent his prestige and that of the journal to Joyce. Many later errors might have been avoided if Larbaud had been read. Unlike Larbaud, Joyce's other significant French critic, Louis Gillet, of the equally prestigious *Revue des Deux Mondes*, wrote with little knowledge of Joyce's early works. He later reappraised his early views, however, and became a leading French spokesman for Joyce. Larbaud had read the earlier works, had benefited from discussing *Ulysses* with Joyce, and had seen the inextricable unity of Joyce's works. He emphasized the Homeric correspondences, the 'interior monologue', the method and material of the book, the relation to Rabelais, and the significance of the the main characters, Stephen Dedalus and Leopold Bloom (No. 118).

Ezra Pound's essay, 'James Joyce et Pécuchet', which appeared in the June 1922 issue of the *Mercure de France*, established Joyce in the tradition of Flaubert, emphasized the satirical aspects and the form of the work, and first suggested that like Flaubert Joyce had learned that the best way to handle the imbecility and idiosyncrasy of his century was to make an encyclopedia of it. Pound also suggested the importance of the father-son theme, a concern which remained dormant for many years thereafter. Though he minimized the Homeric parallels, Pound found *Ulysses* an enormous, finely planned cosmic comment (No. 119).

The third most influential article on *Ulysses* (after Larbaud and Pound), T. S. Eliot's '*Ulysses*, Order and Myth', did not appear until November 1923, in the *Dial*. Eliot was the first to suggest Joyce's scientific impersonality and the second, after Larbaud, to appreciate the significance of the method, the parallel to the *Odyssey* and the 'use of appropriate styles and symbols to each division'. Eliot, having read Pound, disposed of the latter's method as 'scaffolding erected by the author for the purpose of disposing his realistic tale' and also disposed of Richard Aldington's fear of Joyce's chaotic influence. He proposed that in 'using the myth, in manipulating a continuous parallel between contemporaneity and antiquity, Mr. Joyce is pursuing a method which others must pursue after him.' This would be a step 'toward making the modern world possible for art' (No. 120).

Joyce did not answer any reviews or criticisms, because he had his own ideas about what *Ulysses* was. This enormous tome which had started as a short story for *Dubliners*, was, he felt, 'an extremely tiresome book', but the only book he could then write (Gilbert, *Letters*, I, p. 128). 'From my point of view,' he suggested, 'it hardly matters whether the technique is "veracious" or not; it has served me as a bridge over which to march my eighteen episodes' (Ellmann, *James Joyce*, p. 542). He admitted to a 'grocer's assistant's mind' (Ellmann, *Letters*, III, p. 304), and, in letters written when he was composing *Ulysses*, he supplied the motivation for the innovations in structure and style: the Sirens' episode is written with all the eight regular parts of a *fuga per caononem* (Letters, I, p. 129); Nausicaa is written in a 'namby-pamby jammy marmalady drawersy (alto la!) style with effects of incense, mariolatry, masturbation, stewed cockles, painter's palette, chit chat, circumlocution, etc. etc.' (Gilbert, *Letters*, I, p. 135). And when Benoist-Mechin wished to see the plan for the book, Joyce replied: 'If I gave it all up immediately, I'd lose my immortality. I've put in so many enigmas and puzzles that it will keep the professors busy for centuries arguing over what I meant, and that's the only way of insuring one's immortality' (Ellmann, *James Joyce*, p. 535).

None the less, Joyce followed the progress of the book very closely, with his eye apparently on sales. He suggested additions to the collection of reviews Miss Weaver was preparing. He had planned to let Larbaud reveal his intentions in the December 1921 lecture, for he wrote to Miss Weaver that month, 'It will allow me to send out to the world in those parts where he uses critical exegesis certain suggestions as to the scheme and technique which I shall then have the pleasure of rehearsing and rereading when they have gone the rounds' (Gilbert, *Letters*, I, p. 199). He is reported to have said to Djuna Barnes, 'The pity is the public will demand and find a moral in my book, or worse they make take it in some serious way, and on the honor of a gentleman, there is not one single serious line in it.'[20] To Jacques Mercanton he admitted that in *Ulysses* 'there is no past, no future; everything flows in an eternal present.'[21] But on the subject of the interior monologue and his desperate little scheme for the rehabilitation of Edouard Dujardin's having originated it, he said, 'I laugh at it today, now that I have had all the good of it. Let the bridge blow up, provided I have got my troops across.' And on the subject of *Ulysses*: 'Nonetheless, that book was a terrible risk. A transparent leaf separates it from madness.'[22]

Perhaps it was the transparency of this leaf which provoked contemporary authors (with a few exceptions) to such hostility. Virginia Woolf found the book 'underbred', a book of a 'self taught working man', or of a 'queasy undergraduate scratching his pimples'. Even Eliot, in private, was not quite as approving as his *Dial* essay might indicate: 'Bloom tells us nothing. Indeed, this new method of giving the psychology proves to my mind that it doesn't work.' Katherine Mansfield, evidently, was troubled by Joyce: 'Oh, I can't get over a great great deal. I can't get over the feeling of wet linoleum and unemptied pails and far worse horrors in the house of his mind—He's so terribly *unfein*.' Bernard Shaw, whose famous thrift letter is presented in this volume (No. 94), wrote to the editor of the *Picture Post* in June 1939 denying that he was 'disgusted by the unsqueamish realism of *Ulysses*', as Geoffrey Grigson had reported in an earlier article (Ellmann, *Letters*, III, pp. 444–5, note 3).[23] The reactions of other contemporary writers like Gertrude Stein, Edmund Gosse and George Moore are equally worth noting (Nos. 125–31, 145).

There is no adequate but brief way to summarize the course of Joyce's reputation from 1922 up to the American publication of *Ulysses* in 1934. Richard Ellmann suggests that 'the ironic quality of Joyce's fame was that it remained a *gloire de cénacle*, even when the *cénacle* had swelled to vast numbers of people' (*James Joyce*, p. 541). Joyce was not generally read, although there were eight editions of *Ulysses* during this period. Primarily because his book was banned, his pornographic reputation soared, and copies of *Ulysses* were smuggled into England and America. Until Samuel Roth's piracy of *Ulysses* for his *Two Worlds' Monthly* in 1927, there were few American copies. Roth's piracy evoked a famous 'Ulysses Protest' which was signed by hundreds of the world's leading writers. This was also the period of the appearance of the first introductory books: Herbert Gorman's Joyce-written biography in 1924 and books by Paul Jordan Smith, Charles Duff and Louis Golding. Gilbert's *Study* suggested Joyce's conscious artistry for the first time. But, a too-conscious artistry which becomes almost a manipulation seemed a fearful prospect, particularly when 'Work in Progress' began to appear in 1927. Joyce the mysterious and Joyce the intentional confuser became the 'darling' of the critics. Even reputable German critics like Ernst R. Curtius, Bernhard Fehr, Carola Giedion-Welcker and Carl Jung, entered the foray (Nos. 202 and 212; 125, 200, 261 and 262; and 149, 164, 167–8, 201, 202). The French continued to assist at the *gloire*, but the voice of Italian criticism was scarcely heard. Even the Marxian critics Radek, Mirsky and Miller-Budnitsky entered the critical arena in the middle thirties, deploring Joyce for his bourgeois decadence and holding up socialist realism as an example for him (Nos. 265, 275, 279, 294). They were answered by James T. Farrell in a famous attack in 1935 (No. 288).

As early as November of 1922 Sylvia Beach could meet Joyce's suggestion for an article on *Ulysses* with the frank statement that nothing concerning him or a possible third edition should be printed (Gilbert, *Letters* I, pp. 195–6). None the less, the progress of Joyce's reputation marched onward. When Malcolm Cowley came to summarize the criticism of the 1924–34 period, he used the metaphor of a stone dropped into a pool: there was a moment of silence after *Ulysses*, the stone, was dropped, 'then all the frogs who inhabited the pool began to talk at once'.[24] Edmund Wilson summarized Joyce's reputation differently, however, in a review of Gorman's biography: there are those who stupidly denounce him and there are those who perpetuate esoteric follies. Future readers of posterity's criticism will not know which critic to admire the most.[25] The observance of the sixteenth of June became known as 'Bloom's Day' and was annually celebrated, provoking from Joyce the comment that 'I have to convince myself that I wrote that book' (Gilbert, *Letters,* I, p. 216).

In 1927, however, the first major and significant blow at Joyce's rising reputation was delivered by Wyndham Lewis in his review *Enemy* and then in his *Time and Western Man* (No. 165). Joyce is, Lewis says, saturated with the 'time mind' which is inimical to the human arts. Joyce is a pernicious influence and Lewis attacked him on all sides. Joyce's reaction was fairly typical: 'Allowing that the whole of what Lewis says about my book is true, is it more than ten per cent of the truth?' (Ellmann, *James Joyce*, p. 608). When in November of 1931 Harold Nicolson proposed a series of talks on Joyce for the BBC, the outcry (led by Alfred Noyes and others) was such that the programmes were delayed for a month. A general protest arose, however, and Nicolson was finally allowed to go on provided he did not refer to *Ulysses* (No. 251).

Since *Ulysses* was banned, few sincere admirers of Joyce's early work had a means of bridging the gap between *A Portrait of the Artist* and 'Work in Progress'. This lapse was resolved by Judge John Woolsey's decision in December 1933 to allow *Ulysses* to be published in the United States, which it was in 1934. The American reviews were, generally, perceptive, owing to the work of English, French and American critics. This was, after all, the period of E. M. Forster's *Aspects of the Novel* (1927), which emphasized the importance of the mythological journey of Odysseus in the creation of Joyce's characters; of Joseph Warren Beach's *The Twentieth Century Novel* (1932), which examined the break with the entire historical tradition of the novel, and the influence of *Ulysses* on the technique and substance of the novel. It was followed by the period of David Daiches's *New Literary Values* (1936) and *The Novel and the Modern World* (1939), which, in examining all Joyce's works, pointed out the new technique in the building up of characters, the escape from a chronological time-sequence and the 'new and dangerous' treatment of language as a medium. As late as 1939, Edwin Muir, in *The Present Age*, stated that it was still difficult to judge *Ulysses*; but he very cogently summarized the influence *Ulysses* had had upon contemporary prose fiction up to that time: free association for verbal and imaginative freedom, use of legend (and myth) as a framework for action, use of the past and literary forms of the past to 'throw the present into relief', a learned approach to experience, and a view of human nature as timeless.

Critical commentary on *Ulysses* continued to appear in the thirties; but the book was eclipsed by *Finnegans Wake* in 1939. Studies have continued in structure and style, in themes, in naturalism and psychology, and in Joyce viewed as a social historian. To attempt to estimate Joyce's reputation in terms of *Ulysses* during the past three decades would be to catalogue the 'heavy freight' of criticism by which the novel seems occasionally obscured. It is a modern classic, no longer considered unorthodox or outspoken or the product of a madman. More and more, as *Ulysses* is viewed as a psychological novel, a verbal symbolistic poem, a document of a disintegrating society, or a writer's compendium of techniques of fiction, it is used to determine whether Joyce was classical or romantic, medieval or modern, realistic or symbolistic. Frank Kermode perhaps best estimated the present reputation of *Ulysses* in a 1959 review of Richard Ellmann's biography:

> If you were ever flushed and excited by *Ulysses* you are probably now over forty; if you ever tried to live by it, over thirty. Under thirty, people seem to be a little bored by Joyce's endless experimentation, and also by the setting up of a polarity between prose and poetry which is rendered in terms of straight talk about the genitals or swooning pre-Raphelite rhythms.[26]

Joyce's 'greater reality' has declined in reputation even while the whole system and the whole world of itself, the art of *Ulysses*, is still there as it was in 1922. We all create our own meanings for *Ulysses*.

Work in Progress and *Finnegans Wake*

In March of 1923 Joyce began work on what was known until 1939 as 'Work in Progress'. The title of the work, *Finnegans Wake*, a reference to an Irish ballad concerning a hod carrier who is resurrected by whisky at his wake, was confided only to his wife. Although the work was published in parts, in *transition* and other journals, Joyce seems to have had a general notion of the entirety of the work. Others did not have this notion, and the publication of the first part, 'Anna Livia Plurabelle' (or *ALP* as it was known), in 1927, began seventeen years of dissatisfaction among former close friends and sympathetic critics. During this period Joyce wrote letters to Pound, Harriet Shaw Weaver and others, seeking encouragement, asking their opinions. Numerous strategic manoeuvres followed, unlike any of the publicity campaigns and strategies that had preceded his other works. He worked the fable of 'The Ondt and the Gracehoper' (*Finnegans Wake*, pp. 414–19) into the book as a defence against Wyndham Lewis's attack on him as a pernicious influence (No. 165). He published *Pomes Penyeach* in July 1927 to show that he could write in conventional grammar. He encouraged the publication in July 1929 of twelve essays explaining 'Work in Progress', the famous *Our Exagmination Round His Factification for Incamination of Work in Progress.* He suggested that James Stephens finish 'Work in Progress' if he could not. In another area, he humorously sent Harriet Weaver some 'Advance press opinions' of *ALP*:

> My father: he has gone off his head, I am afraid . . . My brother Stanislaus: What are you driving at. To make the English language quite incomprehensible. Literary bolshevism. Too flabby for my taste . . . E.P. [Ezra Pound]: F.M.F. [Ford Madox Ford]: E.W. [Ernest Walsh]: No acknowledgement . . . [Sisley] Huddleston: Why would the English printer not print it? (Gilbert, *Letters*, I, p. 235).

To Robert McAlmon, William Bird, Claud Sykes and others, he defended his book. Finally, in November 1926, Miss Weaver having carefully, guardedly and sympathetically sought to understand what Joyce was doing, raised her own doubts:

> But, dear sir . . . the worst of it is that without comprehensive key and glossary such as you very kindly make out for me, the poor hapless reader loses a very great deal of your intention; flounders, helplessly, is in imminent danger, in fact, of being as totally lost to view as that illfated vegetation you mention . . . would it be utterly against the grain, your convictions and principles to publish (when the day comes), along with an ordinary edition, also an annotated edition (at double to treble price, say?) (Ellmann, *James Joyce*, p. 596).

This key or glossary was not part of Joyce's plan, and it was not until 1944 that *A Skeleton Key to Finnegans Wake* by Campbell and Robinson appeared. But Joyce was 'trying to tell the story of this Chapelizod family in a new way' using the elements that any novelist might use: 'man and woman, birth, childhood, night, sleep, marriage, prayer, death' but building 'many planes of narrative with a single esthetic purpose'.[27] Part of his intention with this work, as with *Ulysses*, was to keep critics busy for three hundred years unravelling the skein. He defended the book as a cyclical, night-dream life, the complexity necessary to the theme; a book of pure music, a book to make its readers laugh. In retrospect, *Finnegans Wake* is the logical extension of the use of consciousness in *Dubliners*, of unconsciousness in *A Portrait* and *Ulysses*, leading to the mind asleep in *Finnegans Wake*. To represent this night-third of human life, he could not use a 'wideawake language, cutanddry grammar and goahead plot' (Ellmann, *James Joyce*, p. 597).

Miss Weaver, however, became less guarded in her reaction: '. . . I am made in such a way that I do not care much for the output from your Wholesale Safety Pun Factory nor for the darkness and unintelligibilities of your deliberately-entangled language system. It seems to me you are wasting your genius' (Ellmann, *Letters*, III, p. 154, note 2). Joyce was, then, more and more aware of the hostility that was building about his experiment, just as he was aware of the yeoman work being done in explanation by the writers for *transition*, the Paris organ of the Revolution of the Word group, led by Elliot Paul and Eugène Jolas. Others like Samuel Beckett, Stuart Gilbert, Louis Gillet, Jacques Mercanton also attempted to try to explain the 'Work in Progress'. Robert McAlmon reports of the awe and respect, and his own bewilderment, shown by the select group which gathered to hear Joyce read *ALP*. And he also mentions one of the few surviving comments by Ernest Hemingway on Joyce (No. 206).

The critical reaction to the serial publication of 'Work in Progress' aroused hostility in critics other than the *transition* group. The exception is Edmund Wilson's early and enlightened essay in *Axel's Castle*. Wilson, relying heavily on the suggestive and ground-breaking essays in *Our Exagmination*, discussed the importance of the night and the subconscious, the language, the hero and the 'plot', and attempted to show that the most bewildering elements of 'Work in Progress' were actually exaggerated elements from *Ulysses*. The reviews included in this volume of 'Anna Livia Plurabelle', of 'Haveth Childers Everywhere' and of 'Tales Told of Shem & Shaun' indicate well the adverse opinions Richard V. Chase summarized later: that the book is irreverent, anti-intellectual, and tries to destroy the past; that it is coterie literature and not a novel; that it is a book of pedantic and irresponsible word-play; that it is a parochial curiosity because it is based on the technical elements of Vico, Freud and Jung; and that it is not worth the effort to read Joyce's language.[28] Much of the adverse criticism was provoked by the association of Joyce with the Revolution of the Word movement which declared that the writer expresses; he does not have to communicate; in other words, 'the plain reader be damned'. Joyce's virtuosity in the use of words was later either seen as an end in itself, or else praised for its 'orchestral magnificence' as an organic part of the creation. Critics lamented the 'barrage of learning, authority, research, collation, argument, thesis and hypothesis' produced by admirers in support of Joyce's dream book.

The reviewers of 'Anna Livia Plurabelle', or *ALP*, emphasized Joyce's method and the new language. Many relied on Padraic Colum's 'Preface' to the New York edition for information about Joyce's conception of the River Liffey, the place of the episode in the whole work, the music of the episode, and Joyce's 'de-formations and the re-formations of words' (No. 177). The unsigned reviewer in the *Irish Statesman* (probably George Russell) remarked that, while a chapter was exciting, the entire book 'may prove a labour too great for any to peruse to its end' (No. 181). A controversy between Eugène Jolas and Sean O'Faolain erupted in the pages of *transition* and of the *Irish Statesman* over Joyce's language, a controversy which O'Faolain later (in 1930) resolved by a further examination of the merits that lay in Joyce's language (Nos. 178, 182–4, 190). Gerald Gould, one of Joyce's earliest advocates, objected to the 'fundamental aesthetic dishonesty' of Joyce's new sort of writing (No. 179). The *Times* reviewer chose to emphasize continued Irish dissatisfaction with the English language (No. 180). But by 1929 and 1930, when *Haveth Childers Everywhere* and *Tales Told of Shem & Shaun* appeared, reviewers were more willing to let Joyce have his way until the finished book appeared. This attitude reflects the lucidity of the essays in *Our Exagmination* and the indebtedness of all critics in the thirties to that collection. Such subjects as the analogies of 'Work in Progress' with the kennings of Eddic poets, the presentation of a cyclical history according to the Viconian theory (another bridge to march troops over, Joyce believed), the composite nature of the characters and of the language, the etymological innovations, the use of time and space, the Catholic element, and an explication of selected paragraphs from 'Work in Progress'—these were the topics of invention the Joyce disciples placed before the critical world. These topics were, as Clive Hart has observed, a 'progression away from generalities and towards an increasingly detailed examination of the text'.[29]

When *Finnegans Wake* finally appeared in 1939, the reviews were, in general, apologetic, tentative, confused and confusing, and 'arrogant'. Eugène Jolas reported later that the reviews that most pleased Joyce were those by William Troy in the *Partisan Review* (No. 312), Harry Levin in *New Directions in Prose and Poetry* (No. 311), Edmund Wilson's two essays in the *New Republic*, later incorporated into *The Wound and the Bow*, Alfred Kazin in the *New York Herald Tribune* (No. 307), and Padraic Colum in the *New York Times* (No. 300). Harold

Nicolson acknowledged in the *Daily Telegraph* that he had 'failed to penetrate the meaning of this enormous allegory'. Harry Levin was to apply Dante's fourfold allegorical interpretation to *Finnegans Wake* in one of the most interesting and lastingly valuable essays on the work. The *Irish Times* found it inconceivable that Joyce should have spent so many years upon a hoax (Oliver St. John Gogarty considered the book the 'most colossal leg pull in literature' (No. 301)). Both Harry Levin and Edmund Wilson assumed that the book had a meaningful basis, a sound aesthetic and logical plan, and that through an assembling of its details, the basic pattern of the work could be described. These reviewers are the antidote to the reviewers (and this group includes most of the other reviews found in this volume) who found Joyce either mad, a charlatan, or an exponent of destruction. Joyce, in the meantime, encouraged articles from such friends as Louis Gillet (No. 321) and Jacques Mercanton. But, alas, the world that Joyce was supposedly trying to destroy was destroying itself. *Finnegans Wake* was overshadowed by a world war, Joyce went into exile again in Zürich, where he died in January 1941. He did not live to discover that within a few years, even at the remaindered price of $1.75, *Finnegans Wake* was not being read.

In the years since its publication *Finnegans Wake*, a myth, the 'Comic Synthesis', the gigantic catalogue—the encyclopedic extension of *Ulysses*, the incredibly rich and rewarding multi-dimensional world vision, has continued to pose a challenge for critics. There are, with good reason perhaps, only a small group of dedicated explorers of *Finnegans Wake*, but the significant studies by Adaline Glasheen, Clive Hart, James Atherton and Fritz Senn have greatly assisted in our 'exagmination' of the 'funferall'.

THE CRITICAL TRADITION AFTER 1941

If the tremendous impositions of scholarship upon Joyce's works have been in some ways detrimental, they have also in the twenty-seven years since Joyce's death produced notable achievements. We now have an accurate (or nearly so) text of *Ulysses* and *A Portrait of the Artist*, the complete (almost) *Letters* and a definitive biography by Richard Ellmann, *The Critical Writings, The Epiphanies* and *Stephen Hero*, and Professor Ellmann's edition of *Giacomo Joyce*. There is probably still no better general introduction to Joyce than Harry Levin's *James Joyce: A Critical Introduction*, though there are excellent books on the separate novels. The earlier works are neglected, while *Finnegans Wake* has become increasingly a scholar's creative plaything. It appears that scholars, with exceptions of course, will continue to avoid the labour of explanation and investigation that the book demands. The Irish are apparently the only ones who are able to see Joyce as real, but few Irishmen will heed Elizabeth Bowen's exhortation in her critical obituary of Joyce, 'Let us strip from Joyce the exaggerations of foolish intellectual worship he got abroad, and the notoriety he got at home, and take him back to ourselves as a writer out of the Irish people, who received much from our tradition and was to hand on more.'[30] Because the Irish refuse to perform this function, the outpourings of Joyce scholarship have. The function grows each year, and occasionally it may seem that 'our Human Conger Eel' is being drowned in unreality and in intricacy, or in what Robert M. Adams has called the 'logically arranged machinery of glittering, sterile edges'.[31] It is up to Joyce scholarship in the next period of growth, the next stage already 'in progress', to discover in the entire interwoven fabric of Joyce's art precisely how he tried himself against the 'powers of the world'. This is a peculiarly difficult task, as it was for the critics whose views are collected in this volume, because one of the 'powers' is criticism itself.

NOTES

1. Herbert M. McLuhan, 'A Survey of Joyce Criticism, *Renascence*, IV (1951), 13.
2. Quoted in Richard Ellmann, *James Joyce* (1959), pp. 154–5; hereafter cited in the text as Ellmann, *James Joyce*.
3. Quoted in Ellmann, *James Joyce*, p. 241, and in Richard Ellmann, ed., *The Letters of James Joyce*, Volume II (1966), p. 182; hereafter cited in the text as Ellmann, *Letters*.
4. This is a point Yeats had also observed, with the corollary that it is the poetry of a 'young man who is practising his instrument, taking pleasure in the mere handling of the stops', quoted in Ellmann, *Letters*, II, p. 23.
5. Quoted in Stuart Gilbert, ed., *The Letters of James Joyce*, Volume I (1957), p. 67; hereafter cited in the text as Gilbert, *Letters*.
6. John Kaestlin, 'Joyce by Candlelight', *Contemporaries*, No. 2 (Summer 1933), 47–54; quoted in Marvin Magalaner and Richard M. Kain, *Joyce: The Man, The Work, The Reputation* (1956), pp. 48–9. I am extremely indebted to this excellent summary of Joyce's reputation for many of my remarks in this Introduction. My only hope is that I have not been slavishly dependent upon this truly remarkable book.

7. Herbert Howarth, '*Chamber Music* and Its Place in the Joyce Canon', in *James Joyce Today*, edited by Thomas F. Staley (1966), p. 11.
8. Stanislaus Joyce, *My Brother's Keeper*, edited by Richard Ellmann (1958), p. 116.
9. Wyndham Lewis, 'Ezra: The Portrait of a Personality', *Quarterly Review of Literature*, V, No. 2 (1949), 136.
10. Comments taken respectively from the *Bellmann*, XXI (3 March 1917), 245, the *English Review*, XXIV (May 1917), 478, and the *Future* (June 1917), 237.
11. H. L. Mencken, in the *Smart Set*, LII (August 1917), n.p.
12. Marvin Magalaner, 'Reflections on *A Portrait of the Artist*', *James Joyce Quarterly*, IV, No. 4 (Summer 1967), 343.
13. Edmund Wilson, 'Stephen Hero', *New Yorker* (6 January 1945), 63.
14. Robert Benchley, 'Back to Form', *Life*, LXXXV (12 March 1925), 20.
15. Joseph Wood Krutch, 'Figures of the Dawn', *Nation*, CXX (March 1925), 272.
16. Jane Heap, *Little Review*, V, No. 2 (June 1918), 54, 57.
17. T. S. Eliot, *Athenæum* (4 July 1919), 553.
18. James Douglas, 'Beauty—And the Beast', *Sunday Express* (28 May 1922), 5.
19. Ellmann, *Letters*, III, p. 104.
20. Djuna Barnes, 'James Joyce', *Vanity Fair*, XVIII (April 1922), 65.
21. Jacques Mercanton, 'The Hours of James Joyce, Part I', *Kenyon Review*, XXIV (1962), 702.
22. Mercanton, op. cit., p. 725.
23. Virginia Woolf's comment in her *Writer's Diary* (1954), pp. 47, 49; T. S. Eliot's comment in Virginia Woolf, *Writer's Diary*, p. 50; Katherine Mansfield's comment in *Letters of Katherine Mansfield*, edited by J. Middleton Murry (London, 1928), Volume II, p. 173.
24. Malcolm Cowley, 'James Joyce', *Bookman*, LIX (July 1934), 518.
25. Edmund Wilson, 'An Introduction to Joyce', *Dial*, LXXVII (November 1924), 430.
26. Frank Kermode, *Puzzles and Epiphanies* (1963), p. 86.
27. These comments are reported in Eugène Jolas, 'My Friend James Joyce', in *James Joyce: Two Decades of Criticism*, edited by Seon Givens (1948), pp. 11–12.
28. Richard V. Chase, '*Finnegans Wake*: An Anthropological Study', *American Scholar*, XIII (Autumn 1944), 418.
29. Clive Hart, '*Finnegans Wake* in Perspective', in *James Joyce Today*, edited by Thomas F. Staley (1966), p. 137.
30. Elizabeth Bowen, 'James Joyce', *Bell*, I, No. 6 (March 1941), 49.
31. Robert M. Adams, 'The Bent Knife Blade: Joyce in the 1960s', *Partisan Review*, XXIX (1962), 518.

1. George Russell (Æ) on James Joyce

1902

George Russell (Æ), in a letter to W. B. Yeats (? 11 August 1902).

From *The Letters From Æ* (1961), ed. Alan Denson, p. 43; also in *The Letters of James Joyce*, Volume II (1966), ed. Richard Ellmann, pp. 11–12.

. . . I want you very much to meet a young fellow named Joyce whom I wrote to Lady Gregory about half jestingly. He is an extremely clever boy who belongs to your clan more than to mine and more still to himself. But he has all the intellectual equipment, culture and education which all our other clever friends here lack. And I think writes amazingly well in prose though I believe he also writes verse and is engaged in writing a comedy which he expects will occupy him five years or thereabouts as he writes slowly. [George] Moore who saw an article of this boy's says it is preposterously clever. [The essay is 'The Day of the Rabblement,' a 1901 attack on the Irish National Theatre Society.] . . . He is I think certainly more promising than Magee [William K. Magee who wrote under the pseudonym of John Eglinton]. . . .

2. Æ on Joyce

1902

George Russell (Æ), in a letter to Sarah Pruser (15 August 1902).

From Æ, *Letters*, ed. Alan Denson, pp. 42–3; also in Joyce, *Letters*, Volume II, ed. Richard Ellmann, p. 13.

. . . I expect to see my young genius on Monday and will find out more about him. I wouldn't be his Messiah for a thousand million pounds. He would be always criticising the bad taste of his deity. . . .

3. Stanislaus Joyce on his brother

1903

Extract from *The Dublin Diary of Stanislaus Joyce* (1962), ed. George H. Healey, pp. 13–14.

One of the earliest, 1903, critical comments on Joyce is this one by his brother Stanislaus in his *Diary* (see Introduction, p. 3).

His intellect is precise and subtle, but not comprehensive. He is no student. His artistic sympathy and judgment are such as would be expected in one of his kind of intellect—if he were not more than a critic, I believe he would be as good a critic of what interests him as any using English today. His literary talent seems to be very great indeed, both in prose and in verse. He has, as Yeats says, a power of very delicate spiritual writing and whether he writes in sorrow or is young and virginal, or whether (as in 'He travels after the wintry sun') [from 'Tilly', published in *Pomes Penyeach*] he writes of what he has seen, the form is always either strong, expressive, graceful or engaging, and his imagination open-eyed and classic. His 'epiphanies'—his prose pieces (which I almost prefer to his lyrics) and his dialogues—are again subtle. He has put himself into these with singular courage, singular memory, and scientific minuteness; he has proved himself capable of taking very great pains to create a very little thing of prose or verse. The keen observation and satanic irony of his character are precisely, but not fully, expressed. Whether he will ever build up anything broad—a drama, an esthetic treatise—I cannot say. His genius is not literary and he will probably run through many of the smaller forms of literary artistic expression.

4. Æ on Joyce

1903

George Russell (Æ), in a letter to T. B. Mosher (3 November 1903).

From Æ, *Letters*, ed. Alan Denson, p. 50.

. . . Another boy named Joyce writes with perfect art poems as delicate and dainty as Watteau pictures. . . .

5. Stanislaus on Joyce

1904

Extract from *The Dublin Diary of Stanislaus Joyce* (1962), ed. George H. Healey, p. 23 (see Introduction, p. 4).

Diary entry for 29 February 1904: . . . I have no doubt that he is a poet, a lyric poet, that he has a still greater mastery of prose. He may be a genius—it seems to me very possible—but that he has not yet found himself is obvious.

6. Æ on Joyce

1905

George Russell (Æ), in a letter to T. B. Mosher (? April 1905).

From Æ, *Letters*, ed. Alan Denson, pp. 55–6.

. . . We have a young scamp named Joyce here who writes with a more perfect art than anyone except Yeats who is I believe going to publish a book of lyrics. He gave it [*Chamber Music*, published in 1907] to Grant Richards who collapsed, and I have not heard anything more of it as the poet has decamped to the continent with a barmaid. It will be a good book when it appears. . . .

CHAMBER MUSIC

May 1907

---

7. Arthur Symons on Joyce

1906

Letter to Elkin Mathews (9 October 1906), quoted in Karl Beckson and John M. Munro, 'Letters from Arthur Symons to James Joyce: 1904–1932', *James Joyce Quarterly*, IV, No. 2 (Winter 1967), 96–7. Also in Richard Ellmann, *James Joyce* (1959), p. 240.

Elkin Mathews was to publish *Chamber Music* in 1907.

. . . Would you care to have, for your Vigo Cabinet, a book of verse which is of the most genuine lyric quality of any new work I have read for many years? It is called *A Book of Thirty Songs for Lovers* [the title was subsequently changed to *Chamber Music*], and the lyrics are almost Elizabethan in their freshness, but quite personal. They are by a young Irishman called J. A. Joyce. He is *not* in the Celtic Movement, and though Yeats admits his ability he is rather against him because Joyce has attacked the movement. . . I am offering you a book which cannot fail to attract notice from everyone capable of knowing poetry when he sees it . . .

8. Thomas Kettle, review, *Freeman's Journal*

1 June 1907

Extract from 'Review', *Freeman's Journal* (1 June 1907), n.p.

. . . His work, never very voluminous, had from the first a rare and exquisite accent. One still goes back to the files of *St. Stephen's*, to the *Saturday Review*, the *Homestead*, to various occasional magazines to find these lyrics and stories which, although at first reading so slight and frail, still hold one curiously by their integrity of form. *Chamber Music* is a collection of the best of these delicate verses, which have, each of them, the bright beauty of a crystal. The title of the book evokes that atmosphere of remoteness, restraint, accomplished execution characteristic of its whole contents.

There is but one theme behind the music, a love, gracious, and, in its way, strangely intense, but fashioned by temperamental and literary moulds, too strict to permit it to pass over into the great tumult of passion. The inspiration of the book is almost entirely literary. There is no trace of the folklore, folk dialect, or even the national feeling that have coloured the work of practically every writer in contemporary Ireland. Neither is there any sense of that modern point of view which consumes all life in the language of problems. It is clear, delicate, distinguished playing with harps, with wood birds, with Paul Verlaine.

But the only possible criticism of poetry is quotation.

[quotes poems I and XXVIII]

Mr. Joyce's book is one that all his old friends will, with a curious pleasure, add to their shelves, and that will earn him many new friends.

9. Arthur Symons, review, *Nation*

22 June 1907, i, 639

'A Book of Songs,' *Nation*, I, No. 17 (22 June 1907), 639 (see Introduction, p. 4).

I advise everyone who cares for poetry to buy *Chamber Music*, by James Joyce, a young Irishman who is in no Irish movement, literary or national, and has not even anything obviously Celtic in his manner. The book is tiny; there are thirty-six pages, with a poem a-piece. And they are all so singularly good, so firm and delicate, and yet so full of music and suggestion, that I can hardly choose among them; they are almost all of an equal merit. Here is one of the faintest:

Gentle lady, do not sing
  Sad songs about the end of love;
Lay aside sadness and sing
  How love that passes is enough.

Sing about the long deep sleep
  Of lovers that are dead, and how
In the grave all love shall sleep:
  Love is a weary now.

No one who has not tried can realise how difficult it is to do such tiny, evanescent things as that; for it is to evoke, not only roses in mid-winter, but the very dew on the roses. Sometimes we are reminded of Elizabethan, more often of Jacobean, lyrics; there is more than sweetness, there is now and then the sharp prose touch, as in Rochester, which gives a kind of malice to sentiment:

For elegant and antique phrase,
  Dearest, my lips wax all too wise;
Nor have I known a love whose praise
  Our piping poets solemnise,
Neither a love where may not be
Ever so little falsity.

ARTHUR SYMONS, REVIEW, *Nation* JUNE 1907

There is a rare kind of poetry to be made out of the kind or unkind insinuations of lovers, who are not always in a state of rapture, even when the mood comes for singing, and may, like this love-poet, be turned to a new harmony—

> And all for some strange name he read,
> In Purchas or in Holinshed.

There is almost no substance at all in these songs, which hardly hint at a story; but they are like a whispering clavichord that someone plays in the evening, when it is getting dark. They are full of ghostly old tunes, that were never young and will never be old, played on an old instrument. If poetry is a thing to be overheard, these songs, certainly, will justify the definition. They are so slight, as a drawing of Whistler is slight, that their entire beauty will not be discovered by those who go to poetry for anything but its perfume. But to those who care only for what is most essentially poetry in a poem, they will seem to have so much the more value by all that they omit. There is only just enough life in them to come into existence, but these instants are, in Browning's phrase, 'made eternity.'

I have little hope that the rare quality of these songs will captivate many readers. Such a song as 'Bright cap and steamers,' or 'Silently she's combing,' ought to catch every fancy, and the graver pieces ought to awaken every imagination. But if anything in art is small, and merely good, without anything but that fact to recommend it, it has usually to wait a long time for recognition. People are so afraid of following even an impulse, fearing that they may be mistaken. How unlikely it seems, does it not, that any new thing should come suddenly into the world, and be beautiful?

10. Unsigned notice, *Bookman*

June 1907, xxxii, 113

A little book of poetry which charms, provokes criticism, and charms again. Mr. Joyce has a touch reminiscent of the sixteenth century poets, with here and there a break in his lines' smoothness which can only be smoothed by an old-time stress on the syllable, such as Vaughan and Herbert demanded. At times there are bold liberties taken with rhyme and rhythm; but there is so much of music and quaintness in the little volume that we give praise instead of censure.

11. Opinions of *Chamber Music*

1907

Press notices of *Chamber Music*, privately printed at Trieste, quoted in Joyce, *Letters*, Volume II, ed. Richard Ellmann, pp. 332–3, note 3.

Joyce had a printer in Trieste print up these excerpts from the reviews of *Chamber Music* which were inserted in press copies of *Dubliners* in 1914.
The reviews by Arthur Symons (No. 9), T. M. Kettle (No. 8) and in *Bookman* (No. 10) are not included here. The extracts are Joyce's.

Chanel in the *Leader:* Mr. Joyce has a wonderful mastery over the technique of poetry. It is not without supreme skill that he produces lines of such apparent ease and simplicity, every word in its right place, the whole beautiful in its unadorned charm with a faint subtle fragrance of earthly loveliness. . . . Mr. Joyce flows in a clear delicious stream that ripples. . . . Mr. Joyce complies will [*sic*] none of my critical principles: he is, in truth, entirely earthly, unthinking of the greater and the further, though let me say in justice that the casual reader will see nothing in his verses to object to, nothing incapable of an innocent explanation. But earthly as he is, he is so simple, so pretty, so alluring, I cannot bring myself to chide him.

Daily News: Light and evanescent, pretty and fragile. . . . His poems are attempts at much: he has tried to express one art in terms of another. His aim has been to catch in his rhythms something of the music of pipe or lute as distinct from the verbal music of the great lyrical masters. . . . His poems have at once the music and the want of music of a harpstring played on by the winds in some forest of Broceliande.

Evening Standard: Pretty lyrics with a delusive title.

Manchester Guardian: A welcome contribution to contemporary poetry. Here are thirty-six lyrics of quite notable beauty. . . . Something of the spirit of Waller and Herrick . . . grace and simplicity . . .

an elegance and delicacy that are as uncommon as they are perilous. At their best they reveal a rare musical quality. His muse is a gentle tender spirit that knows smiles and tears, the rain, the dew and the morning sun.

Nottingham Guardian: Lovers of verse will delight in many of the pieces for their simple unaffected merit. *Chamber Music* has a tuneful ring befitting the title and both the rhythm and the smoothness of his lines are excellent.

Glasgow Herald. .. verse which has an old-fashioned sweetness and flavour, Mr. Joyce sings of the coming and, apparently, inexplicable going of love. The most are but snatches of song and one has to be penetrated by the subtle music of them before their poetic value is perceived. Once that is felt their merit is beyond dispute though only lovers of poetry will be likely to see or acknowledge it. Verse such as this has its own charm but where will it find its audience?

Irish Daily Independent: . . . Music in verse, poems, sweet, reposeful and sublime; poems that lying in the shade amid the scent of new-mown hay one would read and dream on, forgetful of the workaday world.

Scotsman: A volume of graceful verse: it contains some little gems of real beauty.

Country Life: A very promising little volume.

12. Unsigned review, *Egoist*

June-July 1918, V, No. 6, 87

An unsigned review of the second edition, Elkin Mathews, 1918.

This is a second edition; first published in 1907. This verse is good, very good; though it never would have excited much attention but for Joyce's prose, still it would in any case have worn well. We infer from it that Mr. Joyce is probably something of a musician; it is lyric verse, and good lyric verse is very rare. It will be called 'fragile,' but is substantial, with a great deal of thought beneath fine workmanship.

[quotes the first three lines of the second stanza of 'When the shy star . . .' (IV) and the second stanza of 'Be not sad . . .' (XIX)]

13. 'M.A.' review, *New Republic*

8 March 1919, xviii, No. 227, 191

This anonymous review, entitled 'The Lyrics of James Joyce', is a review of the B. W. Huebsch (New York) edition.

This is James Joyce's one book of verse, a small book written some ten years ago. And beyond that fact, which is indicative in itself, there are many other indications within the thirty-four lyrics that he is not essentially a poet. There is little of the dreamer in them, nothing of the enthusiast. They make their fragile points by turns of evanescent thought, or rhetoric thrice refined. If we may judge his personality by the zest and spontaneity of his plays and novels it is fair to say that he was in verse a shadow of himself and others, a dilettante playing a safe and pleasant game. The charm the lyrics possess, a charm undeniable and unfailing, is due in great measure to a skill in rhythms that, if not unique, is arresting, and a cleverness that has lent itself momentarily to the touching of chords at once light and wistful, whimsical and sadly austere. Not that it was a conscious effort, to be repeated at will. It is youth that makes these things possible to men not singers by inner compulsion.

The music of the lyrics is of a casual ballad quality, seemingly artless, but full of subtly gained effects. The shifting stress, the naively lengthened line, the half-rhyme, are used with a surety that could be no other than deliberate. And the consciousness of the art is emphasized by the perfection with which variations of the formal rondeau are used. There is formality and device throughout, though well disguised, and a courtliness that reminds one of Herrick or Lovelace:

> Now, wind, of your good courtesy
>   I pray you go,
> And come into her little garden
>   And sing at her window. . . . [XIII]

One-half stanza, of excellence compact, yet it reminds you of too many other excellent things. Of Rossetti, of Yeats, and of phrases and rhythms more archaic, a trace of each. It would be a pretty problem to unravel all the strains of influence that meet, say in the thirtieth poem, perhaps the best:

> Love came to us in time gone by
> When one at twilight shyly played
> And one in fear was standing nigh—
> For Love at first is all afraid.
>
> We were grave lovers. Love is past.
> That had his sweet hours many a one;
> Welcome to us now at the last
> The ways that we shall go upon.

But though we might unravel them to our satisfaction we should still find it beautiful, and not alone with imported tricks. For the very lack of emotion that holds Joyce's hand from further poetic achievement lent him here a special grace. He was ill at ease in this alien medium; he would not venture to put himself on paper; he avoided committing himself. And the result is a sentiment so faint that it seems fairy-like, a madrigal from the stars, a summer wind in the harp that leaves you groping for the minstrel. A mere disembodied third person, aloof, detached, is the author of *Chamber Music.* And now that Joyce is grown up past recall we shall seek him under heaven, or in the depths of the subconscious, quite in vain.

14. Morton D. Zabel on *Chamber Music*

1930

'The Lyrics of James Joyce', *Poetry*, xxxvi (July 1930), 206–13.

A review of both *Chamber Music* and *Pomes Penyeach.* This is the first extensive criticism of Joyce's poetry (see Introduction, p. 5).

The interest aroused by the ever-expanding design of the *Work in Progress*, as it appears in quarterly installments in *transition*, as well as by the inclusion of three segments of this prose epic among the poems which the Messrs. Ford and Aldington have gathered in their recent *Imagist Anthology, 1930*, is probably sufficient reason for recalling that among Joyce's achievements is a small group of lyrics which certain readers still claim as his most beautiful work. Throughout his career Joyce has been regarded in many quarters as fundamentally a poet . . . His first published book was the collection of lyrics, *Chamber Music* (1907), and in earlier poems like *Tilly* (1904) he had sketched in himself the familiar traits of poetic adolescence, enraged at the stupidity of life:

> Boor, bond of the herd,
> Tonight stretch full by the fire!
> I bleed by the black stream
> For my torn bough.

. . . But, conventional definitions apart, his novels lack specific poetic elements, as well as poetry's absolute sublimation of experience. It is equally apparent that his lyrics are the marginal fragments of his art, minor in theme and too often, for all their precise and orderly felicities, undecided in quality. To the thirty-six poems in *Chamber Music* he added the thirteen which in 1927 came from the press of Shakespeare & Co., Paris, under the title *Pomes Penyeach*, eight having originally appeared in 1917 in *Poetry* [Vol. X (May 1917) and Vol. XI (Nov. 1917)]. Though an extremely small part of his entire production, this body of lyrics is large enough to disclose changes and adjustments through which Joyce's mind has passed, as well as the creative impulses by which it has been guided.

The verse in *Chamber Music* has not the finality of single intention. Its deficiencies have been ascribed to the fact that, where it does not reflect the vaporous mysticism of the early Yeats, Æ, and the other Irish revivalists, it is a patent imitation of the Elizabethan song-books. Examination reveals in these poems little more than a superficial verbal similarity to the poetry of the Celtic twilight whose obvious accents appear only in *XXXVI*, 'Oh, it was out by Donnycarney.' Whatever Joyce retained from the bardic songs (or their modern translations) in the way of simplified expression and elegiac motives, was overlaid with the formal decorum, yet enlivened by the lucid sensibility, of Jonson and Herrick, or of those poems by Byrd, Dowland, and Campion which he knew from boyhood. To read *Chamber Music* with its familiar refrains is to revive sensations first gained from the *Book of Airs* or *A Paradise of Dainty Devices*. Yet the overlay of artificial elegance never conceals wholly a nerve of sharp lyric refinement. Little more than elegance is present in *VI:*

[quotes the first stanza]

Adjusted to the courtly tone of Suckling and the Cavaliers, it reappears in *XII:*

[quotes the first stanza]

It is clear that in such poems one has, instead of direct and unequivocal poetic compulsion, a deliberate archaism and a kind of fawning studiousness which attempt to disguise the absence of profounder elements. Yet the archaism which exists at its extreme level in *X* and *XI*, or, phrased as *vers de société*, in *VII*, was converted into Joyce's own material in two or three lyrics which, for spiritual suavity and logic, approach the minor work of Crashaw, or at least of Crashaw's descendants in the nineteenth century, Thompson and Lionel Johnson. One of them is *XXVI:*

[quotes the entire poem]

It has been remarked before, by Edmund Wilson, that Joyce was closer to continental literature during his apprenticeship than to current English and Irish. In a writer so intentionally derivative, affiliations are natural. They can probably be traced here to the kind of lyric impressionism that grew, by a curious process of inversion, out of Dehmel and Liliencron toward the broken accent of expressionism as one finds it in Werfel, Joyce's closest ally among the figures of later German poetry. Through his lively contemporaneity and his curious sympathy with modern French art, Joyce was undoubtedly attracted by the inferential subtlety of the Symbolists. But his lyricism, like Dowson's or Rilke's, betrays too much diffusion to enable him to approach Mallarmé's faultless penetration or Rimbaud's intense discipline . . . But Joyce was testing his lyric gift by a stricter training, by a reading of Rimbaud and Samain perhaps, or of Meredith. The latter's homelier phrases in *Love in a Valley* are echoed in *XXIV*, and his unexpected power to order the material of allegory lies behind the last poem in *Chamber Music*, the magnificent lyric whose Yeatsian tendency has yielded to the vigor of Meredithian symbolism as one finds it in *Lucifer in Starlight* or *The Promise in Disturbance:*

I hear an army charging upon the land
  And the thunder of the horses plunging, foam about their knees.
Arrogant, in black armor, behind them stand,
  Disdaining the reins, with fluttering whips, the charioteers.

The later lyrics in *Pomes Penyeach* go so far in integrating these disparate elements that Joyce achieved in the little booklet his own poetic character for the first time. The sedulous understudy which kept him from attaining intimacy or a unifying personality in his earlier work is largely avoided. The style may be defined by devices. It consists in the marked alliteration of *On the Beach at Fontana* and *Tutto e sciolto;* in the persistent periphrasis of words like *rockvine, greygolden, slimesilvered, moongrey, loveward,* and *loveblown* (all suggestive of *Ulysses*); and in the transparent choral tonality of *She Weeps over Rahoon* and *Watching the Needleboats at San Sabra.* Archaisms are still present, and the humid emotionalism of impressionist verse still prevails in *Alone* and *Bahnhofstrasse.* But the pattern is constricted by severer form, the lyric accent gains edge, and the emotional content is more secure in its power. Ultimately the tragic surge and wrath of *Ulysses* finds voice in *A Prayer* and in *A Memory of the Players in a Mirror at Midnight:*

[quotes the second stanza]

Even within this narrow range, Joyce's eclecticism, the long reach of his artistic interests, is revealed. Yet one sees likewise the limitations which have kept his lyric output small. The real functions of free-verse have escaped him, and his lyric ideas must otherwise submit to conventional stanzaic formalities. Diffusion mars the outline of many poems, and unnatural sobriety and caution hinder the spontaneity of others. But in four or five pages he has achieved a complete fusion of rapture and lucidity, and written with mastery. *Simples* must rank as one of the purest lyrics of our time:

[quotes the entire poem]

The lyric motive and discipline have not been forgotten by Joyce among the problems and ingenuities of his prose epics. Wherever *Ulysses* avoids parody or satire, it is likely to soar in a lyric utterance; the river symphony at the beginning of the *Work in Progress* is one of the brilliant phonetic evocations in modern literature. His power to synthesize and formulate the swarming resources of his mind has demanded prose for its proper extension. Yet the poetic temper which has played an indubitable part in his career has given us, by the way, a small offering of exquisite poems, valuable both as diversions of one of the first literary geniuses of our day, and as lyrics which at their best have the mark of classic beauty upon them.

15. Louis Golding on Joyce's poetry

1933

'A Sidelight on James Joyce', *Nineteenth Century & After*, cxiii (April 1933), 491–3, 496–7 [491–7].

. . . The James Joyce canon officially begins with the publication in 1907 of a collection of thirty-six poems entitled *Chamber Music*. . . .

I state that the canon *officially* begins with *Chamber Music*, not merely because it was the first work published by Joyce through the ordinary channels, not merely because the most solemn consideration of Joyce as major artist usually includes a respectful or even enthusiastic criticism of *Chamber Music*, but because Joyce himself has made no effort to disavow it. On the contrary, he avows it very explicitly. In the page that faces the title-page of his most famous work, *Ulysses*, it stands up in bold type heading the brief list of works 'by the same writer.' Moreover, so late as 1927, in the year when the first section of the cryptic *Work in Progress* appeared, *Chamber Music* appeared again. It is true it had another name. It was called *Pomes Penyeach* this time . . . From the title of the minute volume, from the fact that *Ulysses* had been finished in 1921, from the fact that *Work in Progress* was in progress, the reader would have been justified in expecting a terrifying distillation of that variety of Rive-Gauche-Greenwich-Village poetry which, consisting to an appreciable extent of figures and signs of punctuation, seems to the uninitiate as coherent as a blind man's lackadaisical tappings upon a typewriter.

But it was not that variety of poetry which met the eye. You read in a poem entitled *Flower Given to My Daughter* and written in Trieste in 1913:

Frail the white rose and frail are
  Her hands that gave
Whose soul is sere and paler
  Than time's wan wave.

In *Alone*, a poem written in Zürich in 1916, a year when the same author was engaged upon a prose masterpiece which exalts him among the most important artists of our day, you read:

> The sly reeds whisper to the night
> A name—her name—
> And all my soul is a delight,
> A swoon of shame.

There are better poems, far better, in this volume. Indeed, the best is the earliest, and was written in Dublin in 1904, the very year in which the celebrated June 16 occurred in which is comprehended the whole action of *Ulysses*. The best is the first, so that in his lyric verse undeliberately, as in *Work in Progress* deliberately, Joyce confutes the categories of time. But the point is not that there are better poems than *Alone* and *A Flower Given to My Daughter* in *Pomes Penyeach*. The point is that there are poems so bad as those; the point is, that Joyce is writing *Chamber Music*, however exiguously, all his life long; the point is, not that he turns out infrequently a fairly beautiful poem, but that he is perpetuating and re-rendering poems so thin, so mawkish, usually so derivative, as those I have quoted—from stage to stage across a career in which, as a prose artist, he exercises so masculine, so subtle, so versatile, so courageous an intellect, in which, as a prose artist, he not merely handles his medium with incomparable skill, but creates it in a fashion associated with very few artists besides himself . . . How much more enigmatic do the two enigmas of *Chamber Music* and *Work in Progress* become when we try—as we must, for Joyce allows no alternative—to explain them in the terms of a single creative personality! We cannot ignore *Chamber Music* because Joyce does not. And Joyce does not, I believe, because the key to Joyce, or to Stephen Dedalus (the name he gives himself in his *Portrait of the Artist as a Young Man*), is locked in it, more truly than the key to Shakespeare is locked up in the Sonnets . . . But Stephen Dedalus is the theme of James Joyce from the beginning to the end. In *Chamber Music* he sings his pitiful little songs. In *Dubliners* we tread his streets and rub shoulders with his familiars. The light moves from the circumference into the centre in *Portrait of the Artist as a Young Man*. In *Exiles* his heart is shown divided between two bodies. In *Ulysses* he is incorporated into myth and attains immortality. His grin, disembodied, extends across the dislocated firmament of *Work in Progress*.

What, then, is the secret hidden away in *Chamber Music* and the much tinier volume *Pomes Penyeach*, which, though twenty years elapse between the writing of its first and last poem, laboriously tots up to fifteen pages?

[Mr. Golding refers, at length, to Miss Rebecca West's essay 'The Strange Necessity' and the 'secret' she discovers: Joyce is a 'great man who is entirely without taste' (No. 199). Golding discusses the tastelessness of the poems.]

I say of poetry that it is the exercise of the subconscious mind, because, whatever the source of it, the element of irresponsibility is stronger in poetry than in the other forms of aesthetic composition in words, even though the conscious mind may quite scientifically, throughout the whole process, organise the technique of its expression. That Stephen Dedalus did not give up all hope that he might some day exercise in poetry the subconscious mind is proved by the pathetic retention of the scraps of verse which constitute *Pomes Penyeach*. It is as if he hoped that by muttering them over to himself he might some day suddenly, in the fortunate coincidence of kabbalistic syllables, find that the iron doors opposed to him had drawn apart. In the meanwhile, the conscious, the prose, mind exercised itself in the production of *Dubliners*, the *Portrait*, *Exiles*, and, supremely, in *Ulysses*. And now at length, as it seems to me, having given up all hope of release through poetry and the subconscious mind, having exorcised his demon so far as prose and the mind permit (producing during that process the greatest prose work in our time), he is endeavouring to exercise in *Work in Progress* a type of cognition which can be described only as a 'superconscious mind.' That is to say, he himself is conscious, and expects his readers to be conscious, on a number of planes and in a number of dimensions at the same time. In space, the river Liffey is simultaneously Ganges and Indus and all earth's rivers; Waterloo is the Garden of Eden. In time, Gladstone and Noah are simultaneously his protagonists. In speech, a given word may be compounded out of elements introduced from three or four languages. In philosophy, the tongue of the Frenchman Bergson projects from the mask of the Neapolitan Giambattista Vico. In approach, the reader must listen intensely with his ears to the spoken achievement, apprehend on the page the composition and disposition of the printed word, rise to the attack with all he possesses of erudition, lie passive to the reception of overtones, undertones, crude jokes, suave innuendo.

It is extremely difficult. But it is not so difficult, I assure you, as the thirty-first poem in *Chamber Music:*

Along with us the summer wind
  Went murmuring—o, happily!—
But softer than the breath of summer
  Was the kiss she gave to me.

There is a sense in which the most tortuous poem of Robert Browning is a nursery rhyme compared with that!

16. Arthur Symons on Joyce's poetry

1933

'Epilogue', in *The Joyce Book* (1933), ed. Herbert Hughes, pp. 79–84; appeared earlier in *Two Worlds' Monthly*, i, No. 1 (1926), 86–92.

The article begins by quoting from Symons's review of *Chamber Music* (No. 9).

. . . Not long ago I received a delightful letter from Joyce written in Paris in which he says (and I venture to give his own words): 'As for *Pomes Penyeach* I don't think they would have been published but for Mrs Symons's suggestion when she was with me'. She was right. There is in these poems a rare lyrical quality, with touches of pure magic, and some give me the effect of a warm wind wafting the scent of heather over me when on the coast of Cornwall I used to lie near the edge of a cliff, basking in the intense heat of the sun. There I could watch the sea, where, when the wind urges it, it heaves into great billows, that rise up green and tilt over, and, as the waves roll up to the shore, they leap suddenly at the rocks, and hammer at them with a loud voluminous softness, and fall back like a blown cataract, every drop distinct in the sunlight. And at times the sea was the colour of lilac deepening into rose, and it lay like a field of heather washed by the rain.

ARTHUR SYMONS ON JOYCE'S POETRY 1933

Wisdom, it has been said, is justified in her children: and why not Joyce? Words and cadences must have an intoxication for him, the intoxication of the scholar; and in his own wandering way he has been a wild vagabond, a vagabond of the mind and of the imagination. He knows that words are living things, which we have not created, and which go their way without demanding from us the right to live. He knows that words are suspicious, not without malice, and that they resist mere force with the impalpable resistance of fire or water. They are to be caught only with guile or trust. And his voice can be heard like a wandering music, which comes troublingly into the mind, bringing with it the solace of its old and recaptured melodies. And I am haunted by the strange wild beauty of two of his poems, *Flood* and *Nightpiece*. Take, for instance, this stanza:

> Saraphim,
> The lost host awaken
> To service till
> In moonless gloom as each lapses muted, dim,
> Raised when she has and shaken
> Her thurible.

Dubliners was published in 1914; *A Portrait of the Artist as a Young Man* in 1916; *Exiles, a Prose Play in Three Acts* in 1918. He wrote *Ulysses* (a book of 732 pages) in Trieste, Zürich, and Paris, between 1914 and 1921—an incredible achievement when one considers the difficulties he experienced during its composition. The novel was printed at Dijon in 1922 by Maurice Darantière, and for the simple reason that the printers in Paris who began to set up the type refused to go on with it on account of what seemed to them masses of indecencies. Some of our modern craftsmen are aghast at passion, afraid of emotion, only anxious that the phrase and the sentiment should be right. Joyce is totally exempt from such fears as these: he is afraid of nothing; no more than his Stephen Dedalus, who said—and the words are the writer's own words, and all the more significant for that: 'I will not serve that which I no longer believe, whether it call itself my home, my fatherland, or my church: and I will try to express myself in my art as freely as I can and as wholly as I can, using for my defence the only arms I allow myself to use, silence, exile, and cunning'. The man and his most creative work are an unholy mixture of these three singular qualities. Without cunning he could never have written *Ulysses*. Without exile he might never have created what he has created—nor in fact could

Byron or Shelley or Landor. Byron was an exile from his country, equally condemned and admired, credited with abnormal genius and abnormal wickedness, confessing himself defiantly to the world, living with ostentatious wildness at Venice.

> We live and die,
> And which is best, you know no more than I.

All the wisdom (experience, love of nature, passion, tenderness, pride, the thirst for knowledge) comes to that in the end, not even a negation. He also suffered, as Pater and Joyce and myself have suffered, from that too vivid sense of humanity which is like a disease, that obsession to which every face is a challenge and every look an acceptance or a rebuff. How is content in life possible to those condemned to go about like magnets, attracting or repelling every animate thing, and tormented by restlessness which their own presence communicates to the air around them? This magnetic nature is not given to man for his happiness. It leaves him at the crowd's mercy, as he ceaselessly feels the shock of every disturbance which he causes them. Driving him into solitude for an escape, it will not let him even then escape the thought of what in himself is so much of an epitome of humanity, for 'quiet to quick bosoms is a hell'.

Joyce's vocabulary is unusually large and it is used too recklessly, but in a surprisingly novel, personal manner; and as for the craftsman, he has never curbed himself to a restraint in the debauch of words, still sufficiently coloured and sounding for an equally personal and novel effect; and with this a daring straightforwardness and pungency of epithet which refreshes one's thirst. Take for instance *A Portrait of the Artist as a Young Man*.

[quotes from *A Portrait*]

. . . Joyce's prose is in a sense fascinating; there is no doubt that he has been and that he will be considered the most complex literary problem of this generation; and, apart from his intricate and elaborate subtleties, it seems to me that he has made such gigantic steps that the only possible comparison which has been hazarded is with Flaubert's *Bouvard et Pecuchet*, itself a satire of so tremendous a nature, and yet withal an unfinished satire, that, when I look backward, I turn to the greatest satire ever written, the *Gargantua* of Rabelais.

[discusses Mallarmé and the 'modern epic' form of the novel]

ARTHUR SYMONS ON JOYCE'S POETRY 1933

. . . Worshipping colour, sound, perfume, for their own sakes, and not for their ministrations to a more divine beauty, Joyce stupefies himself on the threshold of ecstasy. And Joyce, we can scarcely doubt, has passed through the particular kind of haschisch dream which this experience really is. He has realized that the great choice, the choice between the world and something which is not visible in the world, but out of which the visible world has been made, does not lie in the mere contrast of the subtler and grosser senses. He has come to realize what the choice really is, and he has chosen. In his escape from the world, one man chooses religion, and seems to find himself; another, choosing love, may seem also to find himself; and may not another, coming to art as to a religion and as to a woman, seem to find himself not less effectually? The one certainty is, that society is the enemy of man, and that formal art is the enemy of the artist. We shall not find ourselves in drawing-rooms or in museums. A man who goes through a day without some fine emotion has wasted his day, whatever he has gained in it. And it is so easy to go through day after day, busily and agreeably, without ever really living for a single instant. Art begins when a man wishes to immortalize the most vivid moment he has ever lived. Life has already, to one not an artist, become art in that moment. And the making of one's life into art is after all the first duty and privilege of every man. It is to escape from material reality into whatever form of ecstasy is our own form of spiritual existence. There is the choice; and our happiness, our 'success in life', will depend on our choosing rightly, each for himself, among the forms in which that choice will come to us.

17. Italo Svevo on Joyce's *A Portrait of the Artist*

1909

Italo Svevo (Ettore Schmitz), in a letter to Joyce (8 February 1909). From Joyce, *Letters*, Volume II, ed. Richard Ellmann, pp. 226–7.

Schmitz describes his reaction upon reading the first three chapters of *A Portrait of the Artist.*

Really I do not believe of being authorised to tell you the author a resolute opinion about the novel which I could know only partially. I do not only allude to my want of competence but especially to the fact that when you stopped writing you were facing a very important development of Stephen's mind. I have already a sample of what may be a change of this mind described by your pen. Indeed the development of Stephens childish religion to a strong religion felt strongly and vigorously or better lived in all its particulars (after his sin) was so important that no other can be more so. I like very much your second and third chapters and I think you made a great mistake doubting whether you would find a reader who could take pleasure at the sermons of the third chapter. I have read them with a very strong feeling and I know in my own little town a lot of people who would be certainly stroke by the same feeling. Every word of these sermons acquires its artistic significance by the fact of their effect on poor Stephen's mind . . . I object against the first chapter. I did so when I had read only it but I do so still more decidedly after having known the two others. I think that I have at last also discovered the reason why these two chapters are for me so beautiful while the first one which surely is of the same construction, by the same writer who has surely not changed his ways, written evidently with the same artistic aims, fails to impress me as deeply. I think it deals with events devoid of importance and your rigid method of observation and description does not allow you to enrich a fact which is not rich by itself. You should write only about strong things. In your skilled hands they may become still stronger. I do not believe you can give the appearance of strength to things which are in themselves trivial, not important. I must say that if you had to write a whole novel with the only aim of description of everyday life without a problem which could affect strongly your own mind (you would not choose such a novel) you would be obliged to leave your method and find artificial colours to lend to the things the life they wanted in themselves. . . .

DUBLINERS

June 1914[1]

18. An Irish view of *Dubliners*

1908

Joseph Hone, 'A Recollection of James Joyce', *Envoy*, v (May 1951), 44–5. Joyce's difficulties with Maunsel & Company are discussed in the Introduction, p. 8.

It was in 1908—the summer, I think—that I read Joyce's *Dubliners* in manuscript. The stories were written out in cheap notebooks in a copperplate hand that would have won for a schoolboy a prize in calligraphy. They were handed to me by George Roberts, the managing-director of Maunsel & Co., a publishing firm of which I was then a member. Roberts was a very good judge of a book, besides being a fine printer; but one, at least, of the stories gave him pause: such is my recollection. This was 'Ivy Day in the Committee Room,' in which Dublin's grave councillors are depicted in discussing, among other matters, the private life of King Edward VII . . . I took the manuscript home, the issue still undecided, and I am ashamed to think of the length of time I had it in my possession. A month or two at least. It visited with me the house of a friend near Bray, Victor Le Fanu, a nephew of the novelist, Joseph Sheridan Le Fanu, the agent for Lord Meath's estates, and in my mind's eye I can still see it lying open on the table of his book-room, for I had invited his opinion upon it. Le Fanu, formerly a famous rugby international, was a good classical scholar, and in the midst of his country pursuits he found time to read a great deal. Kipling, Meredith, and Stevenson were his favourite novelists, and I did not expect that he would take very kindly to *Dubliners*. Nor did he; the life described was off his beat. But he read the stories carefully, and recognising their remarkable quality, took more interest in them than in the usual Maunsel publications.

[1] For later criticism of *Dubliners* see Nos. 50, 52, 82, 85, 87, 118.

Apparently, Joyce learned that I had been given it to read, and on my way home, while stopping at Marseilles, I had a letter of complaint from him, dated Trieste, and forwarded to me from Dublin. In my reply I may have asked him whether he would assent to the exclusion of 'Ivy Day' from the collection; but, at all events, whatever it was that I said, it furnished him with a pretext for submitting the story in the next year, after King Edward's death, to his successor, George V. Subsequently, he published an account of his grievance against Maunsel and of his appeal to Caesar (which of course was abortive) in a communication to Arthur Griffith's *Sinn Féin*; but I was out of Ireland then, and only heard of this long afterwards, when someone told me, or I read somewhere, that he had quoted 'A Mr. Hone writing from Marseilles' in his covering letter to the King. I have never consulted his version of the episode, and I must confess that I feel a disinclination to do so now, though my memory might be thereby refreshed. . . .

19. Symons on *Dubliners*

1914

Letter to Joyce (29 June 1914), quoted in Karl Beckson and John M. Munro, 'Letters from Arthur Symons to James Joyce: 1904–1932', *James Joyce Quarterly*, iv, No. 2 (Winter 1967), 98.

This letter is in reply to a copy of *Dubliners* Joyce had sent Symons.

No, I have not forgotten you. I still have your verses here. I find a great deal to like in *Dubliners*—unequal as the short stories are, but original, Irish, a kind of French realism, of minute detail, sordid; single sentences tell: I like the kind of abrupt style in the book. 'Counterparts' is quite fine—grim humour—a sense of Dublin as I saw it—a lurid glare over it. It gave me a sensation of Fountain Court and the pubs. But the best is the last: the end imaginative. . . .

20. Unsigned review, *Times Literary Supplement*

18 June 1914, 298

Dubliners is a collection of short stories, the scene of which is laid in Dublin. Too comprehensive for the theme, the title is nevertheless typical of a book which purports, we assume, to describe life as it is and yet regards it from one aspect only. The author, Mr. James Joyce, is not concerned with all Dubliners, but almost exclusively with those of them who would be submerged if the tide of material difficulties were to rise a little higher. It is not so much money they lack as the adaptability which attains some measure of success by accepting the world as it is. It is in so far that they are failures that his characters interest Mr. Joyce. One of them—a capable washerwoman—falls an easy prey to a rogue in a tramcar and is cozened out of the little present she was taking to her family. Another—a trusted cashier—has so ordered a blameless life that he drives to drink and suicide the only person in the world with whom he was in sympathy. A third—an amiable man of letters—learns at the moment he feels most drawn to his wife that her heart was given once and for all to a boy long dead.

Dubliners may be recommended to the large class of readers to whom the drab makes an appeal, for it is admirably written. Mr. Joyce avoids exaggeration. He leaves the conviction that his people are as he describes them. Shunning the emphatic, Mr. Joyce is less concerned with the episode than with the mood which it suggests. Perhaps for this reason he is more successful with his shorter stories. When he writes at greater length the issue seems trivial, and the connecting thread becomes so tenuous as to be scarcely perceptible. The reader's difficulty will be enhanced if he is ignorant of Dublin customs; if he does not know, for instance, that 'a curate' is a man who brings strong waters.

21. Unsigned review, *Athenæum*

20 June 1914, 875

Mr. George Moore says in his *Confessions*, if our memory does not deceive us, that when he and a certain French writer are dead no more 'naturalistic' novels will be written. Whether this is one of his characteristic outbursts of candour as to his and his friend's abilities, or merely a statement to the effect that novelists as a whole have no taste for such writing, we need not discuss. But we can frankly say that Mr. Joyce's work affords a distinct contradiction of the saying.

The fifteen short stories here given under the collective title of *Dubliners* are nothing if not naturalistic. In some ways, indeed, they are unduly so: at least three would have been better buried in oblivion. Life has so much that is beautiful, interesting, educative, amusing, that we do not readily pardon those who insist upon its more sordid and baser aspects. The condemnation is the greater if their skill is of any high degree, since in that case they might use it to better purpose.

Mr. Joyce undoubtedly possesses great skill both of observation and of technique. He has humour, as is shown by the sketch of Mrs. Kearney and her views on religion, her faith 'bounded by her kitchen, but if she was put to it, she could believe also in the banshee and in the Holy Ghost.' He has also knowledge of the beauty of words, of mental landscapes (if we may use such a phrase): the last page of the final story is full evidence thereto. His characterization is exact: speaking with reserve as to the conditions of certain sides of the social life of Dublin, we should say that it is beyond criticism. All the personages are living realities.

But Mr. Joyce has his own specialized outlook on life—on that life in particular; and here we may, perhaps, find the explanation of much that displeases and that puzzles us. That outlook is evidently sombre: he is struck by certain types, certain scenes, by the dark shadows of a low street or the lurid flare of an ignoble tavern, and he reproduces these in crude, strong sketches scarcely relieved by the least touch of joy or repose. Again, his outlook is self-centred, absorbed in itself rather; he ends his sketch abruptly time after time, satisfied with what he has done, brushing aside any intention of explaining what is set down or supplementing what is omitted.

All the stories are worth reading for the work that is in them, for the pictures they present; the best are undoubtedly the last four, especially 'Ivy Day in the Committee Room.' The last of all, 'The Dead,' far longer than the rest, and tinged with a softer tone of pathos and sympathy, leads us to hope that Mr. Joyce may attempt larger and broader work, in which the necessity of asserting the proportions of life may compel him to enlarge his outlook and eliminate such scenes and details as can only shock, without in any useful way impressing or elevating, the reader. . . .

22. Gerald Gould on *Dubliners*

1914

New Statesman, iii (27 June 1914), 374–5.

It is easy to say of Gorky that he is a man of genius. To say the same of Mr. James Joyce requires more courage, since his name is little known; but a man of genius is precisely what he is. He has an original outlook, a special method, a complete reliance on his own powers of delineation and presentment. Whether his powers will develop, his scope widen, his sympathies deepen, or not—whether, in short, his genius is a large one or only a little one, I cannot pretend to say. Maturity and self-confidence in a first book (and I believe that, in prose, this is Mr. Joyce's first book) contain a threat as well as a promise. They hint at a set mode of thought rather than a developing capacity. Certainly the maturity, the individual poise and force of these stories are astonishing. The only recent work with which they suggest comparison is *The House with the Green Shutters*, and even that was very different, for one heard in it the undertone of human complaint—its horrors were partly by way of expressing a personal unhappiness; while Mr. Joyce seems to regard this objective and dirty and crawling world with the cold detachment of an unamiable god.

He has plenty of humour, but it is always the humour of the fact, not of the comment. He dares to let people speak for themselves with the awkward meticulousness, the persistent incompetent repetition, of actual human intercourse. If you have never realised before how direly our daily conversation needs editing, you will realise it from Mr. Joyce's pages. One very powerful story, called 'Grace', consists chiefly of lengthy talk so banal, so true to life, that one can scarcely endure it—though one can still less leave off reading it. Here is one of the liveliest passages:

[quotes from 'Grace']

You see the method? It is not employed only in conversation. The description of mood, of atmosphere, is just as detailed and just as relentless. Horrible sordid realities, of which you are not spared one single pang, close in upon you like the four walls of a torture-chamber. It is all done quite calmly, quite dispassionately, quite competently. It never bores. You sometimes rather wish it did, as a relief.

The best things in the book are 'Araby', a wonderful magical study of boyish affection and wounded pride, and 'The Dead', a long story (placed at the end) in which we begin with a queer old-fashioned dance, where the principal anxiety is whether a certain guest will arrive 'screwed,' and are led on through all the queer breathless banalities of supper and conversation and leave-taking till we find ourselves back with a husband and wife in their hotel bedroom, the husband's emotion stirred, the wife queerly remote and sad, remembering the boy, Michael Furey, whom she had loved and who had died because of her. To quote the end without the innumerable preparatory touches that prepare for it seems unfair; yet it must be quoted for its mere melancholy beauty:

[quotes from 'The Dead']

Frankly, we think it is a pity (perhaps we betray a narrow puritanism in so thinking) that a man who can write like this should insist as constantly as Mr. Joyce insists upon aspects of life which are ordinarily not mentioned. To do him justice, we do not think it is a pose with him: he simply includes the 'unmentionable' in his persistent regard.

23. Unsigned review, *Everyman*

3 July 1914, xc, 380

Mr. James Joyce writes with a sense of style that makes his work distinctive. *Dubliners* is a collection of short stories dealing with undercurrents of Irish character. The author understands the technique of his craft to perfection, and uses words as a sculptor uses clay. Every phrase is pregnant with suggestion, but the suggestion for the most part is unpleasantly and curiously tinged with a pessimism that finds virility and purpose only in the power of evil. 'A Painful Case,' one of the best-written sketches in the volume, strips life of all hope of consolation and leaves the reader faced by a cold, cruel egotism that finds expression in perpetual self-exultation. 'Two Gallants' reveals the shuddering depths of human meanness. The men, villainous of soul and repugnant of aspect, trade on the affections of young servant-girls, and the story reproduces the hopes of the one who waits the results of the wiles of the other. Even for these outcasts some hope might remain. But the author, with a ruthless callousness, decides they shall be doomed and damned. The book may be styled the records of an inferno in which neither pity nor remorse can enter. Wonderfully written, the power of genius is in every line, but it is a genius that, blind to the blue of the heavens, seeks inspiration in the hell of despair.

24. Unsigned review, *Academy*

11 July 1914, lxxxvii, 49

In the matter of literary expression these sketches—of which the book contains fifteen in all—are akin to the work of Mr. Cunninghame Graham and of Mr. George Moore; there is a clarity of phrasing and a restraint such as characterises the work of these two authors, and in every sketch atmosphere is so subtly conveyed that, without mention of a street or of a jaunting car, we feel Dublin about us as we read. In one, 'Counterparts,' is power enough to make us wish for a novel from Mr. Joyce's pen, and in the earlier, schoolboy stories are all the dreaming and mystery of an imaginative boy's life. The book is morbid, to a certain extent, in its tone, but it is of such literary quality that we forgive the defect for the sake of the artistic value. The work is not all morbid, however, for here and there are flashes of humour, rendered more forceful by their settings. Altogether, this is a book to recommend, evidently written by a man of broad sympathies and much human understanding. . . .

25. Ezra Pound on *Dubliners*

1914

'"Dubliners" and Mr. James Joyce,' *Egoist*, i, No. 14 (15 July 1914), 267. Also appeared in Pound's *Pavannes and Divisions* (1918), pp. 156–60, and in *The Literary Essays of Ezra Pound* (1954), ed. T. S. Eliot, pp. 399–401. For an account of Pound's assistance to Joyce, see Introduction, pp. 4, 8–10.

Freedom from sloppiness is so rare in contemporary English prose that one might well say simply, 'Mr. Joyce's book of short stories is prose free from sloppiness,' and leave the intelligent reader ready to run from his study, immediately to spend three and sixpence on the volume.

Unfortunately one's credit as a critic is insufficient to produce this result.

The readers of *The Egoist*, having had Mr. Joyce under their eyes for some months, will scarcely need to have his qualities pointed out to them. Both they and the paper have been very fortunate in his collaboration.

Mr. Joyce writes a clear hard prose. He deals with subjective things, but he presents them with such clarity of outline that he might be dealing with locomotives or with builders' specifications. For that reason one can read Mr. Joyce without feeling that one is conferring a favour. I must put this thing my own way. I know about 168 authors. About once a year I read something contemporary without feeling that I am softening the path for poor Jones or poor Fulano de Tal.

I can lay down a good piece of French writing and pick up a piece of writing by Mr. Joyce without feeling as if my head were being stuffed through a cushion. There are still impressionists about and I dare say they claim Mr. Joyce. I admire impressionist writers. English prose writers who haven't got as far as impressionism (that is to say, 95 per cent. of English writers of prose and verse) are a bore. . . .

Mr. Joyce's merit, I will not say his chief merit but his most engaging merit, is that he carefully avoids telling you a lot that you don't want to know. He presents his people swiftly and vividly, he does not sentimentalise over them, he does not weave convolutions. He is a realist. He does not believe 'life' would be all right if we stopped vivisection or if we instituted a new sort of 'economics.' He gives the thing as it is. He is not bound by the tiresome convention that any part of life, to be interesting, must be shaped into the conventional form of a 'story.' Since De Maupassant we have had so many people trying to write 'stories' and so few people presenting life. Life for the most part does not happen in neat little diagrams and nothing is more tiresome than the continual pretence that it does.

Mr. Joyce's 'Araby,' for instance, is much better than a 'story,' it is a vivid writing.

It is surprising that Mr. Joyce is Irish. One is so tired of the Irish or 'Celtic' imagination (or 'phantasy' as I think they now call it) flopping about. Mr. Joyce does not flop about. He defines. He is not an institution for the promotion of Irish peasant industries. He accepts an international standard of prose writing and lives up to it.

He gives us Dublin as it presumably is. He does not descend to farce. He does not rely upon Dickensian caricature. He gives us things as they are, not only for Dublin, but for every city. Erase the local names and a few specifically local allusions, and a few historic events of the past, and substitute a few different local names, allusions and events, and these stories could be retold of any town.

That is to say, the author is quite capable of dealing with things about him, and dealing directly, yet these details do not engross him, he is capable of getting at the universal element beneath them.

The main situations of 'Madame Bovary' or of 'Doña Perfecta' do not depend on local colour or upon local detail, that is their strength. Good writing, good presentation can be specifically local, but it must not depend on locality. Mr. Joyce does not present 'types' but individuals. I mean he deals with common emotions which run through all races. He does not bank on 'Irish character.' Roughly speaking, Irish literature has gone through three phases in our time, the shamrock period, the dove-grey period, and the Kiltartan period. I think there is a new phase in the works of Mr. Joyce. He writes as a contemporary of continental writers. I do not mean that he writes as a faddist, mad for the last note, he does not imitate Strindberg, for instance, or Bang. He is not ploughing the underworld for horror. He is not presenting a macabre subjectivity. He is classic in that he deals with normal things and with normal people. A committee room, Little Chandler, a nonentity, a boarding house full of clerks—these are his subjects and he treats them all in such a manner that they are worthy subjects of art.

Francis Jammes, Charles Vildrac and D. H. Lawrence have written short narratives in verse, trying, it would seem, to present situations as clearly as prose writers have done, yet more briefly. Mr. Joyce is engaged in a similar condensation. He has kept to prose not needing the privilege supposedly accorded to verse to justify his method.

I think that he excels most of the impressionist writers because of his more rigorous selection, because of his exclusion of all unnecessary detail.

There is a very clear demarcation between unnecessary detail and irrelevant detail. An impressionist friend of mine talks to me a good deal about 'preparing effects,' and on that score he justifies much unnecessary detail, which is not 'irrelevant,' but which ends by being wearisome and by putting one out of conceit with his narrative.

Mr. Joyce's more rigorous selection of the presented detail marks him, I think, as belonging to my own generation, that is, to the 'nineteen-tens,' not to the decade between 'the 'nineties' and today.

At any rate these stories and the novel now appearing in serial form are such as to win for Mr. Joyce a very definite place among English contemporary prose writers, not merely a place in the 'Novels of the Week' column, and our writers of good clear prose are so few that we cannot afford to confuse or to overlook them.

26. Unsigned review, *Irish Book Lover*

November 1914, vi, No. 4, 60–61

Dublin, like other large cities, shelters many peculiar types of men and women, good, bad and indifferent; in fact some, whose knowledge of it is extensive and peculiar, would say more than its fair share. Of some of these Mr. Joyce here gives us pen portraits of great power, and although one naturally shrinks from such characters as are depicted in 'An Encounter' or 'Two Gallants,' and finds their descriptions not quite suited 'virginibus puerisque,' one cannot deny the existence of their prototypes, whilst wishing that the author had directed his undoubted talents in other and pleasanter directions. . . .

27. A French view of *Dubliners*

1926

Edmond Jaloux, 'l'Esprit des livres', *Les Nouvelles littéraires* (29 May 1926), n.p.

An extract from a review of the French translation of *Dubliners*, i.e. *Gens de Dublin*, by Y. Fernandez, H. du Pasquier, J.-P. Raynaud. See the Introduction, pp. 8,18,20, for Joyce's popularity with the French; and see Adrienne Monnier's article, No. 211.

. . . One of the most recent foreigners adopted by us—and, this time, an Irishman—is Mr. James Joyce whose revelation we owe to M. Valéry Larbaud, and whose first novel, *Portrait of an Artist as a Young Man*, appeared two years ago. . . . While waiting for a translation . . . of the enormous *Ulysses*, here are his short stories, *Dubliners*, published in London in June 1914 after many difficulties. Reading them, it is astonishing that they could have shocked or scandalized anyone. There are more liberties in Shakespeare and the Elizabethans, in Wycherly or in Farquhar or Smollet. Are the English no longer reading them therefore?

It is difficult to speak of *Dubliners* because these are realistic short stories, and if one maintains appearances, one would risk not being able to speak about them in a way other than by title alone. Mr. James Joyce, however, like Tchekov or Katherine Mansfield—has something which makes him very different from Maupassant, Flaubert or Huysmans. But in what exactly does this something consist?

It consists, I believe, in the total absence of ulterior motive. There is in the French mind something fundamentally judicial, fundamentally mathematical, fundamentally didactic. To make a judgment, to demonstrate, to instruct—these are for us the very consequences of thinking. However detached from all moral end Flaubert, Maupassant or Huysmans may seem, they do not escape this law. . . . Now take any work of Mr. James Joyce, 'An Encounter', 'Two Gallants', and try to disentangle the author's intention. . . .

[discusses the lack of certitude in these two stories]

'A little piece of gold shines in the palm.' Imagine with what hidden indignation, what sarcasm Maupassant or Huysmans would have told this story . . . There is none of this in the narration of James Joyce, and this is not his indifference; it is the minute and pure application of a botanist or of an entymologist, the seriousness of an Irish Fabré, dedicated to unfortunate human beetles, obstinate not even comical. I think that if anyone has been able to influence Mr. Joyce, the excellent humanist, it is less likely the French or Russian realists as the Roman historians. There is in him like a far-off echo of the Suetonius accent, this metallic impassivity with which the terrible annalist of the Caesars recounts the insanity of Caligula or the systematized luxury of Nero. . . .

One must be a great artist to treat events so simply and to render them nevertheless attractive. These short stories would not even make anecdotes; they become true slices of social cells, the scissor operated by Mr. James Joyce on the events and the people so adroitly that each of these stories takes an extraordinary significance from this technique. . . .

. . . These uncertain stories of a gray color have in reality such an interior energy that they impose themselves definitely upon us. And this secret energy contrasts so much more with the apparent impermeability of Mr. James Joyce—impermeability in some scientific way and which has the implacable character of a cinematographic apparatus or of a microphone recording reality.

When the great fragments of *Ulysses* are published . . . we will be able to see the road covered by Mr. James Joyce from *Dubliners* to his extraordinary encyclopedic epic of an individual; but it is obvious that *Dubliners* was already a solid platform for advancing toward this conception. *Dubliners*, if one considers *Ulysses*, is like a store of accessories where the author first tried to use the human and social resources of which he disposed before reuniting them in a new synthesis. It is an essential work for the literary historian, but it is a curious work, attractive and charmingly enigmatic for readers.

28. Review of the French translation

1926

Jacques Chenevière, 'Les Livres, Traduction', *Bibliothèque universelle et Revue de Genève*, ii (August 1926), 267–8.

A review of the French translation of *Dubliners*.

Mr. James Joyce is still a rather enigmatic writer for the French public. We have already had the translation of his *Portrait of the Artist as a Young Man*, but we are awaiting the enormous and unusual *Ulysses*. The reading of *Dubliners* is an excellent initiation. . . . They [the stories] are preceded by a clear and substantial preface written by Valéry Larbaud. He heralds again a great foreign mind, with a devotion and an ardor which is very rare today in a writer of his importance. What is most striking in these Irish stories is the particular quality of their realism, almost of their nationalism. Domestic situations, boys playing hookey from school, humble piano teachers, employees, café politicians, bourgeois lovers, and even pimps—the subjects, the characters recall those of Maupassant or of the descendants of the group of Medan. But a French novelist—a logician and always, in spite of himself, a moralist even when he considers himself unimpressionable—would begin and end the narrative precisely at the point when even the mysterious would be explicit. Joyce, however, only conducts the reader with a weak hand from which, however, one does not escape. He rarely informs us and does not conclude. It is a moment of daily life, such as it is. He leaves the movements of the acts and the lines of a décor floating. He seems to record from without what is happening; but he suggests all the complexities of the interior being as so much more poignant that they remain uncertain, as in our human truth itself. Sometimes this fog bothers us, accustomed as we are to life, translated literally and appearing logical. How dare art guide us so little and yet remain master of us! Even in a brief story, the visages, the first aspects of a situation, the rapports of being to being only emerge progressively, unequally at first from the unknown, like parts of images on a cliché plunged into the 'revealer.' . . . Such a discretion in the wording of the necessary detail obliges us not to read this book with a negligent eye, a book which imposes itself upon us through its mysterious pervasion, the effacement even of its means, and its stifled accent . . . Joyce, so precise in such detail, expresses himself primarily through allusion. This is a book of an interview, of the unavowed; he treats—and with a hallucinating truth—only secrets: lusts, despairs, secret or even aborted impulses. And one thinks of the comment of Copperfield: 'very often things which do not happen to us have over us, in reality, as much effect as those which are accomplished.'

29. Another French view of *Dubliners*

1926

Andre Billy, *l'Oeuvre* (Paris) (5 October 1926), n.p.

The Irish writer James Joyce . . . began in 1907 with a collection of verse, *Chamber Music*, and then produced nothing until 1914 when he published a collection of short stories entitled *Dubliners*. It is this collection that now appears, with an explanatory preface by Mr. Valéry Larbaud. If they were not the work of the author of *Ulysses*—but in fact, when will we read in French this book considered ingenious—these short stories would have nothing to recommend them to our attention, and I find Mr. Larbaud inaccurate in taking such trouble to make us believe that these short stories are naturalistic without their being so. There was no dishonor in a young Irish writer of the beginning of this century in undergoing the influence of our realistic story-tellers of the preceding century, and all the naturalism of *Dubliners* would not have prevented *Ulysses* from being a masterpiece, if indeed it is one.

30. Review of the French translation

1926

Georges Bourguet, *Les Cahiers du Sud* (6 November 1926), 313–15.

A review of the French translation of *Dubliners* (*Gens de Dublin*).

[a brief historical note on *Dubliners*] This [the publication of *Ulysses*] was a beautiful uproar. The Anglo-Saxons are modest and Joyce calls a cat a cat, which is very indecent. The author had committed the fault of not hiding the weaknesses of his hero and the necessities that nature imposes on his body. . . This does not lack in the comical: for to read some exciting passages the chaste islanders would only have had to cross the channel; and every sailor of any culture, reaching a French port bought the work.

But if Joyce is without modesty, he does not leave a juicy taste in the mouth of his readers, like Rabelais. His boldness is pleasant; it is first of all that of an intellectual. Joyce speculates with his mind, tirelessly.

This cerebral vision is found in particular in *Dedalus* (the French translation of *A Portrait of the Artist*) where the author accumulated intimate details almost, it seems, without transposition. This way of writing does not at all imply a lack of imagination in Joyce. It would be rather the sign of a great timidity, of a great prudence in the artistic creation, and of an absolute moral freedom. . . Thus we do not feel any annoyance, any lassitude with *Dubliners*. However in most of the stories nothing happens; these are 'slices of life' as has been said before. Only the people who live under our eyes live in us also; these are no longer eyes from outside, but rather understanding. Certainly these figures are called Hyner, Doran, Conray, Joe, or Aunt Kate, Ursula, Polly, and they belong to these persons. They enter us also and we become accustomed to seeing them so exactly that soon they seem to go out of our conscience. This means of occupying us indicates a great power in the author.

There is in Joyce, furthermore, an entirely mysterious side, slightly intriguing. You sense that he possesses you through magical means and imagine his long hands with red hair which look at you frightfully, as though rising up on the pages, from their ten eyes which are ten ends of fingers.

Joyce, however, uses the simplest vocabulary. If he does not fear slang, he doesn't abuse it. In sum he makes people talk as they ought to talk in Ireland when they are not nobility. And Ireland bursts forth entirely alive.

The three short stories of the collection which I prefer are: 'A Painful Case,' 'The Boarding House,' 'The Dead.' In the first two narratives, curious rapports are grasped between mediterranean and Irish manners. 'The Dead' carries the writer on his true way. A solid narrative, a little long (which only seems long on the first reading), and then a phantom who eats life; all subsides, there is no longer anything but a warm cinder. But Gabriel drenches this cinder with tears and in the patience of his love reconstructs the idol with this strange material.

There is a mystical and esoteric sense through which Joyce attains grandeur. The sense of the symbol within the symbol, simply because Mr. Bloom sees today what is like yesterday. Thus this writer resembles perhaps no other. The density of his thought and the purity of the means employed give his written work an extensiveness which greatly extends the brutal pleasure of the reading.

31. A later opinion of *Dubliners*

1930

J. C. 'Experimentalists', *Post* (4 March 1930), n.p.

Lately I have been reading again those sketches and short stories of James Joyce's, gathered together under the title *Dubliners*—brave, relentless, sympathetic studies of life in the Irish capital in the years before the war that the author of *Ulysses* produced somewhere about 1913, and that placed him (at least, in the eyes of the discerning) in the foremost rank of realist short story writers. Altogether, it has been a somewhat disconcerting experience—disconcerting to reflect that *Dubliners* and *Portrait of the Artist as a Young Man* (to say nothing of *Ulysses* and the monumental work now under way) came both from the same hand. Even the circumstance that James Joyce is no ordinray author does not adequately explain it. At the time that *Dubliners* was written Joyce was at the beginning of his career. He conformed then to convention—at least, as far as was possible for a man of his peculiar genius.

He wrote short stories, as later Katherine Mansfield and Stacey Aumonier were to write short stories, realist, analytical studies of everyday people in everyday surroundings—in his case, Dublin—the Dublin of the suburbs and the bars, the boarding-houses and the music-halls, the alleys and the courts and the river. To them he brought a descriptive power, a psychological insight, a sense of character, a wealth of beautiful phrasing. *Dubliners*, indeed, seemed both a portent and an event—a portent of greater things still to come, an event in the annals of Anglo-Irish literature unequalled since George Moore produced *The Untilled Field* to help along the prose part of the Literary Renaissance. We waited then as confident of Joyce as we used to be of Gilbert Cannan or Compton Mackenzie, and—the Joyce of *Dubliners* began and ended with a single volume. Later came *Portrait of the Artist as a Young Man*, bearing hardly a touch of the hand that wrote 'The Boarding House' and 'The Sisters,' 'Eveline,' and 'Araby.' There followed *Ulysses*—with the suspicion that Joyce was lost to the short story hardened to a certainty. And now he is at work upon a 'new prose,' a 'new language for a theme that ignores both space and time.' In the cause of literary experiment the short story loses one of its masters; literature in its stead gains—what?

In Joyce's case, two of the strangest works that have ever fallen from the pen of man; but I doubt seriously whether literature altogether is the richer for the experiment. Most of us would readily jettison *Ulysses* and the *Portrait* for another volume like *Dubliners*, even though the stories had a Parisian setting—as they probably would have now. . . .

32. Review of the German translation

1934

Alois Brandl, 'James Joyce, *Dubliners*', *Archiv für das Studium der Neueren Sprachen*, clxv (1934), 145.

A review of the German translation of *Dubliners*.

This small volume includes fifteen sketches of a peculiar type. You cannot call them *novellen* because they are lacking in plot and also in depth of character. Mood pictures of human individuals would perhaps be a much better description, but even for that they contain too many broad biographical elements. Rather than attempt to explain them through definitions, one could express what they are by a few examples. There is, for example, right at the beginning, a clergyman, naturally an Irishman, who as an old celibate is half-dignified and still even more worthy of sympathy, with his large yellow teeth which he uninhibitedly shows when he smiles. He wanders quite a bit into nonsense; it is completely logical that he does not really die but simply falls asleep. Then there is Eveline, who does not get along well with her father; she has found a fiancée whom she wishes to seduce away to Buenos Aires and marry. The lovely lady would entice him but the love for her fiancée is really not there and so it disappears as soon as the ship departs, simply not there to be found. There are the two loose young fellows who in the title are called 'Two Gallants'. The one always goes in for light adventure, as always with caution against being forced into marriage and propagating children, while the other thinks a reasonable home would be much better. That is everything. The streets and the environment of Dublin, Irish customs and also Irish slang usages, and we soon become well enough acquainted with them. What is obvious is, however, the absolute absence of seriousness which hides behind these forms and in the long run it also has a tiring effect. It shows, nevertheless, that without seriousness there really can be no genuine humor.

OPINIONS

1915–16

33. Pound to H. L. Mencken

1915

Letter to H. L. Mencken (18 February 1915) in *The Letters of Ezra Pound* (1950), ed. D. D. Paige, p. 51.

. . . The prose writer I am really interested in is James Joyce. He is in Austria; therefore I can't write to him but you might. . . . His *Dubliners*, a book of short stories, has succeeded since I first wrote to him. *The Egoist* is using a long novel of his [*Portrait of the Artist*] as a serial. It's damn well written.

34. Pound to Mencken

1915

Letter to H. L. Mencken (17 March 1915), in *The Letters of Ezra Pound* (1950), ed. D. D. Paige, p. 56.

. . . Joyce is evidently beginning to be 'the common man' (commercially even), for H. G. Wells' agent wrote in to say that H. G. had put him on to Joyce, and that he wanted to handle his stuff.

35. W. B. Yeats to Edmund Gosse

1915

Letter to Edmund Gosse (24 July 1915), in *The Letters of W. B. Yeats* (1955), ed. Allan Wade, p. 597. The relations between Joyce and Yeats are the subject of a chapter, 'The Hawklike Man', in Richard Ellmann, *Eminent Domain* (1967), pp. 29–56.

I enclose letters and statement about James Joyce of whose need I told you . . . I believe him to be a man of genius . . . He has written *Dubliners* a book of satiric stories of great subtlety, a little like Russian work, and *Chamber Music* a book of verse, a little of it very beautiful and all of it very perfect technically. . . .

36. W. B. Yeats on Joyce

1915

Letter to the Secretary of the Royal Literary Fund (29 July 1915), in *The Letters of W. B. Yeats*, (1955), ed. Allan Wade, pp. 598–9.

. . . I think that Mr. Joyce has a most beautiful gift. There is a poem on the last page of his *Chamber Music* ['I hear an army charging'] which will, I believe, live. It is a technical and emotional masterpiece. I think that his book of short stories *Dubliners* has the promise of a great novelist and a great novelist of a new kind. There is not enough foreground, it is all atmosphere perhaps, but I look upon that as a sign of an original study of life. I have read in a paper called *The Egoist* certain chapters of a new novel, a disguised autobiography [*The Portrait of the Artist*], which increases my conviction that he is the most remarkable new talent in Ireland to-day.

37. George Moore on Joyce

1916

Letter to Edward Marsh (3 August 1916), quoted in Ellmann, *James Joyce*, p. 418, and in Joyce, *Letters*, Volume II, ed. Richard Ellmann, p. 380.

Edward Marsh, as secretary to Prime Minister Asquith, was seeking Moore's opinion about Joyce in order to secure Joyce a Civil List grant.

. . . The only book of Joyce's that I have read is a collection of stories called *Dubliners*, some of them are trivial and disagreeable, but all are written by a clever man, and the book contains one story, the longest story in the book and the last story which seemed to me perfection whilst I read it! I regretted that I was not the author of it ['The Dead']. But this story, which I am sure you would appreciate as much as I did, does not prove that Joyce will go on writing and will end by writing something like a masterpiece. A talent, musical literary, or pictorial, is a pale fluttering thing that a breath will extinguish . . . Of the novel I know nothing. . . .

A PORTRAIT OF THE ARTIST AS A YOUNG MAN

December 1916[1]

---

38. Reader's report on *A Portrait of the Artist*

Edward Garnett, a reader's report for Duckworth & Company, publishers, quoted in a letter from Jonathan Cape to James B. Pinker, in Richard Ellmann, *James Joyce* (1959), pp. 416–17, and in Ellmann, ed., *Letters*, Volume II, pp. 371–2.

James B. Pinker was Joyce's literary agent at this time; Duckworth were considering publishing *A Portrait of the Artist*.

James Joyce's *Portrait of the Artist as a Young Man* wants going through carefully from start to finish. There are many 'longueurs' Passages which, though the publisher's reader may find them entertaining, will be tedious to the ordinary man among the reading public. The public will call the book, as it stands at present, realistic, unprepossessing, unattractive. We call it ably written. The picture is 'curious,' it arouses interest and attention. But the author must revise it and let us see it again. It is too discursive, formless, unrestrained, and ugly things, ugly words, are too prominent; indeed at times they seem to be shoved in one's face, on purpose, unnecessarily. The point of view will be voted 'a little sordid.' The picture of life is good; the period well brought to the reader's eye, and the types and characters are well drawn, but it is too 'unconventional.' This would stand against it in normal times. At the present time, though the old conventions are in the background, we can only see a chance for it if it is pulled into shape and made more definite.

In the earlier portion of the MS. as submitted to us, a good deal of pruning can be done. Unless the author will use restraint and proportion he will not gain readers. His pen and his thoughts seem to have run away with him sometimes.

[1] For later criticism of *A Portrait* see Nos. 81, 82, 85, 87, 118, 139, 258.

And at the end of the book there is a complete falling to bits; the pieces of writing and the thoughts are all in pieces and they fall like damp, ineffective rockets.

The author shows us he has art, strength and originality, but this MS. wants time and trouble spent on it, to make it a more finished piece of work, to shape it more carefully as the product of the craftsmanship, mind and imagination of an artist.

39. Pound on *A Portrait*

1917

'At last the Novel Appears', *Egoist*, iv, No. 2 (February 1917), 21–22. See the Introduction, p. 9, for a discussion of Pound's part in the publishing of *A Portrait*.

It is unlikely that I shall say anything new about Mr. Joyce's novel, *A Portrait of the Artist as a Young Man*. I have already stated that is it a book worth reading and that it is written in good prose. In using these terms I do not employ the looseness of the half-crown reviewer.

I am very glad that it is now possible for a few hundred people to read Mr. Joyce comfortably from a bound book, instead of from a much-handled file of *Egoists* or from a slippery bundle of type-script. After much difficulty *The Egoist* itself turns publisher and produces *A Portrait of the Artist* as a volume, for the hatred of ordinary English publishers for good prose is, like the hatred of the *Quarterly Review* for good poetry, deep-rooted, traditional.

. . . Members of the 'Fly-Fishers' and 'Royal Automobile' clubs, and of the 'Isthmian,' may not read him [William Savage Landor]. They will not read Mr. Joyce. *E pur si muove*. Despite the printers and publishers the British Government has recognized Mr. Joyce's literary merit. That is a definite gain for the party of intelligence. A number of qualified judges have acquiesced in my statement of two years ago, that Mr. Joyce was an excellent and important writer of prose.

The last few years have seen the gradual shaping of a party of intelligence, a party not bound by any central doctrine or theory. We cannot accurately define new writers by applying to them tag-names from old authors, but as there is no adequate means of conveying the general impression of their characteristics one may at times employ such terminology, carefully stating that the terms are nothing more than approximation.

With that qualification, I would say that James Joyce produces the nearest thing to Flaubertian prose that we have now in English, just as Wyndham Lewis has written a novel which is more like, and more fitly compared with, Dostoievsky than is the work of any of his contemporaries. In like manner Mr. T. S. Eliot comes nearer to filling the place of Jules La Forgue in our generation. . . .

My own income was considerably docked because I dared to say that Gaudier-Brzeska was a good sculptor and that Wyndham Lewis was a great master of design. It has, however, reached an almost irreducible minimum, and I am, perhaps, fairly safe in reasserting Joyce's ability as a writer. It will cost me no more than a few violent attacks from several sheltered, and therefore courageous, anonymities. When you tell the Irish that they are slow in recognizing their own men of genius they reply with street riots and politics.

Now, despite the jobbing of bigots and of their sectarian publishing houses, and despite the 'Fly-Fishers' and the types which they represent and despite the unwillingness of the print packers (a word derived from pork-packers) and the initial objections of the Dublin publishers and the later unwillingness of the English publishers, Mr. Joyce's novel appears in book form, and intelligent readers gathering few by few will read it, and it will remain a permanent part of English literature written by an Irishman in Trieste and first published in New York City. I doubt if a comparison of Mr. Joyce to other English writers or Irish writers would much help to define him. One can only say that he is rather unlike them. *The Portrait* is very different from *l'Education Sentimentale*, but it would be easier to compare it with that novel of Flaubert's than with anything else. Flaubert pointed out that if France had studied his work they might have been saved a good deal in 1870. If more people had read *The Portrait* and certain stories in Mr. Joyce's *Dubliners* there might have been less recent trouble in Ireland. A clear diagnosis is never without its value.

Apart from Mr. Joyce's realism—the school life, the life in the University, the family dinner with the discussion of Parnell depicted in his novel—apart from, or of a piece with, all this is the style, the actual writing: hard, clear-cut, with no waste of words, no bundling up of useless phrases, no filling in with pages of slosh.

It is very important that there should be clear, unexaggerated, realistic literature. It is very important that there should be good prose. The hell of contemporary Europe is caused by the lack of representative government in Germany, and by the non-existence of decent prose in the German language. Clear thought and sanity depend on clear prose. They cannot live apart. The former produces the latter. The latter conserves and transmits the former.

The mush of the German sentence, the straddling of the verb out to the end, are just as much a part of the befoozlement of Kultur and the consequent hell, as was the rhetoric of later Rome the seed and the symptom of the Roman Empire's decadence and extinction. A nation that cannot write clearly cannot be trusted to govern, nor yet to think.

Germany has had two decent prose-writers, Frederick the Great and Heine—the one taught by Voltaire, and the other saturated with French and with Paris. Only a nation accustomed to muzzy writing could have been led by the nose and bamboozled as the Germans have been by their controllers.

The terror of clarity is not confined to any one people. The obstructionist and the provincial are everywhere, and in them alone is the permanent danger to civilization. Clear, hard prose is the safeguard and should be valued as such. The mind accustomed to it will not be cheated or stampeded by national phrases and public emotionalities.

These facts are true, even for the detesters of literature. For those who love good writing there is no need of argument. In the present instance it is enough to say to those who will believe one that Mr. Joyce's book is now procurable.

40. Unsigned review, *Everyman*

23 February 1917, 398

This review was titled 'A Study in Garbage'.

Mr. James Joyce is an Irish edition of Mr. Caradoc Evans. These writers, that is to say, have made it their business in life to portray the least estimable features of their respective countrymen, Irish or Welsh. Mr. Joyce's new book, *A Portrait of an Artist as a Young Man* is an astonishingly powerful and extraordinary dirty study of the upbringing of a young man by Jesuits, which ends—so far as we have been at all able to unravel the meaning of the impressionist ending—with his insanity. The description of life in a Jesuit school, and later in a Dublin college, strikes one as being absolutely true to life—but what a life! Parts of the book are perhaps a little too allusive to be readily understood by the English reader. On pp. 265–6, there is an account of what happened at the Abbey Theatre, Dublin, when *The Countess Cathleen*, by Mr. W. B. Yeats, was put on, but the fact is darkly hidden. Mr. Joyce is a clever novelist, but we feel he would be really at his best in a treatise on drains. . . .

41. H. G. Wells, review, *Nation*

1917

'James Joyce', *Nation*, xx (24 February 1917), 710, 712. The same review appeared in *New Republic*, x (10 March 1917), 158–60; in the *New Republic Anthology* (1936), ed. Groff Conklin, pp. 45–48; in *Novelists on Novelists* (1962), ed. Louis Kronenberger, and in the *New Republic*, cxxi (1954), 91–2.

The review begins with a comment on the state of literature during 1916 and on the 'great amount of fresh and experimental writing'.

. . . Even more considerable is *A Portrait of the Artist as a Young Man*, by James Joyce. It is a book to buy and read and lock up, but it is not a book to miss. Its claim to be literature is as good as the claim of the last book of *Gulliver's Travels*.

It is no good trying to minimize a characteristic that seems to be deliberately obtruded. Like Swift and another living Irish writer, Mr. Joyce has a cloacal obsession. He would bring back into the general picture of life aspects which modern drainage and modern decorum have taken out of ordinary intercourse and conversation. Coarse, unfamiliar words are scattered about the book unpleasantly, and it may seem to many, needlessly. If the reader is squeamish upon these matters, then there is nothing for it but to shun this book, but if he will pick his way, as one has to do at times on the outskirts of some picturesque Italian village with a view and a church and all sorts of things of that sort to tempt one, then it is quite worth while. And even upon this unsavory aspect of Swift and himself, Mr. Joyce is suddenly illuminating. He tells at several points how his hero Stephen is swayed and shocked and disgusted by harsh and loud *sounds*, and how he is stirred to intense emotion by music and the rhythms of beautiful words. But no sort of smell offends him like that. He finds olfactory sensations interesting or aesthetically displeasing, but they do not make him sick or excited as sounds do. This is a quite understandable turn over from the more normal state of affairs. Long ago I remember pointing out in a review the difference in the sensory basis of the stories of Robert Louis Stevenson and Sir J. M. Barrie; the former visualized and saw his story primarily as picture, the latter mainly heard it. We shall do Mr. Joyce an injustice if we attribute a normal sensory basis to him and then accuse him of deliberate offense.

But that is by the way. The value of Mr. Joyce's book has little to do with its incidental insanitary condition. Like some of the best novels in the world it is the story of an education; it is by far the most living and convincing picture that exists of an Irish Catholic upbringing. It is a mosaic of jagged fragments that does altogether render with extreme completeness the growth of a rather secretive, imaginative boy in Dublin. The technique is startling, but on the whole it succeeds. Like so many Irish writers from Sterne to Shaw Mr. Joyce is a bold experimentalist with paragraph and punctuation. He breaks away from scene to scene without a hint of the change of time and place; at the end he passes suddenly from the third person to the first; he uses no inverted commas to mark off his speeches. The first trick I found sometimes tiresome here and there, but then my own disposition, perhaps acquired at the blackboard, is to mark off and underline rather fussily, and I do not know whether I was so much put off the thing myself as anxious, which after all is not my business, about its effect on those others; the second trick, I will admit, seems entirely justified in this particular instance by its success; the third reduces Mr. Joyce to a free use of dashes. One conversation in this book is a superb success, the one in which Mr. Dedalus carves the Christmas turkey; I write with all due deliberation that Sterne himself could not have done it better; but most of the talk flickers blindingly with these dashes, one has the same wincing feeling of being flicked at that one used to have in the early cinema shows. I think Mr. Joyce has failed to discredit the inverted comma.

The interest of the book depends entirely upon its quintessential and unfailing reality. One believes in Stephen Dedalus as one believes in few characters in fiction. And the peculiar lie of the interest for the intelligent reader is the convincing revelation it makes of the limitations of a great mass of Irishmen. Mr. Joyce tells us unsparingly of the adolescence of this youngster under conditions that have passed almost altogether out of English life. There is an immense shyness, a profound secrecy, about matters of sex, with its inevitable accompaniment of nightmare revelations and furtive scribblings in unpleasant places, and there is a living belief in a real hell. The description of Stephen listening without a doubt to two fiery sermons on that tremendous theme, his agonies of fear, not disgust at dirtiness such as unorthodox children feel but just fear, his terror-inspired confession of his sins of impurity to a strange priest in a distant part of the city, is like nothing in any boy's experience who has been trained under modern conditions. Compare its stuffy horror with Conrad's account of how under analogous circumstances Lord Jim wept. And a second thing of immense significance is the fact that everyone in this Dublin story, every human being, accepts as a matter of course, as a thing in nature like the sky and the sea, that the English are to be hated. There is no discrimination in that hatred, there is no gleam of recognition that a considerable number of Englishmen have displayed a very earnest disposition to put matters right with Ireland, there is an aboslute absence of any idea of a discussed settlement, any notion of helping the slow-witted Englishman in his three-cornered puzzle between North and South. It is just hate, a cant cultivated to the pitch of monomania, an ungenerous violent direction of the mind. That is the political atmosphere in which Stephen Dedalus grows up, and in which his essentially responsive mind orients itself. I am afraid it is only too true an account of the atmosphere in which a number of brilliant young Irishmen have grown up. What is the good of pretending that the extreme Irish 'patriot' is an equivalent and parallel of the English or American liberal? He is narrower and intenser than any English Tory. He will be the natural ally of the Tory in delaying British social and economic reconstruction after the war. He will play into the hands of the Tories by threatening an outbreak and providing the excuse for a militarist reaction in England. It is time the American observer faced the truth of that. No reason in that why England should not do justice to Ireland, but excellent reason for bearing in mind that these bright-green young people across the Channel are something quite different from the liberal English in training and tradition, and absolutely set against helping them. No single book has ever shown how different they are, as completely as this most memorable novel.

42. A. Clutton-Brock, review, *Times Literary Supplement*

1917

'Wild Youth', *TLS*, No. 789 (1 March 1917), 103–4.

If we begin by complaining of the title of this book, it is only because it may turn some people away from it. Others may be put off by occasional improprieties—there is one on the very first page; and it is useless to say that people ought not to be put off by such things. They are; and we should like the book to have as many readers as possible. It is not about the artist as a young man, but about a child, a boy, a youth. As one reads, one remembers oneself in it, at least one reader does; yet, like all good fiction, it is as particular as it is universal.

It is about a young Irishman, the son of a father whom he describes to a friend as 'a medical student, an oarsman, a tenor, an amateur actor, a shouting politician, a small landlord, a small investor, a drinker, a good fellow, a story-teller, somebody's secretary, something in a distillery, a tax-gatherer, a bankrupt, and at present a praiser of his own past.' He seems neither to love nor to hate his father; he is educated by the Jesuits, and he neither hates nor loves them; he tries to love a woman, or not to love her, and fails both ways. He tries to love God. 'It seems now I failed,' he says. 'It is very difficult to unite my will with the will of God instant by instant. In that I did not always fail. I could perhaps do that still.' Told thus baldly, it sounds futile, but it is not. Mr. Joyce does not talk about futilities because he cannot make anything happen in his story. He can make anything happen that he chooses. He can present the external world excellently, as in the quarrel over Parnell at a Christmas dinner at the beginning of the book. No living writer is better at conversations. But his hero is one of those many Irishmen who cannot reconcile themselves to things; above all, he cannot reconcile himself to himself. He has at times a disgust for himself, a kind of mental queasiness, in which the whole universe seems nauseating as it is presented to him through the medium of his own disgusting self. That perhaps is the cause of those improprieties we have mentioned. What an angel he would like to be, and what a filthy creature, by comparison with that angel, he seems to himself! And so all men and women seem to him filthy creatures. So it was with Hamlet. There is nothing good or bad but thinking makes it so; and thoughts pass through his mind like good or bad smells. He has no control of them.

So it is with all youth; we can all look back on ourselves and remember how disgusting we were to ourselves sometimes. But now we are used to ourselves; and we have established some relation with reality outside us, and made a habit of it, so that we do not permit those self-disgusts. But this youth, Stephen Dedalus is his name, has formed no habits that he consents to. His mind is a mirror in which beauty and ugliness are merely intensified; but how they are intensified in Mr. Joyce's story! Perhaps he is called the artist because everything to him is beauty or ugliness; but that is often so with youths who never become artists. They have their period of passive experience, and suffer because they know it to be passive; and yet they cannot but despise those elders who will themselves out of all experience, to whom nothing happens, or is, except as they wish it to be. But what Mr. Joyce gives us is the unwilled intensity of this youth's experience. He makes it like the unwilled intensity of dreams. And we have the talk of his fellow-students intensified by his experience of it. It is more real than real talk; it is like our memories of youth, but more precise than they ever are to most of us. The students often do not talk nicely; but then they are students, not nice students. They remind us of Dostoevsky's Russians in the manner in which thoughts happen to them, thoughts, irritations, disgusts; and also in the manner in which they can vent these in mere talk without ever passing on to action. Hence their malease, which is strongest in the hero; and yet they have the Irish and Russian contempt for those in whom experience converts itself into action before it has ever been really experience. They cannot but laugh at the man of action; and their chief pleasure in life is in making their laughter articulate, in making a kind of music of it. The phrase satisfies them; yet it does not satisfy, because they want a world in which phrases will act.

The hero is distinguished from the rest of them by a deeper malease. His experience is so intense, such a conflict of beauty and disgust, that it must drive him to do something. For a time it drives him into an immoral life, in which also there is beauty and disgust; but the fear of hell drives him away from this into a period of rigid piety. That again, like his immorality, begins with beauty—in the wonderful scene of his confession—and ends in listlessness. There is always something in himself that laughs at him, and it translates itself into laughers outside him. That is a common experience of youth, but with Stephen Dedalus it is always happening.

[quotes from ch. 5]

. . . he remembered his own sarcasm: the house where young men are called by their Christian names a little too soon.

That kind of sarcasm starts up in his mind about everything, like a whisper of Satan, and it destroys all his values. He has not enough egotism to have any values, and when the book ends suddenly he is setting out to find some. But for all that he is not futile, because of the drifting passion and the flushing and fading beauty of his mind. Mr. Joyce gives us that, and therefore gives us something that is worth having. It is wild youth, as wild as Hamlet's, and full of wild music.

43. Unsigned review, *Literary World*

1 March 1917, lxxxiii, No. 1, 985, 43

For some reason which we shall not try to fathom the publishers enclose a leaflet of Press notices of a volume of short stories by Mr. Joyce. All the critics, big and small, seem to have tumbled over themselves in their haste to acclaim a genius. It is, of course, very impressive, and it behoves us to be cautious and to remember that in a review there are often reservations that liberally discount the praise. We confess that it is very difficult to know quite what to say about this new book by Mr. Joyce. It is rather a study of a temperament than a story in the ordinary sense. Whether it is self-portraiture we do not know, but it has the intimate veracity, or appearance of veracity, of the great writers of confessions. It is concerned mainly with the school and college life—a Jesuit school and Trinity College—of a youth who has no home life to balance him. Stephen Dedalus is not only real, he is like every artistic projection, a type. He is an artist with all the artist's vices and virtues, exquisite sensibility, moral perversity, Christian mysticism and Pagan sensualism, the refinement of human nature at its best and a bestial coarseness. At times the analysis of emotions reminds us of Andreyed in the brutal probing of the depths of uncleanness; at others the writing is pure lyrical beauty. It is not a book we can recommend to anyone; it has the coarseness in places of a young man who is wilfully coarse. But people who stand Mr. Masefield's exploitation of the vulgarity of the farm labourer will not find much to hurt them in the brutal language of college students who are mostly good Catholics. The tradition of English fiction, however, is not in the direction of Russian realism, and we cannot say that we regret it.

44. Review, *Manchester Guardian*

1917

'A.M.', 'A Sensitivist', *Manchester Guardian*, No. 22,018 (2 March 1917), 3.

When one recognizes genius in a book one can perhaps best leave criticism alone . . . There are many pages, and not a few whole scenes, in Mr. Joyce's book which are undoubtedly the work of a man of genius, nevertheless, it leaves us combative. The reader—who is as much ignored, and as contemptuously, as it is possible for him to be in a printed work—revolts and asserts himself from time to time, and refuses to sit down passively under the writer's scorn. Once criticism is let loose, it finds range enough and many marks to hit.

Nor for its apparent formlessness should the book be condemned. A subtle sense of art has worked amidst the chaos, making this hither-and-thither record of a young mind and soul . . . a complete and ordered thing. There are ellipses, though, that go beyond the pardonable. A little too much is asked of the even eager reader in the way of understanding situations that have not been led up to, and obscure allusions. One has to be of the family, so to speak, to 'catch on.' This is part of one distinguishing feature of the book—its astounding bad manners. About this one must speak frankly at the start and have done with it. Not all the scenes are touched by genius. Some read like disagreeable phonographic records of the stupid conversations of ill-born and ill-bred youths, compact of futile obscenities, aimless outrages against reasonable decencies—not immoral, but non-moral in a bad-mannered fashion. Perhaps Mr. Joyce wants to show what may be, and often is, the ugly background of fairer things which consent astonishingly to grow in a sordid neighbourhood. Well, there is too much of this background. Also, an idiosyncrasy of Stephen, the central figure of the book—and some of his companions seem to share it—is a passion for foul-smelling things. A doctor could put a definite name to this disease, not an interesting one to the general reader, though Mr. Joyce by his insistence on it seems to think the contrary. One is driven to the conclusion that this gifted and very modern writer who rejects old theories so contemptuously is a slave to a new and particularly stupid one.

At the end Stephen has not yet proved his title to the name of artist, but is still looking for a formula to work by. He is a sensitivist. For heat and cold and discomfort, for the atmosphere of persons and companies, he has extra-subtle senses. For the pace of the world, for the things of the soul, too, he has a rare keenness of feeling, and his interpreter gives these exquisite expression. Mr. Joyce's literary gift is beyond praise. At his best he is a master. His methods are hard to define. It is almost without narrative that he depicts inimitably the condition of the Dedalus family in its prosperity and the nameless squalor which it falls into when fortune fails. Lounging feebly among this squalor we find Stephen, helpless against the ruin, but with life in him, the life of the mind, keenly concerned for intellectual experience and for a faith his mind can live by. All this is true and pathetic. True also to this kind of youth is the half-expressed notion that mainly by sin he is to win his way to mental salvation. So convenient a theory for the lounger! Yet Stephen is better than his theory. Among the new-fangled heroes of the newest fiction devoted to the psychology of youth he is almost unique in having known at least once a genuine sense of sin and undergone a genuine struggle. There is drama in Stephen. The struggle might conceivably recur, and from the lounger emerges the man and the artist.

45. Francis Hackett, review, *New Republic*

1917

'Green Sickness', *New Republic*, x, No. 122 (3 March 1917), 138–9. Later appeared in *Horizons* (1918), pp. 163–8.

This review is quoted by William Carlos Williams, 'Advent in America of a New Irish Realist', *Current Opinion*, lxii (April 1917), 275.

There is a laconic unreasonableness about the ways of creators. It is quite true that the Irish literary revival was beginning to be recognized at precisely the period of Mr. Joyce's novel, and it is also true that his protagonist is a student in Dublin at the hour of the so-called renaissance, a writer and poet and dreamer of dreams. So perverse is life, however, there is scarcely one glimmer in this landscape of the flame which is supposed to have illuminated Dublin between 1890 and 1900. If Stephen Dedalus, the young man portrayed in this novel, had belonged to the Irish revival, it would be much easier for outsiders to 'place' him. The essential fact is, he belonged to a more characteristic group which this novel alone has incarnated. One almost despairs of conveying it to the person who has conventionalized his idea of Ireland and modern Irish literature, yet there is a poignant Irish reality to be found in few existing plays and no pre-existent novel, presented here with extraordinary candor and beauty and power . . . It is only when a person with the invincible honesty of James Joyce comes to write of Dubliners as they are, a person who is said to be mordant largely because he isn't mushy, that the discrepancy between the people and the myth [the myth that the southern' Irish are a bright and witty people'] is apparent. When one says Dubliners 'as they are', one of course is pronouncing a preference. One is simply insisting that the Irishmen of James Joyce are more nearly like one's own estimate of them than the Irishmen of an amiable fabulist like George Birmingham. But there is the whole of the exquisite *Portrait of the Artist as a Young Man* to substantiate the assertion that a proud, cold, critical, suspicious, meticulous human being is infinitely more to be expected among educated Catholic Irishmen than the sort of squireen whom Lever once glorified. If this is a new type in Ireland, come into existence with the recent higher education of Catholics, one can only say that it is now by far the most important type to recognize. Bernard Shaw suggested it in the London Irishman, Larry Doyle, who appeared in *John Bull's Other Island*, but the main character of the present novel is much more subtly inflected and individualized than Larry Doyle, and is only said to belong to a type to intimate that his general mode is characteristic.

Mr. Joyce's power is not shown in any special inventiveness. A reader of novels will see at once that he has never even thought of 'plot' in the ordinary sense, or considered the advantage or importance of consulting the preferences of his reader. The thing he writes about is the thing he knows best, himself, himself at boarding school and university, and any radical variation on the actual terms of that piercing knowledge he has declined to attempt. He has sought above everything to reveal those circumstances of his life which had poignancy, and the firmest claim on him to being written was not that a thing should be amenable to his intentions as a sophisticated novelist, but that a thing should have complete personal validity. It did not weigh with him at any moment that certain phrases or certain incidents would be intensely repugnant to some readers. Was the phrase interwoven with experience? Was the incident part of the fabric of life? He asked this searchingly, and asked no more. It is not even likely that he made inquiry why, out of all that he could write, he selected particularly to reveal details that seldom find expression. Had he made the inquiry he might well have answered that the mere consciousness of silence is an incitement to expression, that expression is the only vengeance a mortal can take on the restrictions to which he finds himself subject. If others submit to those restrictions it is their own affair. To have the truth one must have a man's revelation of that which was really significant to himself.

Considering that this portrait is concluded before its subject leaves college one may gather that the really significant relations are familiar and religious, and that the adjustment is between a critical spirit and its environment. What gives its intensity to the portrait is the art Mr. Joyce has mastered of communicating the incidents of Stephen's career through the emotions they excited in him. We do not perceive Stephen's father and mother by description. We get them by the ebb and flood of Stephen's feeling, and while there are many passages of singularly life-like conversation—such, for example, as the wrangle about Parnell that ruined the Christmas dinner or the stale banter that enunciated the father's return to Cork—the viridity is in Stephen's soul.

[quotes part of the dinner scene, ch. 1]

It is his mortal sin of masturbation that preys most terribly on this youth, and he suffers all the blasting isolation which is created by the sense of sin in connection with it. Eventually he makes a 'retreat'—he is being educated by the Jesuits—and goes to confession and for a time knows religious happiness. The explicitness of this experience is more telling than the veiled account of sexual stupidity in Samuel Butler's *Way of All Flesh*, and Mr. Joyce is more successful than Samuel Butler in making religious belief seem real. The efforts of a Jesuit father to suggest a religious vocation to Stephen are the beginning of the end of his religion. In 'lucid, supple, periodic prose' Mr. Joyce describes the transition from devotional life and a private specializing in mortification to the acceptance of nature and the earth. 'His soul had arisen from the grave of boyhood, spurning her grave-clothes. Yes! Yes! Yes! He would create proudly out of the freedom and power of his soul, as the great artificer whose name he bore, a living thing, new and soaring and beautiful, impalpable, imperishable.' The 'Yes! Yes! Yes!' gives that touch of intense youthfulness which haunts the entire book, even though Mr. Joyce can be so superb in flaunting Aristotle and Aquinas.

The last chapter of the portrait gives one the *esprit* of the Catholic nationalist students in University College. It is a marvelous version of scurrilous, supercilious, callow youth. Mr. Joyce's subject is not in sympathy with the buzzing internationalist any more than with the arcane Irishman whom he compares to Ireland, 'a batlike soul waking to the consciousness of itself in darkness and secrecy and loneliness.' Stephen walks by himself, disdainful and bitter, in love and not in love, a poet at dawn and a sneerer at sunset, cold exile of 'this stinking dunghill of a world.'

A novel in which a sensitive, critical young man is completely expressed as he is can scarcely be expected to be pleasant. *A Portrait of the Artist as a Young Man* is not entirely pleasant. But it has such beauty, such love of beauty, such intensity of feeling, such pathos, such candor, it goes beyond anything in English that reveals the inevitable malaise of serious youth. Mr. Joyce has a peculiar narrative method, and he would have made things clearer if he had adopted H. G. Wells's scheme of giving a paragraphed section to each episode. As the book is now arranged, it requires some imagination on the part of the reader. The

Catholic 'retreat' also demands attentiveness, it is reported with such acrimonious zeal. But no one who has any conception of the Russian-like frustrations and pessimisms of the thin-skinned and fine-grained Irishman, from early boarding school onward, can miss the tenacious fidelity of James Joyce. He has made a rare effort to transcend every literary convention as to his race and creed, and he has had high success. Many people will furiously resent his candor, whether about religion or nationalism or sex. But candor is a nobility in this instance.

46. Notice, *Nation* (New York)

1917

Extract from H. W. Boynton, 'Outstanding Novels of the Season', *Nation* (New York), civ, No. 2701 (5 April 1917), 403–5.

. . . A perfect picture of genius in the making has just come over from Ireland in *A Portrait of the Artist as a Young Man*. It is also, say the enthusiastic publishers, an important document for those who wish to understand modern Ireland in its social, political, and religious aspects. 'Psychological insight, masterly simplicity of style, and extraordinary naturalism make this book a promise of great things.' What thrusts itself forward, of course, is the 'naturalism.' This consists, unluckily, in a free use of privy-language and a minute study of the sex-torments of adolescence. Apart from this, in spite of it, the book has a measure of force by virtue of its sincere intent and its unconquered though ingrowing and indeterminate idealism. Its hero (who surely discourses like nobody in nature) is to be an artist in words—for the sake of Ireland. . . .

47. Unsigned review, *Freeman's Journal*

7 April 1917, n.p.

Entitled 'A Dyspeptic Portrait'.

. . . *A Portrait of the Artist* has notable positive merits. Mr. Joyce's prose is masterly in its terseness and force; even his most casual descriptions haunt the mind by their vividness and wonderful economy of line. What he sees he can reproduce in words with a precision as rare as it is subtle; the pity is that, in one of his own phrases, the memory of these things has too often 'coated his palate with the scum of disgust.' Take, for instance, this vignette of a tea-table.

[quotes from ch. 4]

Had it been a description of the desolation of No Man's Land on the Somme or the Yser, the horror could hardly have been laid on more thickly, and all through the book food is scarcely mentioned without the same shudder of disgust, which is more reminiscent of the pangs of dyspepsia than of the joy of art. Had the author confined himself to this particular form of ugliness it would not have been so bad, but, as Whistler said of Oscar Wilde, that he could not keep out of the area, so Mr. Joyce plunges and drags his readers after him into the slime of foul sewers. He is not, indeed, like Mr. George Moore, who points to the iridiscence as a proof of the beauty of corruption. Mr. Joyce knows better, but despite his repulsion his pen, instead of pointing to the stars overhead, is degraded into a muck-rake. This is due in a measure to a false theory of aesthetics, but it springs even more from temperamental defects . . .The great masters have not been blind to the aspects of life that Mr. Joyce exploits, but they see them in their true perspective and do not dwell on them to the exclusion of everything else. They know the value of proportion and the importance of sanity and clear judgment and realise that to see life steadily one must see it whole. It is an accident that Mr. Joyce's book should have Dublin as its background. A youth of the temperamental quality of his Stephen Dedalus was bound to react just as sharply against any other environment; had he been brought up in an English cathedral town or an American industrial centre he would have pillioried them in just as repellant a fashion. Yet English critics, with a complacency that makes one despair of their intelligence, are already hailing the author as a typical Irishman, and his book as a faithful picture of Irish life. It would be just as accurate to declare that DeQuincey's *Opium Eater* embodied the experiences of the average English youth or that Carlyle's splenetic railings reflected the emotions of Victorian England.

48. J. C. Squire, review, *New Statesman*

1917

'Mr. James Joyce', in *Books in General* (1919), pp. 245–50. Appeared originally in *New Statesman*, ix (14 April 1917), 40.

Mr. James Joyce is a curious phenomenon. He first appeared in literary Dublin about (I suppose) a dozen years ago: a strangely solitary and self-sufficient and obviously gifted man. He published a small book of verse with one or two good lyrics in it; and those who foresaw a future for him became certain they were right. He published nothing; but his reputation spread even amongst those who had never read a line he had written. He disappeared from Ireland and went to Austria, where he settled. The war came, and soon afterwards his second book—*Dubliners*—was issued and reviewed with a general deference, after wandering about for years among publishers who had been fighting shy of it because of its undoubted unpleasantness and a reference to Edward VII. Another interval and *A Portrait of the Artist as a Young Man* began to run serially in the *Egoist*. 'The Egoist, Ltd.,' has now published this book, and nobody is surprised to find all writing London talking about it. Mr. Joyce has only done what was expected.

A Portrait of the Artist as a Young Man

Whether this book is supposed to be a novel or an autobiography I do not know or care. Presumably some characters and episodes are fictitious, or the author would not even have bothered to employ fictitious names. But one is left with the impression that almost all the way one has been listening to sheer undecorated, unintensified truth. Mr. Joyce's title suggests, well enough, his plan. There is no 'plot.' The subsidiary characters appear and recede, and not one of them is involved throughout in the career of the hero. Stephen Dedalus is born; he goes to school; he goes to college. His struggles are mainly inward: there is nothing unusual in that. He has religious crises: heroes of fiction frequently do. He fights against, succumbs to, and again fights against sexual temptation: we have stories on those lines in hundreds. All the same, we have never had a novel in the least degree resembling this one; whether it is mainly success or mainly failure, it stands by itself.

You recognize its individuality in the very first paragraph. Mr. Joyce tries to put down the vivid and incoherent memories of childhood in a vivid and incoherent way: to show one Stephen Dedalus's memories precisely as one's own memories might appear if one ransacked one's mind. He opens:

[quotes the first paragraph of ch. 1]

'His mother had a nicer smell than his father,' he proceeds. There is verisimilitude in this; but a critic on the look-out for Mr. Joyce's idiosyncrasies would certainly fasten upon his preoccupation with the olfactory—which sometimes leads him to write things he might as well have left to be guessed at—as one of them. Still, it is a minor characteristic. His major characteristics are his intellectual integrity, his sharp eyes, and his ability to set down precisely what he wants to set down. He is a realist of the first order. You feel that he means to allow no personal prejudice or predilection to distort the record of what he sees. His perceptions may be naturally limited; but his honesty in registering their results is complete. It is even a little too complete. There are some things that we are all familiar with and that ordinary civilized manners (not pharisaism) prevent us from importing into general conversation. Mr. Joyce can never resist a dunghill. He is not, in fact, quite above the pleasure of being shocking. Generally speaking, however, he carries conviction. He is telling the truth about a type and about life as it presents itself to that type.

He is a genuine realist: that is to say, he puts in the exaltations as well as the depressions, the inner life as well as the outer. He is not morosely determined to paint everything drab. Spiritual passions are as powerful to him as physical passions; and as far as his own bias goes it may as well be in favour of Catholic asceticism as of sensual materialism. For his detachment as author is almost inhuman. If Stephen is himself, then he is a self who is expelled and impartially scrutinized, without pity or 'allowances,' directly Mr. Joyce the artist gets to work. And of the other characters one may say that they are always given their due, always drawn so as to evoke the sympathy they deserve, yet are never openly granted the sympathy of the author. He is the outsider, the observer, the faithful selector of significant traits, moral and physical; his judgments, if he forms them, are concealed. He never even shows by a quiver of the pen that anything distresses him.

His prose instrument is a remarkable one. Few contemporary writers are effective in such diverse ways; his method varies with the subject-matter and never fails him. His dialogue (as in the remarkable discussions at home about Barnell and Stephen's education) is as close to the dialogue of life as anything I have ever come across; though he does not make the gramophonic mistake of spinning it out as it is usually spun out in life and in novels that aim at a faithful reproduction of life and only succeed in sending one to sleep. And his descriptive and narrative passages include at one pole sounding periods of classical prose and at the other disjointed and almost futuristic sentences. The finest sustained pages in the book contain the sermon in which a dear, simple old priest expounds the unimaginable horrors of hell: the immeasurable solid stench as of a 'huge and rolling human fungus,' the helplessness of the damned, 'not even able to remove from the eye a worm that gnaws it,' the fierceness of the fire in which 'the blood seethes and boils in the veins, the brains are boiling in the skull, the heart in the breast glowing and bursting, the bowels a red-hot mass of burning pulp, the tender eyes flaming like molten balls.' Stephen, after listening to this, 'came down the aisle of the chapel, his legs shaking and the scalp of his head trembling as though it had been touched by ghostly fingers. He passed up the staircase and into the corridor along the walls of which the overcoats and waterproofs hung like gibbeted malefactors, headless and dripping and shapeless.'

No wonder. For myself, I had had an idea that this kind of exposition had died with Drexelius; but after I had read it I suddenly and involuntarily thought, 'Good Lord, suppose it is all true!' That is a sufficient testimony to the power of Mr. Joyce's writing.

This is not everybody's book. The later portion, consisting largely of rather dull student discussions, is dull; nobody could be inspired by the story, and it had better be neglected by any one who is easily disgusted. Its interest is mainly technical, using the word in its broadest sense; and its greatest appeal, consequently, is made to the practising artist in literature. What Mr. Joyce will do with his powers in the future it is impossible to conjecture. I conceive that he does not know himself: that, indeed, the discovery of a form is the greatest problem in front of him. It is doubtful if he will make a novelist.

49. Unsigned review, *Irish Book Lover*

April–May 1917, viii, Nos. 9–10, 113

In spite of the serious drawbacks to be mentioned later, truth compels one to admit that this pseudo autobiography of Stephen Dedalus, a weakling and a dreamer, makes fascinating reading. We read it at a single sitting. The hero's schooldays at Clongowes Wood, and later at Belvedere, are graphically and doubtless, faithfully portrayed, as is the visit to Cork in company with his father, a clever ne'er-do-well, gradually sinking in the social scale. One of the strongest scenes in the book is the description of the Christmas dinner party during the black year of 1891, when Nationalist Ireland was riven to the centre over the Parnell 'split.' Mr. Joyce is unsparing in his realism, and his violent contrasts—the brothel, the confessional—jar on one's finer feelings. So do the quips and jeers of the students, in language unprinted in literature since the days of Swift and Sterne, following on some eloquent and orthodox sermons! That Mr. Joyce is a master of a brilliant descriptive style and handles his dialogue as ably as any living writer is conceded on all hands, and, oh! the pity of it. In writing thus he is just to his fine gifts? Is it even wise, from a worldly point of view—mercenary, if you will—to dissipate one's talents on a book which can only attain a limited circulation?—for no clean-minded person could possibly allow it to remain within reach of his wife, his sons or daughters. Above all, is it Art? We doubt it.

50. John Quinn, review, *Vanity Fair*

May 1917, viii, No. 3, 48, 128

'James Joyce, A New Irish Novelist'.

James Joyce has come to town, and he has come to stay. A new star has appeared in the firmament of Irish letters, a star of the first magnitude. The question that one is now asked is not have you *seen* a portrait, but 'Have you *read The Portrait*?' All of a sudden everyone is reading and talking about *The Portrait*. Everywhere one hears of it. . . .

[a brief biographical sketch and publishing history follows here]

. . . *Dubliners* is one of the most sincere and most realistic books ever written. Its great sincerity is one of its chief attractions. The book does not belong to the flashy school of literature. It is the work of a writer who was moved by what he felt and saw, but apparently remained as cold as stone. It is the reader who catches the infection. I am tempted to say it is the most powerful book of short stories in English published in the last ten years. . . . It is due to the enterprise and courage of an American publisher that Joyce's book has first seen the light of day. The publisher is receiving his reward. The book places James Joyce in the same rank with James Stephens and John M. Synge.

Partial blindness! No wonder the book is a distillation of bitter-sweet. It is not 'unpleasant.' No one could recall the Christmas dinner and the row over Parnell, the wonderful sermon, the confession, and the other episodes in the book, and complain that it lacked special inventiveness. The sermon itself is epical. There is no record of any 'movement' or 'revival' in it, for Joyce is too good an artist to mix propaganda with his art. He knows the vital distinction that poetry is never propaganda.

One often hears in these days of war the remark that very little good literature is written or published. When I hear that, I often refer to the modern Irish writers and say that anything by William Butler Yeats, Lady Gregory, George Russell (A. E.), James Stephens, Padraic Colum, and now I shall add James Joyce, is literature and is always worth reading. Joyce's last book stands out above anything that has been published in this country or in Great Britain in the last two years. . . . Joyce's book is like a series of etchings. In some cases the acid has bit deep into the plate. To read Yeats' book [*Reveries Over Childhood and Youth*] might be compared to going into a finely proportioned room hung with noble paintings by Puvis de Chavannes. To read Joyce is like being in a room decorated with paintings by Daumier or Toulouse-Lautrec. *A Portrait of the Artist as a Young Man* is a great work of art. It will live. There is nothing abstract about Joyce. His style is vital and has the radium that makes art live. He writes with the frankness and freedom that is not uncommon in Ireland. That Irish frankness surprised and shocked a few in Synge's plays, notably in *The Playboy of the Western World*. But Synge's writings have now taken their place as classics. If James Joyce can keep up the pace that this book sets, he is assured of an equally high place. Synge is perhaps the more Irish of the two; more Irish in the richness of his idiom and the color of his thought and the quality of his style, although the culture of both is European. Joyce has not so deep a talent. He has written a play which may be as great a success as *The Portrait* and *Dubliners*, and one can never tell how far a first-rate man will go. I do not say that with two books of prose and a small volume of verse to his credit he is a great writer. But I do say that this last book is a great work of art. Conrad, a friend of mine, is a great creative artist. I do not compare him, a veteran writer, with Joyce, a young one. But Joyce's mind interests me greatly. I like his way of writing tremendously. After all, there is plenty of room for the work of artists like Joseph Conrad and George Moore, as well as for the work of James Joyce, just as in a live gallery there should be room for paintings by Manet and Cézanne and Picasso. . . .

[quotes from Ezra Pound's article 'James Joyce and the Modern Stage', see No. 68]

A Portrait of the Artist as a Young Man was refused by publisher after publisher in London ostensibly because of the frankness with which certain episodes in the life of a young man were treated. It is perhaps not a book for all young women: *pas pour la jeune fille*. And yet no young man or young woman of the right fibre would be harmed by it. Compared to such a soft and false and dangerous book as *Ann Veronica*, by H. G. Wells, for example, not to speak of similar American trash that reeks and smells of sex, Joyce's book is bracing and hard and clean.

Neither is it a book for suffragettes, for Joyce never argues. He does not try to convince. He has no thesis. His book is just life. It is good, clean writing, even if some of his phrases are as startling as many that could be culled from the bible. His is a new style. There is no ornament, no rhetoric, nothing declamatory, no compromise, complete realism, and great sincerity. This way of writing is not easy. The book was not written on a typewriter, one may be sure; nor was it dictated to a stenographer between motor trips or while the author strolled about his room smoking a cigarette or puffing at his pipe.

He has the sincerity of genius. Let a man be ever so frank and plain-spoken, as Joyce is, if he is sincere, he is not vulgar or 'unpleasant.' In *The Portrait* we have a man at grips with himself and with his love of life. The book must not be read line by line as a pedant would read it, or as a conventional reviewer would read it, but as a whole, and then one will realize what a fine, hard, great piece of work it is.

If the book had been translated from the Russian, it would have instantly been hailed as a masterpiece. But it is a finer work of art than any Russian novel written in the last ten years that has been translated into English. The conversations of those young men will be most intelligible to Irish Catholics. Irish Ireland is in some respects a mediaeval country, and the talks of those young students, saturated with their religion in spite of their free-thinking, with the boy-Latin that they talk, is mediaeval and yet quite modern.

When *Dubliners* was published three years ago I handed a copy of it to an Irish friend of mine, an artist and a man of letters, and said to him that here was a new Irish writer that had the real stuff in him. My friend read the book and returning it to me said: 'Good God, Quinn, that is a gray book! One always knew that there were such places in Dublin, but one never wanted to go near or to hear of them. But the man can write.'

I have compared William Butler Yeats' *Reveries Over Childhood and Youth* with Joyce's *A Portrait of the Artist as a Young Man*. Both Yeats and Joyce are poets. Yeats in his Reveries is a poet looking back to his youth fondly, and seeing things through mists of tenderness. Joyce writes his book about his youth in his youth. It has the bite and the harshness of strong youth, but what art! Yeats is a great poet at fifty writing of his youth. Joyce, the most gifted of all the young Irish writers, does the story of his youth at twenty-five. There we have the difference. The older poet has acquired the sense of life. The younger struggles with the stuff of life. Both are frank and very sincere. Some may think Joyce is bitter. But he is not. He is true to life. In one of his lyrics he speaks of

A sage that is but kith and kin
With the comedian Capuchin.

But perhaps the truer key is found in Joyce's words towards the end of his book: 'and I will try to express myself in some mode of life or art as freely as I can and as wholly as I can, using for my defense the only arms I allow myself to use, silence, exile and cunning.'

51. Van Wyck Brooks, review, *The Seven Arts*

May 1917, ii, No. 7, 122

The seven veils are dropping from the face of Ireland and it is a strange reality that face presents, strange at least to those who know nothing of the harsh old Irish world of a past that has been perpetuated as hardly any other European past has been, strange to those who know nothing of the black chieftains and the subterranean sympathies of Catholic Ireland and Catholic Spain. You have to go back generations in any other Western country to find a spiritual equivalent of James Joyce, whose *Portrait of the Artist as a Young Man* (Huebsch) is altogether atavistic from the standpoint of English literature, full as it is of Shandy-isms but Rabelaisian in a pure style that Sterne was born too late to compass. Yet it is a living society that Mr. Joyce pictures, one that conforms to the twentieth century in its worldly apparel but reveals in its table-talk and its more intimate educational and religious recesses a mediaevalism utterly untouched by that industrial experience which has made the rest of the world kin, for good or ill. Mr. Joyce's literary culture is of a piece with his theme; he stems from Cardinal Newman as other men stem from Goethe, and his pages bristle with Aristotle and Thomas Aquinas. . . . Do young men in other countries than Ireland still lift vermin from their collars and soliloquize over them, as Uncle

Toby soliloquized over the fly, and as the goliards used to do at the Sorbonne eight hundred years ago? . . . Emotionally the book is direct, spare, and true in its flight as hardly any Anglo-Saxon books are, and its style goes to bear out Thomas MacDonagh's assertion that the English tongue possesses in Ireland an uncodified suggestiveness, a rich concreteness, that it has largely lost in its own country.

52. John Macy, review of *A Portrait* and *Dubliners*

1917

'James Joyce', *Dial*, lxii, No. 744 (14 June 1917), 525–7.

A review of *A Portrait of the Artist* and of *Dubliners*.

. . . It was only in the last generation that English and Irish novelists, under the influence of French literature, freed themselves from the cowardice of Victorian fiction and assumed that anything human under the sun is proper subject-matter for art. If they have not produced masterpieces (and I do not admit that they have not), they have made a brave beginning. Such a book as *A Portrait of the Artist as a Young Man* would have been impossible forty years ago. . . .

Joyce's work is outspoken, vigorous, original, beautiful. Whether it faithfully reflects Irish politics and the emotional conflicts of the Catholic religion one who is neither Irish nor Catholic cannot judge with certainty. It seems, however, that the noisy controversies over Parnell and the priests in which the boy's elders indulge have the sound of living Irish voices; and the distracted boy's wrestlings with his sins and his faith are so movingly human that they hold the sympathy even of one who is indifferent to the religious arguments. I am afraid that the religious questions and the political questions are too roughly handled to please the incurably devout and patriotic. If they ever put up a statue of Joyce in Dublin, it will not be during his life time. For he is no respecter of anything except art and human nature and language.

There are some who, to turn his own imaginative phrase, will fret in the shadow of his language. He makes boys talk as boys do, as they did in your school and mine, except that we lacked the Irish imagery and whimsicality. If the young hero is abnormal and precocious, that is because he is not an ordinary boy but an artist, gifted with thoughts and phrases above our common abilities. This is a portrait of an artist by an artist, a literary artist of the finest quality.

The style is a joy. 'Cranly's speech,' he writes, 'had neither rare phrases of Elizabethan English nor quaintly turned versions of Irish idioms.' In that Joyce has defined his own style. It is Elizabethan, yet thoroughly modern; it is racily Irish, yet universal English. It is unblushingly plain-spoken and richly fanciful, like Shakespeare and Ben Jonson. The effect of complete possession of the traditional resources of language is combined with an effect of complete indifference to traditional methods of fiction. Episodes, sensations, dreams, emotions trivial and tragic succeed each other neither coherently nor incoherently; each is developed vividly for a moment, then fades away into the next, with or without the mechanical devices of chapter divisions or rows of stars. Life is so; a fellow is pandied by the schoolmaster for no offense; the cricket bats strike the balls, pick, pock, puck; there is a girl to dream about; and Byron was a greater poet than Tennyson anyhow. . . .

The sufferings of the poor little sinner are told with perfect fidelity to his point of view. Since he is an artist his thoughts appropriately find expression in phrases of maturer beauty than the speech of ordinary boys. He is enamored of words, intrigued by their mystery and color; wherefore the biographer plays through the boy's thoughts with all manner of verbal loveliness.

[quotes from ch. 4]

From the fading splendor of an evening as beautifully described as any in English, he tumbles into the sordid day of a house rich in pawn tickets. That is life. 'Welcome, O life!' he bids farewell to his young manhood. 'I go to encounter for the millionth time the reality of experience and to forge in the smithy of my soul the uncreated conscience of my race. Old father, old artificer, stand me now and ever in good stead.'

JOHN MACY, REVIEW OF *A Portrait* AND *Dubliners* 1917

I know nothing of Mr. James Joyce, the man, and I have not yet tried to look up his history; it is pleasanter to read him first and find out about him afterwards. . . .

The sketches in *Dubliners* are perfect, each in its own way, and all in one way: they imply a vast deal that is not said. They are small as the eye-glass of a telescope is small; you look through them to depths and distances. They are a kind of short story unknown to the American magazine if not to the American writer. An American editor might read them for his private pleasure, but from his professional point of view he would not see that there was any story there at all. . . . Joyce's power to disentangle a single thread from the confusion of life and let you run briefly back upon it until you encounter the confusion and are left to think about it yourself—that is a power rare enough in any literature. I have an impression of having felt that power in some of Gissing's sketches, though that is only an impression which I should not care to formulate as a critical judgment until I had read Gissing again. (A good thing to do, by the way.)

Except one story, 'A Painful Case,' I could not tell the plot of any of these sketches. Because there is no plot going from beginning to end. The plot goes from the surface inward, from a near view away into a background. A person appears for a moment—a priest, or a girl, or a small boy, or a streetcorner tough, or a drunken salesman—and does and says things not extraordinary in themselves; and somehow you know all about these people and feel that you could think out their entire lives. Some are stupid, some are pathetic, some are funny in an unhilarious way. The dominant mood is reticent irony. The last story in the book, 'The Dead,' is a masterpiece which will never be popular, because it is all about living people; there is only one dead person in it and he is not mentioned until near the end. That's the kind of trick an Irishman like Synge or Joyce would play on us, and perhaps a Frenchman or a Russian would do it; but we would not stand it from one of our own writers.

53. Unsigned review, *New Age*

12 July 1917, xxi, n.s. No. 11, 254

If this book had been written by Dostoieffsky, it would have been a masterpiece; and we invite Mr. Joyce to read that famous thirteenth chapter of Corinthians and apply to himself the teaching. For his wilful cleverness, his determination to produce kinematographic effects instead of a literary portrait, are due entirely to a lack of clarity. He fears to suffer, and will not, therefore, put himself in the place of his hero; he will record with wonderful fidelity, and frequently with remarkable dramatic skill, what happened around or to Stephen Dedalus, but as it is all objectively viewed and objectively rendered, the character has no continuum, no personality. Even the introspective passages have the same character of objectivity; Stephen only observes the thoughts that come to him, only suffers the impact of external emotions, but never do his experiences reveal him to himself or to the reader. There are passages in this book comparable with the best in English literature; the scene wherein Mr. Dedalus carves the Christmas turkey is perfectly rendered, the Jesuit sermons on Hell are vivid intellectual tortures, Stephen's first experience in a brothel, and the whole history of his sexual obsession are given with pitiless accuracy. But Mr. Joyce never answers the reader's: 'Why?': he keeps on the circumference of his hero's mind, and never dives to the centre of his soul. So this portrait seems to be a mere catalogue of unrelated states; there is everything in it that becomes a man, but it never does become the man, Stephen Dedalus. Samuel hewed Agag to pieces, but the pieces were not Agag; and the fragments here offered of the experience of Stephen Dedalus are no substitute for a 'portrait of the artist as a young man.' It is a composition that does not hang together, a creation into which the creator has forgotten to breathe the breath of life, and, therefore, Stephen Dedalus never becomes a living soul. He never 'shows forth' anything but a furtive lust; his occasional exercises in theories of aesthetics have an interest that is not personal, his mind has no apparent relation to his experience. Yet if it fails as a personal portrait, the value of the book as a portrait of young Ireland, Catholic Ireland, cannot be over-estimated. Beware of the men who have no souls, is the warning conveyed to England by this book; they are not even consumed with a holy hatred of those who are opposed to them, contempt, even, is too violent for them, but they conceal an essential dissimilarity under a superficial resemblance of technical proficiency, and are incalculable in their divergence of purpose.

COMMENTS ON A PORTRAIT

1917–22

54. Stanislaus on *A Portrait*

1904

The Dublin Diary of Stanislaus Joyce (1962), ed. George. H. Healey, p. 25.

From a journal entry for 29 March 1904.

. . . Jim has turned the paper [*A Portrait of the Artist* rejected by the review *Dana*, edited by W. K. Magee ('John Eglinton') and Frederick Ryan] into a novel the title of which—*Stephen Hero*—I also suggested. He has written eleven chapters. The chapters are exceptionally well written in a style which seems to me altogether original. It is a lying autobiography and a raking satire. He is putting nearly all his acquaintances in it, and the Catholic Church comes in for a bad quarter of an hour. . . .

55. Ezra Pound to John Quinn

1917

Letter to John Quinn (18 April 1917), in *The Letters of Ezra Pound* (1950), ed. D. D. Paige, p. 109.

. . . I have read a 12th Century Provençal sermon about hell—same model as the one in *The Portrait*, same old hoax.

I don't put myself up as a sample of how the book will strike most people. But I do think Joyce has done his job so well and so thoroughly that he conveys the *milieu* of the book, and that an Irish Catholic with local knowledge has very little advantage over the outsider with good grounding in literature when it comes to understanding *The Portrait*.

56. An Italian comment on *A Portrait*

1917

Diego Angeli, 'Un Romanzo di Gesuiti', *Il Marzocco* (Florence), xxii, No. 32 (12 August 1917), 2–3; translated by Joyce for *Egoist*, v, No. 2 (February, 1918), 30 (from which the present text is taken).

Mr. James Joyce is a young Irish novelist whose last book, *A Portrait of the Artist as a Young Man*, has raised a great tumult of discussion among English-speaking critics. It is easy to see why. An Irishman, he has found in himself the strength to proclaim himself a citizen of a wider world; a Catholic, he has had the courage to cast his religion from him and to proclaim himself an atheist; and a writer, inheriting the most traditionalist of all European literatures, he has found a way to break free from the tradition of the old English novel and to adopt a new style consonant with a new conception. In a word such an effort was bound to tilt against all the feelings and cherished beliefs of his fellow countrymen but, carried out, as it is here, with a fine and youthful boldness, it has won the day. His book is not alone an admirable work of art and thought; it is also a cry of revolt: it is the desire of a new artist to look upon the world with other eyes, to bring to the front his individual theories and to compel a listless public to reflect that there are another literature and another esthetic apprehension beyond those foisted upon us, with a bountifulness at times nauseating, by the general purveying of pseudo-romantic prose and by fashionable publishers, with their seriocomic booklists, and by the weekly and monthly magazines. And let us admit that such a cry of revolt has been uttered at the right moment and that it is in itself the promise of a fortunate renascence . . . in the midst of the great revolution of the European novel English writers continued to remain in their 'splendid isolation' and could not or would not open their eyes to what was going on around them. Literature, however, like all the other arts underwent a gradual transformation and Mr. Joyce's book marks its definite date in the chronology of English literature. I think it well to put so much on record here not only for that which it signifies actually but also for that which in time it may bring forth.

The phenomenon is all the more important in that Mr. Joyce's *Portrait* contains two separate elements, each of which is significant and worthy of analysis: its ethical content and the form wherewith this content is clothed. When one has read the book to the end one understands why most English and American critics have raised an outcry against both form and content, understanding, for the most part, neither one nor the other. Accustomed as they are to the usual novels, enclosed in a set framework, they found themselves in this case out of their depth and hence their talk of immorality, impiety, naturalism and exaggeration. They have not grasped the subtlety of the psychological analysis nor the synthetic value of certain details and certain sudden arrests of movement. Possibly their own Protestant upbringing renders the moral development of the central character incomprehensible to them. For Mr. Joyce is a Catholic and, more than that, a Catholic brought up in a Jesuit college. One must have passed many years of one's own life in a seminary of the society of Jesus, one must have passed through the same experiences and undergone the same crises to understand the profound analysis, the keenness of observation shown in the character of Stephen Dedalus. No writer, so far as I know, has penetrated deeper in the examination of the influence, sensual rather than spiritual, of the society's exercises.

For this analysis so purely modern, so cruelly and boldly true, the writer needed a style which would break down the tradition of the six shilling novel: and this style Mr. Joyce has fashioned for himself. The brushwork of the novel reminds one of certain modern paintings in which the planes interpenetrate and the external vision seems to partake of the sensations of the onlooker. It is not so much the narrative of a life as its reminiscence but it is a reminiscence whole, complete and absolute, with all those incidents and details which tend to fix indelibly each feature of the whole. He does not lose time explaining the wherefore of these sensations of his nor even tell us their reason or origin: they leap up in his pages as do the memories of a life we ourselves have lived without apparent cause, without logical sequence. But it is exactly such a succession of past visions and memories which makes up the sum of every life. In this evocation of reality Mr. Joyce is truly a master. The majority of English critics remark, with easy superficiality, that he thinks himself a naturalist simply because he does not shrink from painting certain brutal episodes in words more brutal still. This is not so: his naturalism goes much deeper. Certainly there is a difference, formal no less than substantial, between his book and let us say, *La Terre* of Emile Zola. Zola's naturalism is romantic whereas the naturalism of Mr. Joyce is impressionist, the profound synthetic naturalism of some pictures of Cézanne or Maquet, the naturalism of the late impressionists who single out the characteristic elements of a landscape or a scene or a human face. And all this he expresses in a rapid and concise style, free from every picturesque effect, every rhetorical redundancy, every needless image or epithet. Mr. Joyce tells us what he must tell in the least number of words; his palette is limited to a few colours. But he knows what to choose for his end and therefore half a page of his dry precise angular prose expresses much more (and with much more telling effect) than all that wearisome research of images and colour of which we have lately heard and read so much.

And that is why Mr. Joyce's book has raised such a great clamour of discussion. He is a new writer in the glorious company of English literature, a new writer with a new form of his own and new aims, and he comes at a moment when the world is making a new constitution and a new social ordinance. We must welcome him with joy. He is one of those rude craftsmen who open up paths whereon many will yet follow. It is the first streaks of the dawn of a new art visible on the horizon. Let us hail it therefore as the herald of a new day.

57. Jane Heap on Joyce

1917

'James Joyce', *Little Review*, iii, No. 10 (April 1917), 8–9.

I suppose Mr. Joyce had some idea in mind when he gave his book the title of *A Portrait of the* ARTIST *as a Young Man*. But the critics seem to want it their own way and say, 'Mr Joyce paints the Irishman as he really is.' . . . Irishman, doctor, lawyer, merchant, chief, I suppose. Francis Hackett says it 'reveals the inevitable malaise of serious youth.' Why then doesn't this inevitable malaise of all our serious youth end inevitably like this: the call 'to create proudly out of the freedom and power of his soul, a living thing, new and soaring, and beautiful, impalpable, imperishable.'

H. G. Wells assures us that the youth of his country need not suffer such tortures of adolescence because of England's more common-sense treatment of the sex question. And all the time Mr. Joyce was talking about the artist of any land, not the youth of England or any other country. In this country there is only God to thank that the young artist does not go entirely mad over one and all of its institutions. In our country the young artists could suffer tortures far beyond anything suffered by Stephen, over the utter emptiness of the place. But he will always suffer. He will always be 'a naked runner lost in a storm of spears.'

There is too much geography of the body in this education of ours. You can talk about or write about or paint or sculp some parts of the body but others must be treated like the Bad Lands. You can write about what you see that you don't like, what you touch, taste, or hear; but you can't write about what you smell; if you do you are accused of using nasty words. I could say a lot more about the geography of the body, and how its influence goes all the way through until the censor makes a geography for your mind and soul. But I want to talk about nasty words. The result of this education is that we have all the nasty words in the world in our language. How often a European or an Oriental will say: 'Oh to us it is something very nice—beautiful; but to you it would not be nice; it is much different in English.' When they told James Joyce he had words like that in his book he must have been as surprised as a painter would be if he were told that some of his colors were immoral.

His story is told the way a person in a sick room sharply remembers all the over-felt impressions and experiences of a time of fever; until the story itself catches the fever and becomes a thing of more definite, closer-known, keener-felt consciousness—and of a restless oblivion of self-consciousness.

58. Margaret Anderson on Joyce

1917

Little Review, iii, No. 10 (April, 1917), 9–10.

This James Joyce book is the most beautiful piece of writing and the most creative piece of prose anywhere to be seen on the horizon to-day. It is consciously a work of Art in a way that *Jean-Christophe* made no effort to be; it is such head and shoulders above *Jacob Stahl* or Gilbert Cannan's *Mendel* that one must realize those books as very good novels and this as something quite more than that. It can be spoken of in terms that apply to *Pelle the Conqueror*, but only in this way: each is a work of Art and therefore not to be talked of as lesser or greater; but while *Pelle* is made of language as it has been used the *Portrait* is made of language as it will come to be used. There is no doubt that we will have novels before long written without even as much of the conventional structure of language as Mr. Joyce has adhered to—a new kind of 'dimension in language' which is being felt in many places and which George Soule has illustrated beautifully in an article in *The New Republic.*

But that isn't the most important thing. The interest in *Pelle* is in the way its stories are told. The interest in the *Portrait* is in the way its aesthetic content is presented.

[quotes from ch. 1]

59. A Pound editorial on Joyce and Wyndham Lewis

1917

Extract from 'Editorial', *Little Review*, iv, No. 1 (May 1917), 3–6.

. . . In so far as it is possible, I should like *The Little Review* to aid and abet *The Egoist* in its work. I do not think it can be too often pointed out that during the last four years *The Egoist* has published serially, in the face of no inconsiderable difficulties, the only translation of Remy de Gourmont's *Chevaux de Diomedes*; the best translation of *Le Comte de Gabalis*, Mr. Joyce's masterpiece *A Portrait of the Artist as a Young Man*, and is now publishing Mr. Lewis's novel *Tarr*. Even if they had published nothing else there would be no other current periodical which could challenge this record, but *The Egoist* has not stopped there; they have in a most spirited manner carried out the publication in book form of the *Portrait of the Artist*, and are in the act of publishing Mr. Eliot's poems, under the title *Mr. Prufrock and Observations*.

I see no reason for concealing my belief that the two novels, by Joyce and Lewis, and Mr. Eliot's poems are not only the most important contributions to English literature of the past three years, but that they are practically the only works of the time in which the creative element is present, which in any way show invention, or a progress beyond precedent work. The mass of our contemporaries, to say nothing of our debilitated elders, have gone on repeating themselves and each other.

60. Wyndham Lewis on *A Portrait*

1937

Blasting and Bombardiering, (1937), pp. 271–2.

A brief mention of *A Portrait of the Artist* in Lewis's chapter 'First Meeting with James Joyce' (Chapter IV).

. . . *Some* pages of the *Portrait* I had read, when it first appeared as a serial in the *Egoist*. . . . But I took very little interest. At that time, it was of far too tenuous an elegance for my taste. Its flavor was altogether too literary. And as to its emotional content, that I condemned at once as sentimental-Irish. Even now, for that matter, I feel much the same about the *Portrait of the Artist*, with the important difference that I have obliged myself to read a great many more books, in the meanwhile, many of which suffer from the same shortcomings, as I see it. So I do recognize the *Portrait of the Artist as a Young Man* to be one only of a large class, and of its kind a very excellent example.

61. John F. Harris on the unconventional

1918

'A Note on James Joyce', *To-Day*, iii, No. 15 (May 1918), 88–92.

The critic notes the surprise and hostility that greets an 'unlikely' and unconventional book.

. . . Mr. James Joyce, the author of *A Portrait of the Artist as a Young Man*, is an Irishman and one of the modern writers who has the courage of his convictions and of his own artistic methods.

[A brief literary history follows here, up to the announcement of serial publication of *Ulysses* in the *Egoist*.]

A Portrait of the Artist as a Young Man is not only an original book; it strikes us as fundamentally true. It is not the kind of book of which the ordinary subscriber to Mudie's is likely to approve. Indeed, no publisher could be found for it in England, nor was there an English printer who would consent to print it. It was therefore set up in America and has been issued in England by the proprietors of the *Egoist*. We are aware, of course, that these facts do not in themselves necessarily establish any particular merit in Mr. Joyce's novel.

Yet it has taken a very definite place in modern fiction for its fearlessness of expression, its insight into the stress and turmoil of the artist's mind and soul, its exposure of the emotional shams of a certain type of religious upbringing, and its utter disregard of the ordinary customs of polite novel-writing. Mr. Joyce has no literary *gaucherie*. He may be classified as a realist: his realism is naked and unashamed. Yet his improprieties and *mesquineries*, his insistence on the material squalor and ugliness of his hero's surroundings, have their origin in an artistic purpose. And, we may add in parentheses, however much his characters may indulge in furtive nastiness, we are never in doubt about the sensitiveness of the author himself. Only a man with a mind and spirit painfully aware of the hideous brutality and cruelty that is in the world could have written this book.

Stephen Dedalus is the artist whose portrait Mr. Joyce has drawn so convincingly in these pages. . . . Here, then, is the story of an education. We meet Stephen first as a small boy in his own home, then as a schoolboy at Clongowes Wood College; later the scene shifts to a Jesuit School in Dublin. It is in this later phase of the book, which deals with a distinctively Irish and Catholic education, that the author writes with the most surprising intimacy. But before this point is reached there is a scene in a brothel—the central episode of the story—which better that any other gives the measure of Mr. Joyce's powers of artistic description. He passes with characteristic detachment to the most depressing passages in Stephen's development. Stephen, full of disturbing thoughts, is sitting at the schoolroom window staring into the twilight.

[quotes from ch. 3]

And in the chapter that follows Stephen is momentarily released from his temptations by the fierce denunciations of the Roman faith. He hears two revolting sermons on the terrors of Hell: he is driven shrinkingly to the confessional. So obsessed is he with a conviction of sin that he seems unaware of the materialism of a religion which interprets eternal damnation almost entirely in the language and ideas of the material world. But his restless thoughts jump away from the present to the place where he is not: he sees himself in the past with complete mental detachment:

[quotes from ch. 2]

At the conclusion of the narrative Stephen has made his revolt: the confusions of life still press in upon him; but he longs for a wider life. 'Away! Away!' he exclaims in the chaotic diary which fills the last pages of the book. 'The spell of arms and voices: the white arms of roads, their promise of close embraces and the black arms of tall ships ships that stand against the moon, their tale of distant nations. They are held out to say: We are alone—come. . . .'

We have little space left in which to speak of Mr. Joyce as a prose writer. He writes with a marked economy of words; his style is nervous and impressionistic, but it rises at times to a very definite beauty. It has about it some of that 'superb and wild' quality of which Synge has spoken; it reflects the emotional longings and exaltations which from time to time stir men's spirit. It has in it the wild Irish beauty of rivers and clouds and changing seas. There is a passage full of this fierce beauty which pictures Stephen Dedalus, at a disheartened moment which is to change immediately to one of spiritual uplifting, as he gazes at the slow-drifting clouds. 'They were voyaging high over Ireland, westward bound. The Europe they had come from lay out there beyond the Irish Sea, Europe of strange tongues and valleyed and woodbegirt and citadelled and of entrenched and marshalled races. He heard a confused music within him as of memories and names which he was almost conscious of but could not capture even for an instant. . . . Again! Again! Again! A voice from beyond the world was calling.'

Nor is Mr. Joyce less successful in his management of dialogue. His dialogue has all the naturalness of conversations that we have heard and taken part in. Indeed, *A Portrait of the Artist* is a book of contrasts; it has its Rabelaisian moments and its moments of beauty. But over the whole of it is a deep sincerity, a painful searching for truth. It is the work of a genuine artist.

62. Hart Crane on Joyce and Ethics

1918

'Joyce and Ethics', *Little Review*, v, No. 3 (July 1918), 65. Also appeared in *Twice a Year*, Nos. 12–13 (1945), 427–8, in *The Little Review Anthology* (1953), ed. Margaret Anderson, pp. 298–9, and in *The Complete Poems and Selected Letters and Prose of Hart Crane* (1966), ed. Brom Weber, pp. 199–200.

The Los Angeles critic who commented on Joyce in the last issue was adequately answered, I realize,—but the temptation to emphasize such illiteracy, indiscrimination, and poverty still pulls a little too strongly for resistance.

I noticed that Wilde, Baudelaire and Swinburne are 'stacked up' beside Joyce as rivals in 'decadence' and 'intellect'. I am not yet aware that Swinburne ever possessed much beyond his 'art ears', although these were long enough, and adequate to all his beautiful, though often meaningless mouthings. His instability in criticism and every form of literature that did not depend almost exclusively on sound for effect, and his irrelevant metaphors are notorious. And as to Wilde,—after his bundle of paradoxes has been sorted and conned,—very little evidence of intellect remains. 'Decadence' is something much talked about, and sufficiently miscontrued to arouse interest in the works of any fool. Any change in form, viewpoint or mannerism can be so abused by the offending party. Sterility is the only 'decadence' I recognize. An abortion in art takes the same place as it does in society,—it deserves no recognition whatever,—it is simply outside. A piece of work is art, or it isn't: there is no neutral judgment.

However,—let Baudelaire and Joyce stand together, as much as any such thing in literary comparison will allow. The principal eccentricity evinced by both is a penetration into life common to only the greatest. If people resent a thrust which discovers some of their entrails to themselves, I can see no reason for resorting to indiscriminate comparisons, naming colours of the rainbow, or advertising the fact that they have recently been forced to recognize a few of their personal qualities. Those who are capable of being only mildly 'shocked' very naturally term the cost a penny, but were they capable of paying a few pounds for the same thinking, experience and realization by and in themselves, they could reserve their pennies for work minor to Joyce's.

The most nauseating complaint against his work is that of immorality and obscenity. The character of Stephen Dedalus is all too good for this world. It takes a little experience,—a few reactions on his part to understand it, and could this have been accomplished in a detached hermitage, high above the mud, he would no doubt have preferred that residence. *A Portrait of the Artist as a Young Man*, aside from Dante, is spiritually the most inspiring book I have ever read. It is Bunyan raised to art and then raised to the ninth power.

63. Virginia Woolf on modern novels

1919

'Modern Novels', *Times Literary Supplement*, No. 899 (10 April 1919), 189–90; appeared as 'Modern Fiction' in *The Common Reader* (1925), L. and V. Woolf.

This article is extensively quoted in an unsigned review of *A Portrait of the Artist* and the serialized *Ulysses*: 'Over the Top with the New Novelists', *Current Opinion*, lxvi (June 1919), 387–8.

. . . We are not pleading merely for courage and sincerity; but suggesting that the proper stuff for fiction is a little other than custom would have us believe it.

In some such fashion as this do we seek to define the element which distinguishes the work of several young writers, among whom Mr. James Joyce is the most notable, from that of their predecessors. It attempts to come closer to life, and to preserve more sincerely and exactly what interests and moves them by discarding most of the conventions which are commonly observed by the novelists. Let us record the atoms as they fall upon the mind in the order in which they fall, let us trace the pattern, however disconnected and incoherent in appearance, which each sight or incident scores upon the consciousness. Let us not take it for granted that life exists more in what is commonly thought big than in what is commonly thought small. Any one who has read *The Portrait of the Artist as a Young Man* or what promises to be a far more interesting work, *Ulysses*, now appearing in the *Little Review*, will have hazarded some theory of this nature as to Mr. Joyce's intention. On our part it is hazarded rather than affirmed; but whatever the exact intention there can be no question but that it is of the utmost sincerity and that the result, difficult or unpleasant as we may judge it, is undeniably distinct. In contrast to those [H. G. Wells, Arnold Bennett, John Galsworthy] whom we have called materialists Mr. Joyce is spiritual; concerned at all costs to reveal the flickerings of that innermost flame which flashes its myriad messages through the brain, he disregards with complete courage whatever seems to him adventitious, though it be probability or coherence or any other of the handrails to which we cling for support when we set our imaginations free. Faced, as in the Cemetery scene, by so much that, in its restless scintillations, in its irrelevance, its flashes of deep significance succeeded by incoherent inanities, seems to be life itself, we have to fumble rather awkwardly if we want to say what else we wish; and for what reason a work of such originality yet fails to compare, for we must take high examples, with *Youth* or *Jude the Obscure*. It fails, one might say simply because of the comparative poverty of the writer's mind. But it is possible to press a little further and wonder whether we may not refer our sense of being in a bright and yet somehow strictly confined apartment rather than at large beneath the sky to some limitation imposed by the method as well as by the mind. Is it due to the method that we feel neither jovial nor magnanimous, but centred in a self which in spite of its tremor of susceptibility never reaches out or embraces or comprehends what is outside and beyond? Does the emphasis laid perhaps didactically upon indecency contribute to this effect of the angular and isolated? Or is it merely that in any effort of such courage the faults as well as the virtues are left naked to the view? In any case we need not attribute too much importance to the method. Any method is right, every method is right, that expresses what we wish to express. This one has the merit of giving closer shape to what we were prepared to call life itself; did not the reading of *Ulysses* suggest how much of life is excluded and ignored, and did it not come with a shock to open *Tristram Shandy* and even *Pendennis*, and be by them convinced that there are other aspects of life, and larger ones into the bargain? . . .

64. Florent Fels, review of *A Portrait*

1920

'Revues', *Action*, No. 6 (December 1920), 63–4.

A review of *A Portrait of the Artist*, then published by *The Egoist*.

Wandering from Trieste to New York, from Paris to Zürich, he moves his fantasy across the world, following the tradition of the great British writers.

The novel is implacable and cruelly realistic but not with that *stercoraire* realism which began with Huysmans and ends with 'Hell', but a more cerebral kind, which approaches the end of all thought and suffers from analytical pessimism.

. . . As to the thought, there is no other novelist near him but Pascal. . . . Like Pascal, he has some doubts, and his book is a great cry of doubt. He sought to convince himself that his faith was reasonable and in contact with reason. This faith escapes him little by little, and he remains lamentably alone in life, frightened and with an entirely new ideal to reconstruct. The Joyce book does not end in any event, the work leaves us suspended in expectation of the future and of all possible futures; like life it has neither beginning nor end, it is a becoming.

. . . Stephen Dedalus wishes a constant mortification which will prepare him for the holy life. He is an example of contrition and piety; he is going to leave the public existence in order to enter the religious, and here it is that life brings him slowly, gently but surely, and in an imperceptible movement of reflex, and he goes away little by little from Catholicism, then from faith.

Is he an atheist? Not yet, he discovers, for he reasons and reason brings his last scruples of believing. He shows himself definitely irreligious, but believing in life. . . .

65. Ford Madox Ford on Joyce

1922

Ford Madox Huffer (Ford), 'A Haughty and Proud Generation', *Yale Review*, xi (July 1922), 714–17.

The critic is discussing the composure a writer must show in discussing sex.

. . . Indeed, I fancy that Mr. Joyce is the only artist we have to-day who with an utter composure regards processes of reproduction, of nourishment, and of physical renewal. But then Mr. Joyce, the supreme artist, regards with an equal composure—all things. That is why the law of the United States has persecuted his publishers. . . .

And Mr. Joyce is a writer of very beautiful, composed English. To read *The Portrait of the Artist as a Young Man* as against, say, *Interim* of Miss Dorothy Richardson is to recognize the difference between singularly fussy inclusiveness and absolutely aloof selection. There is really more enlightenment as to childhood and youth in the first three pages of Mr. Joyce's book—there is more light thrown on the nature of man—than in all Miss Richardson's volumes.

And that is not to belittle Miss Richardson; for to be infinitely little set over against Mr. Joyce, is to be yet considerable enough. But Mr. Joyce measures his effects by things immense and lasting, Miss Richardson by the passing standards of the lower-middle-class boarding-house. It is as you might say Flaubert against Gissing.

Mr. Joyce's work is a voyaging on a much higher spiritual plane: the embarrassments and glories of Miss Richardson's young women are bound up in material details. . . .

[Ford illustrates this point and goes on to discuss the ordinary and typical perception of the sordid.]

The *Portrait of the Artist as a Young Man* is a book of such beauty of writing, such clarity of perception, such a serene love of and interest in life, and such charity that, being the ungenerous creature man is, one was inclined to say: 'This surely must be a peak! It is unlikely that this man will climb higher!' But even now that Mr. Joyce has published *Ulysses*, it is too early to decide upon that. One can't arrive at one's valuation of a volume so loaded as *Ulysses* after a week of reading and two or three weeks of thought about it. Next year, or in twenty years, one may. For it is as if a new continent with new traditions had appeared, and demanded to be run through in a month. *Ulysses* contains the undiscovered mind of man; it is human consciousness analyzed as it has never before been analyzed. Certain books change the world. This, success or failure, *Ulysses* does: for no novelist with serious aims can henceforth set out upon a task of writing before he has at least formed his own private estimate as to the rightness or wrongness of the methods of the author of *Ulysses*. If it does not make an epoch—and it well may!—it will at least mark the ending of a period.

EXILES

May 1918

66. George Bernard Shaw, the Stage Society and *Exiles*

William White, 'G.B.S. On Joyce's *Exiles*', *Times Literary Supplement* (4 December 1959), 709.

Also see the reply from Stephen Winsten (No. 67) and White's reply to him (No. 67).

As Professor Richard Ellmann's *James Joyce* . . . is likely to be the definitive life of the author of *Ulysses* for some time, it is perhaps worth correcting a comment in it concerning George Bernard Shaw's opinion of Joyce's play *Exiles*.

Professor Ellmann says in a footnote on page 429: 'Joyce wrote Carlo Linati on September 19, 1919, that *Exiles* was placed on the program of the Stage Society, along with *The Way of the World* and *La Città Morta*, but was removed following the protest of Bernard Shaw who found it obscene.'

One wonders where Joyce got this information which the book quotes, but among other Joyce material in the Feinberg Collection, Detroit, is the ballot of the Stage Society considering *Exiles*. The ballot is not dated, but Professor Ellmann writes that Joyce's agent Pinker sent the play to the society on January 27, 1916, and it was rejected on July 11; the society asked for it again on April 1, 1917, and Joyce asked Pinker to withdraw it on July 2. So the balloting on the play,which Professor Ellmann quotes one member as calling 'Filth and Disease,' took place between January 27 and July 11, 1916.

The ballot shows that Dr. Wheeler, Mr. Kennedy, Mr. Lee Mathews, and Mr. Hertz voted against *Exiles*, and Mr. Whalen and Mr. Sturge Moore voted for producing it. But more interesting than these statistics are the signed remarks below the space for voting. Lee Mathews wrote:

'I don't want the S.S. to play this but it has interest. Circulate it & find out if Mr. Joyce has written any more.'

Although Dr. Wheeler also voted to reject the play, he commented: 'I certainly want to know more about Mr. Joyce and should like to see any other work of his.' Mr. Hertz was strongest in his disapproval: 'Reminiscent of Strinberg at his worst. Putrid!'

Of the two who voted 'yes,' Mr. Whalen wrote: 'This play I certainly think we ought to accept at once'; and T. Sturge Moore, who was active in trying to get *Exiles* accepted, remarked on the ballot sheet, 'This seems to me the only kind of good play which the S.S. would be false to its best traditions in not producing.'

Not all members of the Reading Committee of the Stage Society made qualifying statements, and apparently others, who did not vote, could comment. For, at the bottom of the ballot sheet is this line in Shaw's hand:

'Just the thing for the S.S. G.B.S.'

67. G.B.S., the Stage Society and *Exiles*

Stephen Winsten, 'G.B.S. on Joyce's Exiles', *Times Literary Supplement* (18 December 1959), 741, quoting from his *Days with Bernard Shaw* (New York, 1949), p. 129.

This article is a reply to William White's earlier article. White replies to this article in 'Irish Antithesis: Shaw and Joyce', *The Shavian*, ii, No. 3 (February 1961), 27: 'What Mr. Winsten writes may well be true, but William Hull comments in the *Shaw Bulletin* [1 (September 1954), 9] on "Winsten's known inaccuracy" (Mr. Dan Laurence tells me that Shaw's copy of Winsten's book at Ayot St. Lawrence is heavy with marginal refutations).'

. . . It happens that I often discussed James Joyce with G.B.S. and I refer to two or three of the conversations in my *Days with Bernard Shaw*. . . . Here is the reference to *Exiles*:

When I was on the Stage Society [G.B.S. says], James Joyce sent in his plays, and he always felt that they were not complete without a good obscene act. That kind of thing bores me to tears. . . .

Here you may ask why G.B.S. jotted down: 'Just the thing for the S.S.' The facts are as follows: G.B.S. liked *Exiles* but suggested certain harmless alterations, but James Joyce disliked Shaw's old-maidish prudery and refused to alter a word of it. Bernard Shaw should have understood because he had refused not many years back to delete the word 'bloody' from his *Pygmalion*. Anyhow this left G.B.S. with no option but to refuse his support; he went further and used his influence to get it rejected. You will note that it was not prudery but boredom that prompted Shaw's remarks about obscenity. . . .

68. Pound on *Exiles* and the modern drama

1916

'Mr. James Joyce and the Modern Stage', *The Drama*, vi, No. 21 (February 1916), 122–5, 132 [122–32].

. . . Last week I received a play by Mr. James Joyce and that argumentative interest, which once led me to spend two years of my life reading almost nothing but plays, came back upon me, along with a set of questions 'from the bottom up': Is drama worth while? Is the drama of today, or the stage of today, a form or medium by which the best contemporary authors can express themselves in any satisfactory manner?

Mr. Joyce is undoubtedly one of our best contemporary authors. He has written a novel, and I am quite ready to stake anything I have in this world that that novel is permanent. It is permanent as are the works of Stendhal and Flaubert. Two silly publishers have just refused it in favor of froth, another declines to look at it because 'he will not deal through an agent'—yet Mr. Joyce lives on the continent and can scarcely be expected to look after his affairs in England save through a deputy. And Mr. Joyce is the best prose writer of my generation, in English. So far as I know, there is no one better in either Paris or Russia. In English we have Hardy and Henry James and, chronologically, we have Mr. James Joyce. The intervening novelists print books, it is true, but for me or for any man of my erudition, for any man living at my intensity, these books are things of no substance.

Therefore, when Mr. Joyce writes a play, I consider it a reasonable matter of interest. The English agent of the Oliver Morosco company has refused the play, and in so doing the agent has well served her employers, for the play would certainly be of no use to the syndicate that stars *Peg o' My Heart*; neither do I believe that any manager would stage it nor that it could succeed were it staged. Nevertheless, I read it through at a sitting, with intense interest. It is a long play, some one hundred and eighty pages.

It is not so good as a novel; nevertheless it is quite good enough to form a very solid basis for my arraignment of the contemporary theatre. It lays before me certain facts, certain questions; for instance, are the excellences of this play purely novelist's excellences? Perhaps most of them are; yet this play could not have been made as a novel. It is distinctly a play. It has the form of a play—I do not mean that it is written in dialogue with the names of the speakers put in front of their speeches. I mean that it has inner form; that the acts and speeches of one person work into the acts and speeches of another and make the play into an indivisible, integral whole. The action takes place in less than twenty-four hours, in two rooms, both near Dublin, so that even the classical unities are uninjured. The characters are drawn with that hardness of outline which we might compare to that of Durer's painting if we are permitted a comparison with effects of an art so different. There are only four main characters, two subsidiary characters, and a fishwoman who passes a window, so that the whole mechanics of the play have required great closeness of skill. I see no way in which the play could be improved by redoing it as a novel. It could not, in fact, be anything but a play. And yet it is absolutely unfit for the stage as we know it. It is dramatic. Strong, well-wrought sentences flash from the speech and give it 'dramatic-edge' such as we have in Ibsen, when some character comes out with, 'There is no mediator between God and man'; I mean sentences dealing with fundamentals.

It is not unstageable because it deals with adultery; surely, we have plenty of plays, quite stageable plays, that deal with adultery. I have seen it in the nickel-plush theatre done with the last degree of sentimental bestiality. I admit that Mr. Joyce once mentions a garter, but it is done in such a way . . . it is done in the only way . . . it is the only possible means of presenting the exact social tone of at least two of the characters.

'Her place in life was rich and poor between,' as Crabbe says of his Clelia; it might have been done in a skit of a night club and no harm thought; but it is precisely because it occurs neither in fast nor in patrician circles, but in a milieu of Dublin genteelness, that it causes a certain feeling of constraint. Mr. Joyce gives his Dublin as Ibsen gave provincial Norway.

Of course, oh, of course, if, *if* there were an Ibsen stage in full blast, Mr. Joyce's play would go on at once.

But we get only trivialized Ibsen; we get Mr. Shaw, the intellectual cheese-mite.

[At this point, and up to the last page of the article, Pound proceeds with his 'arraignment of the contemporary theatre.']

So Mr. Joyce's play is dangerous and unstageable because he is not *playing* with the subject of adultery, but because he is actually driving in the mind upon the age-long problem of the rights of personality and of the responsibility of the intelligent individual for the conduct of those about him, upon the age-long question of the relative rights of intellect, and emotion, and sensation, and sentiment.

And the question which I am trying to put and which I reform and reiterate is just this: Must our most intelligent writers do this sort of work in the novel, *solely in the novel*, or is it going to be, in our time, possible for them to do it in drama?

On your answer to that question the claims of modern drama must rest.

69. Review, *Freeman's Journal*

1918

J.W.G., 'Ibsen in Ireland', *Freeman's Journal* (15 June 1918), 4.

The obvious thing to say about Mr. James Joyce's *Exiles* is that though the scene is laid in Dublin, the spiritual home of the characters is less Ireland than Norway. This would not in itself detract from the value of the play as a work of art, except perhaps in the eyes of literary chauvinists who have schooled themselves to believe, in defiance of all precedents, that the merit of a writer depends not on how he uses influences for his own end, but on whether these influences are native or alien. One's quarrel with Mr. Joyce is not that he borrows from Ibsen, but that he borrows the wrong things. The cloudy enigmas of 'When the dead awaken' appeal to him, if we may judge from this play, as the high-water mark of Ibsen's achievement. But it is precisely this side of

Ibsen's genius that shows the most signs of wear and tear. His greatness did not lie in the fact that his characters were adepts in the analysis of their emotions, but that this analysis was so presented as to strengthen the impression of dramatic personality. This is exactly what Mr. Joyce fails to do, and his failure is the more curious because it is due to no lack of power. The appalling discussion at the dinner party, in the opening chapters of *Portrait of the Artist as Young Man*, crams into a single page more dramatic reality than is to be found in the three acts of *Exiles*. In his play, where one looks for men and women one finds instead states of mind loosely personified. Vital energy seems to have been drained out of the characters, and they impress one less as individuals than as Æolian harps vibrating to the waves of emotions they are powerless to direct or control. Subtlety is possible in the theatre, but to be effective it must be expressed in terms of the theatre. Mr. Joyce scarcely makes a pretence of attempting to hold the interest of his audience, and though he introduces, as Ibsen certainly would not have done, a suburban sitting-room equipped with no less than four doors, he disdains to conjure up a single dramatic situation in the real sense of the word. The plot of *Exiles* is not unlike that of *Candida*, with the humour left out. Betha Rowan is in much the same plight as Mr. Shaw's heroine was between Marchbanks and Morell, only in Mr. Joyce's play all the three principals see themselves and are presented by their author from the Marchbanks' point of view. Dramatically it is a case of great cry and little wool; and while *Exiles* contains, as one expects from Mr. Joyce, some dialogue that is wonderfully subtle and effective, good dialogue is the beginning, and not the end, of play-making.

70. A. Clutton-Brock, review, *Times Literary Supplement*

1918

A. Clutton-Brock, 'The Mind to Suffer', *Times Literary Supplement* (25 July 1918), 346.

Many men have written interesting books about their childhood and youth, and never succeeded again in the same degree. Not only was esteem for Mr. James Joyce's *Portrait of the Artist as a Young Man* subject to this discount, but it unfortunately raised both friends and enemies whose excitement about it was unconnected with its merits: here brilliant, there tedious, the book itself rendered the stream of opinion yet more turbid. An unacted problem play is not the book to clear the public mind. Yet this work does prove the author's imagination independent of stimulus from self-preoccupation; and, though a first play, roughly straining its means, it reveals resources of spiritual passion and constructive power which should greatly cheer the friends of his talent.

Richard Rowan, like so many gifted young men, has early rebelled against current compromises. He will not stoop either to seduce or to marry Bertha, yet of her own impulse she accompanies him to Rome, where they live in voluntary exile for nine years and bring up their little son. Meanwhile scholarly and brilliant work has won him the first fruits of renown, and by absorbing him has oppressed Bertha with the loneliness of the unequally mated. Her man is one who clings to the soul's absolute integrity as feverishly as others cling to material existence. He suffers agonies of shame and remorse when he finds himself less faithful to her than she has been to him; he confesses everything to her, and insists that she is equally free. When the play opens they are back in Dublin, Robert Hand, the great friend of his youth, a journalist, zealously prepares the University and the Press to ignore the fact that Richard and Bertha's happy union owes nothing to the law, but at the same time he undermines their domestic quietude by covertly courting

Bertha. She, jealous of Richard's relations with an intellectual lady who is able to discuss his ideas in a way she cannot, and constantly indoctrinated as to her absolute freedom, receives Robert's addresses, yet relates every advance as it is made to Richard, partly in hopes of rousing his jealousy, which her own prescribes as its proper antidote, partly because, like himself, she has never hidden anything. He perceives that his old friend is acting like 'a common thief' and precedes Bertha to the first assignation. But Robert, cynic and rake though he is, genuinely loves and admires his friend. His humility touches Richard, in whom, as he listens, dread wakes lest, like the ghost of his own passion, he may stand between Bertha and experiences which are her due. Like another Shelley, he decides that their rivalry must be open and unprejudiced by the past. Does he any longer really possess Bertha's heart? She arrives; he explains to her again her absolute freedom, and leaves her to meet his friend. The second curtain falls before that interview has ended. In the third act both Bertha and Robert, equally admiring and loving Richard, assure him that nothing has happened between them; but he has doubted both and cannot recover his faith—the torture of a night of suspense has been too great.

> I have wounded my soul for you—a deep wound of doubt which can never be healed. . . . I do not wish to know or to believe. . . . It is not in the darkness of belief that I desire you, but in restless living, wounding doubt.

and she can only answer:—

> Forget me and love me. . . . I want my lover. . . . You Dick. O, my strange, wild lover, come back to me again!

So the play ends—a situation after Browning's own heart, and seen more distinctly, less as a case put, than he would probably have seen it; only the machinery used is Ibsen's.

The second act transcends this machinery and is in outline and effect a poetical creation; the other two acts, in which minor characters figure, are less happy. On the stage custom shows people in such situations, light-heartedly, sentimentally, or cynically: to show them seriously and sympathetically alarms some folk as Jesus did when he persisted in dining with harlots and publicans. Intellectual charity is to-day as rare a virtue as human compassion was then. Those for whom certain themes and certain words constitute either a 'taboo' or a 'hall mark' are debarred from exercising it. Sympathy opens both the heart and the eye that discerns beauty; prejudice closes both. In the last act a doubt arises in the reader's mind whether Bertha and Robert are not lying to Richard; probably this is due to inadvertence on the author's part. Their falsehood by increasing their inferiority would deepen the grounds of his lonely suffering, but by proving their response to his lead superficial it would diminish the poignancy of his tragic doubt. Thus an outline is doubled, one intention cancelling the other: such ambiguity is merely distracting, and might easily be removed. But this is a detail, an accident; the whole is lifted and throbs, like *King Lear*, with a capacity for suffering more startling even than the situations in which it is manifested. Of course, work so young and in some ways crude is no match for the varied enchantments of *King Lear*. The woodenness of realism is made painfully apparent by the passion that contrasts to it the bone-structure and blood of a creation—of *Exiles*. Experience in the use of words and the management of scenes may supply what Mr. James Joyce lacks, though, of course, they may not, and a world that crushes and pampers authors with equal blindness may be trusted to make the finest success the most difficult and least likely. Will not the Stage Society or the Pioneers let us and the author see this play, so that its shortcomings may become apparent to him and its virtues be brought home to us with their full force?

71. Desmond MacCarthy, review, *New Statesman*

1918

'Exiles', *New Statesman*, xi (21 September 1918), 492–3. A shortened version of this review appeared as 'Mr. James Joyce's Play', *New Statesman*, xxvi (20 February 1926), 581–2, at the time of the Stage Society's production of *Exiles*. The original, longer article appeared in MacCarthy's *Humanities* (1953), pp. 88–93 (from which the present text is taken).

Exiles is a remarkable play. I am more sure of this than of having understood it. I could never undertake to produce it unless the author were at my elbow; and when a critic feels like that about a play which has excited him it means he has not quite understood it. What I can do is to give an account of the play and show where I was puzzled. But first I must come to terms with a misgiving. It is a treat to be puzzled by a play, so perhaps I overrate this one because it has puzzled me? I do not think that is the case, but that possibility is the grain of salt with which what follows must be taken.

To be made to wonder and to think about characters in a play is a rare experience—outside the drama of Ibsen. It is a pleasure far excelling the simple pleasure of delighted recognition which is all that the character-drawing in the ordinary respect-worthy play provides . . . *Exiles* excited me for the same reason that the plays of Ibsen excite me—the people in it were so interesting. Ibsen's characters have roots which tempt one to pull at them again and again.

[the critic comments upon Ibsen's characterization]

. . . I do not take Ibsen's name in vain in connection with the work of Mr Joyce. It is not (I beg you to believe) that habit so common in critics of chattering about anything but the subject in hand which persuades me to approach *Exiles* through the art of Ibsen. . . . I hail Mr Joyce as one of the few who have grasped the value of two principles in dramatic art of which Ibsen is the master exponent.

The first is that on the stage, as in the novel, character (the individual) is the most interesting thing, the ultimate thing; for nothing *happens* at all unless it happens to a particular person, and action is dependent on character. The dramatist therefore must choose characters who illustrate his theme better and better the more he goes into them. Then, the deeper he digs the clearer will sound in our ears the running water of his theme. . . .

One of the qualities which delighted me in *Exiles* was that evidently nothing would induce Mr Joyce to make his characters less complex and interesting than he saw them to be. He would rather obscure his theme than do that, and though a fault, it is a fault on the right side—on the interesting side. The second respect in which he has learnt from the master is his practice of intensifying our interest in the present by dialogue which implies a past. What a little scrap of people's lives a dramatist can show us—just an hour or two! In life it is usually what has gone before that makes talk between two people significant. . . .

The merits of this play make it hard to tell its story. Summarised, that story would not distinguish it from many a play in which the love relations of two men and a woman wove the plot. Its distinction lies in the relations of the three points in that familiar triangle being complex and intense. Art is usually so superficial, life so profound. I admire Mr Joyce for having tried to deepen our conventional simplification of such relations and bring them nearer to nature. Now and then I lost my way in his characters as in a wood, but that did not make me think they were not true; rather the contrary. When I put my finger on his spinning rainbow top, I do not see the coloured rings which produced that iridescence so definitely as in the case of Ibsen. The theme of *Exiles* is not so clear to me. I conjecture that I get nearest to it in saying that the play is a study in the emotional life of an artist. (I am sure, at any rate, that I am giving the reader a useful tip in bidding him keep one eye *always* upon Richard Rowan, whatever else may be interesting him besides.) And when I say that the play is a study in an artist's life, I mean that its theme is the complication which that endowment adds to emotional crises which are common to all men. It makes sincerity more difficult and at the same time more vitally important. Imagination opens the door to a hundred new subtleties and possibilities of action; it brings a man so near the feelings of others that he has never the excuse of blindness, and keeps him at a distance, so that at moments he can hardly believe he cares for anything but his own mind.

When he acts spontaneously, he knows he is acting spontaneously—

if not at the moment, the moment after—much as some people, thought modest, have hardly a right to be considered so, because they invariably know when they are. *Exiles* is a play in which two men are struggling to preserve each his own essential integrity in a confusing situation where rules of thumb seem clumsy guides; and between them is a bewildered, passionate woman—generous, angry, tender, and lonely. To understand Bertha one need only remember that she has lived nine years with Richard Rowan in that intimacy of mind and feeling which admits of no disguises, merciful or treacherous; that she has known all the satisfactions and disappointments of such an intimacy. Her nature cries out for things to be simple as they once were for her; but she, too, has eaten of the tree of knowledge and knows that they are not.

If you ask how Richard Rowan and Robert Hand stood towards each other, the answer is they were friends. There was a touch of the disciple in Robert. Richard was the intenser, more creative, and also the more difficult nature. He was an exile in this world; Robert was at home in it. But the essence of their relation was that they were friends, and friends who from youth had made life's voyage of discovery together. One was a journalist, the other an artist; but in experience they were equals. Both had lived intensely enough, and had been intimate enough to reach together that pitch of mutual understanding at which consciousness that each is still at bottom solitary is, in a strange way, the tenderest bond between them. Am I over-subtle? I think what I mean is recognisable. After all, it is in friendships of the second order (Heaven forfend that they should be held cheap!) that men are least troubled about the value of what they give. It is between these two friends that competition for the same woman rises, bringing with it jealousy, suspicion, and making candour—the air in which alone such a friendship as theirs can live—almost impossible. Well, very hard. Both make a mighty effort to preserve it; Richard succeeds best; how far Robert Hand failed is not quite clear to me. At first Richard thought his friend a common vulgar thief; against such a one he would protect Bertha tooth and nail. But he has misgivings which in different ways torture him more than natural jealousy. Perhaps Robert can give her something he cannot (O, he knows how unsatisfying and yet how much that has been!); something no human being has a right to prevent another having. This is the first thing he must find out.

The scene in Act II between the two men is wonderful in its gradually deepening sincerity. Hand is a coward at first, but he gets over that. Then Richard is tormented by misgivings about himself. Is not there something in him (for ties, however precious, are also chains) which is attracted by the idea that Bertha might now owe most to another—now, at any rate, that their own first love is over? How far is he sincere in leaving her her liberty? Is it his own that he is really thinking of? Bertha taunts him with that. And Bertha's relation to Robert—what is that? I think it is the attraction of peace. To be adored, to be loved in a simpler, more romantic, coarser way, what a rest! Besides, Robert is the sort of man a woman can easily make happy; Richard certainly is not. Yet, just as she decided between them years ago, in the end it is her strange, elusive lover who comes so close and is so far away whom she chooses. But was she Robert's mistress? The dramatist leaves that ambiguous. He does not mean us to bother much one way or another about that. Richard says at the end he will never know what they were to each other; but I do not think he is thinking of Divorce Court facts. He means how completely Bertha still belongs to him. Bertha tells Robert to tell Richard everything; but does he? She also tells him to think of what has passed between them as something like 'a dream'. That, I think, is the line on which one must fix one's attention to get the focus. Robert is happy; quite content with that. Perhaps because less hot for certainties in life than Richard, he thinks he has enjoyed a solid reality. I do not know.

I have left out much it would be a pleasure to mark. Richard's relation to Beatrice Justice (the other woman in the play)—I could write an article on that; but what I have written will be perhaps enough to persuade you that this is a remarkable play.

72. Padraic Colum, review, *Nation*

1918

'James Joyce as Dramatist', *Nation*, cvii, No. 2780 (12 October 1918), 430–1.

James Joyce's *Portrait of the Artist as a Young Man* is dated 'Dublin 1904, Trieste 1914.' The action of *Exiles* is indicated as passing in 1912. The play, therefore, succeeds the novel in time. But if *Exiles* be more recent than *Portrait of the Artist*, it is far less modern. In the novel James Joyce created a form that was individual and distinctively modern, that suggested new horizons. The play is in Ibsen's form, without the symbolism that haunted Ibsen's plays and without his conclusiveness and his climaxes. Mr. Joyce may return to the drama and bring into it some of the discoveries that make his narrative so startling. Meantime, *Exiles* would make it appear that narrative is his peculiar domain.

The distinction of the play is in the characters presented. Richard Rowan, a writer newly returned to his native Dublin; Bertha, his young wife; and Robert Hand, a journalist, are unusual people. They are Catholic Irish, and two of them, Richard Rowan and Robert Hand, would pass beyond good and evil with words derived from Catholic philosophy on their lips. The play is a triangle, but we forget to name it so because of the oddness of the trio's relation. The characters in the triangle are Richard, Bertha, and Robert. In a way this triangle is duplicated by another, a shadowy one: Richard Rowan, Robert Hand, and Robert's cousin and supposed betrothed, Beatrice Justice. Richard Rowan is a man with a hurt soul. He is deeply in love with Bertha, a girl with whom he eloped some years before, but Bertha is not adequate to the whole of his personality. He corresponds with Beatrice Justice, and his new work is influenced by her. Moreover, he has been unfaithful to Bertha through many casual connections. He knows, too, that Robert Hand, his soul-friend of former days, is making love to Bertha. He will not deny her a particle of freedom, but he is tortured by a doubt as to her faithfulness. The play ends inconclusively—without Richard's having attained that liberation that he has been striving for with such agony . . . Bertha, with her candid, forgiving nature, may cure Richard of his wound. But in the last scene he has hardly been frank with her. For in the second act he has told Robert Hand:

[quotes from Act II]

So he accuses himself, and Robert tells him that the Church has lost a theologian in him. But Robert Hand is something of a theologian, too, and he can quote Duns Scotus with effect. Meanwhile, Beatrice Justice has faded out of the play.

Bertha is the first notable woman character that James Joyce has created. She is a subtle character. We get the suggestion that she has had little education, yet she carries herself with real simplicity and dignity. For all her contact with the super-subtle Richard she remains unspoiled, alluring, unconventional, faithful. She has her outbreaks and she knows where to strike at Richard. Her simplicity and her good sense are shown in her last dialogue with Beatrice Justice, the woman who is able to understand her husband's mind and work. When Beatrice says, 'Do not let them humble you, Mrs. Rowan,' Bertha answers:

> Humble me! I am very proud of myself, if you want to know. What have they ever done for him? I made him a man. What are they all in his life? No more than the dust under his boots. He can despise me too, like the rest of them—now. And you can despise me. But you will never humble me, any of you.

It is in passages such as this that James Joyce shows his power to draw a real and distinctive character.

73. Francis Hackett, review, *New Republic*

12 October 1918, xvi, No. 206, 318–19

So good are the fine qualities of *Exiles* that the defects seem to be an illusion, but the more the play is examined the more fundamental and inexplicable seem its defects. It is part of Mr. Joyce's gift that he appears intuitive and occult. It does not seem possible that all his intuition and penetration could go astray. But *Exiles* neither creates a perfect conviction of being like human experience nor quite recalls experience in terms anything like its own. On the contrary, Mr. Joyce seems definitely to force human beings to do and say unlikely things, and to jumble up the true perspective of their lives. He is exceedingly keen in making people talk like people. He has a genius for idiom and idiosyncrasy and no one could be better than he in the way he dovetails his conversations. His ear is sharp, also, for the click of one personality against another, and for the corroborative phrase. But when it comes to comprehending men and women in their skins and under them, he can hardly be said to be reliable. There is an unreality around certain passages in *Exiles* that suggests the literary alchemist vaguely striving to transmute pretty theories into honest flesh and blood. The flesh and blood of *Exiles*, so far as it is honest, does not fit the theories. They are imposed by their author on subjects unwilling and rebellious. The result is a disharmony that almost defies literary analysis. It condemns *Exiles* to a limbo outside the normal hell and heaven of appraisal.

So far as Richard and Bertha are concerned, the play is clear enough. Bertha is the simple woman who falls desperately in love with Richard, who is a writer, nine years before, and runs off with the 'curious bird,' regardless of everything else. Richard is the man of pride and scorn who does not deign to explain himself to his dying mother and who allows her to judge him hardly and savagely for his refusal to bind Bertha by marriage. The situation of Richard and Bertha, back in Dublin with their child nine years after the event, only becomes obscure and confusing by the introduction of Bertha's old suitor, the journalist Robert Hand. . . .

[The critic here examines the relations of Robert, Richard and Bertha among themselves.]

If there were anything in Robert to give depth to his attitude on romantic love, it would be easy to suppose that Mr. Joyce was balancing it against Richard's attitude. But the triviality of Robert with Bertha, his second-hand epigrams, his stale pleasantries, his general imperviousness to 'the spirit,' make him utterly impossible as a protagonist. The excitement that he creates by making love to Bertha has no genuine significance. If Mr. Joyce had made him less frivolous he might have been supposed to disturb the fine assumptions of Richard's life. As it is he could but rumple their surface, provided Richard had any gravity. But Richard is strangely credulous for a man of insight. He is prepared, if necessary, to give up Bertha. Leaving Bertha to an assignation with Robert in the famous cottage of his own youthful revelries, he writes all night (and thinks) and before dawn goes walking on the strand, 'hearing voices.' He even 'despairs.' 'I have wounded myself for you,' he says to Bertha, 'a deep wound of doubt that can never be healed.' She protests that nothing happened with Robert during their evening together, she has remained faithful. 'I can never know, never in this world,' intones Richard. 'I do not wish to know or to believe. I do not care. It is not in the darkness of belief that I desire you. But in restless living wondering doubt. To hold you by no bonds, even of love, to be united with you in body and soul in utter nakedness—for this I longed. And now I am tired for a while, Bertha. My wound tires me.'

Had Richard possessed humor, his 'wound' would not have tired him. He would have disposed of the debonair Robert more easily, or at least seen more readily the folly of discussing with Robert 'the death of the spirit.' Two such characters, in real life, could not have met in the same sexual plane.

But in spite of this curiously jarring supposition, with all Richard's cold dissection of Robert's kisses and his meticulous desire to release Bertha, there is a strong reality in the woman's love for him and her yearning for him and her jealousy. His desire to be betrayed by her is also intelligible. It is only his interchanges on the subject of love and freedom that seem so unimaginable.

To say 'unimaginable' is merely to protest incredulity. Those who can imagine the proud and scornful Richard tolerating the discourse of Robert will take a different view of *Exiles*. To them it will be much more than an imperfect antithesis of sacred and profane love, much more than a glimpse of the finite munching away at the infinite. It will be a genuine drama with no false intimations, no cross-currents, no theorist frigidity at the core of its being.

74. *Little Review* symposium on *Exiles*

1919

'*Exiles*, A Discussion of James Joyce's Plays', *Little Review*, v No. 9 (January 1919), 20–7.

Extract from a symposium of critics, none of whom 'compared notes or talked over their opinion' (note, p. 20)—John Rodker, Israel Solon, Samuel A. Tannenbaum, Jane Heap.

JOHN RODKER (pp. 20–2)

Again in this play Mr. Joyce exploits that part of mind merging on the subconscious. The drama is one of will versus instinct, the protagonist Richard Rowan, a writer. This particular psychological triangle is one of barely comprehended instincts, desires for freedom (equally undefined), emotions that hardly crystallise before fading out. Inter-action of thought and will is carried so close to this borderline that the reader fears continually lest he miss any implication. Analysis digs continually deeper. At a certain moment it is lost. Mind will go no further.

People are built on no plan and since it is impossible at any moment to say that either will or instinct is dominant, the author lets the curtain fall finally on the hero's temporary surrender to both.

. . . The play is particularly à propos. Everyone talks of individual freedom,—(Stirner is a name to conjure with, though unread),—identifying it in some obscure way with Woman's Suffrage. But the issues are psychological and no spread of popular education will simplify them. In this case Rowan leaves his wife to do as she will. She naturally reviles him for leaving her without the prop of his decisions. After nine years of conjugal life she is unable to make up her mind as to whether she needs a lover. If in the end she does not sin, it is because she uses her virginity as he his profligacy; for pride and humiliation. I have read the play often but without arriving at whether it is an ultimate cowardice or love for her husband that keeps her faithful. To Rowan detail of what has happened does not matter. The atmosphere of their communion would make a more treacherous betrayal than any carnal sideslip. That he can never know.

His anguish at the possible withholding from his wife of any instant of experience which might make her life more full may be interpreted as moral strength or cowardice. Where it is his will demanding Bertha's freedom, he is diffident, but instinct in him speaks fiercely . . .

[quotes from Act III]

The play is very romantic, poetical in a manner rare among plays. It is as fervent as the *Seagull* of Tchekhof. It was no small achievement of Mr. Joyce to have made dramatic such very pure cerebration, and that with a touch so delicate that its most intricate part of the mechanism has suffered by the inquisition. One sees Ibsen ruining such a situation with coarse fingers. Tchekhof got his purity of apprehension from taking people by their instincts. Joyce has done the same thing with a difference. Not that his people have necessarily more brains, but beyond instinct the brain ramifies into obscurer delicacies. The implication of *Exiles* are so numerous—each one subject for minute elucidation—that only with great familiarity would a total impression be possible. Tchekhof's subtleties are plain-sailing, instinctively apparent, so that for stage purposes he is the last word in effectiveness. *Exiles* will have however to become classical—a repertory play, seen often—before any audience can be familiar with it. It is a play which though perfect as literature, might easily lose significance on the stage: it is too full of meat. The most accustomed stomachs only will avoid indigestion.

Nevertheless a production should be full of interest. No manager will, I fancy, care to produce a play without a real suicide, even though it be a 'death of the spirit' that drops the curtain; but a small theatre, of which there are many in America and one or two in this country, might easily gain a reputation for intelligence by its production.

ISRAEL SOLON (pp. 22–3)
Let me say at once that I was most painfully disappointed with James Joyce's *Exiles*. My disappointment was so keen because of what he might have achieved and came near achieving but failed to achieve. His merely good is not good enough where the great was so nearly within his reach. With that theme, the author of the *Portrait* and *Ulysses* should have achieved nothing short of the sublime. No poet since Sophocles has had so dramatic a vehicle. Indeed, I think Joyce's the more dramatic . . . James Joyce in *Exiles* has taken for his dramatic

vehicle the fate of two men who are in love with each other and who are at the same time excessively amenable to all social coercion. Bound by the letter of conventional morality more completely than most men, the disguises winked at by organised society and thereby made available to most men is not available to these two men. They will have nothing they may not have openly. Drawn to each other from within and held back from without, these two men are doomed to keep within sight of each other but beyond the reach of each other. The 'eternal traingle' of our conventional comedy is repulsive to these men. Here is matter worthy of the very best that James Joyce has it within him to lend. Why, then, does James Joyce fail to achieve that measure of greatness we have every right to expect of him and the theme he has chosen?

I believe it is because he has failed to make his characters conscious of what fate has in store for them. Had he made these men fully aware of what their lives held for them, the rôles fate meant them to play, and he, furthermore, made them struggle valiantly against it, then if they had won in the end we should have had great comedy, and if they lost we should have had sublime tragedy. Consciousness would have made of them such responsible human beings as would have engaged our sympathies to the utmost; whereas unconsciousness has left them feeble victims blindly wallowing to no purpose. And since it is unthinkable to me that the author of the *Portrait* and *Ulysses* could be lacking in moral courage, I am forced to the conclusion that James Joyce was not himself aware of the matter of his play.

SAMUEL A. TANNENBAUM, M.D. (pp. 23–5)

Exiles will in all probability prove to be caviare to the general, not only because it is open to the obvious criticism that it is not true to life, but because its subject-matter is one that unconsciously stirs up the most passionate resistances of a reader unaccustomed to the most honest and deep-searching self-analysis. To the psychologist trained in psycho-analysis, on the contrary, the book will be agreeably welcome as an inspired contribution from the depths of an artist's soul to one of the most tabooed and falsified motives of human conduct,—we mean homosexuality. It is true that the reader unlearned in such matters, and perhaps the author too, may not be aware that this is the theme of the play and may look for it in vain. Of course, this is not all there is to the play: just as in a dream the main motive is overladen and disguised with other subsidiary motives and rationalizations, so is it in the drama before us.

The comparison of *Exiles* with a dream may be carried much further. Every work of fiction is its creator's dream: the more fictitious, the more dream-like, the more apparently absurd and unreal, the truer it is to the hidden forces in the maker's soul and the truer too to the generality of mankind for whose repressed springs of action the poet is the mouthpiece. *Exiles* very often reads like a dream and must be interpreted as such. As such it may be said to derive its motive power from the author's repressed but most urgent impulses, to emanate from the unconscious forces within him and to enable him to gratify in this 'harmless' way his unacted and unactable longings. In all this, it need hardly be said, there is not the slightest reproach for or condemnation of the dramatist: every purely fictitious literary work is the self-revelation of a burdened soul that saves itself from a neurosis or from a perversion by the cathartic effect of the creative process.

Richard Rowan's, the protagonist's, homopsychism is never once referred to in the story but is clearly to be deduced from his character and conduct. He has no love for his dead mother and several times refers bitterly to her hardness of heart, at the same time crediting her with having been a remarkable woman; of his 'handsome father', on the contrary, he always speaks with great affection. He is utterly incapable of making love to a woman or of loving one unless she is or has been in love with a man to whom he is attached; for this reason he connives at his life-long friend's, Robert Hand's wooing of his wife and urges her, nay, goads her on to be unfaithful to him. The author subtly and delicately leads us to infer that Richard and Bertha are living a life of abstinence ever since his betrayal of her nine years before and that he gives her full freedom only that they might thus be reunited. Speaking to Robert of the moment when he surprised him wooing Bertha, he says: 'At that moment I felt our whole life together in the past, and I longed to put my arm around your neck'. A little later he says to him: 'In the very core of my ignoble heart I longed to be betrayed by you and by her—in the dark, in the night—secretly, meanly craftily. By you, my best friend, and by her. I longed for that passionately and ignobly'. Being asked why he did so, he replies: 'From pride and from ignoble longing. And from a deeper motive still'. From a psychological point of view it is important, too, to note that before Richard's marriage he and Robert had for years shared a house in the country as a rendez-vous for erotic escapades. Of course Richard rationalizes his motives in his unconscious conflict with his latent passion ('I fear that I will reproach myself for having taken all for myself because I would not suffer her to give to another what was hers and not mine to give; because I accepted from her her loyalty and made her life poorer in love'), but even the few sentences we have quoted prove the correctness of our deduction concerning him. Fully to comprehend this splendid portrait of a type of artistic soul that one meets often enough in real life, though exiled, it is necessary not to overlook Richard's intensely masochistic and voyeur impulses. He delights in putting himself in situations that entail a great deal of anguish for him, and he compels his wife to give him the fullest details of his friend's assaults upon her honor. That he can be cruel too on occasion is not at all surprising; by virtue of the law of bi-polarity the masochist is also a sadist.

The portraits of the Wife, the Friend, the Other Woman and even the Child are interesting characterizations that will repay careful study. They are all intensely individualized and unquestionably human though not conventional. Archie, aged eight, is one of the few life-like children to be found in literature and is introduced into the play very effectively —perhaps because in portraying him the author was inspired by Shakespeare's Prince Mamillius to whom the little lad bears a strong resemblance. (Incidentally it may be remarked that *The Winter's Tale* is largely unintelligible if we fail to see the homopsychic conflict in it and do not recognize the erotic relationship between Leontes and Polixenes. Othello's fate too might have been different had it not been for his unconscious love for Cassius.)

Many of the minute details of this play, such as Richard's slip of the tongue about his interest in Robert's cottage, Beatrice's forgetting to bring her music, Bertha's sudden attack of fear when Robert speaks to her from the bed-room, etc., prove Mr. Joyce to be a fine psychologist and a keen observer of human nature. But his courage to be true and unconventional, combined with the fact that his chief characters are neurotic, exiles, will we fear doom him to a small but select following.

JANE HEAP (pp. 25–7)

I find it difficult to put any of my thoughts on *Exiles* into words. They are not used to words: they die. I feel that Joyce's play has died in words. I do not mean because of the words literally,—all Art is linguistic. But even Art must fail many times before it conquers those things whose nature it is to keep themselves a secret from us forever.

On the surface the play gives itself up to many intepretations. Propagandists declare it is a play on the freedom of the individual. Other reviewers talk of triangles and Ibsen and neurotics. All these things are easy and semi-intelligent things to say. But when it is unanimously agreed that Joyce hasn't 'put over his idea clearly 'or that he hasn't known just what he was trying to put over, I grow a bit nervous and wonder why it doesn't appear to them that perhaps Joyce couldn't reach their darkness. I also wonder why not read *Exiles* with Joyce in mind. The man who wrote *A Portrait of the Artist* and *Ulysses*, a highly-conscious, over-sensitized artist living at the vortex of modern psychology, would scarcely go back to dealing with material in a pre-Nietzsche manner. Joyce is not Galsworthy; on the other hand he is not D. H. Lawrence. And to discuss courage in connection with Joyce is ridiculous. Joyce outlived courage in some other incarnation. . . .

There is much talk of freedom in the play. Everyone wanting everyone else to be free, it is shown that there is at no time any freedom for anyone. The discussion of the wife's decision when she went away with Richard—unasked by him—proves she has no freedom to make a decision. She may have been in love with Robert, but she had no choice: she was Richard. Robert is in love with Richard, has always been: but he is an unthinking, natural man. He follows nature with his brain and thinks he is in love with Richard's wife, a woman being the conventional symbol for a man's love. But when he has a meeting with her and they are left alone by Richard in perfect freedom they are foiled, they are both Richard, both trying to reach Richard, not each other. Richard's old conflict with his mother (just indicated) was based on her refusal to become him. The wife sees the child going the way of all of them.

There is no where in the world for Richard to turn for love. Sex as other men know it can be for him only a boring, distasteful need of the body. Love strikes back at him from every source. His becomes a Midas tragedy.

He is tormented by the commonplace 'beaten path' love-making of Robert and his wife. He asks her infinite questions; he directs the love-making to save his sensibilities. He says to Robert: 'Not like this—this is not for people like us.' Yet he wishes darkly that they had dishonoured him in a common, sneaking way. Not that he cares for either of them, not that he cares for honour or for conventions, but then he might have been free of them. They would have acted for once without his spirit having been the moving force.

We see Richard wearily contemplating his despair. There is much of the child in Richard. He has a need to create some hold on life, some connection with the experiences of other men. He chooses the least uncomplimentary to himself of those in the play as the symbol through which he can make his connection with love. He sees himself less handicapped intellectually in the music teacher, so he loves love through her. When they taunt him with her he answers 'No, not even she would understand'. He writes all night endless pages at this image of himself, and in the morning walks on the beach maddened by emptiness and despair. At the last curtain he falls on to a couch, worn and helpless, in need only of a 'great sweet mother': but he must be forever on the wheel: his wife kneels beside him babbling of her love.

75. A French comment on *Exiles*

1919

Henry Davray, 'Lettres Anglaises', *Mercure de France*, cxxi, No. 495 (1 February 1919), 514–15 [512–18]

Although conceived after the Ibsenian formula, which has become somewhat venerable in our time, James Joyce's play *Exiles* captures the attention. Of a sustained interest and very firm texture, this is the work of an artist and writer. The drama of it is purely psychological. . . .

[A brief summary of the plot and a discussion of character.]

We must congratulate James Joyce on what he has just accomplished. This is to portray the possible consequences of a state of mind which is making too much progress in England among intellectuals imbued with the ideas of Tolstoi. The Russian influences have formed a generation of readers who are deprived of a sense of reality and of social conscience, who are absorbed in a purely personal casuistic where the notions of good and evil, of freedom and justice, have distilled themselves into subtle and dangerous theories because they are liberated from the natural basis which furnishes them with the bonds of family, of nation, and of state. Without sermons and without long dithyrambs James

Joyce unveils the wound. *Exiles* is a strong and sincere work in which the manipulation of the artist is never lacking. . . .

[The article concludes with a brief statement about Joyce's earlier works.]

76. Francis Fergusson on *Exiles* and Ibsen

1932

Extract from 'Exiles and Ibsen's Work', *Hound & Horn*, v (April–June 1932), 345–53.

In *A Portrait of the Artist as a Young Man* we read of Stephen that 'as he went by Baird's stonecutting works in Talbot Place the spirit of Ibsen would blow through him like a keen wind, a spirit of wayward boyish beauty.' This spirit blows through *Exiles* with a super-Ibsen keenness over a colder-than-Ibsen structure of cut stone. Professor Rubek, in *When We Dead Awaken*, asks Irene with weariness and bewilderment, 'Do you remember what you answered when I asked if you would go with me out into the wide world?'

Irene

I held up three fingers in the air and swore that I would go with you to the world's end and to the end of life. And that I would serve you in all things—

Professor Rubek

As the model for my art—

Irene

—In frank, utter nakedness—

But there is no such bewilderment in *Exiles*, and in the last scene Richard can tell Bertha, 'It is not in the darkness of belief that I desire you. But in restless, wounded, living doubt. To hold you by no bonds, even in love, to be united with you in body and soul in utter nakedness—for this I longed.' It is like the analogy between Stephen Dedalus on one side, a bird-man, unique, soaring straight toward the Sun, and on the other, Brand with his gloomy aspiration, and Peer Gynt with his irresponsible histrionics. In each case we gulp, we gape, we are astounded as though by a superb stunt. This 'stunt,' both in *Exiles* and in the Ibsen plays, is a feat of the author's mind, a presentation of new and startling simplifications. All drama depends on some sort of simplification. But, Sophocles and Shakespeare offer us theirs as distillments of common traditional human wisdom, and though their insights may be ever new, the newness, and the author's discovery of it, is never the point. In Ibsen and *Exiles* the newness *is* the point, and in *Exiles* the point is the finality also. . . . Joyce, faced with this problem [of presenting characters who debate, self-consciously, their rights and wrongs], manages differently. His characters all come clear in the mere presence of the compelling and inquisitorial Richard. He makes their halting apologias more credible, as he makes them more complete, once you grant him Richard, in the light of whose mind and under the influence of whose strenuous ethic everything is presented. . . And the characters meet, if at all, on the basis of the barest facts of the inescapable human relations, those of parent to child and of man to woman. There is the lamp of the spirit with a vengeance, but with its flame not 'practically exposed,' but as near to 'utterly naked' as Rowan-Joyce can make it. Richard Rowan will not have it that the world and the flesh can make him a whit different from what he chooses to be. And the mind of this Rowan-Joyce being is far less provincial than James's own.

This is as much as to say that *Exiles* is by no means to be thought of as an Ibsen type of play in the sense in which Strindberg's, for instance, or Andreyev's or some of O'Neill's plays belong in that category. These writers have run the Ibsen prophetic or didactic tradition up several blind alleys, where it is expiring loudly but without vision, force or dignity. Ibsen had no Ibsen to study; and his followers, taking the direction he marked out, have failed to profit by his example. But the author of *Exiles* has precisely profited by Ibsen's example, taking what he needed of Ibsen's technique to state once and for all what is inescapable in Ibsen's story or theme. He finishes off the modern intellectual drama, the drama of 'individualism,' the drama which attempts to dispense with tradition. Yet at the same time he attains a static perfection of vision which carries him quite beyond that genre, and even amounts to destroying it. This may be shown in a number of ways.

Take, for instance, the perfection of Mr. Joyce's portraits in *Exiles*. . . Lacking a traditional theme like those of the Greeks or Elizabethans, Ibsen's actions remain like umbilical cords which he could never cut. But Mr. Joyce substitutes for action a motionless picture, and for a thesis a metaphysical vision of a kind of godless monadology or Pluralistic Universe, of a consistency and strictness which William James the liberal never dreamed of. So it serves the consistency of his vision to bring out all the qualities of his people which make them what they are 'and not another thing'; which distinguish them, above all, from Rowan-Joyce. Ibsen was interested in what people *do*, and in the effort to show their actions as significant sometimes seems to do violence to what they *are*. If Mr. Joyce falsifies his people, it is in the opposite way. However much he may sympathize with them, he *sees* them, much more than he invents them out of his own inner life—sees them as hopeless, 'looks and passes,' like Dante touring Hell; and cuts them off, with the most sober and delicate exactitude, in their actual frivolity and darkness.

An analysis of this kind might be pursued indefinitely, as though along a thousand centripetal spirals leading ever more subtly up to the unity of the work. It leads beyond the play *as play*, as soon as we see that there is no action here as other dramas have taught us to understand action. A hasty reading of the play might lead one to believe that the action was Robert's unsuccessful attempt to seduce Richard's wife. Another reading will show that this is only part of a larger whole . . .

In the last speech of the play, a speech of extreme beauty, wherein a Joycean character comes very near the Ibsen trick of speaking with the author's voice, Bertha places Rowan-Joyce himself among the exiles: 'Forget me, Dick,' she says. 'Forget me and love me again as you did the first time.' Which we see—if we remember that all is shown in the light of Richard's mind—as making the exile-vision absolute, removing it from the relativity or meaningfulness of action. For action is the *lingua franca* on which drama as an art among other arts depends; it is the common guide-line for actors and audience, and it gives the meaning of the play in terms of something outside itself. It is meaning in this sense which Mr. Joyce has been at great pains to eliminate.

Exiles is thus a 'drama to end dramas.' And it invokes to this end the authority of life 'caught in the fact'—an ultimate fact, we are supposed to feel, not the mere real circumstances, which is what Henry James had in mind when he applied this phrase to Ibsen. . . Mr. Joyce has been concerned to save the truth and authority of his image by removing every trace of radiance as symbolism, which amounts to predication, to meaning in relation to other images, whereby *Exiles* would take its place, as a play, not a metaphysical vision, in due relation to other images. Hence that unique glare, as of a spot of brilliant light in surrounding blackness, before which we are supposed to come to rest 'in the silent stasis of esthetic pleasure.'

If the authority of the exile-vision stops you 'cold,' you must come to rest indeed—like Beatrice, perhaps, 'with pride and scorn in your heart,' but like her caught in the fascination of what it claims as intelligibility in terms of itself. If not, you must explain it in terms of Rowan-Joyce as a human being. Nowhere outside *Exiles* will you find human isolation so finely rendered—that obstinate incommensurability of human longings which seems to be the cold little wisdom special to our time—both in its bracing fear and exaltation, and in its pity. Yet even while you mourn and thrill you may begin to feel, as in Ibsen, that the case is too special to be satisfying, and the simplification, however brilliant, somehow arbitrary. This is my experience. The 'silent stasis of esthetic pleasure' gives place, for me, at a certain point, to an obsessive circling of the mind around a fixed, compelling thought, which is the Stephen-Rowan-Joyce thought of himself. It is this being which is both the shadow and the idea of *Exiles*, if we ask it to have a meaning, and it is this being we must question. This may only be done with the help of Mr. Joyce's other works.

The Joycean cycle will doubtless not be understandable till long after it is completed. But it may already help us to make the Richard-Stephen character conceivable. Surely the barren askesis of his life, as we are shown it in *Exiles*, is intolerable?—But *Exiles* shows us only the ethical side of that character, and only a moment in his relation to the other personages. Richard is evidently the continuation of Stephen; Robert seems to be another incarnation of Mulligan. Richard is also in some ways intermediate between the Stephen and the Bloom of *Ulysses*. Most important of all, the other works, which are more directly concerned with his consciousness, show us the perceptions he lives by and for fragments of beauty which are for him equivalents neither of the Dantesque *Esser beato nell' atto che vede* nor of Aristotelian contemplation.

With the aid of the larger Joycean testimony, too, we can get a more exact conception of the relation between *Exiles* and Ibsen . . . The work of Ibsen may speak to our need for a faith even if it leads nowhere, but *Exiles*, rightly understood, appeals only to the eye of the mind. It is a point in the heroic but necessarily unique living out of a 'heresy'; it is like a new geometry, based on the denial of a Euclidean axiom, and worked out, to the enrichment of mathematics, in accordance with mathematical laws.

Meanwhile there remains one's delight in *Exiles* as the most terrible and beautiful of modern plays. This delight, like one's admiration for the Joycean sanity and common sense, is the mark of a certain stage in the understanding of it; but in the same way it has its truth, it is there to return to, and it is to be preserved with the utmost care as a part of the experience of Mr. Joyce's work which consents to take its place alongside other experiences.

77. Bernard Bandler on *Exiles*

1933

'Joyce's Exiles', *Hound & Horn*, vi, No. 2 (January-March 1933), 266–85.

. . . The note of exile recurs frequently in our age. It is the one constant among the voices which have most engaged contemporary attention in literature, dissimilar as those voices otherwise are as in Proust, Eliot, and Joyce. . . .

A familiar solution to the problem of exile is not that the nature of man has been misrepresented but that God has been forgotten. Reintroduce the idea of God and faith in Him, one hears said, and the maladies of our age will depart. No solution could be more irrelevant. Man is exiled from man and that exile is not caused by disbelief in God. The ground of exile is always, I believe, a false interpretation of the relation between the body and the soul; an ignoring of the function of the body and hence an erroneous analysis of the soul; and as a result of this untrue conception of man an incomplete and often destructive ideal is striven for. This thesis cannot be demonstrated apart from multiple examples, but an analysis of *Exiles* by James Joyce, where the problem is most clearly stated, will illustrate my argument.

What first strikes one upon consideration of *Exiles* is the irrelevance of God. There is simply no need for Him. The characters' exile and sorrow is the human one of incompatible desires and unrealized hopes, a sorrow suffered in a universe with God in all times as well as in a universe without Him. Their longing is not for God and their exile is not from Him. . . . The picture which Joyce presents would not be materially affected by the addition of the various gods imagined or conceived by Jews, Greeks, and Christians; the existence of these gods, their attempted grace, even their omnipotence would not alter Joyce's vision of man. For Joyce's people are not only magnificently done, beautifully realized individuals of certain human types, but their dilemma is presented as true of all people, and hence inescapable. Exile as Joyce sees it, is necessarily our lot; it is the result of no accident, nor weakness, nor sin in human nature, the consequence of a fall from a Paradise to which a beneficent providence could restore us . . . To save man, to harmonize one man's desires with his neighbor's, would be to destroy man as Joyce sees him: grace can but give us the strength and fortitude to bear our exile. When Richard Rowen appeals for help, it is not the light of self-knowledge that he seeks, or the knowledge of others, for their goods or salvation, being intrinsically different from his, are unknowable: Richard seeks the strength to be immovably and unchangeably himself. . . .

If *Exiles* were presented in its relative truth, as a play that distilled the sorrow of human isolation, the office of the critic would be limited to understanding and enjoyment. But *Exiles* goes further; the vision claims to be universal and as final and as irrevocable as the Last Judgment. From such a sentence there is no appeal; mercy has no lien on truth; and *Exiles* is held up as the Medusa head of truth. Hence it is the truth itself of *Exiles* that one must question, its absolute truth about human destiny. Why are Beatrice and Bertha, Robert and Richard, exiles? From what are they exiled? . . . If exile is imposed by the lure of a superior personality, what is the nature of that personality, what is his idea of himself and of others, and his demands from life? Does he regard himself as a rational animal, or a fallen angel, or a strange and untrammelled spirit? Is his exile less from mother and wife, friends, Ireland, and the Catholic Church, from their understanding, compassion, and love, as he would have us believe, than from the goods and limitations of human nature itself, society, and every form of order? Is the exile of Richard Rowen so hopeless and terrifying because he is in revolt against the conditions of life itself? . . .

In an artist so conscious as Joyce each character has his full significance. Neither old Brigid nor Archie at eight are exiles. Their roles are secondary and aesthetic, to inform us of the natures and motives of the other characters. Brigid figures seriously only in the opening scene of the third act. She there appears as the mother substitute: even when Richard's mother lived he confided to Brigid his love for Bertha, talked of her letters and discussed his plans. Brigid's weight in the play rests on her material assurance to Bertha that 'there's good times coming still.' Archie plays a more important part. To Brigid he is Master Richard's son; to Beatrice he is an excuse for coming to see Richard; to Bertha he is son and symbol of Richard's love; and to Robert he is lusty, buoyant, hopeful youth. Archie scrambles through windows, crawls out of piano lessons, and arranges to drive early mornings with the milkman.

SOME VIEWS FROM 1918 TO 1921

78. P. Beaumont Wadsworth on Joyce

1917

'Visits with James Joyce', *James Joyce Quarterly*, i, No. 4 (Summer 1964), 14 [14–18].

It was in the spring of 1917 that I first came across the name of James Joyce after his first novel. *A Portrait of the Artist as a Young Man* had been published in London. It was an exciting review in one of the British politico-literary weeklies which aroused my curiosity, and I went out and bought that slim green-backed book at once.

I was a young man myself, just 22; I felt that I was artistic, and identified myself with the adolescence of Stephen Dedalus. With one bound I now marched into the modern movement of Joyce, Eliot,

Wyndham Lewis, Ezra Pound, D. H. Lawrence, Dorothy Richardson, and Virginia Woolf. Proust and Thomas Mann were to come several years later.

Extremely shy at the time, it took me almost a year to pluck up courage to write to Joyce, telling him how much I had enjoyed his novel. . . .

Although his poems, *Chamber Music* and the short stories *Dubliners* had already been published, Joyce was not yet known internationally, and I suppose he was grateful to receive a letter of appreciation from an unknown admirer. I must have been one of the earliest Joyce fans. . . .

79. Pound to Mencken

1918

Letter to H. L. Mencken (25 January 1918) in *The Letters of Ezra Pound* (1950), ed. D. D. Paige, p. 130.

. . . There is great desolation in litterchure at the moment. Joyce's new novel [*Ulysses*] has a corking 1st Chap. (which will get us suppressed), not such a good second one.

80. Pound to John Quinn

1918

Letter to John Quinn (3 April 1918), in *The Letters of Ezra Pound* (1950), ed. D. D. Paige, p. 133.

I can't agree with you about Joyce's first chapter. I don't think the passages about his mother's death and the sea would come with such force if they weren't imbedded in squalor and disgusts.

I may say that I rec'd the fourth chapter some days ago, and deleted about twenty lines before sending it off to N.Y.; and also wrote Joyce my reasons for thinking the said lines excessive.

He does not disgust me as Wells does. . . .

81. Padraic Colum on Joyce and Dublin

1918

'James Joyce', *Pearson's Magazine* (May 1918), 38–42. This article is the first to draw attention to the Catholic tradition and culture that shaped Joyce's early works (See introduction, pp. 5, 16).

People here who are interested in the subject, after talking for a while about the new literature of Ireland, often say to me, 'But who is James Joyce? What a curious book his *Portrait of the Artist as a Young Man* is! And the stories in his *Dubliners* are quite extraordinary! What else has he written? Is he well known in Ireland?'

Generally I reply, 'Joyce is not well known in Ireland. . . Besides *Portrait of the Artist* and *Dubliners* he has written a book of verse which has not been published here—*Chamber Music*. He has also published a play which I have not read . . . What comes vividly to my mind when I think of James Joyce is some melody—some strain of song. Perhaps it is that Irish ballad that Gabriel Conroy's wife heard in the story called 'The Dead':
. . . Or perhaps it is a lyric of Ben Jonson's that I hear repeated in Joyce's modulated voice:

> Still to be neat, still to be drest
> As you were going to a feast;

Or perhaps it is one of Joyce's own lyrics that, to me, are no less excellent than the Elizabethans':

> What counsel hath the hooded moon
> Put in your heart, my shyly sweet?
> Of love in ancient plenilune,
> Glory and stars beneath his feet?
> A sage who is but kith and kin
> To the comedian Capuchin.
>
> Believe me rather that am wise
> In disregard of the divine—
> A glory lightens in your eyes,
> Trembles to starlight. . . . Mine, O mine:
> No more be tears in moon or mist
> For thee, sweet sentimentalist.

These lyric things come to me not merely because I have heard him sing and heard him repeat verse beautifully, but because I know how much his mind dwells upon the melody and because I know that his ideal in literature is that which is simple and free—the liberation of a rhythm. His aesthetic is in that conversation which the hero of *Portrait of the Artist*, Stephen Dedalus, has with the student Lynch. What Stephen says there is, word for word, what Joyce used to say to many of us who were with him in the early twenties:

[quotes from ch. 5]

Joyce was ten years writing the book. I saw him in Dublin when he was mid-way in it and he told me there were parts that gave him physical nausea to write. *Portrait of the Artist as a Young Man* is a biography in which all inessentials are suppressed and people and incidents only stand out as a background for the emergence of a soul. It is a confession in which there are things as ignominious as the things in Rousseau's *Confessions*. But there is heroism in the book, and in spite of corruption and precocity there is youth in it also. Halfway in the life that is shown to us Stephen Dedalus comes to a spiritual morass. He wins through it by virtue of a power of spiritual vision backed by the discipline of the Catholic Church. Later he loses his faith in the sanctions of that Church and at the end of the story he is leaving his country. He is going to discover a mode of life or art whereby his spirit may express itself in unfettered freedom.

What really makes *Portrait of the Artist as a Young Man* strange to English and American people is that it gives a glimpse into a new life—into the life that has been shaped by Catholic culture and Catholic tradition. James Joyce's book is profoundly Catholic. I do not mean that it carries any doctrine or thesis: I mean that, more than any other modern book written in English, it comes out of Catholic culture and tradition—even that culture and tradition that may turn against itself. Even in the way the book is written there is something that makes us think of the Church—a sense of secrecy, of words being said in a mysterious language, of solidity breaking into vision. Stephen Dedalus is unable to analyze his ideas or to shape his life except in terms of the philosophy that the Catholic Church has evolved or adopted. His ideal of beauty is the ideal that has been attained to in the masterpieces of Catholic art. It is the speech of the Church that fills his soul with apprehension because of his secret sins, and it is the absolution of the Church that gives him peace and the way to a new life. . . .

And this city, so thwarted on the side of culture, is low in material circumstances. The misery that comes from low wages and few opportunities pervades the *Portrait of the Artist* as it pervades *Dubliners*. Stephen's bread-and-butter life is not merely sordid, it is on the verge of being squalid. . . .

[quotes from ch. 4]

Against this background of economic decay and incomplete culture and of shut-in sin Stephen Dedalus makes his spiritual assertion. He will win toward freedom and the power to create. He will strive, too, to give a soul to this people. . . .

And out of his squalor, his lack of companionship, his closed future, he created a proud soul. Liberation came to him through his poetry.

Many squalid and vicious things are described in *Portrait of the Artist as a Young Man*, but also the pure ecstasy of poetic creation has been rendered in it as in no other book that I know of: . . .

[quotes from ch. 5]

. . . Stories were told about his arrogance. Did not this youth say to Yeats, 'We have met too late: you are too old to be influenced by me'? And did he not laugh in derision when a celebrated critic spoke of Balzac as a great writer? . . . He gave me his poems to read—they were in a beautiful manuscript. He used to speak very arrogantly about these poems of his, but I remember his saying something that made me know how precious these beautifully wrought lyrics were to him—he talked about walking the streets of Paris, poor and tormented, and about what peace the repetition of his poems had brought him.

His poems were perfect in their form. But could one who expressed himself so perfectly at twenty really go far? Yeats had said to him, 'I do not know whether you are a fountain or a cistern,' and A. E. had remarked, 'I do not see in your beginnings the chaos out of which a world is created. . .' It was then that he told me the name of the book he was writing—the book that was being referred to in Dublin as 'Joyce's Meredithian novel'—it was *Portrait of the Artist as a Young Man*. It was not 'Meredithian' at all. . . .

The last sentences in one of the stories in *Dubliners* seems to me to show the quality of Joyce's writing at its best. I refer to the story called 'The Dead.' It is after a party at which an old song, 'The Maid of Aughrim,' had been sung. Gabriel Conroy's wife had remained strangely abstracted after having heard it. Suddenly she lifts a veil by telling her husband that she had known in Galway a young man who used to sing that song, Michael Furey, and that he had died for love of her. Yes, he had come into her garden one night to speak to her before she went to the convent. It was raining bitterly and the chill he had taken, working on a weakened constitution, had brought him to his grave. She did not love him, but they had been friends. At first the husband is jealous of poor young Michael Furey, but then he is won to a mood of compassion: . . .

[quotes the last two paragraphs of 'The Dead'.]

82. Pound on the early works

1918

'Joyce', *The Future* (May 1918), 161–3. Later appeared in *Instigations* (1920), pp. 203–11. Also appeared in *Literary Essays of Ezra Pound* (1954), ed. T. S. Eliot, pp. 410–17.
A notice of a new edition of *A Portrait* and a brief discussion of *Dubliners* and *Chamber Music*.

Despite the War, despite the paper shortage, and despite those old-established publishers whose god is their belly and whose god-father was the late F. T. Palgrave, there is a new edition of James Joyce's *A Portrait of the Artist as a Young Man*. It is extremely gratifying that this book should have 'reached its fourth thousand,' and the fact is significant in just so far as it marks the beginning of a new phase of English publishing, a phase comparable to that started in France some years ago by the *Mercure*. . . .

Joyce's *A Portrait* is literature; it has become almost the prose bible of a few people, and I think I have encountered at least three hundred admirers of the book, certainly that number of people who, whether they 'like' it or not, are wholly convinced of its merits.

Mr. Wells I have encountered only in print. Mr. Wells says that Joyce has a cloacal obsession, *but* he also says that Mr. Joyce writes literature and that his book is to be ranked with the works of Sterne and of Swift [*Nation*, x (10 March 1917), 158–60; see No. 41] . . . .

Still, from England and America there has come a finer volume of praise for this novel than for any that I can remember. There has also come impotent spitting and objurgation from the back-woods and from Mr. Dent's office boy, and, as offset, interesting comment in modern Greek, French and Italian.

Joyce's poems have been reprinted by Elkin Mathews, his short stories re-issued, and a second novel started in *The Little Review*.

For all the book's being so familiar, it is pleasant to take up *A Portrait* in its new exiguous form, and one enters many speculations, perhaps more than when one read it initially. It is not that one can open to a forgotten page so much as that wherever one opens there is always a place to start. . . I do not mean to imply that a novel is necessarily a bad novel because one can pick it up without being in this manner, caught and dragged into reading; but I do indicate the curiously seductive interest of the clear-cut and definite sentences.

Neither, emphatically, is it to be supposed that Joyce's writing is merely a depiction of the sordid. The sordid is there in all conscience as you would find it in De Goncourt, but Joyce's power is in his scope. . . .

On almost every page of Joyce you will find just such swift alternation of subjective beauty and external shabbiness, squalor, and sordidness. It is the bass and treble of his method. And he has his scope beyond that of the novelists his contemporaries, in just so far as whole stretches of his keyboard are utterly out of their compass. . . .

In the three hundred pages of *A Portrait of the Artist as a Young Man* there is no omission; there is nothing in life so beautiful that Joyce cannot touch it without profanation—without, above all, the profanations of sentiment and sentimentality—and there is nothing so sordid that he cannot treat it with his metallic exactitude. . . .

Joyce's earlier book, *Dubliners*, contained several well-constructed stories, several sketches rather lacking in form. It was a definite promise of what was to come. There is very little to be said in praise of it which would not apply with greater force to *A Portrait*. I find that whoever reads one book inevitably sets out in search of the other.

The quality and distinction of the poems in the first half of Mr. Joyce's *Chamber Music* is due in part to their author's strict musical training. We have here the lyric in some of its best traditions, and one pardons certain trifling inversions, much against the taste of the moment, for the sake of the clean-cut ivory finish, and for the interest of the rhythms, the cross run of the beat and the word, as of a stiff wind cutting the ripple-tops of bright water.

The wording is Elizabethan, the metres at times suggesting Herrick, but in no case have I been able to find a poem which is not in some way Joyce's own, even though he would seem, and that most markedly, to shun apparent originality. . . .

[quotes all of 'Who goes amid . . .', VIII]

Here, as in nearly every poem, the motif is so slight that the poem scarcely exists until one thinks of it as set to music; and the workmanship is so delicate that out of twenty readers scarce one will notice its fineness. Would that Henry Lawes were alive again to make the suitable music, for the cadence is here worthy of his cunning:

O, it is for my true love,
  That is young and fair.

The musician's work is very nearly done for him, and yet how few song-setters could be trusted to finish it and to fill in an accompaniment.

The tone of the book deepens with the poem beginning. . .

[quotes first two stanzas of 'O Sweetheart. . .', xviii]

The collection comes to its end and climax in two profoundly emotional poems; quite different in tonality and in rhythm-quality from the lyrics in the first part of the book:

All day I hear the noise of waters
    Making moan,
Sad as the sea-bird is, when going
    Forth alone,
He hears the wind cry to the waters'
    Monotone.

The grey winds, the cold winds are blowing
    Where I go.
I hear the noise of many waters
    Far below.
All day, all night, I hear them flowing
    To and fro.

The third and fifth lines should not be read with an end stop. I think the rush of the words will escape the notice of scarcely anyone. The phantom hearing in this poem is coupled, in the next poem, to phantom vision as well, and to a *robustezza* of expression:. . .

[quotes 'I hear an army. . .', xxxvi]

In both these poems we have a strength and a fibrousness of sound which almost prohibits the thought of their being 'set to music,' or to any music but that which is in them when spoken; but we notice a similarity of technique with the earlier poems, in so far as the beauty of movement is produced by a very skilful, or perhaps we should say a deeply intuitive, interruption of metric mechanical regularity. It is the irregularity which has shown always in the best periods.

The book is an excellent antidote for those who find Mr. Joyce's prose 'disagreeable' and who at once fly (*à la* Mr. Wells, for example) to conclusions about Mr. Joyce's 'cloacal obsessions,' &c. I have yet to find in Joyce's published works a violent or malodorous phrase which does not justify itself not only by its verity, but by its heightening of some opposite effect, by the poignancy which it imparts to some emotion or to some thwarted desire for beauty. Disgust with the sordid is but another expression of a sensitiveness to the finer thing. There is no perception of beauty without a corresponding disgust. If the price for such artists as James Joyce is exceeding heavy, it is the artist himself who pays. . . .

83. Silvio Benco on Joyce and Trieste

1918

Extract from 'James Joyce in Trieste', *Pegaso*, No 2 (August 1930), 150–65. Also appeared in *The Bookman* (New York), lxxii (December 1930), 375–80 (from which the present text is taken), and in *Umana* (Trieste), i, No. 4 (6 July 1918), 1–3.

. . . The success of *Dubliners*, at a distance; the princely price paid in America for the manuscript, and even for the proof sheets, of *A Portrait of the Artist as a Young Man*; complete material ease for today and tomorrow; final independence earned by the work of the mind. He was in good humor (so says my friend Antonio Battara who was his companion in his Swiss exile), and delightful hours were passed in reading his aphorisms and paradoxes. He spent much time in bed, writing *Ulysses*; often he mixed with the other Irish exiles, and helped them to found a company of 'Irish Players', which, having improvised a theatre, gave his comedy, *Exiles*. . . .

On my return to Trieste in the spring of 1918, I found *Exiles* and a little later *A Portrait of the Artist* came from Zürich. In the comedy I at once recognized the Ibsenian inspiration (Ibsen, the great love of Joyce's youth), but cruelly developed, somewhat in the manner of Strinberg, according to the natural law of the destruction of the soul when it is exposed to fire. Perhaps Strindberg would have ended with the bursting into flame; Joyce ironically viewed the complete destruction. In the *Portrait* I was struck by the precision and extreme lucidity of the draughtsmanship, the 'resemblance' to its original revealed through the logic of its structure. It is too terse, too rigidly fresh and intellectually exact to be a favorite book with Italians. . . .

That evening I got a general idea of the work, not sufficient however to give me even a vague conception of its real value. My measure of Joyce was still in the *Portrait of the Artist*: my expectations were naturally modelled on that criterion. But after a few more visits (no longer busy with his lessons, Joyce often came to my office), my curiosity increased until it was at its height. Then the magic talisman of *Ulysses* was revealed to me, the key to its secret, which all can now readily find in Stuart Gilbert's volume, that excellent commentary which, with the aid of the author himself, interprets every phase of James Joyce's novel.

After that initiation, he wanted me to read what was already written of *Ulysses*. . . . He showed me the loose sheets on which he prepared the material of each episode, notes as to composition, quotations, references, ideas, essays in various styles. When the rough material was ready, he devoted himself to writing out the complete episode, and this he usually did in less than a month. Following this method, *Ulysses* had been begun in Trieste before the war, continued in Zürich, and now resumed in Trieste. . .

84. Yeats to John Quinn

1918

Letter to John Quinn (23 July 1918), after reading a chapter of *Ulysses* then appearing in the *Little Review*. Quoted in *The Letters of W. B. Yeats* (1955), ed. Allan Wade, p. 651.

. . . If I had had this tower of mine when Joyce began to write, I daresay I might have been of use to him, have got him to meet those who might have helped him. I think him a most remarkable man, and his new story in the *Little Review* looks like becoming the best work he has done. It is an entirely new thing—neither what the eye sees nor the ear hears, but what the rambling mind thinks and imagines from moment to moment. He has certainly surpassed in intensity any novelist of our time.

85. Scofield Thayer on Joyce's works

1918

'James Joyce', *Dial*, lxv, No. 773 (19 September 1918), 201–3.

A general article on *A Portrait, Dubliners, Exiles*, and *Chamber Music*.

Stephen Dedalus, the hero of *A Portrait of the Artist as a Young Man*, desires to try out all possible means of expression. Whether or not the somewhat scattered personality of this hero be a child wholly after his father's heart, at any rate Mr. Joyce himself is publicly trying out his own mettle in the short story, the novel, the Elizabethan lyric, and the Ibsenesque drama. The most recent of his publications in this country is *Exiles*, a prose play in three acts. . . . The play appears to be intended to illustrate a problem and perhaps to throw light upon it; the question is so intricate that I for one am quite unable to follow even the speeches of the characters, still less to fathom the author's own intention or conclusion. The problem is the seasoned one of marriage and freedom, but just what takes place and why and what the upshot of it all is does not emerge from the emotional scenes and the final disintegration of the protagonist. On the stage, which stops for no man, this drama would be an impregnable puzzle; and even when it is held fast on the printed page, hopelessly conflicting solutions vie with one another. Next time Mr. Joyce would do well to try his hand at exegesis and to take this play as his subject.

Chamber Music is—all but the intensely contemporary and distinguished final poem—a remarkably perfect echo of the best in early seventeenth century prosody. These little songs are so intimately alluring that no one but a schoolmaster would cavil at their harping upon one note, and that the secular one of courteous-mannered love.

And I but render and confess
The malice of thy tenderness

disarms all strictures that might be made upon the futility of repeating an already deviously explored manner. . . Indeed in the case of these lyrics our reminiscence of earlier pipings does but enhance our pleasure: it is good to know that a mind so crammed with the impertinences of modern city life as the creator of *Dubliners* can yet achieve the liquid grace of a less handicapped age.

This collection of short stories published under the title *Dubliners* is certainly Mr. Joyce's finest piece of work; indeed I should not know where to go for their betters. The title is a very appropriate one, for these stories are not so much narratives of events as they are evolvements of character. To be sure, these people of Joyce are not painted as standing still for our perusal of their complicated lineaments; they are caught, so to speak, on the wing, and the portrait is the more successful for this fact. In the changing light and shadow of their veering flight we are able to look them over pretty thoroughly, and Mr. Joyce sees to it that we look to the right place at the right time. Judged from Aristotle's point of view, the vague plots of these stories are so unsymmetrical as to be definite malformations: they are the hunchbacks of fiction. Yet the sparse incidents that make them up are casual only in their relations to each other and to the rest of incidental, practical life; they are uncannily indicative, even ratiocinative, when rightly taken for what they are—media for the expression of character.

There is therefore almost no plot tension; and however much we may sympathize with certain of the characters, curiosity as to the outcome of the predicament is scarcely awakened. As in some dreams, we ourselves are unaccountably detached not only from the incidents narrated but also from practical interest of every kind. With an hypnotic attention we perceive these characters evolve and our whole will is so strangely absorbed in their contemplation that otherwise we neither wonder nor desire. . . .

Controlled by the genius of Mr. Joyce, the short story is an art not less pure than music: we do not ask how the piece will end, still less that it should end sunnily; that our emotions and our imaginations are so proudly stirred gives us a profound content.

The people of Mr. Joyce are for the most part not less casual than the tales in which they figure More obviously flotsam even than the majority of mankind, they are yet almost at home on the shifting, contradictory currents of their life. . . . At the last we are reminded that they are not fishes: we are aware of their body smells.

The *Portrait of the Artist as a Young Man* is, paradoxically, less a portrait than these stories in *Dubliners*. Ostensibly and successfully the biography of a young man of sensitive imagination bent upon the difficult career of letters, it is yet primarily a cross-section of contemporary Irish middle-class life. When the boy is at home, it is so overpoweringly an Irish one that we almost forget home and boy together in the glory of this immense gulp of Celtic domesticity. When fate submits poor Stephen to the smooth, disagreeable machinery of boarding-school, the pallid boy is easily lost sight of against the highly coloured Jesuitical background. Even in the latter half of the book, where the harsh insistence of sex replaces the home and school interest, we almost forget the patient, so intent are we upon this catastrophic disease of puberty. . . . For in his prose style the intelligent Irishman is not less protean than in his flittings among literary genres. . . While the limber quality of Joyce's speech is most peculiarly apposite in dialogue, yet his clear, nervous language is not less well illustrated by a paragraph in which Dedalus, whom we may surely take at least here as the mouthpiece of our author, reflects to himself upon his enforced use of our Anglo-Saxon tongue: . . .

[quotes from ch. 5]

The last pages of the *Portrait* are in the form of a diary and written in a style jotty and spasmodic. . . . This style, suggestive fancifully at least of pointillist painting, is a perfect expression of the mood of the sick boy. But a novel written in this jerky way becomes very tiring, and that seems to be the case with Mr. Joyce's *Ulysses*, now appearing in *The Little Review*. It has something in common with not a few of Shakespeare's prose passages. But while the poet is inclined to employ this disconnected utterance only for brief intervals set off between the smooth periods of his verse, Joyce now makes of it a narrative style. This is not, however, perverse. For Shakespeare's characters are of course speaking aloud, and naturally, except in rare instances of madmen and women who keep inns, speak connectedly; while Joyce's novel is really a long inward soliloquy broken only by haphazard small talk. . . The great Frenchman [Flaubert] did his best to depict things as he saw them, and that is all the word 'impressionist,' at least in literature, heretofore implied. Joyce has become impressionist in a much more subtle sense. He gives us, especially in *Ulysses*, the streaming impressions, often only subconsciously cognate to one another, of our habitual life—that vague, tepid river of consciousness to which only our ephemeral moments of real will or appetite can give coherence. Joyce succeeds in this undertaking to a remarkable degree. The chief fault of this method is its jerkiness, peculiarly inapt to interpret the calm flow of our sensations merging so noiselessly one into another. Some of us feel it a pity that he who could write the strangely sinuous final pages of 'The Dead' should now have adopted so different a medium. But there is a time for all things.

The Ireland of this *Dubliners* is a long shot from the land of legend and of poetry; for Joyce, despite his own verses, is persistently occupied with such muddy raptures as in this life we do attain. The creation of which he is author has gold in its teeth and walks not so much on feet as in decayed sport shoes. It is a world of battered derbies and bleared souls, where if there be gallants at all they are of the sort who wait outside areaways for the sovereigns of amorous housemaids. Mr. Joyce exhibits the cynicism of a fine nature habituated but not subdued to the sordidity of our industrial civilization, and his pictures are too acrid not to persuade us of their truth. In the end we come uncomfortably near feeling that human life itself may be insolvent. . . .

86. Pound to John Quinn

1920

Letter to John Quinn (19 June 1920), in *The Letters of Ezra Pound* (1950), ed. D. D. Paige, p. 153.

Joyce—pleasing; after the first shell of cantankerous Irishman, I got the impression that the real man is the author of *Chamber Music*, the sensitive. The rest is the genius; the registration of realities on the temperament, the delicate temperament of the early poems. A concentration and absorption passing Yeats'—Yeats has never taken on anything requiring the condensation of *Ulysses*.

87. Evelyn Scott on Joyce and modernity

1920

Extract from 'Contemporary of the Future', *Dial*, lxix (October 1920), 353–67.

. . . As the character of feeling displayed by Emma Bovary and Evelyn Innes is that of minds controlled in their operations by no experience of the past or anticipation of the future, it is the type of feeling which psychology has associated with the mentality of the child; and when James Joyce, in his *Portrait of the Artist as a Young Man*, gives us the early life of Stephen Dedalus in a similar vein we find exquisite appropriateness in the method so used. It is a mind which has not yet developed complexities that responds so simply yet so delicately to the obvious aspects of its surroundings. . . .

It is because Stephen has not catalogued these people that they live for us in his imagination. From his contract with Mr and Mrs Dedalus, Mrs Riordon, Uncle Charles, and Eileen is sprung the first spark of self-awareness. That part of our environment which lives is the part which makes emotional demands on us. When the figures of childhood fade from Stephen's emotional vision, they cease to exist, and the vitality of the father and mother and the priests and boys at Clongowes is transmuted into the vitality of the whore in the mean street. . . .

When Stephen Dedalus casts off the thraldom of the religion which has dominated his childhood, he becomes a man, and probably a great man—certainly an artist—by asserting himself in this negative sense. In the freedom of denial which never belongs fully to any one but the artist, he is able to feel the life about him with exquisite and intimate detachment. For ever apart from him, the clouds, the sea, the young girl with the long white legs like a stork's, are intimate, perfect, and indivisible incidents of his being.

If only Mr Joyce had possessed the artistic courage to end his book with these most intense paragraphs of emotional realization, and had not diffused the effects of a priceless moment in some one hundred pages of brilliant but disintegrating comment! The aesthetic formulas which originate in Stephen's maturing mind articulate so small a part of the reality which is Stephen, a reality which we have not touched curiously from the outside but have entered into.

However, as extraneous as is Mr Joyce's exposition of art to the very effective impressionism of the creation which goes before, he gives us, on the lips of the maturing adolescent, more than one hint, from the critic standpoint, of a tendency which later fulfils itself in *Ulysses*, the first imaginative attempt at a complete history of consciousness.

Mr Joyce might be described as the only artist who has seen himself through. Even in his volume of poems, *Chamber Music*—made up of plaintive little Elizabethan numbers of irrelevant perfection—there is discernible that balance between sense and consideration which should characterize the seeker for reality. One imagines it impossible for Mr Joyce to intoxicate himself with the approximate expression; and the clarity of his vision, always so precise, is at the same time quietly and endlessly intense, like a continuous pain.

Mr Joyce is still a young writer, but even in *Dubliners*, one of his first published volumes, there is in his style an extreme lucidity and composure which give one the impression of fulfilment rather than promise. In this book he broke no new ground, but at least he showed us that the absence of spiritual nuance in most of the prose written in the English tongue was not due to any lack in the potentialities of the language, but was rather the result of a crassness of mentality in the people who used it.

To-day, when this author's technique has developed unique aspects that threaten to indicate a revolution of style for the future, the spirit of his work suggests the culmination of a long and slowly evolving line rather than the ebullition of a fresh impulse. Most of the *Dubliners* are presented to us statically through a quality of mind comparable only to the poetic quality in emotions. That is to say these are true sketches which escape the suggestion of direction; though occasionally one moves toward an irrevocable climax in the manner of the short story formula.

No man is wholly himself who is wholly aware of himself, and it is only through the delicacy of his method that the most exquisite ironist escapes a taint of complaisance. Mr Joyce, who in this single instance resembles Chekhov, is sometimes ironical, and on these occasions is, one might say, almost imperceptibly obvious. Some of the studies seem a bit opaque, like faithful transparencies which require the gilding of sense to throw them into relief. There is more than one hint of that submerged drama in which half of the human race is still-born—the drama of the incomplete act. The man without imagination is able to act entirely; but our past asserts itself through our refinements and chains us in a sterility of the emotions. . . .

In *A Portrait of the Artist as a Young Man* the material is broad and simple and the author's triumph, as in *Dubliners*, is in his superior application of a method already half established by precedent. When Mr Joyce set out to write a play, on the contrary, he initially distinguished his effort by his daring selection of a theme which is exquisitely complex. And in presenting his situation he dares to express himself through the medium of a *vis-à-vis* who is on a perfect equality—emotional and intellectual—with his creator. . . .

Before reading *Exiles*, Mr Joyce's work, I looked upon Strindberg as the single instance in contemporary and nearly-contemporary drama, of the artist able to include the finest counter-currents of reaction in the general forward motion of the drama, without halting or impeding the culmination of this movement. . . .

When Mr Joyce drew Richard Rowan, however, he gave us a character highly self-perceptive and ruthlessly so, one whose experience of life is complete, each instant born of the senses dying a beautiful and perfect death in the mind. So clearly does Richard Rowan appreciate the value of moments detached from each other, as they must be in realization, that he is no longer capable of what might be termed the lie of action. Action is a simple and entire expression of the individual, and becomes possible only through a temporary obliviousness to complex values. The tendency of a high state of perception is to arrest the motive force which is behind the will. . . .

In *Ulysses* there is the touch of a Rabelaisian humour, felt occasionally in the *Portrait*, but entirely missing from *Exiles* and *Dubliners*. It furnishes a base in permanent and simple requirements for the superstructure of refined perceptions; and contradicts the tendency of the sophisticated mind toward a sterile disassociation from essentials. In the literature of an average intelligence is the tradition of a humour which would be flavourless without the conventions, the humour of man's astonishment when Nature intrudes.

Mr Joyce's humour anticipates the conventions. It is the humour of dirt, of Nature herself as she regards man in his fastidiousness. This is the humour of the god and of the child. It does not discriminate in a secondary sense, and is not surprised by a disarrangement of particular conventions, but by the phenomena of convention as a single incongruity. This is expressed in the freshness of Bloom's curiosity as he examines his sensations, and, with an added sharpness, it is in Buck Mulligan's contemplation of himself and his friend. I do not know of any contemporary prose writer of specious gusto whose work shows a hardihood which could sustain it. Certainly the red-blooded *littérateurs* of America would faint with the odour of Mr Joyce's sanity.

After the first several episodes, *Ulysses* changes *tempo* and takes on a quality of intricacy which can be neither condemned nor justified until we are presented with the volume entire and are able to gauge the scope of its pretensions. In representing mass-consciousness by cross current impressions of individuals reacting almost simultaneously to a common stumulus, Mr Joyce sometimes arrives at a doubtful effect; but putting aside an end, which at this writing is still beyond us, there remain the means through which the Irish artist is recreating a portion of the English language.

By a compounding of nouns with adjectives and even of adjectives with adverbs—'Eglintoneyes, looked up shybrightly,' and so forth—he conveys to us a simultaneous rather than a cumulative occurrence in which the senses cooperate, of many qualities at once as if they were one, and the result is a reaction that is simple yet full of nuance.

In attributing quotations he also places the adverb of modification before rather than after the name of the person speaking, which is, except in the shock of meeting on a street corner, the true order of recognition. Again convention falsely lays the emphasis of our attention on a recognition of the speaker's identity.

There is no great courage that does not reflect a proportionate fear. The dauntless self-recognition of the great artist is the despairing protest of his egotism. Against the blankness of emotion with which one must regard annihilation, are thrown into relief the sharp details of existence. If James Joyce were not clear-thinking and deliberate in his pessimism, he could not register so exquisitely the delicate ramifications of living.

It is the defect of many a compelling and responsive personality that it intoxicates itself with life until it cannot longer make accurately the great distinction between this world and the next. This is the psychology of the martyr's triumph. James Joyce escapes the intoxication of self through the marvelous fineness of his psychological balance.

The human race accepts slowly its subconscious convictions, which then rise almost imperceptibly to the lips of its great artists and become articulate in their work. James Joyce, to my mind, expresses, more clearly than any other writer of English prose in this time, the conviction of modernity—a new and complex knowledge of self which has passed its period of racial gestation and is ready for birth in art. . . .

88. J. C. Squire on Joyce

1921

Solomon Eagle (J. C. Squire), 'The Critic at Large: Irish Literature Today', *Outlook* (16 July 1921), 53.
Joyce is mentioned in a review of L. D'O. Walters, *Irish Poets of To-Day*.

. . . Among the younger Irish writers (I am speaking only of 'creative' writers) who have appeared above the horizon only Mr. James Joyce arouses much curiosity. The author of *Portrait of the Artist as a Young Man* and *Ulysses* is scarcely likely to become a popular novelist. But he writes like an artist; his stylistic explorations are interesting, even if they may lead him into a cul-de-sac, and he has a powerful and original mind. He appears, by the way, to have shaken the dust of Ireland off his feet, and he discloses remarkably little interest in the political or any other moment. He is a lonely and self-sufficient worker if ever there was one.

89. Arthur Power on Joyce

1921

Extract from 'Conversations with Joyce', *James Joyce Quarterly*, iii, No. 1 (Fall, 1965), 41–6.

While living in Dublin I had read *Dubliners*, and later *A Portrait of the Artist as a Young Man*, and I was intrigued to meet one of our most important authors. . . .

'That is the emotional aspect. There is also the intellectual attitude which dissects life instead of puffing it up with romanticism, which is a fundamental false attitude. In *Ulysses* I have tried to write literature out of my own experience and not out of emotion, for you cannot write well if you allow yourself to be blown around by your passions.'

'I think you wrote better when you were blown around by your passions as you express it,' I said, 'as for example, in the *Portrait*.'

'That was the book of my youth,' said Joyce, 'but *Ulysses* is the book of my maturity. Youth is a time of torment in which we can see nothing clearly, but in *Ulysses* I have seen life clearly, I think, and as a whole. It has taken me half a lifetime to reach the necessary equilibrium to express it, for my youth was exceptionally painful and violent . . .

'In my Mabbot Street scene I have, in my opinion, approached reality closer than anywhere else in the book (except perhaps for the last chapter) since sensation is the object heightened even to the point of the hallucination which is the exalted vision of the mystics. . . .'

90. Joyce and jazz prose

1921

Clive Bell, 'Plus de Jazz', *New Republic*, xxviii (21 September 1921), 94–5 [92–6].

The influence of the jazz movement upon other arts is examined, with Joyce serving as the example of jazz prose.

. . . In literature Jazz manifests itself both formally and in content. Formally its distinctive characteristic is the familiar one—syncopation. It has given us a ragtime literature which flouts traditional rhythms and sequences and grammar and logic. . . . In prose I think Mr. Joyce will serve as a perhaps not very good example: I choose him because he is probably better known to readers than any other writer who affects similar methods. In his later publications Mr. Joyce does deliberately go to work to break up the traditional sentence, throwing overboard sequence, syntax, and, indeed, most of those conventions which men habitually employ for the exchange of precise ideas. Effectually and with a will he rags the literary instrument: unluckily, this will has at its service talents which are only moderate.

ULYSSES

February 1922[1]

91. Valéry Larbaud, reaction to *Ulysses*

1921

'Sur *Ulysses*', *Mercure de France*, cccxlvii (August–September 1963), 99–101.

Two letters written to Sylvia Beach in 1921 (translated by Marcelle Sibon).

15 February 1921

Dear Sylvia,

a thousand thanks for the beautiful flowers! How kind of you. They've done me a lot of good, and as soon as I saw them I felt better. But why take the trouble of sending the typewriter?

Thanks, too, for the *Little Review*. I am reading *Ulysses*. Indeed I cannot read anything else, cannot even think of anything else. Just the thing for me. I like it even better than *A Portrait*. Breaks new ground, goes deeper.

Did Mlle Linossier tell you I have got your copy of *Exiles*? as soon as I am able to go out I'll bring it back to rue Dupuytren. . . .

22 February 1921

Dear Sylvia, I am *raving mad* over *Ulysses*. Since I read Whitman when I was 18 I have not been so enthusiastic about any book. I have read all there is in the *Little Review* (but I want to keep it a little longer—to read a few other things—may I?) and I am reading now the typescript of Episode XIV. I think I should like to translate a few pages for *La N.R.F.* or if they don't want it, *Les Ecrits Nouveaux*. Perhaps the place where Mr. Bloom is in the Restaurant. Just 8 or 10 pages in all,

[1] For reviews of the French translation see Nos. 211, 213, 215, 216, 218, 249. For late criticism of *Ulysses* see Nos. 85, 87, 136–9, 149–52, 163–8, 197–204, 209–22, 240–1, 247–51, 259–63, 266–9, 277–80, 287–8, 293–4, 324.

just to show how wonderful it is. But I shall want time for that. Will you ask Joyce about it, I mean will he allow me? . . . It is wonderful! As great as Rabelais: Mr. Bloom is an immortal like Falstaff. [*Deux mots illisibles, peut-être:* Très grand.]

92. *Ulysses* and censorship

1921

R.H.C., 'Readers and Writers', *New Age* (28 April 1921), 89.

Just when we in Europe were beginning to envy America her promise, contrasting it with the winter of our own discontent, 'the authorities' (as one might say the furies, the parcæ or the weird sisters) have descended upon our unfortunate but deserving friend, the *Little Review*, and suspended its mail service on account of its publication of a chapter of Mr. James Joyce's new novel, *Ulysses*. That such an absurd act of puritanic spleen should be possible after and before years of world-war is evidence that, after all, spiritual meanness is hard to transcend; and it confirms the justice or, at least the apprehension expressed in Mr. Ezra Pound's bon mot that the U.S.A. should be renamed the Y.M.C.A. Not only is the *Little Review* perfectly harmless; would to heaven, indeed, that it were or could be otherwise, for never can any good be done by something incapable of doing harm; but the *Ulysses* of Mr. James Joyce is one of the most interesting literary symptoms in the whole literary world, and its publication is very nearly a public obligation. Such sincerity, such energy, such fearlessness as Mr. Joyce's are rare in any epoch, and most of all in our own; and on that very account they demand to be given at least the freedom of the Press. What the giant American can *fear* from Mr. Joyce or from his publication in the *Little Review* passes understanding. Abounding in every variety of crime and stupidity as America is, even if *Ulysses* were a literary crime committed in a journal of the largest circulation, one more or less could not make much difference to America. But *Ulysses* is of course, no crime; but, on the contrary, a noble experiment; and its suppression will, in consequence, sadden the virtuous at the same time that it gratifies the base. America, we may say, is not going to 'get culture' by stamping upon every germ of new life, America's present degree of cultural toleration may ensure a herb-garden, but not a flower will grow upon the soil of Comstock. It only remains for some reputable English publisher to produce *Ulysses* to secure a notable triumph for the Empire over America. . . . The immediate publication of *Ulysses* in England is imperative; and every literary craftsman in the country should make a point of insisting upon it. . . .

93. Richard Aldington on the influence of Joyce

1921

'The Influence of Mr. James Joyce', *English Review*, xxxii (April 1921), 333–41; also appeared in his *Literary Studies and Reviews* (1924), pp. 192–207.

Obviously no valid criticism can be made of Mr. Joyce's *Ulysses* until the whole work has been published in book form. It seems to me that the serial publication has lasted an abnormally long time, and that there is some excuse for my impatience in speaking of *Ulysses* while it is still fragmentary. Mr. Joyce's attempt is most interesting both for its achievement and for the influence it must have; the achievement, I am convinced, is remarkable, its influence, I fear, may be deplorable. If young writers could be persuaded to applaud and honour Mr. Joyce without copying him, all would be well; but such a thing is unlikely. . . . From the manner of Mr. Joyce to Dadaisme is but a step, and from Dadaisme to imbecility is hardly that. Where Mr. Joyce has succeeded, with occasional lapses, others must fail, lacking his intellectuality, his amazing observation, memory and intuition, his control over the processes of his art.

Mr. Joyce is a modern Naturaliste, possessing a greater knowledge of intimate psychology, but without the Naturaliste preoccupation with *l'écriture artiste*. He is less conscious, more intuitive than the Naturalistes; if the expression is not too strained, he has made realism mystic. *Dubliners*, influenced by French writers, was a book to which Zola would have given his *nihil obstat*. It was neither better nor worse than a great many French Naturaliste books; the stories in *Dubliners* were very nearly the sort of thing that Octave Mirbeau has written. The book attracted attention for the reason that Naturalisme was a literary mode little practised by writers of English fiction who were also artists. . . .

[A long digression on English Naturaliste writers follows here. *A Portrait* is then briefly discussed.]

Undoubtedly the 'triumph' of large sales and the admiration of silly women were not forthcoming, but Mr. Joyce had the admiration and respect of almost all his contemporaries and many of his elders. His next book was awaited with great interest. This proved to be *Ulysses*.

Consider for a moment Mr. Joyce's position in the interval between *The Portrait* and *Ulysses*. He appeared to have outgrown the immature Naturalisme of *Dubliners* and had certainly improved immensely as a writer of fiction. True, *The Portrait* was sordid, but it had fine passages; the contest between the 'idealism' of Daedalus and the outer world of crass stupidity and ugliness was very moving. The spiritual conflict lifted the story out of squalor into tragedy, though there was a lingering over unsavoury details which spoiled the balance of the book. It was nasty in many spots, but with a kind of tonic nastiness. One felt that here was a man of extreme sensitiveness and talent getting rid of 'perilous stuff,' throwing off the evil dreams and influences of mawkish youth to reach a saner, clearer view of human life. Many people must have had great hopes of Mr. Joyce. I did not for one moment desire him to accept a particle of that official optimism which is so poisonous; I did not want him to be 'sugary,' or to affect a Renanesque benevolence and calm which were obviously foreign to his character. But I did hope to see him write real tragedy, and not return to the bastard genre of the Naturalistes who mingle satire and tragedy, and produce something wholly false; I hoped to see his characters emerge into a clearer air from the sordid arena in which they were subdued by Fate in a débris of decayed vegetables and putrid exhalations.

Clearly I hoped the wrong thing. *Ulysses* is more bitter, more sordid, more ferociously satirical than anything Mr. Joyce has yet written. It is a tremendous libel on humanity which I at least am not clever enough to refute, but which I am convinced is a libel. There is laughter in *Ulysses*, but it is a harsh, sneering kind, very different from the *gros rire* of Rabelais. . . .

[Another long digression, on the subject that man is not as debased as Joyce says, nor does postwar man deserve such debasement in his literature.]

. . . I say, moreover that when Mr. Joyce, with his marvellous gifts, uses them to disgust us with mankind, he is doing something which is false and a libel on humanity.

That is my opinion of Mr. Joyce's *Ulysses*. From the point of view of art there is some justification for Mr. Joyce; he has succeeded in writing a most remarkable book; but from the point of view of human life I am sure he is wrong. Moreover, the style of *Ulysses*, which Mr. Joyce usually handles successfully, will be as deplorably false in his imitators as his philosophy. *Ulysses* is a gigantic soliloquy. . . .

[Another digression on contemporary prose styles.]

I have not wandered from Mr. Joyce. His influence, which I dare to prophesy will be considerable, cannot be a wholly good one. He is disgusting with a reason; others will be disgusting without reason. He is obscure and justifies his obscurity; but how many others will write mere confusion and think it sublime? How many dire absurdities will be brought forth, with *Ulysses* as midwife? Mr. Joyce himself is little influenced by his contemporaries, though he is obviously steeped in Church writers, the classics and French literature. He has read the Russians perhaps more than is good for him. But he is not one of those superficial people who pick up some shallow artifice as the canon of a new form of art; he will be the prey of coteries, but he himself is far above them. . . . The young writer should not neglect his contemporaries, but his chief companions ought to be the classics. *Ulysses* is dangerous reading for anyone whose style is unformed. If I had a younger friend who wanted to write, and would accept my advice, I would conceal from him the works of Mr. Joyce and set him on Pascal and Voltaire, with Mr. George Moore and Flaubert as light reading.

And when he knew the value of clarity, sobriety, precision—the good manners of literature—I would hand him Mr. Joyce's books with the highest eulogy and little fear of the consequences.

94. Shaw's reaction to the *Ulysses* prospectus

1921

Letter to Sylvia Beach (11 June 1921). This famous letter can be found in the following: Sylvia Beach, *Shakespeare and Company* (1959), p. 52, a translation of the letter which had appeared in the *Mercure de France*, xxxix (May 1950), 23; David Dempsey, 'G.B.S. on Joyce, Joyce on G.B.S.' *New York Times Book Review* (23 July 1950), 8, with four sentences missing; William Hull, 'Shaw on the Joyce he Scarcely Read', *Shaw Bulletin*, i (September 1954), 17; William White, 'Irish Antithesis: Shaw and Joyce', *Shavian*, ii, No. 3 (February 1961), 28–9 and note 6 (from which the present text is taken), also in Joyce, *Letters*, Volume III, edited by Richard Ellmann, p. 50.

Dear Madam,

I have read several fragments of *Ulysses* in its serial form. It is a revolting record of a disgusting phase of civilisation; but it is a truthful one; and I should like to put a cordon round Dublin; round up every male person in it between the ages of 15 and 30; force them to read it; and ask them whether on reflection they could see anything amusing in all that foul mouthed, foul minded derision and obscenity. To you, possibly, it may appeal as art: you are probably (you see I don't know you) a young barbarian beglamoured by the excitements and enthusiasms that art stirs up in passionate material; but to me it is all hideously real: I have walked those streets and know those shops and have heard and taken part in those conversations. I escaped from them to England at the age of twenty; and forty years later have learnt from the books of Mr. Joyce that Dublin is still what it was, and young men are still drivelling in slackjawed blackguardism just as they were in 1870. It is, however, some consolation to find that at last somebody has felt deeply enough about it to face the horror of writing it all down and using his literary genius to force people to face it. In Ireland they try to make a cat cleanly by rubbing its nose in its own filth. Mr. Joyce has tried the same treatment on the human subject. I hope it may prove successful.

I am aware that there are other qualities and other passages in *Ulysses*; but they do not call for any special comment from me.

I must add, as the prospectus implies an invitation to purchase, that I am an elderly Irish gentleman, and that if you imagine that any Irishman, much less an elderly one, would pay 150 francs for a book, you little know my countrymen.

ULYSSES: REVIEWS

95. Review, *Daily Express*

1922

S. P. B. Mais, 'An Irish Revel: And Some Flappers', *Daily Express* (25 March 1922), n.p.

A few days ago Mr. Gilbert Cannan warned us on this page that the modern novelist's function was to 'follow life to places and recesses in the human soul and heart inaccessible to the camera.'

Mr. James Joyce, an Irish novelist to whom no one would deny originality, has followed it in *Ulysses* . . . to recesses which few of us altogether care to probe. It is significant that most of the younger writers defy conventional reticences in so far as they describe all that most of us do and say. Mr. Joyce goes much further: from his pages there leap out at us all our most secret and most unsavoury private thoughts. Our first impression is that of sheer disgust, our second of irritability because we never know whether a character is speaking or merely thinking, our third of boredom at the continual harping on obscenities (nothing cloys a reader's appetite so quickly as dirt); our fourth, of real interest at watching the vagaries of a mind sensitive to all scents and sounds and colours. But art (if this is art) consists no longer in selection . . . Reading Mr. Joyce is like making an excursion into Bolshevist Russia: all standards go by the board: reading Mr. Coleridge's excellent selections [in *Letters to my Grandson on the Glory of English Prose*, by Stephen Coleridge] is to be soothed into sanity again and to be made aware of the necessity for putting up a fight to preserve the noble qualities of balance, rhythm, harmony, and reverence for simple majesty that have been for three centuries the glory of our written tongue. . . .

96. Review, *Sporting Times (Pink 'Un)*

1922

'Aramis', 'The Scandal of *Ulysses*', *Sporting Times*, No. 34 (1 April 1922), 4

After a rather boresome perusal of James Joyce's *Ulysses*, published in Paris for private subscribers at the rate of three guineas in francs, I can realise one reason at least for Puritan America's Society for the Prevention of Vice, and can understand why the Yankee judges fined the publishers of *The Little Review* one hundred dollars for the original publication of a very rancid chapter of the Joyce stuff, which appears to have been written by a perverted lunatic who has made a speciality of the literature of the latrine.

As readers of the *Pink 'Un* know, I have dealt appreciatively with many unconventional books in these pages; but I have no stomach for *Ulysses*, and do not care to expose my editor to the imminent risk of appearance in court for countenancing the unprintable. James Joyce is a writer of talent, but in *Ulysses* he has ruled out all the elementary decencies of life and dwells appreciatively on things that sniggering louts of schoolboys guffaw about. In addition to this stupid glorification of mere filth, the book suffers from being written in the manner of a demented George Meredith. There are whole chapters of it without any punctuation or other guide to what the writer is really getting at. Two-thirds of it is incoherent, and the passages that are plainly written are devoid of wit, displaying only a coarse salacrity intended for humour.

As the book has been boomed in the most extraordinary way, and as Mr. Joyce's admirers have acclaimed it as a work of supreme art, I will quote a few of the passages that are intelligible and moderately decent, just to show how tiresome the book is. The boredom does not arise from the comparative decency: the filthiest passages are just as dreary. The action of the book is mostly in Dublin, and a good deal of it occurs in a Dublin bar. Joyce must have had secret haunts of his own in the city by the Liffey, as I have never encountered such Boches as he introduces, even in the old days of Tyrone Street. The lowest demi-mondaines in Dublin—or, for that matter, in London, Glasgow or Cardiff—would be revolted by many things that Joyce writes of. As I have said, I can only quote a few isolated passages, which are almost colourless—for Joyce. Here is a conversation between two bronze-haired barmaids, Miss Douce and Miss Kennedy. I give it exactly as it is printed:

[quotes from the Sirens episode, p. 255, p. 259]

This is very difficult reading. It is all difficult reading. Miss Douce, it appears, has some particular trick with a piece of elastic which she only displays to her favourite swains—one is inclined to say swines. Such favoured ones are greasy Lenehan and Blazes Boylan, a wealthy lad in smart tan shoes:

[quotes from the Sirens episode, pp. 260, 261–2; pp. 265–6]

Joyce is more than a bit like that himself. Lenehan and Boylan are clean little cherubs compared with him.

In his more delicate moments James Joyce imitates George Moore and writes sentimentally about pale young girls and their underclothing:

[quotes without indicating omitted text from pp. 342–7, pp. 348–53, the Nausicaa episode]

The latter extract displays Joyce in a mood of kindergarten delicacy. The main contents of the book are enough to make a Hottentot sick. *Ulysses* would have been boycotted in the palmiest days of Holywell Street. And yet there are quite a number of the New York intelligentsia who declare that Joyce has written the best book in the world, and that *Ulysses* is the topmost of them.

Over the one supremely nauseous chapter that the publishers of *The Little Review* were indicted on, a great deal of highbrow nonsense was talked in court by the witnesses for the defence. Mr. Philip Moeller, in bland tones, said that the chapter was 'an unveiling of the subconscious mind in the Freudian manner, and that he saw no possibility of these revelations being aphrodisiac in their influence.'

The court gasped, and one of the judges protested: 'Here, here, you might as well talk Russian. Speak plain English if you want us to understand what you're saying.'

Moeller was then asked what he thought would be the effect of the objectionable chapter on the mind of the average reader. The suave and lofty littérateur replied: 'I think it would mystify him.'

I fancy that it would also have the very simple effect of an ordinary emetic. *Ulysses* is not alone sordidly pornographic, but it is intensely dull. As the volume is about the size of the *London Directory*, I do not envy anyone who reads it for pleasure.

97. Unsigned review, *Evening News*

8 April 1922, 4

This review, 'A New *Ulysses*', is part of the column 'Diary of a Man about Town'.

Copies have just arrived in London from Paris of the new book *Ulysses* by the Irish novelist, James Joyce, whom, ever since his *Dubliners* and *A Portrait of the Artist as a Young Man*, it has been the fashion of enthusiastic youth to dub the peer of Swift, Smollett, and Fielding.

This *Ulysses*, which has nothing at all to do with Homer, is not ('happily' a good many of us will say) generally on sale. The volume is to be had by those who take the trouble to seek it out for about £3 10s., and most of those who are troubling to seek it out are buying it as an investment—they flatter themselves that a first edition of this remarkable author will bring them a handsome profit within a few years.

The book itself in its blue paper cover looks at first glance like nothing so much as a telephone directory. It contains 730 pages—all about the doings, within 24 hours, of two Dublin journalists, Stephen Dedalus and Leopold Bloom. Bloom 'Ulysses' and Dedalus 'Telemachus.'

The modern author, like Homer, does not fail to take his hero to Circe's isle—hence the trouble in New York when the *Little Review* published extracts.

Mr. Joyce is as cruel and unflinching in respect to poor humanity as Zola. His style is in the new fashionable kinematographic vein, very jerky and elliptical.

Mr. Joyce was born in 1882 in Dublin; he has lived in Zürich, Trieste, and Rome; and now has settled down with his family in Paris.

His *Portrait of the Artist* was published during the war. No one who read it will forget such mordant pages as the family quarrel between the Parnellites and the anti-Parnellites—one of the best things in Irish literature. Mr. Joyce is, politically, an Independent.

Ulysses is published by an American woman, Miss Sylvia Beach, whose shop, 'Shakespeare and Co.,' in the Rue de L'Odéon is a great resort of the younger literary folk.

It seems a pity that Mr. Joyce, who might be a universally admired writer, restricts the appeal of his work by so many Zolaesque expressions, which are, to say the least, disfiguring.

98. John M. Murry, review, *Nation & Athenæum*

22 April 1922, xxxi, 124–5

The cant phrase of judgment upon Mr. Joyce's *magnum opus* has been launched by a French critic. 'With this book,' says M. Valéry Larbaud, 'Ireland makes a sensational re-entrance into high European literature.' [See No. 118.] Whether anyone, even M. Larbaud himself, knows what is meant by the last three words, we cannot tell. A phrase does not have to be intelligible in order to succeed, and we already hear echoes of this pronouncement. *Ulysses* somehow is European; everything else is not.

Well, well. *Ulysses* is many things: it is very big, it is hard to read, difficult to procure, unlike any other book that has been written, extraordinarily interesting to those who have patience (and they need it), the work of an intensely serious man. But European? That, we should have thought, is the last epithet to apply to it. Indeed, in trying to define it, we return again and again, no matter by what road we set out, to the conception that it is non-European. It is not the less important for that. *The Brothers Karamazov*, for instance, is not European; and, precisely because of the non-European elements which it contains, it is a mighty work. And *Ulysses* is, perhaps, even less European than *Karamazov*.

[The critic here establishes what a 'European' work is: an artistic acknowledgement of and submission to the social tradition of Europe.]

Mr. Joyce does none of these things. He is the extreme individualist. He acknowledges no social morality, and he completely rejects the claim of social morality to determine what he shall, or shall not, write. He is the egocentric rebel *in excelsis*, the arch-esoteric. European! He is the man with the bomb who would blow what remains of Europe into the sky. But he is so individual that very few people will know when the bomb has exploded. His intention, so far as he has any social intention, is completely anarchic. But in order to be a successful anarchist you must work within the comprehension of society. You have to use the time-tables and the language of ordinary men. By the excess of his anarchy, Mr. Joyce makes himself socially harmless. There is not the faintest need to be concerned about his influence. He will have some, no doubt; but it will be canalized and concentrated. The head that is strong enough to read *Ulysses* will not be turned by it.

Upon such a head, indeed, the influence of *Ulysses* may be wholly excellent. For the driving impulse of this remarkable book is an immense, an unprecedented, liberation of suppressions . . . *Ulysses* is, fundamentally (though it is much besides), an immense, a prodigious self-laceration, the tearing-away from himself, by a half-demented man of genius, of inhibitions and limitations which have grown to be flesh of his flesh. And those who read it will profit by the vicarious sacrifice.

But limitations and inhibitions are necessary to the European. Not, indeed, the extraordinary ones which oppressed the author of *Ulysses*, the explosiveness of whose anarchy is in direct proportion to the closeness of the constraint, but some. The best European is the one who bears his restrictions with the best grace, as recognizing their necessity. Mr. Joyce's book will possibly serve others as an indication of the limits they must not pass. It may help them to free themselves of inhibitions which are really destructive of vitality, and, at the same time, make it easier for them to accept those which are the conditions of civilization, and perhaps of art itself. For just as Mr. Joyce is in rebellion against the social morality of civilization, he is in rebellion against the lucidity and comprehensibility of civilized art. . . . Still, if we ask the essential question: Is *Ulysses* a reflection of life through an individual consciousness, there can be no doubt of the reply. It is. It is a reflection of life through a singularly complex consciousness; and this reflection is concentrated and crystallized into a day of the existence of three human beings: Stephen Dedalus (the hero of *The Portrait of the Artist as a Young Man*), Leopold Bloom, a Hungarian Jew by descent, now an advertisement canvasser in Dublin, and Bloom's wife, Marion. One might almost say that all the thoughts and all the experiences of those beings, real or imaginary, from their waking to their sleeping on a spring day in Dublin in 1904, are somehow given by Mr. Joyce: and not only the conscious thoughts—and they are very differently conscious—but the very fringe of their sentience . . . This transcendental buffoonery, this sudden uprush of the *vis comica* into a world wherein the tragic incompatibility of the practical and the instinctive is embodied, is a very great achievement. It is the vital centre of Mr. Joyce's book, and the intensity of life which it contains is sufficient to animate the whole of it.

And much of it needs animation. The curse of nimiety, of too-muchness, hangs over it as a whole. Mr. Joyce has made a superhuman effort to empty the whole of his consciousness into it . . . In one of his sections he goes so far as to put his narrative in the form of successive parodies of English prose, from the Anglo-Saxon chronicles to the latest American slang. Every trick that a keen-witted man could conceivably play with the English language, and some that were inconceivable until Mr. Joyce arrived, is played somewhere in his book. Every thought that a super-subtle modern can think seems to be hidden somewhere in its inspissated obscurities. We have done our utmost during the best part of a fortnight to master *Ulysses*, yet even now we should hesitate to say that we understand—in the sense of understanding not merely the thing said, but the motive of its being said—more than four-fifths of it.

It may, therefore, be said that our negative judgments are only provisional, and that fuller illumination would make the dark places clear. Possibly. But we cannot spend our life with *Ulysses*. . . . Again and again in *Ulysses* we lose the circumstance in the circumstantiality. Had it been half the size it might have been twice as big. But then Mr. Joyce might not have been able to give rein to all his inhibitions.

That purpose, we repeat, seems to have determined Mr. Joyce's creation. *Ulysses* has form, a subtle form, but the form is not strong enough to resist overloading, not sufficient to prevent Mr. Joyce from being the victim of his own anarchy. One cannot be too conservative in one's methods of proclaiming the 'Weltvernichtungsidee.' Mr. Joyce should ride his genius like a hippogriff. If he bitted it with a chain-cable it would still be a tremendous steed—but not a European one. That never!

Whether the day of the European is over is another question.

99. Holbrook Jackson, review, *To-Day*

June 1922, ix, 47–9

'Ulysses à la Joyce.' Also appeared in *Bruno's Review of Two Worlds* (New York), ii, No. 4 (July–August 1922), 37–38, and as *Ulysses à la Joyce* (1961), 12 pp.

Mr. James Joyce's *Ulysses* is an affront and an achievement. It is not indecent. There is not a salacious line in it. It is simply naked: naked and unconscious of shame. Some of those who have read the novel either in the *Little Review* or in its present volume form have considered it immoral. They are wrong. It is neither moral nor immoral. Mr. Joyce writes, not as though morals had never existed, but as one who deliberately ignores moral codes and conventions. Such frankness as his would have been impossible if such frankness had not been forbidden. Everything that is never done or never mentioned is done and said by him. Compared with Joyce, Zola is respectable and George Moore merely mincing. He is the first unromantic writer of fiction, for, after all, the Realists were only Romantics striving to free themselves from Medievalism. . . .

He is not even out to amuse, like George Moore and the story-tellers, or to criticise, like Meredith, or satirise, like Swift. He simply records like Homer, or, indeed, Froissart.

The attitude has its dangers. Mr. Joyce has faced them, or, rather, ignored them. He has been perfectly logical. He has recorded everything—everything in a single day of the life of an uninteresting and, to me, unpleasant, and, if we forget the parable of the sparrows, negligible human being. This modern Ulysses is one Bloom, the Irish-Jewish advertisement canvasser of a Dublin newspaper. To read the novel is to spend a full day in the company of this person from the time he rises in the morning and gives his wife breakfast in bed to the time of retiring to his bed late at night, whither his wife has already preceded him. You spend no ordinary day in his company; it is a day of the most embarrassing intimacy. You live with him minute by minute; go with him everywhere, physically and mentally; you are made privy to his thoughts and emotions; you are introduced to his friends and enemies; you learn what he thinks of each, every action and reaction of his psychology is laid bare with Freudian nastiness until you know his whole life through and through; know him, in fact, better than you know any other being in art or life—and detest him heartily. The creation of Bloom is an achievement of genius. . . . You do not feel grateful to Mr. Joyce for the introduction [of Bloom]. It is not clear why he troubled to introduce him. At times I could not help feeling that the object was not so objectless as I had believed. Is *Ulysses* a stone flung at humanity—is Bloom the Twentieth Century Yahoo? . . . an ungainly, loose-limbed book which falls to pieces as you read it—as, indeed, you do. The very format of the book is an affront. Bloom could have been drawn effectively in a quarter the words. There are the deadliest of Dead Seas in this ocean of prose. You get becalmed in them—bored, drowsed, bewildered. And there are gulfs and bays which are muddy and noisome with the sewage of civilisation. On the other hand there are wide stretches of magnificent prose even when it is made up of unsavoury ingredients. Mr. James Joyce can write.

But the greatest affront of all is the arrangement of the book, *Ulysses* is a chaos. All the conventions of organised prose which have grown with our race and out of our racial consciousness which have been reverently handed on by the masters with such improvements as they have been able to make, have been cast aside as so much dross. Quotation marks for conversational passages are omitted; punctuation follows new and unknown rules; sentences begin and forget to end; chapters have no apparent relation to one another, and neither numbers nor titles; and one chapter, the last, runs to 42 pages (25,000 words) with not a single punctuation of any kind, and where the enormous stretches of type are condescendingly broken into occasional paragraphs, no capitals are used. Mr. Joyce evidently believes in making it difficult for his readers—but perhaps he wants to scare them away. I am bound to admit, however, that this chapter, perhaps the best in the book, and one of the most disgusting, is by no means so difficult to read as one might expect.

This absence of the ordinary guide-posts of literature injures author as well as reader, for one may fairly assume that the author has something to say to his reader or he would not go to the trouble of writing and printing his work. He knows also that he is saying it in a new way. It seems gratuitous to put unnecessary difficulties in the way of a proper understanding of his message, story or record. For instance, much of the action of *Ulysses* is sub-conscious. Innumerable passages, and often whole pages together, record inward mental impressions, reactions from some external happening—a word, a sight of thing or person, a smell, a sound,—no hint or guide is given as to where these interpolations begin or end. They run on without warning from the known and familiar to the unknown and strange, on the assumption that the reader is as well-informed on the subject as James Joyce. The result is that the reader is continually losing his way and having to retrace his steps. *Ulysses* is like a country without roads. But it is a novel, and if it will not amuse the idle novel reader, or even attract the lewd by its unsavoury franknesses, it must claim the attention of those who look upon fiction as something more than confectionery. With all its faults, it is the biggest event in the history of the English novel since *Jude*.

100. Review, *Dublin Review*

September 1922, clxxi, 112–19

'Domini Canis' (Shane Leslie), '*Ulysses*'.

Since a leading French critic [Valéry Larbaud] has announced that with Mr. James Joyce's *Ulysses* 'Ireland makes a sensational re-entrance into high European literature,' and since reputable English guides like Mr. Middleton Murry and Mr. Arnold Bennett [See Nos. 98, 106] seem to be wandering in his track, and since the entire setting of this book is Catholic Dublin, and since the seven hundred pages contain a fearful travesty on persons, happenings and intimate life of the most morbid and sickening description, we say not only for the *Dublin Review* but for Dublin *écrasez l'infâme*!

The Irish literary movement may have arisen in the bogs of Aran and Mayo, but it is not going to find its stifling climax in a French sink. The vain folk who speak of this book as the greatest English writing since Shakespeare may take what attitude they like concerning English literature, but as for *Ulysses* being a great creation of the Irish Celt, a Cuchulain of the sewer even, or an Ossian of obscenity, it may safely be repudiated, before reading, by the Irish people, who certainly do not get either the rulers or writers they deserve. The bulk of this enormous book is quite unquotable and we hope that, as the edition is limited and the price is rapidly ascending in the 'curious' market, it will remain out of the reach of the bulk of the author's fellow-countrymen. We are prepared to do justice to the power and litheness of the style, when intelligible, to the occasional beauty of a paragraph and to the adventurous headlong experiments in new literary form, but as a whole we regard it as the screed of one possessed; a commoner complaint than is generally realized in these days, but one seldom taking a literary channel of expression. Samuel Butler bitterly, but truly, said that God had written all the books, meaning no doubt that he would like to see what the devil had to say for himself. That opportunity has been now afforded, and we must say that Mr. Joyce has rather added than otherwise to the sorrows of Satan. . . . In this work the spiritually offensive and the physically unclean are united. We speak advisedly when we say that though no formal condemnation has been pronounced, the Inquisition can only require its destruction or, at least, its removal from Catholic houses. Without grave reason or indeed the knowledge of the Ordinary no Catholic publicist can even afford to be possessed of a copy of this book, for in its reading lies not only the description but the commission of sin against the Holy Ghost. Having tasted and rejected the devilish drench, we most earnestly hope that this book be not only placed on the *Index Expurgatorius*, but that its reading and communication be made a reserved case. . . . The theme of the book may be stated, ridiculous as it is. It covers to the extent of half a million of words the experiences and current thoughts, acts, idiocies and natural intimacies of a pupil of Clongowes School during twenty-four hours of mortal life in Dublin. The day consists of the preparation for breakfast, the bath, attendance at a Glasnevin funeral, some hours in the advertising department of the *Freeman's Journal*, lunch in a Dublin eating-house, a visit to the National Library with an interesting Shakespearean discussion, a concert in the Ormond Hotel, an altercation in a public house, a car-drive, a scene in the Women's Hospital and the birth of a child, a visit to a house of ill-fame in Tyrone Street, followed by a brawl, a visit to a cabman's shelter, and finally a very horrible dissection of a very horrible woman's thought. There is also an account of the Black Mass to which the *vis comica* and the *vis diabolica* have contributed in equal quantities.

As for the vaunted new experimentation in literary forms, we doubt if the present generation is likely to adopt them by writing, for instance, forty-two pages without a capital or a stop, or by abandoning all reasoned sequence of thought and throwing the flash and flow of every discordant, flippant, allusive or crazy suggestiveness upon paper without grammar and generally without sense. Of course, when the allusion can be caught, and the language is restrained, the effect can be striking and even beautiful, but how few of such passages can be meshed in the dreary muck-ridden tide. We will give the devil his due and appreciate the idyll of Father Conmee, S.J., who with most people mentioned in the course of the book, is really a Dubliner. Many pages are saturated with Catholic lore and citation, which must tend to make the book more or less unintelligible to critics, who are neither of Catholic or Dublin origin. Nothing could be more ridiculous than the youthful dilettantes in Paris or London who profess knowledge and understanding of a work which is often mercifully obscure even to the Dublin-bred. . . .

Reading a textbook and boiling it down into lists is no new device and depends for its success on the eliminating touch with which Mr. Joyce is most inartistically unendowed. In fact, the reader in struggling from oasis to oasis will find himself caught in a Sahara that is as dry as it is stinking. It is only when he varies his cataloguing with rare or new words that he is endurable, as of the Dublin vegetable market:

[quotes from the Cyclops episode, p. 289, p. 294]

This may, or may not, be literature. It is certainly good cataloguing, but fifty pages have to be squeezed to find a like passage, so that the reader need not expect to be sustained by a genuine spate of words, wherever he dips. . . . The parody of a Celtic Saga is pleasanter, and winds up with an amusing caricature of the national facility for tracing Irish blood in so many of the great ones of the world. The hero is thus approximated in Ossianic style:

[quotes from the Cyclops episode, p. 291, p. 296]

His method of allusion is something between Pelmanism and morbid psycho-analysis. Outside the obsession of sex it is sometimes intelligible. . . . The Dublin causerie about Shakespeare, 'the chap that writes like Synge,' is a real reflection of the best in Irish circles, especially when John Eglinton commands the floor:

[quotes from the Scylla and Charybdis episode, p. 202, pp. 204–5]

. . . And the seaweed in Dublin Bay brings a reminiscence from the Fathers so perfect that we lament the ocean of inferior writing which surrounds it all the more:

[quotes from the Proteus episode, p. 50, p. 49]

. . . We have made these quotations to save anyone the trouble of poring over a volume in which such are scarce rarities. We do not think it worth while to bolt the mud in the sieve to find an occasional phrase like 'Agenbite of inwit' for conscience, 'turlehide whales,' 'dykedropt,' 'antelucan hour,' 'chryselephantine papal standard.' Our search was cursory and we have tried to do justice to this abomination of desolation. By doing so we hope we have quenched the curiosity of the *literati* and *dilettanti*. As for the general reader, it is, as it were, so much rotten caviare, and the public is in no particular danger of understanding or being corrupted thereby. Doubtless this book was intended to make angels weep and to amuse fiends, but we are not sure that 'those embattled angels of the Church, Michael's host,' will not laugh aloud to see the failure of this frustrated Titan as he revolves and splutters hopelessly under the flood of his own vomit.

101. Reaction to a review

1922

C. C. Martindale, S. J., '*Ulysses*', *Dublin Review*, clxxi (1922), 273–6.

When we read *Ulysses*, reviewed in the last issue of the *Dublin*, we were haunted by a puzzle on which the reviewer did not touch. Why, we asked ourselves, is the whole method of this book wrong? What is its interior untruth which vitiates its art far more radically than the surface faults so easy to discern? At last an early Futurist exhibition occurred to us, and the reason why we had disapproved it. Those artists did not, of course, claim to reproduce what they knew their subject to be, but all that in any way it set stirring in their mind.

[The critic discusses the lack of 'Form' in Futurist painting.]

. . . But in the Futurist painting you had no idea of what the next ripple in the painter's impressions might be or not be; not only in the picture there was no 'whole,' but you were quite unable to surmise a future Whole, and so you felt as mad as the picture looked.

Mr. Joyce is guilty of both these atrocities, in words instead of paint. He goes down to that level where seething instinct is not yet illuminated by intellect, or only just enough to be not quite invisible. . . . Great tracts of his enormous book consist of a man's stuff-for-thought—not thoughts—blindly plunging forward through the space of a day. Hence the elimination of stops—the unfinished sentences—the sentences with half of the next sentence inserted in the midst; the mixture of styles, of languages. Hence the refusal to reject anything that instinct, by action or reaction, may supply. He has plunged below the level where ideas shine, energize, select, construct. . . Well, Mr Joyce gets as far down as he can to this level of animality which exists, of course, as an ultimate in every man, and then, consciously and by art, tries to reproduce it. And this requires the most strong mental effort. For he has to *hold together* what yet must somehow *remain* incoherent; never to forget what the conscious memory has never been in possession of; to put into the impressions of the evening all that the morning held but was never known to hold, and to put it there, not in the shape in which morning offered it, but in the shape into which noon and all the hours between have distorted it. Thus the author, by a visibly violent effort of memory and intelligence, had to show us what essentially was never consciously known, still less remembered. Hence an angry sense of contradiction in the reader. Mr. Joyce is trying to think *as if* he were insane.

Again, since he introduces several characters and seeks to show the sort of instinctive reaction they severally experience on the same event, he has to present the simultaneous consecutively. But neither paint nor words can thus convey, by means of a series, the simultaneous. We do not even float equably down the dim disgusting sewer, but continually find ourselves hitched back, with a jerk, to where we started from. Hence a new impression of desperate nightmare.

Mr. Joyce would therefore seem not only to have tried to achieve a psychological impossibility but to have tried to do so in what would, anyhow, have been the wrong medium. He would most nearly have succeeded by using music, and counterpoint. . . .

However, we did, in reading, collect one impression: that is, that in calling his book, and in a sense his hero, *Ulysses*, Mr. Joyce meant to portray in him that 'No Man' who yet is 'Everyman,' just because Mr. Joyce considers he has got down to the universal substratum in man which yet cannot be identified with any man in particular. We surmise, too, that there is a deal of Ulysses-symbolism running through the book; but we were not nearly interested enough to try to work it out. But what we object to is this: if that 'ultimate,' that human Abyss, is to be seen at all, described at all, *some* light some intellectual energy, must have played upon it. But here it is most certainly not the Spirit of the Creator that has so played. What black fires may not the Ape of God light up? Into what insane caricatures of humanity may not the Unholy Ghost, plunging gustily upon animal instinct, fashion it? This book suggests an answer. At best the author's eyes are like the slit eyes of Ibsen's Trolls. They see, but they omit what is best worth seeing; they see, but they see all things crooked. Take a concrete instance: Mr. Joyce has, in this book too, the offensive habit of introducing real people by name. We know some of them. One such person (now dead, it is true) we knew well enough to see that Mr. Joyce, who describes him in no unfriendly way, yet cannot *see*. We absolve him of wilful calumny.

But we realize that he is at least more likely than not to have a mis-seen not only one person, but whole places, like Dublin, or Clongowes; whole categories, like students; whole literatures, like the Irish, or the Latin.

Alas, then, that a man who can write such exquisite prose-music when he chooses, who has so much erudition, such power of original criticism, such subtlety of intuition, and of construction, and the possibility of mental energy so long-continued, should either by preference or because by now he cannot help it, immerse his mind into the hateful dreams of drunkenness, the phantom-world of the neuropath; should be best when he portrays collapse; should be at his most convincing in his chosen line when murmuring through half a hundred pages the dream-memories of an uneducated woman.

102. Shane Leslie, review, *Quarterly Review*

1922

Extract from Shane Leslie, '*Ulysses*', *Quarterly Review*, ccxxxviii (October 1922), 219–34.

. . . When a massive volume, whose resemblance in size and colour to the *London Telephone Book* must make it a danger to the unsuspecting, is written by a well-known Dublin author, printed at Dijon, and published in Paris at an excessive price, it is liable to escape the dignity of general notice unless for particular reasons. *Ulysses*, however, has achieved the success of a scandal behind the scenes. In the first place, it has been brought out in a limited edition, and in the second the author has passed all limits of restraint or convention. . . . For while it contains some gruesome and realistic pictures of low life in Dublin, which would duly form part of the sociological history of the Irish capital, it also contains passages fantastically opposed to all ideas of good taste and morality.

SHANE LESLIE, REVIEW, *Quarterly Review* 1922

As a whole, the book must remain impossible to read, and in general undesirable to quote. It is possible for the fairly intelligent to fail to obtain any intelligible glimmer even from a prolonged perusal. It is an Odyssey no doubt; but divided into twenty-four hours instead of books. Apparently anything that can happen, every thought that might occur to the mind, and anything that could be said in conversation during a twenty-four hours of Dublin life, has been crowded upon this colossal canvas; and yet the conscious conscientiousness required in trying to secure and enscroll for ever a day out of the past, down to its lowest detail and most remote allusion, has failed, as the Tower of Babel failed, of very topheaviness as well as of antitheistic endeavour, and the writer ceases to be comprehensible, possibly even to himself. Of whole passages he can only feel as Browning did of some of his verses that however well God may have known their meaning the writer, at least, had forgotten. To a fair bulk of *Ulysses* no adequate meaning can be attached at first reading, and for this reason the book, which is an assault upon Divine Decency as well as on human intelligence, will fail of its purpose, if purpose it has to grip and corrupt either the reading public or the impressionable race of contemporary scribes.

Our own opinion is that a gigantic effort has been made to fool the world of readers and even the Pretorian guard of critics. Of the latter a number have fallen both in France and England, and the greatness of their fall has been in proportion to their inability to understand what perhaps they cannot have been intended to understand. For the well-meaning but open-mouthed critics in France, who have seriously accepted *Ulysses* as a pendant to Shakespeare and as Ireland's contribution to the modern world's reading, we can only feel sympathy. It is vain to say that in *Ulysses* '*maius nascitur Iliade.*' The great name of Ulysses is horribly profaned. We have only an Odyssey of the sewer.... Here we shall not be far wrong if we describe Mr Joyce's work as literary Bolshevism. It is experimental, anti-conventional, anti-Christian, chaotic, totally unmoral. And it is no less liable to prove the entangling shroud of its author. From it he can never escape. We can well believe that Mr Joyce has put the best years of his life into its pages, toiling during the world's toil and refusing to collapse with the collapse of civilisation. The genius and literary ability of the author of the *Portrait of the Artist as a Young Man* have always been apparent. They have since been remorselessly pressed and driven into the soul-destroying work of writing entire pages, which alienists might only attribute to one cause. Over half a million words crowd the disconcerting paginal result, for the form and scale of which 'Balzacian' and 'Zolaesque' would be appropriate but insufficient epithets. But in the matter of psychology or realism Balzac is beggared and Zola bankrupted. . . . And all this effort has been made, not to make any profound revelation or to deliver a literary message, but to bless the wondering world with an accurate account of one day and one night passed by the author in Dublin's fair City, Lord Dudley being Viceroy (the account of his driving through the streets of Dublin is probably one of the few passages intelligible to the ordinary English reader). The selected day and night are divided into the following series of episodes, if we may quote what appears to be a summary given towards the close of the book:

the preparation of breakfast, intestinal congestion, the bath, the funeral, the advertisement of Alexander Keyes, the unsubstantial lunch, the visit to Museum and National Library, the book-hunt along Bedford Row, Merchants' Arch, Wellington Quay, the music in the Ormond Hotel, the altercation with a truculent troglodyte in Bernard Keiran's premises, a blank period of time including a car-drive, a visit to a house of mourning, a leave-taking, . . . the prolonged delivery of Mrs Nina Purefoy, the visit to a disorderly house . . . and subsequent brawl and chance medley in Beaver Street, nocturnal perambulation to and from the cabman's shelter, Butt Bridge.

The advertisement of Alexander Keyes covers a chapter, tedious beyond recapitulation, in the office of the *Freeman's Journal.* The visit to the National Library expands into a Shakespearean discussion.

The thesis reads like that of a novel from the Mud and Purple school of Dublin novelists, who prefer to lay emphasis on the second adjective in the familiar phrase 'dear dirty Dublin.' . . .

[Here the critic digresses on the Irish Literary Renaissance, concluding with the statement that Synge's was 'real literature'.]

. . . Not so his influence, which can be detected in *Ulysses.* One whole chapter describing a Lying-in Hospital in Dublin and the birth of a child is written not in mock-Elizabethan, but in the pseudo-style of English and Norse Saga which William Morris affected. What is the following, then? . . .

[quotes from the Oxen of the Sun episode, p. 379, pp. 385–6]

. . . Reams of such-like follow, to ring even falser when the Dublin medical students eat sardines and drink whisky thus, . . .

[quotes from the same episode, p. 381, p. 387]

SHANE LESLIE, REVIEW, *Quarterly Review* 1922

In this curious jargon the most modern questions in medico-eugenics are discussed. The mediaeval view against restriction of the race finds mediaeval expression and almost beautiful form in the words,

> Murmur, Sirs, is eke oft among layfolk. Both babe and parent now glorify their Maker, the one in limbo gloom the other in purge fire. But gramercy, what of those God-possibled souls that we nightly impossibilise, which is the sin against the Holy Ghost, Very God, Lord and Giver of Life.'

The language becomes interesting as the chart of Astrology is set in the heavens . . .

[quotes from the same episode, p. 407, p. 414]

. . . Parody is so discernible in the book that of itself it should convince the reader that a gigantic joke has been played on the French, English and Irish public, and, except for the last-named, with fair success. The French and many of the English have taken it seriously. From Dublin as yet we have only heard jocular contempt. Dublin has had a way, however, of rejecting her best writers as well as her politicians; her prophets and her procurers.

The Catholic reader will close the volume at the parodies of the Creed and of the Litany of the Virgin; the Puritan will resent even an adaptation of the *Pilgrim's Progress*, though outside the book it does not read too ill, . . .

[quotes from the same episode, p. 389, p. 395]

. . . The writer has little care for the *sacra* of Catholic or Protestant Christianity. . . The practice of introducing the names of real people into circumstances of monstrous and ludicrous fiction seems to us to touch the lowest depth of Rabelaisian realism. When we are given the details of the skin disease of an Irish peer, famous for his benefactions, we feel a genuine dislike of the writer. There are some things which cannot and, we should like to be able to say, shall not be done.

From any Christian point of view this book must be proclaimed anathema, simply because it tries to pour ridicule on the most sacred themes and characters in what has been the religion of Europe for nearly two thousand years. And this is the book which ignorant French critics hail as the proof of Ireland's re-entry into European literature! . . . Certainly, it takes a Dubliner to pick out the familiar names and allusions of twenty years ago, though the references to men who have become as important as Arthur Griffith assume a more universal hearing. And we are sorry to say that it would take a theologian, even

Jesuit, to understand all the theological references. . . . Mr Joyce's method of allusion, cross-reminiscence and thought-sequence makes most of the book tediously obscure and irrelevantly trivial. He simply dots down whatever succession of thoughts might occur to his mind in certain circumstances. Sometimes the reader catches a flash as in the allusion . . . 'white teeth with gold points. Chrysostomos' . . . A discussion about the Jews leads to the corollary that the reason why Ireland never persecuted them was because she never let them in; . . . Such pictures as can be rescued from the *cloaca* are distinct and sometimes unforgettable. When the style is lucid and restrained, literature is the result in patches; but who can wade through the spate in order to pick out what little is at the same time intelligible and not unquotable?

We are led to make quotations because the confusion of the book is so great that there is no circumventing its clumsiness and unwinding its deliberate bamboozlement of the reader. With an occasional lucid bait the attention is gripped, and then the expectant eye is lost in incoherent fantasies. For sheer realism we have never read such a passage as the paragraphs describing the drowned man in Dublin Bay, and we add that they are unequalled elsewhere in the book. . . .

Through the mist of sexual analysis and psycho-unravelment we can only pass quickly for good. We are sorry that such stuff should have ever reached the dignity even of surreptitious print, and are glad that the limited copies and their exaggerated cost will continue to prevent the vast majority of the reading public from sampling even faintly such unpleasant ware. It will suffice for those who are interested, to know whether Mr Joyce has invented new styles of literature or written a book to be classed as a literary milestone with *Madame Bovary* or *Crime and Punishment*, to take a few more insights into Dublin life, the favoured subject of Mr Joyce's scalpel. . . .

[illustrates this point with a few passages]

. . . Mr Joyce's turn for epigram is keen. He probably looks upon it as an elephant-killer regards the pursuit of sparrows with peas. Here and there stray sayings reveal an ancient sense of humour quite apart from the terrible Comic Force which is his strongest weapon. We smile languidly when we hear that 'the Irishman's house is his coffin,' or that 'we haven't the chance of a snowball in hell,' unless maybe we go 'out of the frying pan of life into the fire of purgatory.' But these may all be second hand, and indeed epigrams can always be picked like blackberries in Dublin. . . .

SHANE LESLIE, REVIEW, *Quarterly Review* 1922

. . . We come back to our complaint that without form there cannot be art. Art must be logical, almost mathematical. Its material, its conditions, its effects must be calculable. Windiness, inconsequence and confusion argue the riot of Nature. We will make one more effort to understand the drift of James Joyce, and quote whole his outburst concerning water, which is a presumed parody of Whitman (and there must be two score other authors parodied in different parts of the book). Of water this apparently may be considered: . . .

[quotes extensively from the Ithaca episode, pp. 655–6, pp. 671–2]

. . . Well, that is that, one feels. Such is water, and there is enough and satisfyingly enough said. Time will show what place and influence *Ulysses* will take in the thought and script of men. In spite of a thin parallelism with the movement of the Odyssey, for the episodes of Circe, Æolus, Nausicaa, are visible amongst others less easily traceable, there has been an abandonment of form and a mad Shelleyan effort to extend the known confines of the English language. Pages without punctuation or paragraph show an attempt to beat up a sustained and overwhelming orchestral effect. French and possibly American critics will utter their chorus of praise in proportion to their failure to understand. English critics will be divided and remain in amicable but squabbling disagreement. Ireland's writers, whose own language was legislatively and slowly destroyed by England, will cynically contemplate an attempted Clerkenwell explosion in the well-guarded, well-built, classical prison of English literature. The bomb has exploded, and creeping round Grub Street we have picked up a few fragments by way of curiosity.

We have had some hesitation (bewilderment almost) in noticing *Ulysses* in the pages of the *Quarterly Review*, and would not have done so, had we thought that such notice would lead the prurient-minded to read the book. . . . The question before the critic of *Ulysses* is whether the literary power is a sufficiently extenuating circumstance. All that is unmentionable according to civilised standards has been brought to the light of day without any veil of decency. Our quotations, being chosen for their interest and decency, are intended to give a possible view of the author's literary ability, concerning which there may be as many views as critics. We believe that the cumbrousness of the style in which these things are revealed may prove their most effective screen from prying eyes, for the author has done his best to make his book unreadable and unquotable, and, we must add, unreviewable. . . .

103. George Rehm, review, *Chicago Tribune* (European edition)

13 February 1922, 2

Ulysses, long attended upon, waited for these several years with bated breath or hopeful curiosity has at last appeared.

What it will mean to the reader is a question. Too many are the possibilities of this human flesh when finally in contact with the crude, disgusting and unpalatable facts of our short existence. One thing to be thankful for is that the volume is in a limited edition, therefore suppressed to the stenographer or high school boy. But another thing to be thankful for is that it might be the precursor to a new understanding of the printed word, a new 'coup de grace' for the salacious prudishness of our present day conventions. Great harm can be done or great good will be done by *Ulysses*.

James Joyce, an Irishman, has been hailed as a genius by several of our truly capable cognoscenti. Generally, he has been condemned, both in Great Britain and the United States by the highly moral, but unperceiving element of Comstockery that reigns with iron hand, turning down an unkempt, sticky thumb on every gladiatorial attempt to break away from the suffocating restrictions laid down by its censorship.

Yet there are passages in *Ulysses* that force a murmur of approval from the most thoroughly ordered Christian—passages deep in their understanding, profound in their knowledge, sparkling in their expression. And then there are excerpts to cause the most ultra-modern brain to gasp and question the verity of eyesight.

All known borders encircling the hemisphere of literature have been traversed with a cynical grin tossed to wordly criticism. Religion, government, ideals, life and death, all are scathingly ridiculed. I am shocked, so will you be, but I am also disturbed to find I am so easily shocked. Bah! I know that Mrs. Bloom could only think within the narrow cycle depicted by Joyce. I know that Buck Mulligan with his blasphemy against religion and convention has existed for centuries and that Stephen, firmly seated on his erudite throne, will ever decry and curse the precepts and silly credo of this life and all that has been gleaned from its past. Then why be upset?

Actually it is the unaccustomed eye and not the calloused brain that takes exception to the crude black imprint of hitherto unknown type.

The theme of *Ulysses* might be outlined as the thoughts and reflections of a number of characters, some ordinary, some extraordinary, but all genuine. The rawness of expression, the employment of words chosen from the seamy, filthy side of our vocabulary, may seem without excuse, but it is true that the prized volumes of our latter-day geniuses are permitted to repose in honored manner on library shelves only by means of a subtler turning of word and phrase.

Similar thoughts, expressions and actions have long been placed before the public but in politer terms. Joyce has gone farther, raised these thoughts, expressions and actions to their true and sometimes nasty reality.

Where is the value? Better to wait a few generations. Give the Phillistine an opportunity to rise above his level or disappear. Allow worthy judges to pass sentence on such a work, be it masterpiece or rot, and so prevent the usual mauling and manhandling invariably accorded to a comparable production by our dearly beloved public.

In all events, it is fitting to extend congratulations to Shakespeare and company and Sylvia Beach for having finally published the book.

104. Sisley Huddleston, review, *Observer*

1922

'*Ulysses*', No. 6823 (5 March 1922), 4. Later appeared as part of an article in *Articles de Paris* (1928), pp. 41–7.

No book has never been more eagerly and curiously awaited by the strange little inner circle of book-lovers and littérateurs than James Joyce's *Ulysses*. It is folly to be afraid of uttering big words because big words are abused and have become almost empty of meaning in many mouths; and with all my courage I will repeat what a few folk in somewhat precious *cénacles* have been saying—that Mr. James Joyce is a man or genius. I believe the assertion to be strictly justified, though Mr. Joyce must remain, for special reasons, caviare to the general. I confess that I cannot see how the work upon which Mr. Joyce spent seven strenuous years, years of wrestling and of agony, can ever be given to the public.

What, it will be asked, is the good of a book which must be carefully locked up, which only a handful of people will read, and which will be found unspeakably shocking even by that little handful? But one must not talk about the utility, the wisdom, the necessity, of a work of art. It is enough to know that Mr. Joyce felt that he had to write *Ulysses*, and that accordingly he wrote *Ulysses*. Of his sincerity—the sincerity of an artist—there can be no doubt. I suppose he wants readers, but he is perfectly prepared to do without readers. An expurgated edition? Not if his labour were to be entirely lost would he consent to cancel half a line! He would rather that nothing were printed than that all were not printed. Personally I may consider him misguided; personally I might find much to write about the folly of a fixed idea. But one does not, one must not, argue with authors. Whatever virtue there is in Mr. Joyce, whatever value in his work, is there because he will listen to no advice and brook no impertinent discussions. You may like or you may dislike *Ulysses*, and you are entitled to express your opinion of its merits or demerits, but you are not entitled to demand that it should be other than it is; you are not entitled to dictate to Mr. Joyce what he should do. You have to take it or leave it. This is how he is. This is what he feels about the human comedy.

He makes the painter who plumes himself on putting in the warts exceedingly foolish and outmoded, for he paints not from the outside but from the inside. Obscenity? Yes. This is undoubtedly an obscene book; but that, says Mr. Joyce, is not his fault. If the thoughts of men and women are such as may be properly described as obscene then how can you show what life is unless you put in the obscenity? This may not be your view or mine, but if it is Mr. Joyce's he has no option but to fulfil his mission as a writer. If I understand him aright he sets out to depict not merely the fair show of things but the inner truth, and whether it is dubbed ugly or beautiful, or is a heart-wracking inextricable mixture and mystery of ugliness and beauty, has nothing to do with him as artist. He would be untrue to himself and to his subject were he to tone down and leave out. Surely it is not necessary to say that his purpose is not pornographic? The pornographic writer can always get his books published. If it is desirable he will employ the blue pencil.

But Mr. Joyce, unable to obtain publication, would certainly have grown indignant at the idea of the blue pencil. The story of his difficulties has been told; the prosecution of the *Little Review* of America, which printed some chapters; the stony stare of commercial publishers; the largely accidental meeting with private persons willing to take the risk of having this gigantic volume of over 700 pages printed in France for uncertain subscribers.

The expectation that these difficulties and the belief in the exceptional genius of Mr. Joyce aroused in the restricted circles of literary craftsmen is, in my experience, unprecedented. Those who have read the earlier books of Mr. Joyce have realised that here is a man who can write. 'We are mighty fine fellows nowadays,' cried Stevenson, 'but we cannot write like Hazlitt!' and many of us have felt like that about Joyce. There are phrases in which the words are packed tightly, as trim, as taut, as perfect as these things can be. There are fine ellipses in which a great sweep of meaning is concentrated into a single just-right sentence. There is a spot of colour which sets the page aglow. There is a point of light which gives life to the world as the lamp-lighter gives sudden life to the street. Here is erudition transfigured by imagination. A piece of out-of-the-way book knowledge or two lines of a silly jingle which we heard when we were boys—they fall wonderfully into their place. I detect a certain slackness here and there, as is inevitable in a book of such length; but I think that the craftsman will, forgetful altogether of the ethics of this book, its amazing a-morality, and completely careless of the content, best appreciate the sheer power of craftsmanship.

As for the matter, I think I can best convey some idea of *Ulysses* by reminding the reader how odd is the association of ideas when one allows all kinds of what are called thoughts, but which have nothing to do with thinking, to pass in higgledy-piggledy procession through one's mind—one's subconscious mind, I suppose it is called in present-day jargon. Psycho-analysis is, I believe, very strong about this. . . . Now the purpose of Mr. Joyce is, of course, much larger than to jot down all the incongruous notions that rattle around the arena of the cranium; but, described narrowly, that is what he does. Has anybody done it before? I do not know, but I am certain that no one ever did it at such length and with such thoroughness. It is obvious that if one tries to put down everything in the life of a man, a single day in that life will fill many volumes. The external events are really of little importance except as forming a starting-point for reflection. Mr. Joyce's style is such that it is sometimes difficult to distinguish between what is taking place externally and what is taking place internally. The internal action is put on the same plane as the external action. Mr. Joyce indicates both with infinite humour and with extraordinary precision. One feels that these things are essentially, ineluctably, true. These are exact notations of trivial but tremendous motions, and these are truly the inconsequential but significant things that one says to oneself. There is Mr. Bloom at the funeral wondering how he can discreetly shift the tablet of soap which he has purchased and put in his tail pocket. As he passes the gasworks in the mourning carriage he wonders whether it's true that to live near a gasworks prevents whooping-cough. A rat in the cemetery inspires horrible and humorous speculations. There are comic and sublime contrasts. The irrelevance and irreverence of the attitude of mankind before the great facts are remorselessly laid bare. Gross animality and subtle spirituality intermingle. Blasphemy and beauty, poetry and piggishness, jostle each other. But, on the whole, one becomes tired of beastliness always breaking in. There is one chapter devoted to the reverie of a woman, and her *monologue intérieur* is, I imagine—and am bound in all honesty to say—the vilest, according to ordinary standards, in all literature, And yet its very obscenity is somehow beautiful and wrings the soul to pity. Is that not high art? I cannot, however, believe that sex plays such a preponderant part in life as Mr. Joyce represents. He may aim at putting everything in, but he has, of course, like everybody else, selected carefully what he puts in. Has he not exaggerated the vulgarity and magnified the madness of mankind and the mysterious materiality of the universe?

105. George Slocombe, review, *Daily Herald*

17 March 1922, n.s., No. 921, 4

An important event in Paris this week has been the appearance, long-heralded and joyfully acclaimed, of Mr. James Joyce's *Ulysses*. Mr. Joyce is a young Irishman who is better known in the United States than in his native country, and better known in Paris perhaps than in either. When the early portents of *Ulysses* broke upon a dazed and incredulous world of very wide-awake and credulous young men, in the pages of the defunct *Little Review*, there was one very occasional reader of that publication who read the first instalments of this astonishing work very carefully five times, and then pressed firmly on the button labelled 'Literary Censorship and Public Morals.' Whereupon a squad of six large Irish policeman sprang up kinema-fashion from their porterhouse-steak breakfasts and sallied forth to suppress. . . .

And here it is at last, as large as a telephone directory or a family Bible, and with many of the literary and social characteristics of each. It took, I understand, nearly six years of Mr. Joyce's life to write, and it will take nearly six years of ours to read. And, after all, that is not much for the task, which apparently Mr. Joyce set himself, of writing the complete physical and spiritual life of a man during a day and a night. No other writer in the world, save perhaps an eighteenth-century clergyman writing Universal Treatises on forty pounds a year, has ever attempted anything so stupendous. And few writers have flung at the world Mr. Joyce's amazing precocity, untrammelled licence, prodigious patience, and shameless unreserve.

The real book begins with the uprising in the morning of a humble, though not obscure, man in the city of Dublin, and ends with his return home in the small hours of the following morning. During that interval the spiritual projection of Mr. Joyce, expressed in the interesting mind of Mr. Leopold Bloom, ranges like Moby Dick throughout the watery globe, and communes with incommunicable things under the stars.

Yet during that interval the body and the chained spirit of Mr. Bloom have merely partaken of, or assisted in, a bath at a public bathing establishment, a funeral, a luncheon in an odorous eating-house, an argument in the editorial offices of the *Freeman's Journal*, a discussion in a public-house, another meal and the song of a man at a piano, drinks with medical students in the common room of a lying-in hospital (with a woman three days in labour overhead), a discussion at the house of 'Æ,' a walk to the rocky shore at Howth, the return to town, a meeting with friends wandering drunkenly in a slum, a dispute with English soldiers, and a talk with a sailor in a cabmen's shelter.

And of these thin incidents Mr. Joyce makes a book that is a man's life; not every man's life, perhaps, but the life of Everyman. Among other things which we knew before, and some that we did not want to know, the book shows chiefly (1) that no man is an ordinary man, and (2) that all a man's thoughts do not make a book, though some of them may, as witness the incomparable Book of Job.

Mr. Joyce would have us see the wide waters and the illimitable stars of this universe through the rather muddied if wondering eye of his introspective Jewish husband in Dublin. We do not see the universe, but we end by seeing the man, approaching him through scorn to pity. And approaching his wife through pity to scorn, we see her too, a shallower water running fast.

There is much in this book to be forgiven to Mr. Joyce. For hundreds of pages he will write desperately, erudite nonsense, that, unfortunately, is not nonsense to himself. Often he writes as if his pen were dipped in obscenity and there were a whole ink-bottle of it to be exhausted before his thoughts would run clear. And his pen is often a scratchy pen, and scratchiness worries us for chapter after chapter as if (it being Sunday and the shops closed) no other pen were available.

But all in all, and by and large, and reading the end first, and skipping the interminable and elaborate syntheses of the middle part, the book is a staggering feat which, once attempted and more than half achieved, may never be attempted again—the way of a cosmic atom under heaven during a day and a night.

106. Arnold Bennett, review, *Outlook*

1922

'James Joyce's *Ulysses*', *Outlook* (London) (29 April 1922), 337–9. Appeared as 'Concerning James Joyce's *Ulysses*', *Bookman* (New York, lv (August 1922), 567–70. Later appeared in his *Things that have Interested Me* (1936), pp. 185–94. A representative middle-class review.

The fame of James Joyce was founded in this country mainly by H. G. Wells, whose praise of *A Portrait of the Artist as a Young Man* had very considerable influence upon the young. . . I read *A Portrait of the Artist as a Young Man* under the hypnotic influence of H. G. Wells. Indeed he commanded me to read it and to admire it extremely. I did both. I said: 'Yes, it is great stuff.' But in the horrid inaccessible thickets of my mind I heard a voice saying: 'On the whole the book has bored you.' And on the whole it had; and with the efflux of time I began to announce this truth. There are scenes of genius in the novel; from end to end it shows a sense of style; but large portions of it are dull, pompous, absurd, confused, and undirected. . . . A year or two later one of the intellectual young exhibited to me a copy of *The Little Review*, which monthly was then being mentioned in the best circles. . . . *The Little Review* contained an instalment of James Joyce's *Ulysses*. I obediently glanced through the instalment and concluded that it was an affected triviality which must have been planned in what the French so delicately call a *châlet de nécessité*. . . . And then the other day, opening *La Nouvelle Revue Française*, I beheld blazing on its brow an article by Valéry Larbaud entitled 'James Joyce'. I was shaken. . . And here was Valéry Larbaud producing a long article on James Joyce, and *La Nouvelle Revue Française* giving it the place of honor! . . . And the conclusion of it is that *Ulysses* is a masterpiece, considered, shapely, and thoroughly achieved. I was left with no alternative but to read the thing. . . .

Much has been made of the fact that the author takes more than seven hundred big pages to describe the passage of less than twenty hours. But I see nothing very wonderful in this. Given sufficient time, paper, childish caprice, and obstinacy, one might easily write over seven thousand pages about twenty hours of life. . . There is no clear proof that James Joyce chose for his theme any particular day. He is evidently of a sardonic temper, and I expect that he found malicious pleasure in picking up the first common day that came to hand. It happened to be nearly the dailiest day possible. . . The uninstructed reader can perceive no form, no artistic plan, no 'organization' (Henry James's excellent word) in the chosen day.

But the uninstructed reader is blind. According to Valéry Larbaud the day was very elaborately planned and organized. James Joyce loved the *Odyssey* in his youth, and the spirit of Homer presided over the shaping of the present work, which is alleged to be full of Homeric parellels. It may be so. Obviously Valéry Larbaud has discussed the work at length with the author. I should suspect the author of pulling Valéry Larbaud's leg, were it not that Larbaud has seen with his own eyes the author's drafts. . . I therefore concede him a plan, successful or unsuccessful. And in doing so I must animadvert upon his damnable lack of manners. For he gives absolutely no help to the reader. . . He apparently thinks there is something truly artistic and high minded in playing the lout to the innocent and defenseless reader. As a fact, there isn't. In playing the lout there is something low minded and inartistic. *Ulysses* would have been a better book and a much better appreciated book, if the author had extended to his public the common courtesies of literature. After all, to comprehend *Ulysses* is not among the recognized learned professions, and nobody should give his entire existence to the job.

A more serious objection to the novel is its pervading difficult dulness.

[quotes from Lestrygonians episode, pp. 180, 183]

Scores and hundreds of pages are filled with this kind of composition. Of course the author is trying to reproduce the thoughts of the personage, and his verbal method can be justified—does indeed richly justify itself here and there in the story. But upon the whole, though the reproduction is successful, the things reproduced appear too often to be trivial and perfectly futile in the narrative. I would not accuse him of what is absurdly called 'photographic realism'. But I would say that much of the book is more like an official shorthand writer's 'note' than a novel. In some of his moods the author is resolved at any price not to select, not to make even the shortest leap from one point of interest to another. He has taken oath with himself to put it all down and be hanged to it. . . He would probably defend himself and find disciples to defend him. But unless the experience of creative artists since the recorded beginning of art is quite worthless, James Joyce is quite wrong headed. Anyhow, with his wilfulness, he has made novel reading into a fair imitation of penal servitude. . . . The author seems to have no geographical sense, little sense of environment, no sense of the general kindness of human nature, and not much poetical sense. Worse than all, he has positively no sense of perspective. But my criticism of the artist in him goes deeper. His vision of the world and its inhabitants is mean, hostile, and uncharitable. . . .

Withal, James Joyce is a very astonishing phenomenon in letters. He is sometimes dazzlingly original. If he does not see life whole he sees it piercingly. His ingenuity is marvelous. He has wit. He has a prodigious humor. He is afraid of naught. . . .

The best portions of the novel (unfortunately they constitute only a fraction of the whole) are immortal. I single out the long orgiastic scene, and the long unspoken monologue of Mrs. Bloom which closes the book. The former will easily bear comparison with Rabelais at his fantastical finest; it leaves Petronius out of sight. It has plenary inspiration. It is the richest stuff, handled with a vituosity to match the quality of the material. The latter (forty difficult pages, some twenty-five thousand words without any punctuation at all) might in its utterly convincing realism be an actual document, the magical record of inmost thoughts thought by a woman that existed. Talk about understanding 'feminine psychology' . . . I have never read anything to surpass it, and I doubt if I have ever read anything to equal it. My blame may have seemed extravagant, and my praise may seem extravagant; but that is how I feel about James Joyce.

It would be unfair to the public not to refer to the indecency of *Ulysses*. The book is not pornographic, and can produce on nobody the effects of a pornographic book. But it is more indecent, obscene, scatological, and licentious than the majority of professedly pornographical books. James Joyce sticks at nothing, literally. He forbids himself no word. He says everything—everything. The code is smashed to bits. Many persons could not continue reading *Ulysses*; they would be obliged, by mere shock, to drop it. . . . It must cause reflection in the minds of all those of us who have hitherto held and preached that honest works of art ought to be exempt from police interference. Is the staggering indecency justified by results obtained? The great majority of Britons would say that nothing could justify it. For myself I think that in the main it is not justified by results obtained; but I must plainly add, at the risk of opprobrium, that in the finest passages it is in my opinion justified. . . .

107. Joseph Collins, review, *New York Times*

1922

'James Joyce's Amazing Chronicle', *New York Times Book Review* (28 May 1922), 6, 17.

A few intuitive, sensitive visionaries may understand and comprehend *Ulysses*, James Joyce's new and mammoth volume, without going through a course of training or instruction, but the average intelligent reader will glean little or nothing from it—even from careful perusal, one might properly say study, of it—save bewilderment and a sense of disgust. It should be companioned with a key and a glossary like the Berlitz books. Then the attentive and diligent reader would eventually get some comprehension of Mr. Joyce's message.

That he has a message there can be no doubt. He seeks to tell the world of the people that he has encountered in the forty years of sentient existence; to describe their conduct and speech and to analyze their motives, and to relate the effect the 'world', sordid, turbulent, disorderly, with mephitic atmosphere engendered by alcohol and the dominant ecclesiasticism of his country, had upon him, an emotional Celt, an egocentric genius, whose chief diversion and keenest pleasure is self-analysis and whose lifelong important occupation has been keeping a notebook in which has been recorded incident encountered and speech heard with photographic accuracy and Boswellian fidelity. Moreover, he is determined to tell it in a new way. Not in straightforward, narrative fashion, with a certain sequentiality of idea, fact, occurrence, in sentence, phrase and paragraph that is comprehensible to a person of education and culture, but in parodies of classic prose and current slang, in perversions of sacred literature, in carefully metered prose with studied incoherence, in symbols so occult and mystic that only the initiated and profoundly versed can understand—in short, by means of every trick and illusion that a master artificer, or even magician, can play with the English language.

Before proceeding with a brief analysis of *Ulysses*, and comment on its construction and its content. I wish to characterize it. *Ulysses* is the most important contribution that has been made to fictional literature in the twentieth century. It will immortalize its author with the same certainty that Gargantua and Pantagruel immortalized Rabelais, and *The Brothers Karamazof* Dostoyevsky. It is likely that there is no one writing English today that could parallel Mr. Joyce's feat, and it is also likely that few would care to do it were they capable. That statement requires that it be said at once that Mr. Joyce has seen fit to use words and phrases that the entire world has covenanted and people in general, cultured and uncultured, civilized and savage, believer and heathen, have agreed shall not be used, and which are base, vulgar, vicious and depraved. Mr. Joyce's reply to this is: 'This race and this country and this life produced me—I shall express myself as I am.'

An endurance test should always be preceded by training. It requires real endurance to finish *Ulysses*. The best training for it is careful perusal or reperusal of *The Portrait of the Artist as a Young Man*, the volume published six or seven years ago, which revealed Mr. Joyce's capacity to externalize his consciousness, to set it down in words. It is the story of his own life before he exiled himself from his native land, told with uncommon candor and extraordinary revelation of thought, impulse and action, many an incident of a nature and texture which most persons do not feel free to reveal, or which they do not feel it is decent and proper to confide to the world.

The salient facts of Mr. Joyce's life with which the reader who seeks to comprehend his writings should be familiar are as follows:

[The critic provides biographical information.]

. . . As a boy Mr. Joyce's favorite hero was Odysseus. He approved of his subterfuge for evading military service, he envied him the companionship of Penelope, all his latent vengeance was vicariously satisfied by reading of the way in which he revenged himself on Palamedes, while the craftiness and resourcefulness of the final artificer of the siege of Troy made him permanently big with admiration and affection. But it was the ten years of his hero's life after he had eaten of the lotus plant that wholly seduced Mr. Joyce, child and man and appeased his emotional soul. . . . In early life Mr. Joyce had definitely identified himself as Dedalus, the Athenian architect, sculptor and magician. This probably took place about the time that he became convinced he was not the child of his parents but a person of distinction and they his foster parents. A very common occurrence in potential psychopaths and budding geniuses. . . .

Mr. Joyce is an alert, keen-witted, brilliant man who has made it a lifelong habit to jot down every thought that he has had, whether he is depressed or exalted, despairing or hopeful, hungry or satiated, and likewise to put down what he has seen or heard others do or say. It is not unlikely that every thought that Mr. Joyce has had, every experience he has ever encountered, every person he has ever met, one might almost say everything he has ever read in sacred or profane literature, is to be encountered in the obscurities and in the franknesses of *Ulysses*. If personality is the sum total of all one's experiences, all one's thoughts and emotions, inhibitions and liberations, acquisitions and inheritances, then it may truthfully be said *Ulysses* comes nearer to being the perfect revelation of a personality than any book in existence. Rousseau's *Confessions*, Amiel's *Diary*, Bashkirtseff's vaporings and Cassanova's *Memoirs* are first readers compared with it.

He is the only individual that the writer has encountered outside of a madhouse who has let flow from his pen random and purposeful thoughts just as they are produced. He does not seek to give them orderliness, sequence or interdependence. His literary output would seem to substantiate some of Freud's contentions. The majority of writers, practically all, transfer their conscious, deliberate thought to paper. Mr. Joyce transfers the product of his unconscious mind to paper without submitting it to the conscious mind, or, if he submits it, it is to receive approval and encouragement, perhaps even praise. He holds with Freud that the unconscious mind represents the real man, the man of nature, and the conscious mind the artificed man, the man of convention, of expediency, the slave of Mrs. Grundy, the sycophant of the Church, the plastic puppet of society and State. For him the movements which work revolutions in the world are born out of the dreams and visions in a peasant's heart on the hillside. 'Peasant's heart' psychologically is the unconscious mind. When a master technician of words and phrases sets himself the task of revealing the product of the unconscious mind of a moral monster, a pervert and an invert, an apostate to his race and his religion, the simulacrum of a man who has neither cultural background nor personal self-respect, who can neither be taught by experience nor lessoned by example, as Mr. Joyce has done in drawing the picture of Leopold Bloom, and giving a faithful reproduction of his thoughts, purposeful, vagrant and obsessive, he undoubtedly knew full well what he was undertaking, and how unacceptable the vile contents of that unconscious mind would be to ninety-nine men out of a hundred, and how incensed they would be at having the disgusting product thrown in their faces. But that has nothing to do with that with which I am here concerned, viz. has the job been done well and is it a work of art, to which there can be only an affirmative answer.

It is particularly in one of the strangest chapters of all literature, without title, that Mr. Joyce succeeds in displaying the high-water mark of his art. Dedalus and Bloom have passed in review on a mystic stage, all their intimates and enemies, all their detractors and sycophants, the scum of Dublin and the spawn of the devil. Mr. Joyce resurrects Saint Walpurga, galvanizes her into life after twelve centuries of death intimacy with Beelzebub, and substituting a squalid section of Dublin for Brocken, proceeds to depict a festival, with the devil as host.

[discusses the scene in the brothel]

It may be said that this chapter does not represent life, but I venture to say that it represents life with photographic accuracy as Mr. Joyce has seen it and and lived it, and that every scene has come within his gaze and that every speech has been heard or said, and every sentiment experienced or thrust upon him. It is a mirror held up to life, life which we could sincerely wish and devoutly pray that we were spared. . . .

Mr. Joyce had the good fortune to be born with a quality which the world calls genius. Nature exacts a penalty, a galling income tax from geniuses, and as a rule she co-endows them with unamenability to law and order. . . . It is very interesting, and most important to have the revelations of such a personality, to have them first-hand and not dressed up. Heretofore our only avenues of information of such personalities led through the asylums for the insane, for it was there that such revelations as those of Mr. Joyce were made without reserve. Lest any one should construe this statement to be a subterfuge on my part to impugn the sanity of Mr. Joyce, let me say at once, that he is one of the sanest geniuses that I have ever known.

He had the profound misfortune to lose his faith and he cannot rid himself of the obsession that the Jesuits did it for him, and he is trying to get square with them by saying disagreeable things about them and holding their teachings up to scorn and obloquy. He was so unfortunate as to be born without a sense of duty, of service, of conformity to the State, to the community, to society, and he is convinced that he ought to tell about it, just as some who have experienced a surgical operation feel that they must relate minutely all the details of it, particularly at dinner parties and to casual acquaintances.

Finally, I venture a prophecy: Not ten men or women out of a hundred can read *Ulysses* through, and of the ten who succeed in doing so, five of them will do it as a *tour de force*, I am probably the only person, aside from the author, that has ever read it twice from beginning to end. I have learned more psychology and psychiatry from it than I did in ten years at the Neurological Institute. There are other angles at which *Ulysses* can be viewed profitably, but they are not many.

Stephen Dedalus in his Parisian tranquility (if the modern Minos has been given the lethal warm bath) will pretend indifference to the publication of a laudatory study of *Ulysses* a hundred years hence, but he is as sure to get it as Dostoyevsky, and surer than Mallarmé.

108. Edmund Wilson, review, *New Republic*

1922

Extract from *Ulysses*, *New Republic*, xxxi, No. 396 (5 July 1922), 164–6.

Mary Colum makes the statement in her *Life and the Dream* (1947) p. 306, that this review and those by Mary Colum (in the *Freeman*, No. 109) and by Gilbert Seldes (in the *Nation*, No. 110) pleased Joyce most.

. . . Stated in the baldest possible terms, this is the story of *Ulysses*—an ironic and amusing anecdote without philosophic moral. In describing the novel thus, I have the authority of the author himself, who said to Miss Djuna Barnes, in an interview published in *Vanity Fair*: 'The pity is the public will demand and find a moral in my book—or worse they may take it in some more serious way, and on the honor of a gentleman, there is not one single serious line in it.' The thing that makes *Ulysses* imposing is, in fact, not the theme but the scale upon which it is developed. It has taken Mr. Joyce seven years to write *Ulysses* and he has done it in seven hundred and thirty pages which are probably the most completely 'written' pages to be seen in any novel since Flaubert. Not only is the anecdote expanded to its fullest possible bulk—there is an elaborate account of nearly everything done or thought by Mr. Bloom from morning to night of the day in question— . . .

[Wilson refers to the 'psychologized' method used by Flaubert and Henry James.]

In Joyce you have not only life from the outside described with Flaubertian virtuosity but also the consciousness of each of the characters and of each of the character's moods made to speak in the idiom proper to it, the language it uses to itself. If Flaubert taught de Maupassant to find the adjective which would distinguish a given hackney-cab from every other hackney-cab in the world, James Joyce has prescribed that one must find the dialect which would distinguish the thoughts of a given Dubliner from those of every other Dubliner.

[Wilson illustrates the various dialects.]

. . . And these voices are used to record all the eddies and stagnancies of thought; though exercising a severe selection which makes the book a technical triumph, Mr. Joyce manages to give the effect of unedited human minds, drifting aimlessly along from one triviality to another, confused and diverted by memory, by sensation and by inhibition. It is, in short, perhaps the most faithful X-ray ever taken of the ordinary human consciousness.

And as a result of this enormous scale and this microscopic fidelity the chief characters in *Ulysses* take on heroic proportions. Each one is a room, a house, a city in which the reader can move around. The inside of each one of them is a novel in itself. You stand within a world infinitely populated with the swarming life of experience. . . . I cannot agree with Mr. Arnold Bennett that James Joyce 'has a colossal "down" on humanity.' I feel that Mr. Bennett has really been shocked because Mr. Joyce has told the whole truth. Fundamentally *Ulysses* is not at all like Bouvard et Pécuchet (as some people have tried to pretend) [The reference here is to Pound]. Flaubert says in effect that he will prove to you that humanity is mean by enumerating all the ignobilities of which it has ever been capable. But Joyce, including all the ignobilities, makes his bourgeois figures command our sympathy and respect by letting us see in them the throes of the human mind straining always to perpetuate and perfect itself and of the body always laboring and throbbing to throw up some beauty from its darkness.

Nonetheless, there are some valid criticisms to be brought against *Ulysses*. It seems to me great rather for the things that are in it than for its success as a whole. It is almost as if in distending the story to ten times its natural size he had finally managed to burst it and leave it partially deflated. There must be something wrong with a design which involves so much that is dull—and I doubt whether anyone will defend parts of *Ulysses* against the charge of extreme dullness. In the first place, it is evidently not enough to have invented three tremendous characters (with any quantity of lesser ones); in order to produce an effective book they must be made to do something interesting. Now in precisely what is the interest of *Ulysses* supposed to consist? In the spiritual relationship between Dedalus and Bloom? But too little is done with this. When it is finally realized there is one poignant moment, then a vast tract of anti-climax. This single situation in itself could hardly justify the previous presentation of everything else that has happened to Bloom before on the same day. No, the major theme of the book is to be found in its parallel with the Odyssey: . . . It is these and not the inherent necessities of the subject which have dictated the size and shape of *Ulysses.*

[Wilson discusses the Homeric parallels.]

. . . Yet I cannot but feel that Mr. Joyce made a mistake to have the whole plan of his story depend on the structure of the *Odyssey* rather than on the natural demands of the situation. I feel that though his taste for symbolism is closely allied with his extraordinary poetic faculty for investing particular incidents with universal significance, nevertheless—because it is the homeless symbolism of a Catholic who has renounced the faith—it sometimes overruns the bounds of art into an arid ingenuity which would make a mystic correspondence do duty for an artistic reason. The result is that one sometimes feels as if the brilliant succession of episodes were taking place on the periphery of a wheel which has no hub.

[Illustrates his point by reference to the monologue of Molly.]

. . . These sterilities and practical jokes form my second theme of complaint. Not content with inventing new idioms to reproduce the minds of his characters, Mr. Joyce has hit upon the idea of pressing literary parody into service to create certain kinds of impressions. It is not so bad when in order to convey the atmosphere of a newspaper office he merely breaks up his chapter with newspaper heads, but when he insists upon describing a drinking party in an interminable series of imitations which progresses through English prose from the style of the Anglo-Saxon chronicles to that of Carlyle one begins to feel uncomfortable. What is wrong is that Mr. Joyce has attempted an impossible genre. You cannot be a realistic novelist in Mr. Joyce's particular vein and write burlesques at the same time. . . . He has been praised for being Rabelaisian but he is at the other end of the world from Rabelais. In the first place, he has not the style for it—he can never be reckless enough with words. His style is thin—by which I do not mean that it is not strong but that it is like a thin metallic pipe through which the narrative is run—a pipe of which every joint has been fitted by a master plumber. You cannot inflate such a style or splash it about. Mr. Joyce's native temperament and the method which it has naturally chosen have no room for superabundance or extravagant fancy. It is the method of

Flaubert—and of Turgenev and de Maupassant . . . In this genre—which has probably brought novel-writing to its highest dignity as an art—Mr. Joyce has long proved himself a master. And in *Ulysses* most of his finest scenes adhere strictly to this formula. Nothing, for example, could be better in this kind than the way in which the reader is made to find out, without any overt statement of the fact, that Bloom is different from his neighbors, or the scene in which we are made to feel that this difference has become a profound antagonism before it culminates in the open outburst against Bloom of the Cyclops-Sinn Feiner. The trouble is that this last episode is continually being held up by long parodies which break in upon the text like a kind of mocking commentary . . . No: surely Mr. Joyce has done ill in attempting to graft burlesque upon realism; he has written some of the most unreadable chapters in the whole history of fiction.—(If it be urged that Joyce's gift for fantasy is attested by the superb drunken scene, I reply that this scene is successful, not because it is reckless nonsense but because it is an accurate record of drunken states of mind.) . . .

Yet, for all its appalling longueurs, *Ulysses* is a work of high genius. Its importance seems to me to lie, not so much in its opening new doors to knowledge—unless in setting an example to Anglo-Saxon writers of putting down everything without compunction—or in inventing new literary forms—Joyce's formula is really, as I have indicated, nearly seventy-five years old—as in its once more setting the standard of the novel so high that it need not be ashamed to take its place beside poetry and drama. *Ulysses* has the effect at once of making everything else look brassy. Since I have read it, the texture of other novelists seems intolerably loose and careless; when I come suddenly unawares upon a page that I have written myself I quake like a guilty thing surprised. The only question now is whether Joyce will ever write a tragic masterpiece to set beside this comic one. There is a rumor that he will write no more—that he claims to have nothing left to say—and it is true that there is a paleness about parts of his work which suggests a rather limited emotional experience. His imagination is all intensive; he has but little vitality to give away. His minor characters, though carefully differentiated, are sometimes too drily differentiated, insufficiently animated with life, and he sometimes gives the impression of eking out his picture with the data of a too laborious note-taking. At his worst he recalls Flaubert at his worst—in *L'Education Sentimentale*. But if he repeats Flaubert's vices—as not a few have done—he also repeats his triumphs—which almost nobody has done. Who else has had the supreme devotion and accomplished the definitive beauty? If he has really laid down his pen never to take it up again he must know that the hand which laid it down upon the great affirmative of Mrs. Bloom, though it never write another word, is already the hand of a master.

109. Mary Colum, review, *Freeman*

1922

'The Confessions of James Joyce', *Freeman*, v, No. 123 (19 July 1922), 450–2. Later appeared in *The Freeman Book* (1924), pp. 327–55.

In her *Life and the Dream* (1947), p. 306, Mrs. Colum states that this review and those by Edmund Wilson (in the *New Republic*, No. 108) and by Gilbert Seldes (in the *Nation*, No. 110) pleased Joyce most.

Mr. James Joyce's *Ulysses* belongs to that class of literature which has always aroused more interest than any other. Although *Ulysses* is new and original in its form, it is old in its class or type: it actually, if not obviously, belongs to the Confession class of literature, and although everything in it takes place in less than twenty-four hours, it really contains the life of a man. It is the Confessions of James Joyce, a most sincere and cunningly-wrought autobiographical book; it is as if he had said, 'Here I am; here is what country and race have bred me, what religion and life and literature have done to me.' Not only his previous book, *Portrait of the Artist*, but all of Joyce's work, gives the impression of being literally derived from experience; and from internal evidence in *Ulysses*, notably the conversation of Stephen Dedalus on Shakespeare in the National Library, one suspects that Joyce believes only in the autobiographical in art.

Such being the nature of the book, it is clear that the difficulty of comprehending it will not be allowed to stand in the way by anybody who can get possession of it. Joyce has so many strange things to say that people would struggle to understand him, no matter in what form or tongue he wrote. Yet the difficulties in the way are very real; *Ulysses* is one of the most racial books ever written, and one of the most Catholic books ever written; this in spite of the fact that one would not be surprised to hear that some official of the Irish Government or of the Church had ordered it to be publicly burned. It hardly seems possible that it can be really understood by anybody not brought up in the half-secret tradition of the heroism, tragedy, folly and anger of Irish nationalism, or unfamiliar with the philosophy, history and rubrics of the Roman Catholic Church; or by one who does not know Dublin and certain conspicuous Dubliners. The author himself takes no pains at all to make it easy of comprehension. Then, too, the book presupposes a knowledge of many literatures; a knowledge which for some reason, perhaps the cheapness of leisure, is not uncommon in Dublin, and, for whatever reason, perhaps the dearness of leisure, is rather uncommon in New York. In addition, it is almost an encyclopædia of odd bits and forms of knowledge; for the author has a mind of the most restless curiosity, and no sort of knowledge is alien to him.

Ulysses is a kind of epic of Dublin. Never was a city so involved in the workings of any writer's mind as Dublin is in Joyce's; he can think only in terms of it. In his views of newspaper-offices, public houses, the National Library, the streets, the cemetery, he has got the psychology of that battered, beautiful eighteenth-century city in its last years of servitude. . . .

[The critic briefly summarizes the first part of the first chapter.]

Wherever Stephen comes in, we have the vision of his dying mother; her death was the great episode of his life. True to his race, death is the one thing that rocks him to the foundations of his being; *la gloire* may be the great emotional interest of the French, love of the English, but death is that of the Celt. Stephen further reveals himself in the conversation with Haines the Englishman. 'I am the servant of two masters . . . an English and an Italian . . . the imperial British State and the Holy Roman Catholic and Apostolic Church.'

He is the servant of these two; and where has the peculiar spiritual humiliation that the English occupation of Ireland inflicted on sensitive and brilliant Irishmen ever been expressed as in this book? Where has the æsthetic and intellectual fascination of the Roman Catholic Church ever found subtler fascination? 'The proud potent titles clanged over Stephen's memory the triumph of their brazen bells . . . *et unam sanctam catholicam et apostolicam ecclesiam*! The slow growth and change of rite and dogma like his own rare thoughts.' Has the Catholic Church ever been described with such eloquence as in the paragraph that has that beginning? . . .

[describes Haines]

[The critic summarizes the rest of the book.]

There is little in the way of incident, but everything in the way of revelation of life and character. Joyce gives us the characters of Stephen and Bloom as they appear externally and in their own subconsciousness. One of the remarkable feats of the book is the manner in which the separate subconsciousnesses of Stephen and Bloom are revealed, with every aimless thought, every half-formed idea and every unformed phrase indicative of their separate character and personality, and of the influences that have gone into their making. This is most marked when they think of the same things.

[illustrates this point]

. . . Almost every section of the book has a different form and manner.

[illustrates this point by reference and illustration: Kiernan's public house and the hospital]

. . . From this half-way chapter to the end, *Ulysses* ceases to be of paramount literary interest; to what extent a writer can parody different styles in the historic development of English is not of literary interest, it is of scientific interest. The catechism relating to Bloom and Stephen, being merely informing, is not of literary interest. The revelation of the mind of Marion Bloom in the last section would doubtless interest the laboratory, but to normal people it would seem an exhibition of the mind of a female gorilla who has been corrupted by contact with humans. The Walpurgis night scene (not called by that name) is too long and too incomprehensible; one feels that Joyce has here driven his mind too far beyond the boundary-line that separates fantasy and grotesquerie from pure madness.

[describes the brothel scene]

. . . One of the chief occupations of critics of this book is making parallels between the sections and characters of *Ulysses*, and the *Odyssey*. The chief reason for this performance is that the author exhibits a note-book with all these parallels and many other symbolical explanations. When it comes to symbolizing, authors have from all time talked the greatest nonsense; think of the nonsense that Goethe achieved when explaining the second part of *Faust*! Just as plausible correspondences could be made between *Faust* and *Ulysses* as between the *Odyssey* and *Ulysses*.

What actually has James Joyce accomplished in this monumental work? He has achieved what comes pretty near to being a satire on all literature. He has written down a page of his country's history. He has given the minds of a couple of men with a kind of actuality not hitherto found in literature. He has given us an impression of his own life and mind such as no other writer has given before; not even Rousseau, whom he resembles.

The Confession-mind in literature is of two classes. We have the Saint Augustine-Tolstoy type and the Rousseau-Strindberg-Joyce type. The difference between Rousseau and Joyce is, of course, extraordinary, but the resemblances are also extraordinary—a psychoanalyst would say they had the same complexes.

[The critic discusses the resemblance between Rousseau and Joyce.]

. . . Some attempt is being made by admirers to absolve Joyce from accusations of obscenity in this book. Why attempt to absolve him? It is obscene, bawdy, corrupt. But it is doubtful that obscenity in literature ever really corrupted anybody. The alarming thing about *Ulysses* is very different; it is that it shows the amazing inroads that science is making on literature. Mr. Joyce's book is of as much interest as science as it is as literature; in some parts it is of purely scientific and non-artistic interest. It seems to me a real and not a fantastic fear that science will oust literature altogether as a part of human expression; and from that point of view *Ulysses* is a dangerous indication. From that point of view, also, I do not consider it as important to literature as *Portrait of the Artist*. After *Ulysses*, I can not see how anyone can go on calling books written in the subconscious method, novels. It is as plain as day that a new literary form has appeared, from which the accepted form of the novel has nothing to fear; the novel is as distinct from this form as in his day Samuel Richardson's invention was from the drama.

110. Gilbert Seldes, review, *Nation*

30 August 1922, cxv, No. 2982, 211–12

Mary M. Colum in her *Life and the Dream* (1947), p. 306, makes the statement that this review and those by Mary M. Colum (in the *Freeman*, No. 109) and by Edmund Wilson (in the *New Republic*, No. 108) pleased Joyce most.

'Welcome, O life! I go to encounter for the millionth time the reality of experience and to forge in the smithy of my soul the uncreated conscience of my race. . . . Old father, old artificer, stand me now and ever in good stead.' With this invocation ended James Joyce's first novel, *A Portrait of the Artist as a Young Man*. It has stood for eight years as the pledge of Joyce's further achievement; today he has brought forth *Ulysses*, a monstrous and magnificent travesty, which makes him possibly the most interesting and the most formidable writer of our time . . . It is the novel as they [Henry James and Flaubert] created it which Joyce has brought to its culmination; he has, it seems likely, indicated the turn the novel will take into a new form. *Ulysses* is at the same time the culmination of many other things: of an epoch in the life of Stephen Dedalus, the protagonist of the *Portrait*; of an epoch in the artistic life of Joyce himself; and, if I am not mistaken, of a period in the intellectual life of our generation.

[Seldes devotes a paragraph to the Stephen Dedalus of the *Portrait*.]

. . . *Ulysses* is, among other things, a day in the life of this same Stephen Dedalus, an average day after his return to Dublin from Paris. As an average day it marks the defeat of the poet; he has encountered and been overcome by the reality of experience; the ecstasy and lyric beauty are no more; instead of it we have a gigantic travesty. That is, as I see it, the spiritual plot of *Ulysses*. And as Stephen, in addition to being a created character, is both 'the artist' generically and specifically James Joyce, *Ulysses* naturally takes on the proportions of a burlesque epic of this same defeat. It is not surprising that, built on the framework of the

Odyssey, it burlesques the structure of the original as a satyr-play burlesqued the tragic cycle to which it was appended; nor that a travesty of the whole of English prose should form part of the method of its presentation. Whether a masterpiece can be written in caricature has ceased to be an academic question.

The narrative of *Ulysses* is simple.

[A paragraph of summary follows here.]

This is what is technically known as a slender plot for a book which is the length of five ordinary novels. But the narrative is only the thread in the labyrinth. Around and about it is the real material of the psychological story, presented largely in the form of interior monologues—the unspoken thoughts of the three principal characters and at times of some of the others, separately or, in one case, simultaneously. In a few words, at most a few pages, the essential setting is objectively presented; thereafter we are actually in the consciousness of a specified or suggested individual, and the stream of consciousness, the rendered thoughts and feelings of that individual, are actually the subject matter of the book. There is no 'telling about' things by an outsider, nor even the looking over the hero's shoulder which Henry James so beautifully managed; there is virtually complete identification. The links in the chain of association are tempered by the nature and circumstances of the individual; there is no mistaking the meditations of Stephen for those of Bloom, those of either for the dark flood of Marion's consciousness. I quote a specimen moment from this specimen day: . . .

[quotes from the Proteus episode, p. 41, p. 40]

The swift destructive parody in the last sentence is a foretaste of what arrives later in the book. In the episode at the *Freeman's Journal* Joyce has sown headlines through the narrative, the headlines themselves being a history by implication of the vulgarization of the press. In the public house a variety of bombastic styles sets off the flatness of the actual conversation; on the beach the greater part of the episode is conveyed through a merciless parody of the sentimental serial story: 'Strength of character had never been Reggy Wylie's strong point and he who would woo and win Gerty MacDowell must be a man among men' and so on. Here the parody creates itself not in the mind of Bloom, but in that of the object in his mind, and renders the young-girlish sentimentality of Gerty with exceptional immediacy and directness. The burlesque of English prose, historically given, against which great complaint has been made, is actually only some sixty pages long; the parodies themselves I find brilliant, but their function is more important than their merit. They create with rapidity and as rapidly destroy the whole series of noble aspirations, hopes, and illusions of which the centuries have left their record in prose. And they lead naturally, therefore, to the scene in the brothel where hell opens.

This is the scene which, by common consent, is called a masterpiece. The method is a variation from that of the preceding; the apparent form is that of a play with spoken dialogue and italicized stage directions. The characters at the beginning are the inhabitants of nighttown; they and the soldiers and Bloom and Stephen have this real existence. But the play is populated by the phantasms and nightmares of their brains . . . In the Witches' Sabbath brute creation and inanimate things give voice; the End of the World appears and dances on an invisible tight-rope; and the Walpurgisnacht ends in a hanging of totally unnamable horror. It is here that Bloom recognizes Stephen as his spiritual kin.

The galvanic fury in which this episode is played is, one feels certain, not equalled in literature; it is a transcription of drunken delirium, with all the elements of thought and imagination broken, spasmodic, tortured out of shape, twitching with electric energy. The soft catlike languor of the whores, the foulness of the soldiers, the whole revel of drink and lust, are only reliefs to the implacable terrors in the subconscious minds of Stephen and Bloom. At the end of it Bloom accepts Stephen as the man his own son, and so himself, might have been; Stephen, more vaguely, seems to see in Bloom the man he himself may become. The orgy dies out in a cabman's shelter, in dreary listlessness, and after a description of their affinities and differences, given in the form of an examination paper, the two men part. The poet defeated by his self-scorn and introspection, the sensualist, with his endless curiosity, defeated by weakness, disappear; and in the thoughts of Mrs. Bloom something coarse and healthy and coarsely beautiful and healthily foul asserts itself. Like the Wife of Bath, she can thank God that she has had her world, as in her time.

Although her last words are an affirmation that her body is a flower, although she morally rejects her brutal lovers in favor of Stephen and ends with a memory of her first surrender to Bloom, there is no moral triumph here. For Mrs. Bloom there can be no defeat similar to that of the others, since there has been no struggle. Their impotence is contrasted with her wanton fornication; she occurs, a mockery of the faithful Penelope, to mark their frustration. In their several ways Bloom and Stephen have been seekers, one for experience and the other for the reality of experience; and finding it they have been crushed and made sterile by it.

If it is true, as Mr. Yeats has said, that the poet creates the mask of his opposite, we have in *Ulysses* the dual mask—Bloom and Stephen—of James Joyce, and in it we have, if I am not mistaken, the mask of a generation: the broken poet turning to sympathy with the outward-going scientific mind. (Bloom is completely rendered by Joyce, with infinite humor and kindness and irony, to give point to this turning.) Conscious despair turns to unconscious futility; in the end, to be sure, Stephen leaves the house of Bloom, to be homeless the last few hours of the night. And this homelessness, beside which is the homelessness of Joyce himself, strikes us as a joyful tragedy in Stephen's freedom and solitude and exaltation. The one thing one does not find in *Ulysses* is dismal pessimism; there is no 'down' on humanity. Lust and superstition, Mr. Santayana has told us, are cancelled by the high breathlessness of beauty; in this book love and hate seem equally forgotten in an enormous absorption in things, by an enormous relish and savoring of palpable actuality. I think that Nietzsche would have cared for the tragic gaiety of *Ulysses*.

I have not the space to discuss the aesthetic questions which the book brings up nor to indicate what its effect upon the novel may be. I have called Joyce formidable because it is already clear that the innovations in method and the developments in structure which he has used with a skill approaching perfection are going to have an incalculable effect upon the writers of the future; he is formidable because his imitators will make use of his freedom without imposing upon themselves the duties and disciplines he has suffered; I cannot see how any novelist will be able (nor why he should altogether want) entirely to escape his influence. The book has literally hundreds of points of interest not even suggested here. One must take for granted the ordinary equipment of the novelist; one must assume also that there are faults, idiosyncrasies, difficulties. More important still are the interests associated with 'the uncreated conscience of my race'—the Catholic and Irish. I have written this analysis of *Ulysses* as one not too familiar with either—as an indication that the book can have absolute validity and interest, in the sense that all which is local and private in the *Divine Comedy* does not detract from its interest and validity. But these and other points have been made in the brilliant reviews which *Ulysses* has already evoked. One cannot leave it without noting again that in the change of Stephen

Dedalus from his affinity with the old artificer to his kinship with Ulysses-Bloom, Joyce has created an image of contemporary life; nor without testifying that this epic of defeat, in which there is not a scamped page nor a moment of weakness, in which whole chapters are monuments to the power and the glory of the written word, is in itself a victory of the creative intelligence over the chaos of uncreated things and a triumph of devotion, to my mind one of the most significant and beautiful of our time.

ULYSSES: REVIEWS OF AMERICAN EDITION

1934

111. Horace Gregory, review, *New York Herald Tribune*

21 January 1934, Book Section, pp. 1–2

. . . The misadventures of Molly Bloom are no longer thrust into prominence by the lean hand of the censor, and we are allowed to relax in her presence. As for the esoteric mysteries of Stephen Dedalus and his companions of a memorable sixteen hours, even these have been cleared away within twelve long years of commentary. We can now approach the large, sparsely punctuated pages of this Homeric idyll in the same spirit that we read *Tristram Shandy* and from them a curious experience emerges. . . . As I have already suggested, we are now moving away from the direct influence of Joyce's *Odyssey*, and as we drop discussion of its technical values, we will find a fresh enjoyment of its comedy and then accept the figure of Leopold Bloom as one of the great comic characters of all literature. It will then be natural to regard him as the peer of Uncle Toby or Falstaff or Mr. Micawber and the creation of his world is quite as complete as theirs. Once we are in it, there is no release from its singular atmosphere; we admit dull passages, but what great novel is entirely free of this defect? Surely not *Don Quixote* or *Tristram Shandy* or *Gil Blas*. I wish to make this prophecy: As Joyce's influence wanes and as the history of *Ulysses* becomes merely another chapter in an encyclopedia of English literature, our enjoyment of the book as major fiction will increase. As we read onward through that June day in 1904, Leopold Bloom's 'stream of consciousness' will again enter our blood and lacking the need to consider Joyce's method in bringing him to life, we shall discover him as part of our heritage and he will be of greater vitality than the friend we boast of knowing all too well. Again we shall see him relish a breakfast of kidneys, feed the cat and follow his wife's directions in brewing a pot of tea, and we shall know by these signs that his day has begun. We shall be less aware, perhaps, of his author's purpose in creating him, but no matter, Bloom will outlive us all and will remain (as Uncle Toby has survived) as the arch symbol of humanity in a transient world. . . .

112. Gilbert Seldes, review, *New York Evening Journal*

27 January 1934, 11

Although the new book by Sinclair Lewis is the event of the week, the free publication of James Joyce's *Ulysses* in America has to be noted as the event of the year. I have written perhaps too much about this book; there is certainly no need for me to review it now. But I am appalled to see that on the jacket of the very handsome volume, beautifully designed and printed and bound (Random House), I am quoted—from a review written about ten years ago. I am not appalled by an excuse of enthusiasm expressed at the time; the reverse. Like Warren Hastings, I am astonished at my own moderation. 'To my mind,' I wrote, *Ulysses* is one of the most significant and beautiful works of our time.' Mealy-mouthed words, weasel words, little, timid words introduced by an apologetic 'to my mind.' I am sure I said other, better, bolder things about *Ulysses*. I must have given the impression at least that for weeks I had lived in that book as I had lived in no other since I read *War and Peace*; I remember definitely saying that every page in the book is a tribute to the grandeur and beauty of the language in which all of our deepest thoughts and highest aspirations had been recorded. I denied that the book was ugly or black pessimism. I felt it to be a great affirmation to everything in life—the good and the evil. I still feel so. . . .

113. Review, *The Carnegie Magazine*

1934

Extract from S.H.C., 'Ulysses', *The Carnegie Magazine*, vii, No. 2 (February 1934), 279–81. See also the sharp rebuttal given in 'World's Worst Comment on *Ulysses* Appears', *Chicago Tribune* (Paris) (12 March 1934), 2.

[Discussion of United States censorship and Woolsey's decision.]

And now what is this book that has brought about a striking of the shackles from the world's literary expression? We have read the book, and after reading it we declare our opinion that it is unreadable—not so much because of the nature of its contents but because it is so deadly dull that no mind can go through the mazes of its barbaric style and the length of its interminable pages except when moved by a sense of justice to read it before judging it.

The book comprises nearly eight hundred pages, set in small type. It tells the conversations and the thoughts of its characters, with an intimation of what they are doing, in their homes and haunts in Dublin during a day and a night in June, 1904. There is no story, no plot, no narrative; there is no conflict of motive; and the persons named appear from time to time in the book only to be lost in a sea of words. And the words are without form, and void. The author, consciously or unconsciously, follows the style of Thomas Carlyle in breaking up his incidents for the introduction of rhapsody; but while Carlyle uses his pages for rhapsodies which illuminate life in a flood of brilliant interpretations, the author here rambles into confused soliloquies which are without meaning in themselves and are inexplicable, having neither beauty of thought nor charm of diction and no relation to the things that have gone before or that are to come after.

We make the statement in good faith that it would be possible to tear out one hundred pages from this book near its opening words, another hundred at the middle, and a third hundred near the end, even including half the pages of the closing soliloquy, and that then the remaining five hundred pages could be read without any loss of sequence; furthermore, that the destroyed pages would contain no paragraph that is lucid, informative, or comprehensible under the rule of directness and force.

Here is his style at its clearest:

'Ineluctable modality of the visible: At least that if no more, thought through my eyes. Signatures of all things I am here to read, seaspawn and seawrack, the nearing tide, that rusty boot . . .[Necessary omission] Limits of the diaphane. But he adds: in bodies. Then he was aware of them against them, sure. Go easy. Bald he was and a millionaire. Limit of the diaphane in. Why in? Diaphane, adiaphane. If you can put your five fingers through it, it is a gate, if not a door. Shut your eyes and see.'

Nearly eight hundred pages of trash like this, and Americans buying the book, according to the publisher's announcement, at five thousand a week.

The chief morsel for those who will stagger through hundreds of skipped pages will be found in the last forty-five pages, in which a prostitute closes this work with what might be called her famed, but not famous, soliloquy. In this final portion she introduces all the words that are known to the lowest followers of her trade. The author has not dared to present this piece of his work with the usual accompaniment of paragraphs and punctuation marks. There are no capitals, commas, semicolons, periods, interrogation or exclamation points. The whole thing is a hodgepodge of type, closely run together, mostly without sense, difficult to read, and flowing on to the end of the book, like a sewer that had burst loose and overwhelmed a city with foul and pestilential vapors. If he or his publishers had had the hardihood to print these passages with the usual set-off of paragraphs, punctuation, and divided sentences we greatly doubt whether the book would have passed its judicial ordeal.

Judge Woolsey says that the book provokes disgust to the point of nausea. He is right. The book seems to us to be the output of the mind of a stableboy, trained amid the lowest habits of speech and conduct, who has then read with extraordinary attention a large collection of literature, ancient and modern, and who undertakes to write a book based upon this study and observation, and goes through his task with a stableboy's mind interpreting every part of the work. It is kaleidoscopic in a sense—that is, if we could imagine a kaleidoscope presenting foul and ugly pictures, instead of beautiful objects, it would be kaleidoscopic;

for there is no continuity of purpose or connected expression in the entire volume. The people here introduced discuss various topics—at one point Shakespeare. But after fifty pages of rambling and licentious talk the only point from Shakespeare that is covered by them is the query as to whether Hamlet was Shakespeare's father or Shakespeare was Hamlet's father. He uses a hundred pages in the night-club scene—we call the place a night club in deference to our readers—to present his characters in a sort of Greek play; but there is no objective—it is insane in its picturization, full of fustian, wearisome to exhaustion, and violates throughout the inexorable Greek rule that a play must have a beginning, a middle, and an end. And no matter what his topic may be—opera, play, society, morals, or the Bible—there is scarcely a page in this bewildering wilderness of words which does not reek with this stableboy's abominable mind.

How absurd then it is to say, as some of the reviewers are extravagantly saying, and as the author himself encourages them in saying, that this book is a tour de force in literature, a profound study in philosophy, a presentation of life that is mysterious and recondite, an achievement that reaches up into the very stratosphere of thought, a transcendental portraiture that goes beyond the average limit of human understanding and, like a new Einstein Theory, can be comprehended by only twelve men in the world! There is nothing at all of any of these qualities about it. As a work of art we can compare it with nothing but that picture which provoked laughter in the galleries a few years ago, 'Nude Descending a Staircase,' in which there was neither nude nor staircase and where art was the only thing that was descending. The book has no more relation to Ulysses than it has to Oliver Cromwell or Lord Byron. Any novel of George Eliot's or Thackeray's could be named *Ulysses* more fittingly in its picture of life. The printed 'key' which promises to unlock this esoteric achievement is not needed. We do not have to read far until we get the key for ourselves: the stableboy's words blaze themselves so shamelessly on every page that we soon choose the only key that will unlock the mystery, and that is the word—neurosis—a diseased mind that sees and feels life only in its deformed relationship to sex. . . .

114. Robert Cantwell, review, *New Outlook*

March 1934, clxiii, 57–8

There have been a number of good novels offered on the spring lists, beginning, of course, with *Ulysses* (Random House), now released from its shameful twelve-year censorship. Nothing need be said about it, except that of all the literature produced in our time, it seems the surest of a place with the best of English writing—of writing in English; that it towers so high it has already cast its shadow on the important writing done since it appeared. Perhaps its tremendous influence will be clarified now that the book is widely available, for writers have usually had to form their opinions of it from borrowed copies (few writers having money enough to buy the illegal editions) and writers are seldom deeply influenced by that sort of hasty reading. They really respond, a real dent is made in their imaginations, when they grow troubled and uncertain about their own small efforts and turn automatically to study the great works of their time. . . .

115. Edwin Baird, review, *Real America*

April 1934, iii, No. 2, 44

Probably no book of the last decade has been so widely discussed, and none so misunderstood, as James Joyce's *Ulysses*. Certainly I know of none that has provoked so much bilge and blather. Solemn asses have written learned treatises on it; others have written 'interpretations.' Literary societies have used it for debate; reading circles for whispered innuendo. It has been hailed as 'the greatest novel in English.' It has been condemned as 'a filthy book, unfit for print.' And I have an idea that all the while Joyce was secretly laughing at all of them.

Of course, as every author and publisher knows, the best way to get publicity for a book is to have it banned as an obscene work. *Ulysses* was banned as obscene, though I have never been able to understand why. Except for half a dozen words rarely if ever encountered in print, I find nothing in its 767 pages that would shock the most sensitive reader. Indeed, such a reader would probably be less shocked than bored. And I venture to say that not one person in twenty who reads it will know what the devil it's all about.

Well, the ban has finally been lifted—by Federal Judge John M. Woolsey of the U.S. District Court of New York—and now you no longer need pay a fancy price for a booklegger's copy. You can purchase it in any book store, just as you would purchase *Alice in Wonderland* or *Little Women*. And Joyce, for the first time, will start drawing some royalties. (He never received a cent from any of the copies sold in America at exorbitant figures.)

But the smut hounds are in for the biggest surprise of their lives when they start sniffing for the dirt in this book. They will be as bewildered as a school boy trying to read Chinese. Even the most intelligent reader finds the going pretty hard in spots. Some parts are wholly unintelligible. Others are downright nasty. None arouse lasciviousness. . . .

Don't think, however, that Joyce can't write plain English. His letter to Bennett A. Cerf, his American publisher, is as clear and practical as a note from your landlord about the rent.

Ulysses, in my opinion, is not 'the greatest novel in English.' Nor is it 'a filthy book.' It's a literary curiosity. As such I recommend it. . . .

116. Review of the English edition, *New Statesman*

1936

G. W. Stonier, 'Leviathan', *New Statesman and Nation*, xii, No. 294 (10 October 1936), 551–2.

A review of the English edition of *Ulysses*.

Ulysses was originally published by Shakespeare and Company, of Paris, in 1922. Since then it has run through many editions; it has been confiscated, banned, burnt, read and re-read, translated into half a dozen languages. The first English edition appeared rather suddenly last week. . . . The list of misprints has disappeared from the end; instead, there is an appendix giving the legal history of *Ulysses* in America. These documents are extraordinarily interesting, for they reveal the rare case of a book condemned for its obscenity being afterwards reclaimed by the weight of literary opinion. . . .

[quotes from Judge Woolsey's decision]

What judge or magistrate has ever before admitted the necessity of understanding the work of art on which he is to pass judgment? (It was a trial without jury, of course.) Judge Woolsey goes on to say that he does not detect anywhere in *Ulysses* 'the leer of the sensualist,' in spite of its unusual frankness, and therefore it is not pornographic. He reviews the book at some length, commenting on its originality, on the 'astonishing success' of its method, and the integrity of the author. To test the value of his own impressions he consulted separately two friends who had read *Ulysses* and whose 'opinion on life and literature' he valued highly: note again the insistence on an aesthetic as well as a moral valuation. . . .

Ulysses itself remains a monstrous and fascinating book. What has surprised me most, re-reading it, is that the word 'classical' should ever have been brought up by Joyce's more fervent admirers. No book for centuries has been so wildly, so elaborately and grotesquely twirled. Having been given the classical key to *Ulysses*, we may as well throw it away. Or—to vary the metaphor—it is as though we were asked to look at a building and to notice particularly the criss-cross of a builder's framework which years ago has been taken down. That is all, so far as I can see, that the Homeric structure, elaborately expounded by Messrs. Larbaud and Gilbert, amounts to. Joyce himself is well aware that the classical obsession, though necessary for writing the book, is not part of it. This passage is obviously autobiographical:

> Buck Mulligan bent across the table gravely.
> —They drove his wits away, he said, by visions of hell. He will never capture the Attic note. The note of Swinburne, of all poets, the white death and the ruddy birth. That is his tragedy. He can never be a poet.

We may take *Chamber Music* and *Pomes Pennyeach* as the attempt at 'the Attic note,' by way of the English classicists, Jonson and Dryden. They are curiously perfect, dead little poems. *Ulysses* is the repository of a whole corpus of unwritten poetry, doggerel as it bobs to the surface of the mind, soliloquies of a modern Hamlet, phrases and fag-ends of lines, the brooding commentary of Stephen Daedalus and the Bouvard-like reveries of Bloom. In the opening pages there are more passages of blank verse than in any other English prose-writer except Dickens. The effect of a pensive melancholy, overflowing the pointillist detail of the style, is curious, new, and perhaps the most original of the many original contributions of *Ulysses* to literature. . . .

[quotes from the Telemachus episode, p. 15, 13]

That is a very fair specimen of the prose in the early part of the book. It interrupts a boisterous conversation. Note even in this short passage how Joyce mixes his effects. The sixth sentence ('Crouching by a patient cow, etc.'), so packed and pictorial, might have been written by Flaubert. It is situated surprisingly in the middle of slow musical sentences, almost metrical in their lull, which end in fact with several lines of blank verse. The whole passage communicates, as well as its picture of the old woman, the brooding temper of Stephen Daedalus. There are Hellenisms, but the note is not Attic.

Poetry, then, in all its forms, from the embryonic to the purple, is what strikes one first on a re-reading. Next, the amazing use of parody. Joyce uses a mixture of parody and pastiche in order to achieve effects of his own, and not only the Oxford Book of English prose, but newspapers, novelettes, scientific reports, advertisements are echoed ironically to suit the scene. The famous chapter of parodies ('The Oxen of the Sun') I have read for the first time straight through. It is an extraordinary fantasia, beginning with Beowulf and ending with polyglot slang, in which the language at times obliterates the characters and their setting . . .

[discusses the episode]

. . . Joyce is a master of all styles, but he is not a stylist. His disgust with life extends also to literature; and in a sense *Ulysses* is a bonfire of literature, a glowing revenge. The process is carried still further in *Work in Progress*, where no one but the author finally can enter.

Yet along with the gigantic literary preoccupation of *Ulysses*, and saving it from Euphuism, there is Joyce's encyclopaedic love of fact. About some of the characters—Bloom, for example—we are told everything, from their thoughts to the tram tickets in their pockets. And as the two hundred or so characters file across the pages, the whole of Dublin with its narrow smoky streets seems to rise. Mr. Frank Budgen relates that when he was walking once with Joyce in Trieste, and they reached the university terrace overlooking the town, Joyce turned to him and said: 'I want to give a picture of Dublin so complete that if the city one day suddenly disappeared from the earth it could be reconstructed out of my book.' Like most of his quoted remarks this one is intensely egotistic. Yes, Joyce has the egotism, without the charm, of Sterne; *Ulysses* is *Tristram Shandy* written by a Brobdingnagian. . . .

117. Unsigned review of the English edition, *Times Literary Supplement*

23 January 1937

Mr. Joyce's major work is at any rate obscure enough to have invited several interpretations, and its structure is sufficiently unlike that of the ordinary novel to have suggested hidden messages and meanings. It has, for example, been supposed to have a pattern analogous to that of the *Odyssey*, to give an accurate and realistic account of the 'stream of consciousness' in the human mind, and by a new technique of writing to have expressed the nature of the characters' thoughts without the usual distortion of common sense and literary forms. But such explanations commonly arise when a new artistic method is invented; when the post-impressionists first startled the world with their pictures it was commonly believed that in some mysterious fashion they described essential as opposed to accidental properties of natural appearances. Later the artistic purpose of the new method emerges, and there is no longer any need to justify it either by supposing that it conceals as in a cryptogram an intelligible plan like that of previous and familiar works, or as a mode of scientific investigation.

There is, of course, a deliberate attempt to impose order on the incoherence of *Ulysses* by making all its events belong to a single day and by making the same episodes and characters appear and reappear in the kaleidoscope. But when one chapter contains a succession of masterly parodies of English prose in chronological order, from *Beowulf* to modern slang, when another is an amusing and satirical excursion on the Irish literary movement, another an irresistibly funny transcription of a young girl's day-dream in terms of the novelettes she has been reading, then the use of the same characters and episodes has the appearance of a merely conventional link between all the sections of the book. No doubt the link has a certain use in helping the reader along, but there is no reason to suppose that it makes the book a coherent whole from which no part can be removed without disaster. It is of no use to look for secret connexions, for in a work of art if the relations of the parts are not apparent enough to be felt, then the parts are not artistically related. Mr. Joyce's unit, in fact, is not the book as a whole but the chapter, often the paragraph, and sometimes, one might almost say, the phrase, or even the word. *Ulysses* is evidently the production of a man fascinated by language rather than by thought or observation; the progress of his style towards the final word-making and word-taking of the unintelligible *Work in Progress* has always been away from observation of life and towards the word as a complete substitute for the flesh. Like the lunatic whose speech degrades into a set of arbitrary sounds more and more remotely connected with his interior preoccupations, Mr. Joyce has played with language—it is perhaps the last development of the Irishman's habit of inventing new languages which shall not be English—until it has become his private construction. This is not, because he is content, like the lunatic, with any private or delusory world; but it is a curious fact, which several writers have noticed, that there is a remarkable similarity between Mr. Joyce's compositions and the prose style of certain lunatics. In the two instances the ordinary structure of the language is broken down for quite different reasons, but the results are oddly alike. And with the lunatic it may be worth while looking for the hidden connexion and meaning of apparently disorderly phrases; but with Mr. Joyce we are not to analyse the latent content of his verbal constructions, we are only concerned with the artistic and therefore immediate effect of his language.

But *Ulysses* only marks a stage in this progress, and his release from the ordinary linguistic conventions only enables Mr. Joyce to exercise all his talent, his almost incredible virtuosity, to the full. Passages that are genuine poetry alternate with the harshest and most deliberately contemptuous parodies, uproarious burlesque with subtle indications of character in a phrase. It is still a work of much observation, and of observation sharpened by disgust; but it is above all the profusion and fertility of language that will fascinate the reader. In this, the first edition published in England, there is an appendix giving, among other details of controversy, the decisions of the United States District Court and of the United States Court of Appeals which allowed *Ulysses* to be published in that country.

CONTEMPORARY CRITICAL OPINIONS

118. Valéry Larbaud on Joyce

1922

'James Joyce', *Nouvelle Revue Française,* xviii (April 1922), 385–405. Section IV of this article was translated as 'The *Ulysses* of James Joyce', in the *Criterion*, i, No. 1 (October 1922), 94–103 (from which the *Ulysses* section of this translation is taken). Also appeared as the 'Preface' to the French translation of *Dubliners* (*Gens de Dublin*, 1926). See the Introduction, p. 18, for a discussion of this important piece of criticism.

What follows is the text of a conference held last December 7 [1921] at the Maison des Amis des Livres [the bookshop of Adrienne Monnier in Paris]. . . . Such as it is, it gives an idea of the work of Joyce, brief without doubt but quite exact.

For two or three years among men of letters of his generation, James Joyce has held an extraordinary notoriety. There is hardly a critic who is not interested in his work, and even the most lettered of the English and American public are beginning to speak of it . . . In fact, he is for some the greatest currently living writer of the English language, the equal of Swift, Sterne and of Fielding, and everyone who has read his *Portrait* recognizes . . . the importance of this work, while those who have read the fragments of *Ulysses* published in a New York review [the *Little Review*] in 1919 and 1920 foretell that the renown and influence of James Joyce will be considerable. . . .

What happened to Joyce in the United States is the same as what happened to Flaubert and Baudelaire. There were several proceedings entered against the *Little Review* regarding *Ulysses.* The debates have sometimes been dramatic and more often comical, but always to the credit of the directress of the *Little Review*, Miss Margaret Anderson, who fought valiantly for misunderstood art and persecuted thought . . .

[A paragraph follows here on the incomprehensibility Larbaud feels about accepting a 'pornographic work for a literary work'.]

I am now going to try to describe the works of James Joyce as exactly as possible, without seeking to make a critical study of them: I will have enough to do in disengaging or trying to disengage for the first time the great lines of this work [*Ulysses*] and in giving a precise idea of it. . . .

[At this point, pp. 387–8, Larbaud gives the 'indispensable biographical notice'.]

. . . In sum, he does not please them [i.e. those who would have him be political or nationalistic]. One must note, however, that in writing *Dubliners, Portrait of the Artist* and *Ulysses,* he did as much as did all the heroes of Irish nationalism to attract the respect of intellectuals of every other country toward Ireland. His work restored Ireland, or rather gave to young Ireland, an artistic countenance, an intellectual identity; it did for Ireland what Ibsen's work did in his time for Norway, what Strindberg did for Sweden, what Nietzsche did for Germany at the end of the nineteenth century, and what the books of Gabriel Miró and Ramón Gomez have just done for contemporary Spain. The fact that Joyce's work is written in English should not trouble us: English is the language of modern Ireland . . . which shows how little nationalistic a literary language can be . . . In short, one might say that with the work of James Joyce and in particular with this *Ulysses* which is soon going to appear in Paris, Ireland is making a sensational re-entrance into high European literature.

I would like to speak to you now about *Ulysses,* but I believe that it would be better to follow a chronological order. Furthermore, *Ulysses,* which is by itself a difficult book, would be almost inexplicable without the knowledge of the earlier works of Joyce. . . .

Chamber Music [pp. 390–1]

His first work is a collection of thirty-six poems, none of which occupies more than a page. (This pamphlet appeared in May 1907. At first glance, it was thought to be a group of short lyric poems having love for their principal theme. However, the connoisseurs and notably Arthur Symons [see No. 9], saw immediately what they were about.) These short poems . . . continued, or more exactly revived, a great tradition, that of the Elizabethan song.

[Larbaud here discusses the obscurity that Elizabethan songs had fallen into because of the prominence of the drama of that period.]

. . . But no one [in 1900] considered seriously a renaissance of this genre; one could scarcely hope even for clever imitations. Indeed, what Joyce did in these thirty-six poems was to revive the genre without falling into imitation. He obeyed the same prosodic laws as Dowland and Campion, and like them he sang, under the guise of love, the joy of living, health, grace and beauty. However, he knew how to be modern in expression as well as in sentiment. The success obtained among the lettered was great, this thin pamphlet sufficed to place Joyce among the best Irish poets of the . . . generation. . . .

We will find the lyric poet again in the later work of Joyce, but only through glimpses and thus indirectly. He will have passed this stage. Other aspects of life, other forms of thought and imagination, will attract him. He will impart, he will relinquish, his lyric gift to his characters: as he did, for example, in the last three pages of the fourth chapter and in certain pages of the fifth chapter of the *Portrait of the Artist*, and very often in the monologues of *Ulysses*. But even at the moment when he composed the last of these poems . . . his imagination turned more and more toward those other aspects of life, more grave and human than the sentiments which served as themes for lyric poetry. I meant that he felt himself more and more possessed by the desire to express and to depict characters, some men, some women. . . .

Dubliners [pp. 392–5]

. . . This collection is composed of fifteen short stories which were completed and ready for publication in 1907, if not sooner. The second entitled 'An Encounter' treats in a perfectly decent manner and one which cannot shock any reader, a rather delicate subject: in fact it tells how two schoolboys play truant and meet a man whose allure and strange discourse—principally on bodily punishments and little amorous intrigues of schoolboys and schoolgirls—astonishes and then frightens them. In another, the sixth, the author presents two Dubliners of an undetermined social position and of a doubtful profession, who are, in fact, the Irish confrères of our Bubu-de-Montparnasse. These are the only two short stories of the collection whose subjects . . . the novelists and short story writers of the English language have avoided. However, they could furnish editors with a pretext for refusing the manuscript. But for want of this pretext, the Irish editors could find some more serious reasons for refusing to publish the book as it was. First of all, not only is all the topography of Dublin exactly reproduced . . . but above all in the short story 'Ivy Day in the Committee Room,' the bourgeois of Dublin, journalists, elected officials, speak liberally of politics, give their opinions on the problem of Irish autonomy and make some rather disrespectful remarks, or rather very familiar remarks, on Queen Victoria and on the private life of Edward VII. For these reasons, even the editor most desirous of publishing *Dubliners* hesitated. . . .

[Larbaud then describes, at some length, Joyce's difficulties about the Edward VII references, the burning of the Dublin edition of *Dubliners*, and the final appearance in June 1914 at London.]

(Most of the critics who discuss this book speak a great deal about Flaubert and Maupassant and about the French Naturalistes. And in fact it seems that it is from them that Joyce departs, not from the English and Russian novelists who preceded them, nor from the French novelists who have become the great masters of naturalism. However, in order to adequately judge this issue, one must perform some serious research into the sources of each of the stories. This is only a hypothesis that I submit to you. In any case, it is with our Naturalistes that Joyce, from his first prose work, has the most affinities. It is always necessary to keep from considering him as a late naturalist, as an imitator or popularizer in the English language of the methods of Flaubert or of Maupassant, or of the Médan group. . . . Even the epithet of neo-naturalist would not suit him because then one would have attempted to take him for a Zola or a Huysmans, or even a Jean Richepin with purely verbal audacities after an entirely superficial knowledge of his work. For even while admitting that he departs from naturalism, one is obliged to recognize that he has not tried to break away from this discipline, but to perfect it and to mould it in such a way that in *Ulysses* one further recognizes the influence of a naturalism that one would rather consider from Rimbaud and Lautremont, whom Joyce has not read.)

The world of *Dubliners* is already the world of *Portrait of the Artist* and of *Ulysses*. It is Dublin and the men and women of Dublin. Their forms are focused with great relief on the background of streets, of squares, of the port and the bay of Dublin. (Never has the atmosphere been better rendered, and in each of these short stories the people who know Dublin will find again a quantity of impressions that they thought they had forgotten.) But it is not the city which is the principal character, and the book does not have any unity: each story is a separate unit, it is a portrait, or a group, and there are some well-marked individualities which Joyce makes live. We will find, furthermore, some of them which we will recognize, as much for their words and traits of character as for their names, in the later works.

(The last of the fifteen stories is perhaps, from a technical point of view, the most interesting: as in the others Joyce conforms to the naturalist discipline, to write without appealing to the public, to tell a story while turning his back to his audience; but at the same time, by the sturdiness of his construction, by the disproportion that there is between the preparation and the dénouement, he leads up to his future innovations, when he will abandon almost completely the narration and substitute for it some unusual and sometimes unknown forms from novelists who have preceded him: the dialogue, the minute notation without logical bonds of facts, colors, odors and sounds, the interior monologue of characters, and even a form borrowed from catechism: question, answer; question, response.)

A Portrait of the Artist as a Young Man [pp. 395–8]

. . . In this book, which has the form of a novel, Joyce proposed to reconstruct the infancy and adolescence of an artist . . . At the same time, the title tells us that this is also, in a certain sense, the story of the youth of the artist, that is of all men gifted with the artistic temperament.

The hero—the artist—is called Stephen Dedalus. And here we approach one of the difficulties of Joyce's work: his symbolism, which we will encounter again in *Ulysses* and which will actually be the plot of that extraordinary book.

First of all, the name of Stephen Dedalus is symbolic: his patron saint is St. Stephen, the proto-martyr, and his family name is Dedalus, the name of the architect of the Labyrinth and of the father of Icarus. But, according to the author, he also has two other names; he is the symbol of two other persons. One of these is James Joyce. . . . But he is also—we shall see it again in *Ulysses*—Telemachus, the man whose Greek name means Far from the War, the artist who remains apart from the mêlée of interests and desires which motivate men of action; he is the man of science and the man of dreams who remains on the defensive, all his forces absorbed by the task of knowing, of understanding and of expressing.

Thus the hero of the novel is both a symbolic character and a real one, as will be all the characters of *Ulysses.*

[Larbaud next discusses the authenticity of the other characters in the novel.]

The English critics who are concerned with the *Portrait of the Artist* have, again, spoken of the naturalism, in a realization that is almost as if it were a question of such and such novel by Mirabeau. It was not that writer. They could equally well have spoken of Samuel Butler. In fact, I spoke of this resemblance the other day with a friend who had arrived at the same conclusion: there are certain fortuitous resemblances, commanded by the situation and by the genius of the two writers, between the religious crisis of Ernest Pontifex [in Butler's *The Way of All Flesh*] and that of Stephen Dedalus, and also between the long monologues of Christina and the interior monologue which takes place in Joyce. But it is too much to consider Butler as the precursor of Joyce on only these particular points.

No, the critics are misled. From the *Portrait of the Artist* forward, Joyce is himself and nothing but himself.

They are also deceived who only wanted to see in this book an autobiography . . . It is not that, for Joyce has drawn Stephen Dedalus from himself but at the same time he has created him. . . .

The success of this book has been great, and since its publication Joyce has become known to the lettered public. It has been 'un succès de scandale'. The critics, for the most part English and Protestant, were shocked by its frankness, and the absence of human decency which these 'confessions' bear witness to. . . . It is certain that in a Catholic country the tone of the press would have been very different . . . In fact, the best article dedicated to the *Portrait* was that in the *Dublin Review*, one of the great reviews of the Catholic world, directed or at least inspired by some priests.

The style of the *Portrait* is a great advance over that of *Dubliners*; the interior monologue and dialogue are substituted more and more for narration. We are more frequently carried to the essence of the thought of the characters: we see these thoughts forming, we follow them, we assist at their arrival at the level of conscience and it is through what the character thinks that we learn who he is, what he does, or where he is and what happens around him. The number of images, of analogies, and of symbols increases . . . all the symbolism of the Church, the different meanings of each object used in the cult, of each gesture made by the priest, without speaking of prefigurations, of prophecies and of concordances. . . . All that, furthermore, applies even better to *Ulysses* than to the *Portrait of the Artist*.

I must, to my great regret, leave out . . . the beautiful drama published in 1918, entitled *Exiles*, and I now proceed to *Ulysses*.

The reader who approaches this book without the *Odyssey* clearly in mind will be thrown into dismay. I refer, of course, to the cultivated reader who can fully appreciate such authors as Rabelais, Montaigne, and Descartes; for the uncultivated or half-cultivated reader will throw *Ulysses* aside after the first three pages. I say that the reader is at first dismayed: for he is plunged into the middle of a conversation which will seem to him incoherent, between people whom he cannot distinguish, in a place which is neither named nor described; and from this conversation he is to learn little by little where he is and who the interlocuters are. Furthermore, here is a book which is entitled *Ulysses*, and no character in it bears this name; the name of Ulysses only appears four times. But gradually the reader begins to see his way. Incidentally, he learns that he is in Dublin. He identifies the hero of the *Portrait of the Artist*, Stephen Dedalus, returned from Paris and living among the intellectuals of the Irish capital. . . .

[A brief summary follows here.]

Accordingly this huge book chronicles a single day; or, to be exact, begins at eight o'clock in the morning and ends towards three in the next morning.

As we have indicated, the reader follows the course of Bloom through his long day; for even if much eludes him at the first reading he will perceive enough to keep his curiosity and interest constantly awake. He remarks that, with the appearance of Bloom, the action begins again at eight o'clock, and that the three first chapters of Bloom's progress through his day are synchronous with the three first chapters of the book in which he has followed Stephen Dedalus. . . .

[Another summary of Bloom's activities.]

None of this, as I have already said, is told us in narrative form, and the book is a great deal more than the detailed history of Stephen's and Bloom's day in Dublin. It contains a vast number of other things, characters, incidents, descriptions, conversations, visions. But for us the readers, Bloom and Stephen are, so to speak, the vehicles in which we pass across the book. Stationed in the intimacy of their minds, and sometimes in the minds of the other characters, we see through their eyes and hear through their ears what happens and what is said around them. In this way, in this book, all the elements are constantly melting into each other, and the illusion of life, of the thing in the act, is complete: the whole is movement.

But the cultivated reader whom I have postulated will not let himself be wholly carried along by this movement. With the habit of reading and a long experience of books, he looks for the method and the material of what he reads. He will analyse *Ulysses* as he reads. And this is what will certainly be the result of his analysis after a first reading. He will say: This is still the society of *Dubliners*, and the eighteen parts of *Ulysses* can provisionally be considered as eighteen tales with different aspects of the life of the Irish capital as their subjects. Nevertheless, each of these eighteen parts differs from any of the fifteen tales of *Dubliners* on many points, and particularly by its scope, by its form, and by the distinction of the characters. Thus, the characters who take the principal rôles in the tales of *Dubliners* would be in *Ulysses* only supers, minor characters, or—it comes to the same thing—people seen by the author from the outside. In *Ulysses* the protagonists are all (in a literary sense) princes, characters who emerge from the depths of the author's inner life, constructed with his experience and his sensibility, and endowed by him with his own emotion, his own intelligence, and his own lyricism. Here, the conversations are something more than typical of individuals of such and such social classes; some of them are genuine essays in philosophy, theology, literary criticism, political satire, history. Scientific theories are expounded or debated. These pieces, which we might treat as digressions, or rather as appendices, essays composed outside of the book and artificially interpolated into all of the 'tales,' are so exquisitely adapted to the plot, the movement, and the atmosphere of the different parts in which they appear that we are obliged to admit that they belong to the book, by the same rights as the characters in whose mouths or whose minds they are put. But already we can no longer consider these eighteen parts as detached tales: Bloom, Stephen, and a few other characters remain, sometimes together and sometimes apart, the principal figures; and the story, the drama, and the comedy of their day are enacted through them. It must be acknowledged that, although each of these eighteen parts differs from all of the others in form and language, the whole forms none the less an organism, a book.

As we arrive at this conclusion, all sorts of coincidences, analogies, and correspondences between these different parts come to light; just as, in looking fixedly at the sky at night, we find that the number of stars appears to increase. We begin to discover and to anticipate symbols, a design, a plan, in what appeared to us at first a brilliant but confused mass of notations, phrases, data, profound thoughts, fantasticalities, splendid images, absurdities, comic or dramatic situations; and we realise that we are before a much more complicated book than we had supposed, that everything which appeared arbitrary and sometimes extravagant is really deliberate and premeditated; in short, that we are before a book which has a key.

Where then is the key? It is, I venture to say, in the door, or rather on the cover. It is the title: *Ulysses.*

Is it possible that this Leopold Bloom, this personage whom the author handles with so little consideration, whom he exhibits in all sorts of ridiculous or humiliating postures, is the son of Laertes, the subtle Ulysses?

We shall see. Meantime, I return to the *un*cultivated reader who was put off by the first pages of the book, too difficult for him; and I imagine that after reading him several passages taken from different episodes, we tell him: 'You understand that Stephen Dedalus is Telemachus, and Bloom is Ulysses.' He will now think that he does understand; the work of Joyce will no longer seem to him disconcerting or shocking. He will say: 'I see! it's a parody of the *Odyssey*!' For indeed, to such a reader the *Odyssey* is a great awe-inspiring machine, and Ulysses and Telemachus are *heroes*, men of marble invented by the chilly ancient world to serve as moral ensamples and subjects for scholastic theses . . . The only distinction between him and the uncultivated reader is that for him the *Odyssey* is not majestic and pompous, but simply uninteresting; and consequently he will not be so ingenuous as to laugh when he sees it burlesqued. The parody will bore him as much as the work itself. . . .

[discusses Joyce's early attraction to the Odyssey]

. . . Joyce extricated Ulysses from the text, and still more from the mighty fortifications which criticism and learning have erected about the text; and instead of trying to return to Ulysses in time, to reascend the stream of history, he made Ulysses his own contemporary, his ideal companion, his spiritual father.

What, then, in the *Odyssey*, is the moral figure of Ulysses? . . . He is a man, and the most completely human of all the heroes of the epic cycle: it is this characteristic which first endeared him to the schoolboy.

Then, little by little, always bringing Ulysses nearer to himself, the young poet recreated this humanity, this human, comic, and pathetic character of his hero. And recreating him, he has set him among the circumstances of life which the author had before his own eyes—in Dublin, in our time, in the complexity of modern life, and amidst the beliefs, the sciences, and problems of our time.

From the moment that he recreates Ulysses he must logically recreate all the characters who have, in the *Odyssey*, more or less to do with Ulysses. From this point, to recreate an Odyssey on the same plane, a modern Odyssey, was only a step to take. . . . Accordingly, in *Ulysses*, the three first episodes correspond to the Telemachy; Stephen Dedalus, the spiritual son and heir of Ulysses, is constantly on the scene.

From Book V to Book XIII are unfolded the adventures of Ulysses. Joyce distinguishes twelve chief adventures, to which correspond the twelve central chapters or episodes of his book. . . .

Naturally, Joyce has traced for himself, and not for the reader, this minutely detailed scheme, these eighteen sub-divided panels, this close web. There is no explanatory heading or sub-heading. It is for us to decipher, if we care to take the trouble. On this web, or rather in the compartments thus prepared, Joyce has arranged his text. It is a genuine example of the art of mosaic. . . .

. . . This plan, which cannot be detached from the book, because it is the very web of it, constitutes one of its most curious and fascinating features. If one reads *Ulysses* with attention, one cannot fail to discover this plan in time. But when one considers its rigidity, and the discipline which the author imposed upon himself, one asks how it can be that out of such a formidable labour of manipulation so living and moving a work could issue.

The manifest reason is that the author has never lost sight of the humanity of his characters, of their whole composition of virtues and faults, turpitude, and greatness; man, the creature of flesh, living out his day. And this is what one finds in reading *Ulysses*.

Among all the points which I ought to deal with, and have not space to deal with here, there are two on which it is indispensable to say a few words. One is the supposedly licentious character of certain passages—passages which in America provoked the intervention of the Society for the Suppression of Vice. The word 'licentious' is inappropriate; it is both vague and weak: it should be *obscene*. In *Ulysses* Joyce wished to display moral, intellectual, and physical man entire, and in order to do so he was forced to find a place, in the moral sphere, for the sexual instinct and its various manifestations and perversions; and, in the physiological sphere, for the reproductive organs and their functions. He does not hesitate to handle this subject any more than the great casuists do, and he handles it in English in the same way that they have handled it in Latin, without respect for the conventions and scruples of the laity. His intention is neither salacious nor lewd; he simply describes and represents; and in his book the manifestations of sexual instinct do not occupy more or less place, and have neither more nor less importance, than such emotions as pity or scientific curiosity. It is of course especially in the interior monologues, the trains of thought, of the characters, and not in their conversations, that sexual instinct and erotic revery emerge; for example, in the long interior monologue of Penelope—that is to say, Bloom's wife, who is also the symbol of Gæa, the Earth. The English language has a very great store of obscene words and expressions, and the author of *Ulysses* has enriched his book generously and boldly from this vocabulary.

The other point is this: why is Bloom a Jew? There are symbolical, mystical, and ethnological reasons which limitations of space prevent me from examining here—but which should be quite clear to readers of the book. All that I can say is that if Joyce has made his chosen hero, the spiritual father of this Stephen Dedalus who is his second self, a Jew—it is not because of anti-Semitism.

119. Pound on *Ulysses* and Flaubert

1922

Extract from 'James Joyce et Pécuchet', *Mercure de France*, clvi (June 1922), 307–20. Also appeared in Pound's *Polite Essays* (1937), pp. 82–97; translated by Fred Bornhauser in *Shenandoah*, iii (Autumn 1952), 9–20 (from which the present text is taken). See the Introduction, p. 21, for the place of this significant criticism of *Ulysses*.

. . . The Flaubert centenary year, first of a new era, also sees the publication of a new book by Joyce, *Ulysses*, which from certain points of view can be considered as the first work that, descending from Flaubert, continues the development of the Flaubertian art from where he left it off in his last, unfinished book.

Although *Bouvard et Pécuchet* does not pass for the master's 'best thing,' it can be maintained that *Bovary* and *l'Education* are but the apogee of an earlier form; and that the *Trois Contes* give a kind of summary of everything Flaubert had accomplished in writing his other novels, *Salammbo*, *Bovary*, *l'Education*, and the first versions of *Saint Antoine*. The three tableaux—pagan, medieval, and modern—form a whole revolving around the sentence: 'And the idea came to him to devote his life to the service of others,' which is in the middle of *Saint Julien*, the first of the three tales to be written.

Bouvard et Pécuchet continues the Flaubertian art and thought, but does not continue this tradition of the novel or the short story. 'Encyclopedia in the form of farce,' which carries as a subtitle, 'Failings of method in the sciences,' can be regarded as the inauguration of a new form, a form which had no precedent. Neither *Gargantua*, nor *Don Quixote*, nor Sterne's *Tristram Shandy* had furnished the archetype. . . .

What is James Joyce's *Ulysses*? This novel belongs to that large class of novels in sonata form, that is to say, in the form: theme, countertheme, recapitulation, development, finale. And in the sub-division: father and son novel. It follows in the great line of the *Odyssey*, and offers many points of more or less exact correspondence with the incidents of Homer's poem. We find there Telemachus, his father, the sirens, the Cyclops, under unexpected disguises, bizarre, argotic, veracious and gigantesque.

Novelists like to spend only three months, six months on a novel. Joyce spent fifteen years on his. And *Ulysses* is more condensed (732 pages) than any whole work whatsoever by Flaubert; more architecture is discovered.

There are some incomparable pages in *Bovary*, some incomparable condensed paragraphs in *Bouvard* (see the one where the sacred hearts, the pious images, etc., are bought). There are some pages of Flaubert which reveal their matter as rapidly as pages of Joyce, but Joyce has perfected the great collection of objects for ridicule. In a single chapter he discharges all the clichés of the English language like an uninterrupted river. In another chapter he compresses the whole history of English verbal expression since the first alliterative poetry (it is the chapter in the hospital where Mrs. Purefoy's delivery is awaited.) In another we have the headlines from the *Freeman's Journal* since 1760, that is to say the history of journalism; and he does this without interrupting the flow of his book.

He expresses himself differently in different parts of his book (as even Aristotle permits), but this does not mean, as the distinguished Larbaud contends, that he abandons unity of style. Each character not only speaks in his own manner, but thinks in his own manner, and that is no more abandoning unity of style than when the various characters of a novel in the so-called unified style speak in various ways: the quotation marks are left out, that's all.

Bloom, advertising agent, the Ulysses of the novel, the sensual average man, the basis—like Bouvard and Pécuchet—of democracy, the man who believes what he reads in the papers, suffers *after his soul's desire*. He is interested in everything, wants to explain everything, to impress everybody. Not only does his celerity and aptness for picking up what is said and thought everywhere, chewed over by everyone a hundred times a week, serve Joyce as a literary device, but the other characters are chosen to support him, in order to pick up the vanities of circles other than his.

Bouvard and Pécuchet are separated from the world, in a sort of still backwater. Bloom, on the contrary, moves in much more infectious surroundings.

Joyce uses a scaffold taken from Homer, and the remains of a medieval allegorical culture; it matters little, it is a question of cooking, which does not restrict the action, nor inconvenience it, nor harm the realism, nor the contemporaneity of the action. It is a means of regulating the form. The book has more form than those of Flaubert.

Telemachus (Stephen), the spiritual son of Bloom, reflects at the beginning on a medieval vanity, picked up in a Catholic school; he carries on with a university vanity, the relationship between Hamlet and Shakespeare. Always realistic in the strictest Flaubertian sense, always documented, always posted on life itself, Joyce never goes beyond the average. Realism seeks a generalization which concerns not only number or multiplicity, but permanence. Joyce combines the middle ages, the classical eras, even Jewish antiquity, in a current action; Flaubert strings out the epochs.

With his insistent elimination of quotation marks, Joyce presents the episode of the Cyclops in ordinary words, but next to it he sets down the grandiloquence, the parody; and measures the difference between realism and bulging romanticism. I have said that true criticism comes from authors; thus Joyce, with regard to Saint Anthony: 'It could be believed if he (Flaubert) had presented us Anthony in Alexandria gobbling down women and luxuries.'

A single chapter of *Ulysses* (157 pages) corresponds to *la Tentation de Saint Antoine*. Stephen, Bloom, and Lynch are drunk in a brothel; all the grotesquerie of their thought is laid bare; for the first time since Dante the harpies, the furies are found living, symbols taken in the real, the contemporary; nothing depends on mythology or dogmatic faith. Proportions are reaffirmed.

The limitation of *Bouvard et Pécuchet*, a limitation that even M. Descharmes notes, is that the incidents do not follow one another with an imperious enough necessity; the plan is not lacking in logic, but another would have sufficed. A more laudatory case can be made for Flaubert, but brief, clear and condensed as *Bouvard et Pécuchet* is, the ensemble is somewhat lacking in animation.

Joyce remedied that; at every instant the reader is kept ready for anything, at every instant the unexpected happens; even during the longest and most catalogued tirades one is kept constantly alert.

The action takes place in one day (732 pages) in a single place, Dublin. Telemachus wanders *beside the shore of the loud and roaring sea*; he sees the midwives with their professional bags. Ulysses breakfasts, circulates; mass, funeral, bath house, race track talk; the other characters circulate; the soap circulates; he hunts for advertising, the 'ad' of the House of Keyes, he visits the national library to verify an anatomical detail of mythology, he comes to the isle of Aeolus (a newspaper office), all the noises burst forth, tramways, trucks, post office wagons, etc.; Nausicaä appears, they dine at the hospital; the meeting of Ulysses and Telemachus, the brothel, the brawl, the return to Bloom's, and then the author presents Penelope, symbol of the earth, whose night thoughts end the story as counterweight to the ingenuities of the male. . . .

. . . Among the more passionately-felt pages one can cite the scene of the executioner, a more mordant satire than any other since Swift proposed a remedy for want in Ireland: to eat the children. Everywhere in the litanies, in the genealogy of Bloom, in the paraphrase of eloquence, the work is carefully done, not a line, not a half-line which does not receive an intellectual intensity incomparable in a work of so long a span; or known to be comparable only with the pages of Flaubert and the Goncourts.

That will give an idea of the enormous work of those fifteen years afflicted by poverty, bad health, and war: the whole first edition of his book *Dubliners* burned, the flight from Trieste, an operation on his eye; such facts will explain nothing about the novel, whose entire action takes place in Dublin on the 16th of June, 1904. Some characters can be found dissected in a page, as in *Bovary* (see Father Connice, the lad Dignam, etc.). One can examine the encyclopedic descriptions, the house dreamed about by Bloom, with the text of the imaginary lease; all the pseudo-intellectual bouillabaisse of the proletarians is presented, all equilibrated by Penelope, the woman who does not in the least respect this mass of nomenclature, the vagina, symbol of the earth, dead seas into which the male intelligence falls back.

It is the realistic novel par excellence, each character speaks in his own way, and corresponds to an external reality. Ireland is presented under the British yoke, the world under the yoke of measureless usury. Descharmes asks (page 267):

> Who, pray, has succeeded in this almost superhuman attempt to show, in the form of a novel and a work of art, universal imbecility?

I offer the reply: if it is not James Joyce, it is an author we must still await; but the reply of this Irishman merits deeply studied examination. *Ulysses* is not a book everybody is going to admire, any more than everybody admires *Bouvard et Pécuchet*, but it is a book that every serious writer needs to read, and that he, in our writer's profession, will be constrained to read in order to have a clear idea of the point of development of our art.

Not at all surprising that Joyce's books were not welcomed in Ireland in 1908; the rustic public and the provincials of Dublin were then in the act of demonstrating against the plays of Synge, finding them an insult to the national dignity. The same plays have just been presented this year in Paris as propaganda and as proof of the culture of the Irish race. Ibsen, if I recall, did not live in Norway; Galdos, in *Dona Perfecta*, shows us the danger of possessing a culture, not even international, but only Madridlian, in a provincial city that one guesses to be Saragossa. As for the romantic 'elders' in Ireland, I simply believe them incapable of understanding what realism is. As for George Moore and Shaw, it is human nature not to wish to see themselves eclipsed by a writer of greater importance. One knows that in Dublin Joyce is read in secret. This lack of cordiality has nothing astonishing about it. But the American law under which the *Little Review* was suppressed four times because of the fragments of *Ulysses* is a curiosity so curious, such a demonstration of the mentality of untutored jurists, of illiterate specialists, that it certainly deserves the attention of European psychologists, or rather of meningitis specialists. No, my dear friends, democracy (which we must so safeguard, according to our late calamity, Wilson) has nothing in common with personal liberty, nor with the fraternal deference of Koung-fu-Tseu. . . .

120. T. S. Eliot on *Ulysses* and myth

1923

'*Ulysses*, Order and Myth', *Dial*, lxxv (November 1923), 480–3. Also appeared in *Criticism: The Foundation of Modern Literary Judgment* (1948), ed. Mark Shorer, Josephine Miles and Gordon McKenzie, and in *James Joyce: Two Decades of Criticism* (1948, 1963), ed. Seon Givens, pp. 198–202.

Mr Joyce's book has been out long enough for no more general expression of praise, or expostulation with its detractors, to be necessary; and it has not been out long enough for any attempt at a complete measurement of its place and significance to be possible. All that one can usefully do at this time, and it is a great deal to do, for such a book, is to elucidate any aspect of the book—and the number of aspects is indefinite—which has not yet been fixed. I hold this book to be the most important expression which the present age has found; it is a book to which we are all indebted, and from which none of us can escape. These are postulates for anything that I have to say about it, and I have no wish to waste the reader's time by elaborating my eulogies; it has given me all the surprise, delight, and terror that I can require, and I will leave it at that.

Amongst all the criticisms I have seen of the book, I have seen nothing—unless we except, in its way, M. Valéry Larbaud's valuable paper [No. 118] which is rather an Introduction than a criticism—which seemed to me to appreciate the significance of the method employed—the parallel to the *Odyssey*, and the use of appropriate styles and symbols to each division. Yet one might expect this to be the first peculiarity to attract attention; but it has been treated as an amusing dodge, or scaffolding erected by the author for the purpose of disposing his realistic tale, of no interest in the completed structure. The criticism which Mr Aldington directed upon *Ulysses* several years ago seems to me to fail by this oversight—but, as Mr Aldington wrote before the complete work had appeared, fails more honourably than the attempts of those who had the whole book before them [No. 93]. Mr Aldington treated Mr Joyce as a prophet of chaos; and wailed at the flood of Dadaism which his prescient eye saw bursting forth at the tap of the magician's rod. Of course, the influence which Mr Joyce's book may have is from my point of view an irrelevance. A very great book may have a very bad influence indeed; and a mediocre book may be in the event most salutary. The next generation is responsible for its own soul; a man of genius is responsible to his peers, not to a studio-full of uneducated and undisciplined coxcombs. Still, Mr Aldington's pathetic solicitude for the half-witted seems to me to carry certain implications about the nature of the book itself to which I cannot assent; and this is the important issue. He finds the book, if I understand him, to be an invitation to chaos, and an expression of feelings which are perverse, partial, and a distortion of reality.

[quotes from Aldington's article (see No. 93).]

. . . Whether it is possible to libel humanity (in distinction to libel in the usual sense, which is libelling an individual or a group in contrast with the rest of humanity) is a question for philosophical societies to discuss; but of course if *Ulysses* were a 'libel' it would simply be a forged document, a powerless fraud, which would never have extracted from Mr Aldington a moment's attention. I do not wish to linger over this point: the interesting question is that begged by Mr Aldington when he refers to Mr Joyce's 'great *undisciplined* talent.'

I think that Mr Aldington and I are more or less agreed as to what we want in principle, and agreed to call it classicism. It is because of this agreement that I have chosen Mr Aldington to attack on the present issue. We are agreed as to what we want, but not as to how to get it, or as to what contemporary writing exhibits a tendency in that direction. We agree, I hope, that 'classicism' is not an alternative to 'romanticism,' as of political parties, Conservative and Liberal, Republican and Democrat, on a 'turn-the-rascals-out' platform. It is a goal toward which all good literature strives, so far as it is good, according to the possibilities of its place and time. One can be 'classical,' in a sense, by turning away from nine-tenths of the material which lies at hand, and selecting only mummified stuff from a museum—like some contemporary writers, about whom one could say some nasty things in this connexion, if it were worth while (Mr Aldington is not one of them). Or one can be classical in tendency by doing the best one can with the material at hand. The confusion springs from the fact that the term is applied to literature and to the whole complex of interests and modes of behaviour and society of which literature is a part; and it has not the same bearing in both applications. It is much easier to be a classicist in literary criticism than in creative art—because in criticism you are responsible only for what you want, and in creation you are responsible for what you can do with material which you must simply accept. And in this material I include the emotions and feelings of the writer himself, which, for that writer, are simply material which he must accept—not virtues to be enlarged or vices to be diminished. The question, then, about Mr Joyce, is: how much living material does he deal with, and how does he deal with it: deal with, not as a legislator or exhorter, but as an artist?

It is here that Mr Joyce's parallel use of the *Odyssey* has a great importance. It has the importance of a scientific discovery. No one else has built a novel upon such a foundation before: it has never before been necessary. I am not begging the question in calling *Ulysses* a 'novel'; and if you call it an epic it will not matter. If it is not a novel, that is simply because the novel is a form which will no longer serve; it is because the novel, instead of being a form, was simply the expression of an age which had not sufficiently lost all form to feel the need of something stricter. Mr Joyce has written one novel—the *Portrait*; Mr Wyndham Lewis has written one novel—*Tarr*. I do not suppose that either of them will ever write another 'novel.' The novel ended with Flaubert and with James. It is, I think, because Mr Joyce and Mr Lewis, being 'in advance' of their time, felt a conscious or probably unconscious dissatisfaction with the form, that their novels are more formless than those of a dozen clever writers who are unaware of its obsolescence.

In using the myth, in manipulating a continuous parallel between contemporaneity and antiquity, Mr Joyce is pursuing a method which others must pursue after him. They will not be imitators, any more than the scientist who uses the discoveries of an Einstein in pursuing his own, independent, further investigations. It is simply a way of controlling, of ordering, of giving a shape and a significance to the immense panorama of futility and anarchy which is contemporary history. It is a method already adumbrated by Mr Yeats, and of the need for which I believe Mr Yeats to have been the first contemporary to be conscious. It is a method for which the horoscope is auspicious. Psychology (such as it is, and whether our reaction to it be comic or serious), ethnology, and *The Golden Bough* have concurred to make possible what was impossible even a few years ago. Instead of narrative method, we may now use the mythical method. It is, I seriously believe, a step toward making the modern world possible for art, toward that order and form which Mr Aldington so earnestly desires. And only those who have won their own discipline in secret and without aid, in a world which offers very little assistance to that end, can be of any use in furthering this advance.

121. John Eglinton on Joyce's method

1922

Extract from 'Dublin Letter', *Dial*, lxxii, No. 6 (June 1922), 619–22; later appeared in *The Dial Miscellany* (1963), ed. William Wasserstrom, pp. 113–16.

In a survey of contemporary Irish letters, the critic refers briefly to Joyce.

. . . I do not know whether it is becoming in a contributor to *The Dial* to speak unsympathetically of the new work of that distinguished Irish exile, Mr James Joyce. Mr Joyce has wished to devise a species of literary notation which will express the interruptedness of life. We cannot hold our minds to any one purpose or idea for more than a few moments at a time . . . One 'specimen day' of such a mind Mr Joyce attempts to set down on paper, with an effort of concentration which reminds one of the ascetic practices of those Indian Yogis, who in attempting to recall their past lives, begin from the present moment, and travelling back laboriously to the moment of birth, are then able to leap the mysterious gulf dividing them from their last incarnation. Mr Joyce's feat in this book I should find admirable, if it were executed with some such practical purpose: but his purpose is to produce a work of virgin art! . . . There is an effort and strain in the composition of this book which makes one at times feel a concern for the author. But why should we half-kill ourselves to write masterpieces? There is a growing divergence between the literary ideals of our artists and the books which human beings want to read. . . .

I am by no means sure, however, that I have understood Mr Joyce's method, which is sufficiently puzzling even where he relates incidents in which I have myself taken a humble part.

122. Cecil Maitland on the Catholic tradition

1922

'Mr. Joyce and the Catholic Tradition', *New Witness*, xx (4 August 1922), 70–1.

. . . It would be absurd to try to make a thorough analysis of *Ulysses* in a short article, and I shall not attempt to do so here. For the convenience of readers unacquainted with Mr. Joyce's early work, I shall try briefly to indicate his place in the modern movement of literature and then to make an analysis of one particular aspect of the book . . . This gap between literature and reality Mr. Joyce has tried to fill. An effort of this sort would have been interesting in any case, but Mr. Joyce succeeded in making works of art of his experiments. His first novel tells the story of the infancy, childhood and youth of Stephen Dedalus, an Irish writer, in a style that admits of the presentation of half-thoughts, broken images, emotions, vivid or obscure, and each dirty, profound, trivial or obscene thought that passes through his mind. This book is, however, only a prelude to *Ulysses*. Masterpiece of compression though it is, the *Portrait* was experimental. *Ulysses* shows the author in absolute control of his medium, and with this book he has definitely produced a new form of novel that owes nothing to tradition. A superficial critic might assert that Mr. Joyce owes something of the elasticity of his prose to Sterne. Personally I should not be surprised if he had never read

Tristram Shandy. The resemblance between the two writers is more apparent than real, for while Sterne's style is an affectation, designed to display his wit and conceal his superficiality, Mr. Joyce elicits the subtlest processes of the mind, so that they are actually present to the reader and not merely recorded.

Ulysses is the *Odyssey* retold, episode by episode, as the story of a day's life in the streets, pubs and brothels of Dublin, and is an attempt to give a complete account of the nature of man. It is apparently almost miraculously successful, for he has reproduced the minds and impressions of his characters so vividly that the reader finds difficulty in separating his consciousness from theirs; and thus his conception of humanity from the author's, the boundaries of whose imagination become his own. These boundaries are very wide; at times Mr. Joyce gathers the thoughts of his characters into a whole that represents the consciousness of Dublin; but though municipal they are not cosmic. Indeed, these frontiers of the imagination are very rigid, for though there is in this book enough fun to make the reputation of a dozen humorous writers, there is no hint of a conception of the human body as anything but dirty, of any pride of life, or of any nobility but that of a pride of intellect. This vision of human beings as walking drain-pipes, this focussing of life exclusively round the excremental and sexual mechanism, appears on the surface inexplicable in so profoundly imaginative and observant a student of humanity as Mr. Joyce. He has, in fact, outdone the psycho-analysts, who admit 'sublimation,' and returned to the ecclesiastical view of man . . . No one who is acquainted with Catholic education in Catholic countries could fail to recognise the source of Mr. Joyce's 'Weltanschauung'. He sees the world as theologians showed it to him. His humour is the cloacal humour of the refectory; his contempt the priests' denigration of the body, and his view of sex has the obscenity of a confessor's manual, reinforced by the profound perception and consequent disgust of a great imaginative writer.

If we consider Mr. Joyce's work from this point of view, it becomes clear that while his study of humanity remains incomplete, the defect is not due to any inherent lack of imagination on his part. Rather it arises from the fact that to a Catholic who no longer believes that he has an immortal soul, fashioned in the image of God, a human being becomes merely a specially cunning animal. I suggest then that Mr. Joyce's failure is not his own, but that of the Catholic system, which has not had the strength to hold him to its transcendentalism, and from whose errors he has not been able to set himself free.

123. Alfred Noyes on literary Bolshevism

1922

'Rottenness in Literature', *Sunday Chronicle* (29 October 1922), 2. From the newspaper headline: 'The literary Bolshevism of to-day formed the theme of a scathing attack by Mr. Alfred Noyes, the well-known poet, in the course of a lecture before the Royal Society of Literature a few days ago . . . Mr Noyes singles out for particular attack Mr. James Joyce's *Ulysses*.'

I have picked out *Ulysses* because it brings to a head all the different questions that have been perplexing literary criticism for some time past. There is no answer possible in this case. It is simply the foulest book that has ever found its way into print. It has received columns of attention from many of our leading journals, and its author has been proclaimed a slightly mad genius perhaps, but still a genius.

The writing of the book is bad simply as writing, and much of it is obscure through sheer disorder of the syntax. But—there is no foulness conceivable to the mind of madman or ape that has not been poured into its imbecile pages.

This is not a question of Puritanism. If it were not so serious a matter there would be considerable irony in the fact that the only sound analysis of the book in this country was made by the *Sporting Times*, which described it as 'the work of a madman,' and said that it was 'couched in language that would make a Hottentot sick' [No. 96].

Yet some of the 'intellectuals,' including one of our leading novelists, have been stating that its author comes within measurable distance of having written the best book in the world. An important review devoted eight columns to this book, and a more or less important novelist announced that Mr. Joyce had only just missed being the most superb member of his own craft, not only in his own times but in any other.

The *Quarterly Review* is perhaps justified in printing its exposure of the critics who proclaimed this insane product, but even the *Quarterly* was unable to tell the whole truth about it [No. 102]. Nobody can tell the whole truth about it; for, to put it plainly, if the book were submitted to the judges of any criminal court in this country, it would be pronounced to be simply a corrupt mass of indescribable degradation.

No word or thought conceivable in the gutters of Dublin or the New York Bowery is omitted, and the foulest references are made to real persons in this country, attributing vile diseases to them, amongst other equally disgusting suggestions.

I have recited the case of this book because it is the extreme case of complete reduction to absurdity of what I have called the 'literary Bolshevism of the Hour.' It can do little harm, however, because the police are, on the whole, circumventing our pseudo-intellectuals. It still remains that copies of Mr. Joyce's book are being smuggled into the country to find purchasers at five guineas apiece.

But what concerns us all, and most urgently demands consideration, is the appalling fact that our Metropolitan criticism should have been treating such works as those of Mr. Joyce seriously as works of genius at the very moment when journal after journal is helping to depreciate the value of some of the noblest pages in our literary history.

The battle that is being waged round the works of Tennyson, for instance, the assault that has been made upon all the great Victorian writers—and it is interesting to note that Bolshevik Russia has recently been declaring that Dickens is more dangerous than Denikin—are indications of a destructive spirit which may lead us far along the road to barbarism.

[The critic continues with his thesis that the younger London literary group is out of touch with reality.]

124. Ford Madox Ford on *Ulysses* and indecency

1922

Extract from '*Ulysses* and the Handling of Indecencies', *English Review*, xxxv (December 1922), 538–48.

I have been pressed to write for the English public something about the immense book of Mr. Joyce. I do not wish to do so; I do not wish to do so at all for four or five—or twenty—years, since a work of such importance cannot properly be approached without several readings and without a great deal of thought. To write, therefore, of all aspects of *Ulysses*, rushing into print and jotting down ideas before a hostile audience is a course of action to which I do not choose to commit myself. The same imperious correspondents as force me to write at all forward me a set of Press-cuttings, the tributes of my distinguished brothers of the pen to this huge statue in the mists.

One may make a few notes, nevertheless, in token of good will and as a witness of admiration that is almost reverence for the incredible labours of this incredible genius. For indeed, holding *Ulysses* in one's hand, the last thing one can do about it is to believe in it.

Let us, if you will, postulate that it is a failure—just to placate anybody that wants placating in that special way. For it does not in the least matter whether *Ulysses* is a success or a failure. *We* shall never know and the verdict will be out of our hands: it is no question of flying from London to Manchester under the hour. That we *could* judge. It fails then.

Other things remain. It is, for instance, obvious that the public—the lay, non-writing public of to-day—will not read *Ulysses* even in the meagre measure with which it reads anything at all, the best or the worst that is put before it. Perhaps no lay, non-writing public will ever read it even in the measure with which it reads Rabelais, Montaigne, or the *Imaginary Conversations* of Walter Savage Landor. (I am not comparing Mr. Joyce with these writers.) That perhaps would be failure.

Or perhaps it would not. For myself, I care nothing about readers for writers. . . .

And yet, even though the great uninstructed public should never read *Ulysses*, we need not call it a failure. There are other worlds. It is, for instance, perfectly safe to say that no writer after to-day will be able to neglect *Ulysses*. Writers may dislike the book, or may be for it as enthusiastic as you will; ignore it they cannot, any more than passengers after the 'forties of last century could ignore the railway as a means of transit.

I have called attention in another place to the writers' technical revolution that in *Ulysses* Mr. Joyce initiates. The literary interest of this work, then, arises from the fact that, for the first time in literature on an extended scale, a writer has attempted to treat man as the complex creature that man—every man!—is.

[The critic here discusses the stream of consciousness technique generally.]

[The critic has been discussing sexuality in literature.]

. . . Before the war, when I was less of a hermit but much more ingenuous, I used to be shocked by the fact that a great many ladies whom I respected and liked possessed copies of, and gloated as it appeared over, a volume of dream-interpretations by a writer called Freud—a volume that seemed to me to be infinitely more objectionable, in the fullest sense of the term, than *Ulysses* at its coarsest now seems to me. For I can hardly picture to myself the woman who will be 'taught to be immodest' by the novel; I could hardly in those days imagine anyone who could escape that fate when reading that—real or pseudo!—work of science. Yet I find to-day that the very persons who then *schwaermed* over Freud now advocate the harshest of martyrdoms for Mr. Joyce.

That is obviously because Mr. Joyce is composed, whilst Mr. Freud has all the want of balance of a scientist on the track of a new theory.

[The critic here discusses censorship and quotes extensively from the Circe episode, pp. 581–2, pp. 597–8.]

. . . That appears to have been an ordinary Dublin Night's Entertainment; the English reader may find it disagreeable to peruse. But I do not see that the adoption of a suppressive policy towards such matters does anyone much good. I ought to say that in Mr. Joyce's pages the epithets that my more coy pen has indicated with dots are written out in full.

I don't see why they should not be: that is the English language as we have made it and as we use it—all except a very thin fringe of our More Select Classes. And that, in effect, is our civilisation of to-day—after a hundred years of efforts at repression on the part of those with Refined Poetic Imaginations. . . .

[The critic continues with his discussion of 'obscene' language.]

There is not very much about Mr. Joyce in all this—*et pour cause*! Mr. Joyce stands apart from this particular world of ambassador-publishers, lay and ecclesiastical editors, intelligentsia, and Comstockian orgies. To call a work that deals with city life in all its aspects 'serene' would probably be to use the wrong word. And yet a great deal of *Ulysses* is serene, and possibly, except to our Anglo-Saxon minds, even the 'disgusting passages' would not really prove disgusting. That is what one means when one calls *Ulysses* at last a European work written in English.

For indeed a book purporting to investigate and to render the whole of a human life cannot but contain 'disgusting' passages; we come, every one of us, into a world as the result of an action that the Church—and no doubt very properly!—declares to be mortal sin; the great proportion of the food we eat and of the food eaten by the beasts that we eat is dung; we are resolved eventually into festering masses of pollution for the delectation of worms.

And it is probably better that from time to time we should contemplate these facts, hidden though they be from the usual contemplation of urban peoples. Otherwise, when, as inevitably we must, we come up against them we are apt to become overwhelmed to an unmanly degree. As against this weakness it would probably be good to read *Ulysses*. But I am not prescribing the reading of *Ulysses* as a remedy to a sick commonwealth.

Nor indeed do I recommend *Ulysses* to any human being. In the matter of readers my indifference is of the deepest. It is sufficient that *Ulysses*, a book of profound knowledge and of profound renderings of humanity, should exist—in the most locked of book-cases. . . .

125. Paul Claudel on *Ulysses*

1922

Adrienne Monnier, 'Lectures chez Sylvia', *Nouvelle Revue Française*, cclxxiv (1 August 1936), 250–2; reprinted in *Mercure de France*, cccxlvii (August–September 1963), 133–5.

Miss Monnier quotes Paul Claudel's comment on *Ulysses*.

They would have loved to see the name of our great Claudel on this Committee [to save Sylvia Beach's Shakespeare & Company from a financial crisis], but we did not dare solicit it: we knew that he would not pardon us for having published Joyce's *Ulysses*. Had he not written to us on this subject: '*Ulysses* like the *Portrait* is full of the most foul blasphemy where all the hatred of a renegade is felt—affected besides with an absence of truly diabolic talent.'

126. Robert McAlmon on Joyce and *Ulysses*

1920–2

Extracts from *Being Geniuses Together: An Autobiography* (1938), pp. 12, 14, 20, 87–8, 90–1, 127–8, 268, 293.

The following comments, all made between 1920 and 1922, have been extracted from these memoirs of a friend and, noting the comments on pages 90 to 91, collaborator.

In Paris I had a note from Harriet Weaver, publisher, of the Egoist Press, to present to James Joyce. His *Dubliners* I much liked. The Stephen Dedalus of his *Portrait of the Artist as a Young Man* struck me as precious, full of noble attitudinizings and not very admirable in its soulful protestations. He seemed to enjoy his agonies with a self-righteousness which would not let the reader in on his actual ascetic ecstacies. Nevertheless, the short stories made me feel that Joyce would be approachable, as indeed did passages of *Ulysses*, which had already appeared in the *Little Review* . . . [p. 12].

I don't think I ever did get to telling Joyce that the high-minded struttings and the word prettifications and the Greek beauty part of his writings palled on me, as did Stephen Dedalus when he grew noble and too forebearing. Stephen's agonies about carnal sin seemed melodramatic, but perhaps they were not so . . . [p. 14].

Where Joyce goes Irish-twilightly and uses words for their isolated beauty of the word alone as it stands in the dictionary, Ezra [Pound] gives entire passages, which evoke historic and legendary memories, and satirizes cooly . . . [p. 20].

A sad and funny episode about this time with James Joyce. *Ulysses* was out and he had not, to my knowledge, started his new work . . .

His friend, on the other hand, was poor and much impressed by the reclame with which *Ulysses* had been greeted. The staid English papers were duly horrified and righteous, while patronizingly admitting a talent. The London *Pink 'Un* [No. 96] was less intellectual. It merely stated that 'The main contents are enough to make a Hottentot sick

. . . not alone sordidly pornographic, but it is intensely dull.' The book *is* dull. It takes a person highly curious about life and letters, one of those super-morons, an intellectual, to read it through. . . . [pp. 87–8].

For a long time Norah had been intent upon moving into an apartment, and Joyce now, who was given to expecting that things would be done for him, hoped that not only would I cover his tales to Norah but that I would locate him an apartment. He got fooled there. If he'd been bright he would have secured a promise from me when I was drunk and I might have made an effort, as I kept my word about typing the last fifty pages of *Ulysses*, the Molly Bloom interior-monologue.

The husband of the English typist who was typing his work had destroyed some forty pages of the original script of *Ulysses*, because it was obscene. Joyce was naturally scared about handing work out to typists, and most typists would insist upon putting in punctuation which he did not desire. He knew that I typed not well, but quickly, and spoke suggestively of the point as we were drinking. I thought then, fifty pages, that's nothing, sure I'll type it for you.

The next day he gave me the handwritten script, and his handwriting is minute and hen-scrawly; very difficult to decipher. With the script he gave me some four notebooks, and throughout the script were marks in red, yellow, blue, purple, and green, referring me to phrases which must be inserted from one of the notebooks. For about three pages I was painstaking and actually re-typed one page to get the insertion in the right place. After that I thought 'Molly might just as well think this or that a page or two later or not at all,' and made the insertions wherever I happened to be typing. Years later upon asking Joyce if he'd noticed that I'd altered the mystic arrangement of Molly's thought he said that he had, but agreed with my viewpoint. Molly's thoughts were irregular in several ways at best. . . . [pp. 90–1].

Henry Seidel Canby and Canfield (of Harper's) were dining one night at the Eiffel Tower when Curtiss Moffatt asked several of us to go to a party at Viola Tree Parsons'. We got into a taxi and started off. Dr. Canby began to talk about *Ulysses*, seemingly worried about what he should think of it. One guessed that he'd like definitely to prove it valueless, but one must have culture and know what is being talked about and be able to converse intelligently. Many people would look the book over, decide either that it is dull or it is interesting and accordingly read it or not read it. One gathers that Dr. Canby by now has gone the way of the others since *Ulysses* has more or less joined the ranks of the unread classics. He mentions it as a work of genius and does not worry about its pornography or its strange technique. . . . [pp. 127–8].

Sylvia Beach gave Sato copies of *Ulysses* to sell in Japan. This letter was to her. 'Mr. Joyce's book has such an original clever and wonderfully unique style. His wording is simply wonderful . . . if it (*Portrait of the Artist*) is translated into Japanese it may be a successful one. Just now the sexual question is very popular among the young peoples. So the struggle of the hero with his sin might hit a popularity in Japan. I will keep on to find him and if I have succeeded to find him a publisher I will tell him hurry my translation of his book. . . .' [p. 268].

Mr. [Ludwig] Lewisohn commented on Mr. Joyce's *Ulysses*, but in a very fatherly, scientific and gentle way. It seems that what Mr. Hoyce needs is psychoanalysis. Had he been given a thorough-going psychoanalytic treatment in the years past he would never have perpetrated the book. I suggested that perhaps the Jesuits and the Catholic church, all institutionalized religions in fact, need psychoanalysis and that perhaps Joyce had given Catholicism and the Jesuits just that in *Ulysses*. . . . [p. 293].

127. Oliver St. John Gogarty comment on *Ulysses*

1922

A comment on *Ulysses* by Oliver St. John Gogarty, quoted in Ulick O'Connor, 'James Joyce and Oliver St. John Gogarty: A Famous Friendship', *Texas Quarterly*, iii (Summer 1960), 191.

When *Ulysses* appeared in 1922 and Gogarty saw himself depicted as Mulligan, he was furious. It seemed to him in the nature of a betrayal that Joyce should have written about him as he did. 'That bloody Joyce whom I kept in my youth has written a book you can read on all the lavatory walls of Dublin,' he snarled to a friend who questioned him about the book shortly after it appeared. When Norah Hault, wishing to place Gogarty as a character in one of her novels, gave him smoke-blue eyes because, as she said, Joyce was always right about such things, Gogarty replied indignantly that this was not so.

128. Gertrude Stein on Joyce

A comment by Gertrude Stein in Samuel Putnam, *Paris was our Mistress* (1947), p. 138.

. . . 'What about Joyce?'

'Joyce,' she admitted, 'is *good.*' (The italics were in her voice.) 'He is a *good* writer. People like him because he is incomprehensible and anybody can understand him. But who came first, Gertrude Stein or James Joyce? Do not forget that my first great book, *Three Lives*, was published in 1908. That was long before *Ulysses*. But Joyce *has* done *something*. His influence, however, is local. Like Synge, another Irish writer, he has had his day. . . .'

129. Yeats to Olivia Shakespear

1922

Letter to Olivia Shakespear (8 March 1922), in *The Letters of W. B. Yeats* (1955), ed. Allan Wade, p. 679.

I am reading the new Joyce [*Ulysses*]—I hate it when I dip here and there but when I read it in the right order I am much impressed. However I have but read some thirty pages in that order. It has our Irish cruelty and also our kind of strength and the Martello Tower pages are full of beauty. A cruel playful mind like a great soft tiger cat—I hear, as I read, the report of the rebel sergeant in '98: 'Oh he was a fine fellow, a fine fellow. It was a pleasure to shoot him.'

130. Hart Crane on *Ulysses*

1922

Extract from a letter from Hart Crane (addressee unidentified). From *The Letters of Hart Crane* (1952), ed. Brom Weber, pp. 94–5. (27 July 1922)

I feel like shouting EUREKA! When [Gorham] Munson went yesterday after a two weeks visit, he left my copy of *Ulysses*, a huge tome printed on Verge d'arche paper. But do you know—since reading it partially, I do not think I will care to trust it to any book-binder I know of. It sounds ridiculous, but the book is so strong in its marvelous oaths and blasphemies, that I wouldn't have an easy moment while it was out of the house. You will pardon my strength of opinion on the thing, but it appears to me easily the epic of the age. It is as great a thing as Goethe's *Faust* to which it has a distinct resemblance in many ways. The sharp beauty and sensitivity of the thing! The matchless details! . . . His book is steeped in the Elizabethans, his early love, and Latin Church, and some Greek. . . .

Joyce is still very poor. Recently some French writers headed by Valéry Larbaud, gave a dinner and reading for his benefit. It is my opinion that some fanatic will kill Joyce sometime soon for the wonderful things said in *Ulysses* . . . He is the one above all others I should like to talk to. . . .

131. Ford Madox Ford on *Ulysses*

1922

Letter to Edgar Jepson (15 August 1922), in *The Letters of Ford Madox Ford* (1965), ed. Richard M. Ludwig, p. 143.

Ulysses we shall no doubt differ about till the end of the chapter; personally I'm quite content to leave to Joyce the leading novelist-ship of this country, think he deserves the position, and hope it will profit him. . . .

132. George Slocombe on Joyce

1923

Extract from *The Tumult and the Shouting* (1936), pp. 220–1.

I made his acquaintance early in 1923. I had already read, admired and reviewed his prodigious *Ulysses*, in one of the earliest notices—perhaps the earliest of all—of that work to appear in the English Press [No. 105]. Some years afterwards, when he published an elfin volume of verse under the characteristically Joycean title of *Pomes Penyeach*, a baker's dozen for a shilling, he told me that I had the melancholy distinction of being the only English writer to have reviewed it [No. 155]. Neither he, his publisher Sylvia Beach, nor I ever discovered the reason for this almost universal neglect. I am inclined to suspect that the postal authorities in England, remembering the dreadful example of *Ulysses*, and without examining the contents of his thin and utterly conservative volume, cast all the review copies addressed to English newspapers into the flames. All of the poems then denied to, or ignored by, English reviewers have since figured in anthologies.

The amazing erudition revealed by *Ulysses* intimidated most people in conversation with Joyce. But apart from a disinclination to discuss that work, and a charming readiness to entertain baffled friends with the theme, treatment and significance of his even more erudite, and far less comprehensive *Work in Progress*, Joyce is singularly free from exclusiveness, pride, reserve, or pedantry. . . .

133. Aleister Crowley on the novel of the mind

1923

Extract from 'The Genius of Mr. James Joyce', *New Pearson's Magazine*, xlix (July 1923), 52–3.

In a discussion of a new form of literature, the 'novel of the mind', the critic notes that this kind of fiction may 'depart from artistic creation'.

. . . This form of writing has been saved, by the genius of Mr. James Joyce, from its worst fate, that of becoming a mere amateur contribution to medical text-books.

Every new discovery produces a genius. Its enemies might say that psycho-analysis—the latest and deepest theory to account for the vagaries of human behaviour—has found the genius it deserves. Although Mr. Joyce is known only to a limited circle in England and America, his work has been ranked with that of Swift, Sterne, and Rabelais by such critics as M. Valery, Mr. Ezra Pound and Mr. T. S. Eliot.

There is caution to be exercised in appraising the work of a contemporary. . . . I am convinced personally that Mr. Joyce is a genius all the world will have to recognize. I rest my proof upon his most important book *Ulysses*, and upon his first novel, *A Portrait of the Artist as a Young Man*, and on such portions of *Ulysses* as have appeared. Before these he wrote two books, *Chamber Music*, a collection of most delicate songs, and *Dubliners*, sketches of Dublin life distinguished by its savage bitterness, and the subsequent hostility it excited. *The Portrait* when it appeared was hailed as a masterpiece, but it has been boycotted by libraries and booksellers for no discernible reason other than the fact that the profound descriptions tell the truth from a new, and therefore to the majority a disturbing, point of view. . . .

[A two-paragraph summary follows.]

The book is written with the utmost delicacy and vigor. When Stephen is a baby, Mr. Joyce selected the exact incidents that would impress the hardly conscious minds in such a way that the reader finds that his own infantile memories are astir. He recalls his own mind when it was incapable of synthesis and conscious only of alternation between nourishment and excretion. Gradually the child becomes aware of the relation between one thing and another, with adolescence his consciousness becomes complete, and the struggle of the individual to express and reconcile himself to life begins. As his mind changes Mr. Joyce changes his style, the unperceiving mind is shown so that the actual texture of its unperceptiveness is felt, an incomplete thought is given in its incompleteness. But when Mr. Joyce leaves his characters to their stream of unsorted perceptions and speaks for himself, he writes classical English prose with the particular beauty proper to a new master. . . .

The end of the *Portrait* leaves Stephen still at Dublin University. He is the eldest, a swarm of brothers and sisters sit round the table and drink tea out of jam pots. His mother 'is ashamed a University student should be so dirty, his own mother has to wash him.' He is the poorest of poor students, the most gifted, proud and perverse. We leave him, knowing that there is worse in store for him and turn to *Ulysses.*

Ulysses, as the title suggests, is another Odyssey of a small Jewish commercial traveller round about the Dublin streets on one day. . . .

[A four-paragraph summary follows here.]

I have no space to enter upon the real profundity of this book or its amazing achievement in sheer virtuosity. Mr. Joyce has taken Homer's *Odyssey* and made an analogy, episode by episode, translating the great supernatural epic into terms of slang and betting slips, into the filth, meanness and wit and passion of Dublin today. Then the subtle little alien is shown exploiting, as once the '*Zeus-born, son of Laertes, Odysseus of many wiles*' exploited, the ladies and goddesses of the 'finest story in the world.'

At present Mr. Joyce is all but unknown except to the inmost ring of English and French lovers of the arts. In his own country prejudiced Dublin opinion is making a determined effort to boycott him. It would certainly reflect no discredit on the Commonwealth of Australia if she were to be one of the first to recognize a writer who will in time compel recognition from the whole civilised world. . . .

134. An interview with Valéry Larbaud

1923

Frederic LeFevre, 'An Hour with M. Valéry Larbaud', *Les Nouvelles littéraires*, ii, No. 51 (6 October 1923), 1–2.

. . . I believe that we have been unremittingly anglicized and that it would be good now to change course . . . There is now only the influence of James Joyce (who is Irish) who has not yet had all his repercussions. Aside from Joyce and in spite of all the translations that have been done, literary anglo-mania is falling off. I have at least that definite impression and it is indeed so. . . .

James Joyce descends from the naturalists, but he has expanded their territory. His most important work, which I should have translated a long time ago and published fragments, is *Ulysses*, where it pleases me to salute the first masterpiece of the interior monologue. I thus label a form in which the reader finds himself installed in the thought of the character and learns in this way the progression of circumstances in which this character finds himself. James Joyce has told me many times that he owed this form to the French writer Edouard Dujardin, who had first used it in *Les Lauriers sont coupés*. Through Joyce I have returned, myself, to Edouard Dujardin and it is to acquit this debt of recognition that I dedicate to him: 'My most secret counsel. . .'

Outside of the interior monologue which characterizes Joyce's work, there is a continual invention of forms: in *Ulysses*, there is a chapter done in the manner of all the classical English writers. There is even a chapter which is like a catechism, with questions and answers. . . .

135. Yeats and the Dublin Philosophical Society

1923

Extract from an unsigned notice, 'The Modern Novel. An Irish Author Discussed', *Irish Times* (9 November 1923), 4.

A journalistic account of the opening meeting of the Dublin University Philosophical Society, at which Mr. W. Beare presented a paper, 'The Modern Novel', in which Joyce is mentioned favourably. W. B. Yeats responded with a few remarks of his own about Joyce. Mr. Beare's comments on Joyce reflect his division of Irish literature into 'two widely divergent classes—that of the sternest realism, and that of the most ideal romanticism. . . .'

. . . Future historians would, perhaps, decide that the most original and influential writer of our day was James Joyce. His *Ulysses* seemed to reach the ultimate limit of realism, but the example set by Mr. Joyce would hardly be very widely followed. In spite of the author's power, humour, and psychological insight, *Ulysses* was open to the charge of dullness.

[Yeats] One writer the Auditor [Mr. Beare] had mentioned—James Joyce—was certainly as voluminous as Johnson's dictionary and as foul as Rabelais; but he was the only Irishman who had the intensity of the great novelist. The novel was not his (Mr. Yeats's) *forte*. All he could say was that there was the intensity of the great writer in Joyce. The miracle was possibly there: that was all he felt he had a right to say, and, perhaps, the intensity was there for the same reason as the intensity of Tolstoi and Balzac.

When James Joyce began to write in Ireland they had not come to their recent peril of the robbery and the murder and the things that came with it, but he thought that the shadow of peril was over everyone when men were driven to intensity. The book *Ulysses* was a description of a single day in Dublin twenty years ago. He thought it was possible that Ireland had had that intensity out of which great literature might arise, and it was possible that James Joyce was merely the first drop of a shower. . . .

1923: ULYSSES

136. An Irish comment on *Ulysses*

1923

Extract from Laurence K. Emery, 'The *Ulysses* of Mr. James Joyce', *Claxon* (Winter 1923–4), 14–20.

The phenomenon of James Joyce seems to most people inexplicable. Why seek the scabrous for a subject when the sweet and pure can be so beautifully expressed? Why walk on dungheaped roads when a rose-walk can be had for a twopenny tram drive? Irishmen, together with Englishmen and Americans, or rather the Irish, English and American *public*, asked these pointed questions and ostracised Mr. Joyce without staying for an answer. Fortunately, however, it is not necessary for an artist to develop on his native soil to produce his best work . . .

A slow and careful worker, Mr. Joyce worked for ten years on the *Portrait of the Artist as a Young Man*. It is usually described as an autobiography, a series of confessions *à la mode*, dressed in the form of a novel. These may be confessions, but Mr. Joyce is too much of an artist faithfully to record his own life. There is in all his work a cold objectivity. He has an uncanny keenness of perception which he does not let his ego influence. This perception he must have applied to himself, and he can synthesise a character from details observed in his own person.

The result can never be self-revelatory, for, like a true artist, this synthesis is coupled with the unusual touch that Shakespeare gives to Hamlet or Balzac to Pons.

Ulysses continues where the *Portrait* left off. At the end of the latter novel Stephen Dedalus left for Paris, and *Ulysses* begins at the point of his return from that city. Chronologically we only advance one day from page 1 to page 732. But actually there is such a world of learning, scientific, metaphysic, æsthetic, of life real and imagined, of force comic and tragic, of description, of lyricism, patter and rhetoric, heroics and eloquence, as to make the day longer than any conceived on this planet.

The incidents round which this immensity hangs are ordinary enough, are quite within the compass of twenty-four hours and are credible without Einstein. . . .

[briefly summarizes the plot]

On this skeleton hangs the variegated fabric of *Ulysses*. I could not, tried I ever so hard, give an adequate notion of the vast number of characters, descriptions, parodies and visions that crowd so comfortably into the 800 pages without actually quoting the whole book, which is manifestly impossible. . . . *Ulysses* cannot be termed pornographic. One might as well label the Venus de Milo indecent, and just as that piece of sculpture has been the urge to centuries of artists, so *Ulysses*, with its strange modernity, will carry away young writers on its irrepressible tide. But I do wrong to talk about a classic nude in relation to *Ulysses*. It has no more in common with the idealised naked beauties of a Cabanel or a Solomon J. Solomon, or the holy etherealisations of the Pre-Raphaelites, than Ibsen with St. Francis of Assisi. Mr. Joyce is essentially the product of his age, or perhaps, as with all genius, a little ahead of it. In him we find collected all the strivings of the modern world. That which stands out most is the kinship between him and modern painters. This year's pictures at the Salon d'Automne have precisely the same effect as *Ulysses* on the conventional mind. It calls the true ugly, because truth comes in the shape of a squatting lady with an abundance of fat . . . Mr. Joyce, however, does not rush with the crowd, and has made skilful use of what the psychologists have taught him. He can open up a thought as a surgeon does a body.

There are so many aspects of Joyce's work that one does not know where to begin. It is comparable to the Bible, with which it has much in common, in the respect that one part differs so much from the other. One might argue, some hundreds of years later, that *Ulysses* was the work of many hands, were it not for the fact that in the seeming medley of chapters and styles there is a form as rigid as that of a sonnet. Here we come to an aspect of *Ulysses* which is not generally noticed. The name of the work is taken from the title of the Homeric hero, and the chapters follow the scenes of the earlier epic. I shall not here attempt to trace the parallelism between the modern and the classic work, save only to mention that Bloom is undoubtedly a humanised conception of Ulysses conceived in a modern vein, and tempered with a modern humour—and Stephen, an artistic Telemachus, aloof and serene, curious commentator on passing life. Nor shall I dwell long on the symbolism that lies hidden in each chapter, and which would have been as unsuspected by me as the mysteries underlying the marble verses of Mallarmé for his first readers, were it not that they were communicated to me by Mr. Joyce himself. It matters not one fiddlestick, however, whether Mr. Joyce's epic sonata sings its new word-music in the borrowed tones of Homer, or whether every chapter hangs on the symbol of some organ of the human body, as in the 17th century *Purple Island* of Phineas Fletcher, or whether the brothel in Dublin's under-world is the parallel of Ulysses' descent into hell: the whole has sufficient significance in itself to make it a work of immortality and in the best traditions of classic form.

Mr. Joyce might have been the comrade of Boccacio and supped at the table of Petronius. As a humorist he is a direct descendant of these men. He is akin to Rabelais and the Balzac of the *Contes Drolatiques*. But his uncanny aloofness distinguishes him from these.

His digressions, despite their apparent remoteness, belong to the action. They are either commentaries, a prose comic chorus, or the full-winged flight of a character's thought. Often scientific theories are discussed or literature. . . .

[discusses, briefly, the Scylla and Charybdis episode]

. . . The form of burlesque which runs through the whole of *Ulysses* is a point of contact with the writings of some young Frenchmen known as Dadaists. Max Jacob in a curious prose poem has a titanic battle in the stalls of a theatre, where thousands are numbered amongst the slain, and the current Dada weeklies warm with this type of gigantic hyperbole. Mr. Joyce has a little more in common with the Dadaists: his inventions of onamatopaeic words and the mixing of science with literature. Joyce and the Dadaist arrived independently, of course, at the similarities. They merely prove how true a son of his age is the author of *Ulysses*. Laurence Sterne I have always considered the first Dadaist. . . . Sterne is an eighteenth century Joyce. They both go to antiquity for quips and quibbles, and have the same taste for salaciousness and the use of names for comic effect. Sterne, however, is the more homely, and enjoys himself what Joyce would have us enjoy. The relationship of Joyce to modernism is a vast subject which I have only barely touched here, but which holds great scope for the critic. He has in him points of similarity with the painter Picasso: the early follower of tradition breaking into new modes and expressing life from a new angle with a changed vision.

Perhaps the most curious chapter in *Ulysses* is the night in the brothel, which most newspapers, for some superficial reason, have agreed to call the *Walpurgisnacht*. The only resemblance between it and Faust's adventures on the Brocken is the disregard of ordinary sequence of time. There are no witches with brooms in Joyce's night-town, but there are some very bawdy hags. Perhaps, too, the symbolism in Goethe in the introduction of contemporaries in strange guise may justify the comparison. But the whole tenor, the zig-zag movement, the supreme obscenity, the exposure of sexual repressions, is characteristically Joyceian. It may be, however, from a desire to give some impression of this cinematographical, orthographical, physiological, erotic, psychological, scatological fantasy in play form that the *Walpurgisnacht* was invoked. It must, however, be read, and, of course, in conjunction with what has gone before, to be appreciated. . . .

[discusses the Circe episode]

When we come finally to the Penelope monologue, or the exhibition of what clergymen call the 'true inwardness' of Mrs. Bloom, we are amazed at the concentration of the author on female psychology. I do not know whether the psychology is true. The author of *The Pretty Lady* picks this out as the finest part of the book. I have no great admiration for Mr. Bennett, and believe that he yields too often to temptation, and keeps his literary pot too long on the boil, but he should be qualified to judge on so delicate a subject. For myself, who can only speak instinctively, and hence tentatively, on such matters, and am of necessity swayed by the conflicting views of male psychologists, I am in a state of uncertainty. Molly Bloom, however, sounds real. What Croce affirms of Ibsen's characters is truer still of Mrs. Bloom. She says aloud, or rather thinks aloud, what we hardly ever dare whisper to ourselves and never bend an ear to listen.

Ulysses is essentially a book for the male. It is impossible for a woman to stomach the egregious grossness. Through the book one hears the coarse oaths and rude jests of the corner-boy and the subtle salaciousness of the cultured. There is a tradition in these things . . . It is not woman but man who has a secret, and Mr. Joyce is guilty of a breach of the male freemasonry in publishing the signs by which one man recognises a healthy living brother. . . .

It is impossible for any discerning mind to deny genius to Mr. Joyce, and that of a very high order. His work will persist in spite of the efforts to suppress it of such literary critics as the Society for the

Suppression of Vice in America and the reviewer of the *Pink 'Un*. The style alone is sufficient to attract readers. The quaint Greek compounds, the melodious words, the rare vocabulary, apart altogether from the profundities and indecencies, will keep *Ulysses* alive for posterity. M. Valéry Larbaud believes Mr. Joyce to be as great as Rabelais. Naturally his reception in Paris was more cordial, for all the greatest French writers look upon life with their eyes open . . . I say this, however, that only an artist could handle his material as Mr. Joyce has done. In other hands there would really be a grave risk of a descent into the morbid and the pornographic. He will have influence, but I doubt if there will be imitators. In the Dorothy Richardsons and May Sinclairs I see already the influence of the Joyce literary style.

In truth, there is no real parallel to Mr. Joyce in literature. He has that touch of individuality that puts genius on a peak. Rabelaisian, he hasn't the *joie de vivre* of the French priest; Sternesque, he is devoid of the personal touch of the Irish clergyman. Trained by the Jesuits, he can't guffaw like Balzac when he tells a good story. He is a scientist in his detachedness, but *Ulysses* is nevertheless, a human book, filled with pity as with the sexual instinct, and the latter in no greater proportion and of no greater importance in the book than any of the other fundamental human attributes.

137. An Irish opinion of Joyce

1923

Extract from Joseph M. Hone, 'A Letter from Ireland,' *London Mercury*, v (January 1923), 306–8.

This article is of interest, not so much for what it does not say about *Ulysses*, but for what at least one Irishman thought about Joyce's reputation.

. . . According to Mr. Joyce himself none of his previous work counts besides *Ulysses*; *Dubliners* and *A Portrait of the Artist* are to be regarded merely as preliminary exercises. The earlier pages of *Ulysses*, as they were published in the *Little Review*, together with accounts given by the author's friends who have seen the whole of the book, help us to understand what Mr. Joyce means. In the matter of artistic radicalism, as in that of linguistic indecency, even *A Portrait of the Artist*, set beside *Ulysses*, will look like a violet hiding a modest head. Moreover, the later book is even more crowded than the earlier with indication of Mr. Joyce's encyclopædic learning and culture. . . . Yet Mr. Joyce still draws from Irish models, still depicts the Irish scene. These retain—for him—their potent fascination across long years of exile in which he has stocked his mind fuller and fuller with the stuff of science and philosophy and has tested in preparation for a masterpiece all the modern experiments in style.

'With *Ulysses*,' says a writer in the *Nouvelle Revue Française*, 'Ireland re-enters his European literature.' [Valéry Larbaud, No. 118.] Ireland is gratified to hear it, and yet a little nervous, nervous as she has not been over any literary event since those far-off days when Synge was producing his original and provocative interpretations of the peasant life of Aran and Connemara. We have many other literary exiles, but none of them provoke the same acute interest. . . . There is nothing genial in Mr. Joyce's comment. He may be detached from our local passions; but it is not a detachment born of English influences or of cosmopolitanism. His struggle for freedom had been fought before he left

Ireland; and the marks of the struggle are in each of the books that he has written, so methodically—this deliberate, determined man has acquired a knowledge of eighteen languages!—between long intervals: in *Dubliners*, in *A Portrait of the Artist*, and now in *Ulysses*. . . .

Mr. Joyce's books exhibit a type of young Irishman of the towns—mostly originating from the semi-anglicised farming or shopkeeping class of the east and centre—a type which has been created largely by the modern legislation which provides Catholic democracy in Ireland with opportunities for an inexpensive university education. This young Irishman is now a dominating figure in the public life of Ireland; he was less important in Mr. Joyce's day, but had already exhibited a certain amount of liveliness. Daniel O'Connell described him, before he had come to the towns and got an education, as smug, saucy, and venturous; and the portrait is still recognisable, though he was then only in the embryo stage of self-consciousness. As social documents, therefore, Mr. Joyce's novels and stories are much more important than Synge's plays and stories; for the later writer describes, intimately and realistically, a growing Ireland, not, as Synge did, an Ireland that is passing away with the Gaelic communities of Aran and Connemara. He writes of a side of life in which—ugly though his picture may be—there is the greatest spiritual energy, a side of Irish life of which our 'Protestant' novelists, like Mr. Ervine and Mr. Birmingham, scarcely wot of except in its political manifestations. This young Irishman has, however, entered literature in a few other recent books besides those of Mr. Joyce—in the books, for example, of Mr. Daniel Corkery, a talented writer from Cork, whose *Hounds of Bamba*, a collection of stories about the Volunteers, has been much admired. . . . When I first read *A Portrait of the Artist as a Young Man* it seemed to me that the book announced the passing of that literary Ireland in which everyone was well bred except a few politicians.

The value of Mr. Joyce's experiments in technique will, no doubt, be warmly contested by the adherents of this or that school among modern novelists. But no one will deny that Ireland has produced in him a man of first-rate intellect and perceptions, not even those who are most keenly aware of the one-sided character of his realism. He is biased, of course; but not by opinions or by the desire to do service to a cause, but by a temperament which is peculiarly sensitive to the brutal and sordid things of experience. Take his account of the extraordinary Christmas dinner in *A Portrait of the Artist*, where Stephen Dedalus's relatives fight over Parnell and the priests. Mr. Joyce spares us no detail:

[quotes from ch. 1 of *A Portrait*]

. . . For us in Ireland Mr. Joyce's significance lies in this, that he is the first man of literary genius, expressing himself in perfect freedom, that Catholic Ireland has produced in modern times. Mr. Joyce is as Irish as M. Anatole France—whom he resembles rather in the quality of his learning—is French. It was perhaps not really strange that when this writer did appear, his implied criticism of Irish life should be so much bolder than anything that could be found in the books of his Protestant contemporaries. Certainly no Irish Protestant writer was likely to have expressed the secular Irish emotions of politics and religion with Mr. Joyce's passionate force and understanding and his entire lack of sentimentality.

138. Stephen Gwynn on modern Irish literature

1923

Extract from 'Modern Irish Literature', *Manchester Guardian* (15 March 1923), 38–9 [36–40]. Later appeared in *Irish Literature and Drama in the English Language: A Short History* (1936), pp. 192–202.

. . . But my business here is with what people call pure literature—work of invention by writers of what I suppose I must not call the Georgian period in Irish literature. Yet it would give me pleasure to associate the reign of King George with the flourishing of Mr. James Stephens and Mr. James Joyce, for these are the outstanding figures . . .

. . . In considering modern Irish literature one has to face the fact that the first notable force to appear in it from the Catholic population has been Mr. Joyce. . . . If the current of feeling drives one author to present such a picture of priests without charity, women without mercy, and drink-sodden, useless men, the same forces will surely push another into open defiance of the religion on which that life is presumed to rest. That is the revolt which you find in Mr. Joyce. I do not know that he detests the life of Dublin in particular with the same intensity as Mr. [Brinsley] Macnamara loathes his valley. But through Mr. Macnamara's book runs a suggestion of freer regions, in which all the windows do not squint and pry. For Mr. Joyce, as I take it, Dublin is life, life is Dublin, and he, being alive, is bound to the body of this death. In *Dubliners*, his first book, you find him making his hand; establishing a miraculous power to reproduce a scene so that not the pettiest detail appears to be left out. For the most part, the people whom he depicts are as futile and as drunken as Mr. Macnamara's, but they have a kind of slack-twisted good nature instead of a slow-blooded spite. Next came his *Portrait of the Artist as a Young Man*, and the art is no longer detached and impersonal; there is declared revolt, suggestion that the detailed control over life exercised through the confessional turns sex into an obsession.

I do not pretend to like Mr. Joyce's work, and, admitting its power, it seems to me, even in this second book, that his preoccupation with images of nastiness borders on the insane. But the power of the writing is astonishing. In *Ulysses* it comes to the full. He uses language rather like an orchestra than an instrument. Half a dozen voices speak at once, inner voices and outer voices; he will plunge into mimicry and from mimicry pass to stark dramatisation. Of course *Ulysses* recalls Sterne—who also was of Irish race. But Sterne stayed in the Church; eighteenth-century consciences had a robust digestion; there is nothing behind Sterne except a sometimes uneasy laughter. What gives value to *Ulysses* is passion; all through it runs the cry of a tortured soul. Mr. Joyce's Stephen Dedalus is the Catholic by nature and by tradition, who must revolt under the stress of an intellectual compulsion, to whom truth—the thing which he sees as true—speaks inexorably. Yet what he would shake off clings to his flesh like the poisoned shirt of Hercules. He wallows, it burns the more, but revolt persists. He can touch, taste, and handle every abomination; only one thing is impossible, to profess a belief that he rejects. Ancient pieties hold him to it, ties of his nearest life: his mother dying of cancer, dumbly prays of him to pray with her, and she dies without that solace; years pass, her thought, haunting him everywhere and always, only urges him to spit again on whatever she and her like thought holiest. It is revolt the more desperate because it sees no chance of deliverance; and against this fool, this Dedalus, with the stored complex of his brain oversubtilised and overcharged by the very training of that scholastic philosophy from which he breaks away, Mr. Joyce sets his wise man Ulysses, the fortunately happy, whom life cannot injure, lacerate, or bruise, because he has no shame; who must enjoy, so full is his sensuous develpment; who can enjoy, being without conscience. He likes music almost as genuinely as the nastinesses through which, with every elaboration of their detail, you are privileged to follow him. Seven hundred pages of a tome like a Blue-book are occupied with the events and sensations in one day of a renegade Jew, whose trade is touting for advertisements, but whose subsistence comes through marriage; I need not be more precise. . . .

139. Ernest Boyd on Ireland's literary renaissance

1923

Ireland's Literary Renaissance, revised edition, (1923), pp. 402–12. Portions of this work appeared as 'The Expressionism of James Joyce', *New York Tribune* (28 May 1922), 29.

Joyce is not mentioned in the 1916 edition. Valéry Larbaud's article (No. 118) is being attacked in this critique (see the Introduction, p. 19).

. . . With the exception of *Chamber Music* and his one play, *Exiles* (1918), the publication of Joyce's books has failed to answer to that definition of happiness which consists in having no history.

Charming as his little poems are they would no more have established James Joyce as one of the most original figures in the whole world of contemporary letters than would his remarkable psychological drama in three acts, which is undoubtedly the only Irish play to realise the first intentions of Edward Martyn in helping to launch the Dramatic Movement. In its morbid and profound dissection of the soul, *Exiles* suggests the social analysis of Ibsen combined with the acute sexual perceptions of Strindberg. The originality of Joyce and the justification of the high esteem in which he is held must be sought in those three volumes of fiction, *Dubliners, A Portrait of the Artist as a Young Man* and *Ulysses*, which have rightly aroused the attention of the intelligent public in Europe and America, even though a French critic [Valéry Larbaud] has rashly declared that with them 'Ireland makes a sensational re-entry into European literature.' Apart from its affecting and ingenuous belief in the myth of a 'European' literature, this statement of M. Valéry Larbaud's has the obvious defect of resting upon two false assumptions . . . In other words, to the Irish mind no lack of appreciation of James Joyce is involved by some slight consideration for the facts of Ireland's literary and intellectual evolution, and the effort now being made to cut him off from the stream of which he is a tributary is singularly futile. The logical outcome of this doctrinaire zeal of the coterie is to leave this profoundly Irish genius in the possession of a prematurely cosmopolitan reputation, the unkind fate which has always overtaken writers isolated from the conditions of which they are a part, and presented to the world without any perspective.

Fortunately, the work of James Joyce stands to refute most of the theories for which it has furnished a pretext, notably the theory that it is an unanswerable challenge to the separate existence of Anglo-Irish literature. The fact is, no Irish writer is more Irish than Joyce; none shows more unmistakably the imprint of his race and traditions . . . The syllogism seems to be: J. M. Synge and James Stephens and W. B. Yeats are Irish, therefore James Joyce is not. Whereas the simple truth is that *A Portrait of the Artist as a Young Man* is to the Irish novel what *The Wanderings of Oisin* was to Irish poetry and *The Playboy of the Western World* to Irish drama, the unique and significant work which lifts the *genre* out of the commonplace into the national literature. Like most of his fellow-craftsmen in Ireland, as we have seen, Joyce began characteristically with a volume of short stories. *Dubliners* differed from the others, not in technique, but in quality, and above all, in its affinity with the best work of the French Naturalists, from whom Joyce learned his craft as George Moore did before him. . . . The genesis of all that the author has since published is in that superb collection of studies of middle-class Dublin life.

Dublin is the frescoe upon which James Joyce has woven all the amazing patterns designed by an imagination which is at once romantic and realistic, brilliant and petty, full of powerful fantasy, yet preserving an almost incredible faculty of detailed material observation. He is governed by a horror and detestation of the circumstances which moulded the life of his Stephen Dedalus, in that city which he has carried away with him during the long years of his expatriation, and whose record he has consigned to the pages of *A Portrait of the Artist* and *Ulysses*. With a frankness and veracity as impressive as they are appalling Joyce sets forth the relentless chronicle of a soul stifled by material and intellectual squalor . . . The autobiographical and realistic character of the history of Stephen Dedalus is dismissed by certain critics as of no importance, but except for some disguises of name, the two volumes of his adventures are as effectively indiscreet as *Hail and Farewell*.

The gradual downfall of the Dedalus family provides the framework of the first book. A deep undertone of filth and sordid shiftlessness is the fitting accompaniment to the disintegration of Stephen's life. The atmosphere in which he is expected to respond to the stimulus of higher education is sardonically suggested in the chapter where he is shown preparing to attend his lectures: . . .

[quotes from ch. 2]

This hideous interior is typical of the material surroundings in which Stephen Dedalus lives. When he leaves the house we are told: . . .

[quotes from ch. 4]

It is not an escape, however, which the university provides, for he simply exchanges physical ugliness for intellectual ugliness, so far as Joyce reports his life there . . . It is apparently the author's purpose to empty Catholicism of all its spiritual content, in order to provide his hero with a congruous religious background. Similarly he is tempted to depart from the strictly horrible veracity of his pictures in order to romanticise the unclean initiation of Stephen into the adventure of love . . . So long as he describes the exterior of Dublin's underworld, Joyce is too good an observer to suggest anything more than its repulsiveness. It is the supreme irony of his portrait that the artist proceeds to Swinburnian romantics based upon material so unspeakably frowsy. The romance in Stephen's life is designedly of this degrading and degraded quality. For James Joyce shows himself throughout preoccupied with all that is mean and furtive in Dublin society, and so far as he permits his own views to emerge, he professes the greatest contempt for a social organisation which permits so much vileness to flourish squalidly, beneath a rigid formality of conduct. . . .

In *Ulysses* the analysis of Stephen Dedalus in particular, and of Dublin in general, is carried a step further, how much further may be imagined from the fact that this vast work, of more than seven hundred and twenty-five quarto pages, covers the events of less than twenty-four hours. It recounts a day in the life of Stephen Dedalus and Leopold Bloom, and shows in a marvellous microcosm the movement of the city's existence, in ever spreading circles and ripples of activity, correlated by a method which recalls that of Jules Romains and the *Unanimistes*. But its form is more akin to that of the German Expressionists. The technical innovations which began to show in *A Portrait of the Artist as a Young Man* are here advanced to the point of a deliberate stylistic method, whose cumulative effect is wonderful. The occasional use of monologue, the notation of random and unspoken thoughts as they pass through the mind of each character, the introduction without warning of snatches of conversation, of prolonged dialogues, now almost entirely takes the place of narrative. The final chapter, for instance, is a reverie of forty-two pages, without any kind of punctuation except the break of paragraphs, in which the whole sexual life of Leopold Bloom's wife rushes pell-mell into her consciousness. It is almost always in these passages of introspection that the author reveals the sex interests and experiences of his people, and in the emptying out of their minds naturally a great deal is uncovered to the discomfiture of convention. The charges of 'immorality' which Joyce has had to face have been based as a rule upon such passages.

Yet, rarely in literature has eroticism appeared in such harsh and disillusioned guise as in the work of James Joyce, where it oscillates between contemptuous, Rabelaisian ribaldry, and the crude horror and fascination of the body as seen by the great Catholic ascetics. . . *Ulysses* is simultaneously a masterpiece of realism, of documentation, and a most original dissection of the Irish mind in certain of its phases usually hitherto ignored, except for the hints of George Moore. Dedalus and Bloom are two types of Dubliner such as were studies in Joyce's first book of stories, remarkable pieces of national and human portraiture. At the same time they serve as the medium between the reader and the *vie unanime* of a whole community, whose existence is unrolled before their eyes, through which we see, and reaches our consciousness as it filters into their souls. As an experiment in form *Ulysses* more effectively accomplishes its purpose than Jules Romains did in *La Mort de Quelqu'un*, for out of the innumerable fragments of which this mosaic is composed Joyce has created a living whole, the complete representation of life. The book might have been called *La Vie de Quelqu'un*, for it is not the personal existence of Dedalus and Bloom that matters so much as the social organism of which they are a part. . . .

Much has been written about the symbolic intention of this work, of its relation to the Odyssey, to which the plan of the three first and last chapters, with the twelve cantos of the adventures of Ulysses in the middle, is supposed to correspond. Irish criticism can hardly be impressed by this aspect of a work which, in its meticulous detailed documentation of Dublin, rivals Zola in photographic realism. In its bewildering juxtaposition of the real and the imaginary, of the commonplace and the fantastic, Joyce's work obviously declares its kinship with the Expressionists, with Walter Hasenclever or Georg Kaiser.

With *Ulysses* James Joyce has made a daring and valuable experiment, breaking new ground in English for the future development of prose narrative. But the 'European' interest of the work must of necessity be largely technical, for the matter is as local as the form is universal. In fact, so local is it that many pages remind the Irish reader of *Hail and Farewell*, except that the allusions are to matters and personalities more obscure. To claim for this book a European significance simultaneously denied to J. M. Synge and James Stephens is to confess complete ignorance of its genesis, and to invest its content with a mysterious import which the actuality of references would seem to deny. While James Joyce is endowed with the wonderful fantastic imagination which conceived the fantasmagoria of the fifteenth chapter of *Ulysses*, a vision of a Dublin Brocken, whose scene is the underworld, he also has the defects and qualities of Naturalism, which prompts him to catalogue the Dublin tramways, and to explain with the precision of a guidebook how the city obtains its water supply. In fine, Joyce is essentially a realist as Flaubert was, but, just as the author of *Madame Bovary* never was bound by the formula subsequently erected into the dogma of realism, the creator of Stephen Dedalus has escaped from the same bondage. Flaubert's escape was by way of the Romanticism from which he started, Joyce's is by way of Expressionism, to which he has advanced.

140. F. M. Ford on the cadence of Joyce's prose

1924

Extract from 'Literary Causeries: vii: So She Went into the Garden', *Chicago Tribune Sunday Magazine* (6 April 1924), 3, 11.

The other day a critic, a Frenchman and therefore a man of some intelligence and politeness, varied the form of the enquiry and asked: 'How is it possible that you take pleasure in the work of Mr. Joyce? You, a Classic?' . . . And you observe that he conceded without question the fact of my pleasure in the Advanced.

And indeed I do take that pleasure. And I am not paid to do it and to do so does not pay. . . .

I am driven into these speculations by being asked by my editor to explain to his readers, precisely the pleasure that I take in the work of Mr. Joyce . . .

For myself then, the pleasure—the very great pleasure—that I get from going through the sentences of Mr. Joyce is that given me simply by the cadence of his prose, and I fancy that the greatest and highest enjoyment that can be got from any writing is simply that given by the cadence of the prose. . . .

Now I must not be taken as saying that there is any kinship or resemblance between the writings of Mr. Joyce, the Scriptures or the prose of Mr. Conrad. All that I am saying is that immense pleasure *can* be obtained from letting the cadences of Mr. Joyce pass through the mind. . . .

The reader will by now be saying: 'Well, but this fellow says nothing about what we want to hear of. There is not a single word about the obscenities, the blasphemies, the Bolshevism of which we have heard so much.' And there is not, simply because I have been asked to explain what makes me take pleasure in the work of Mr. Joyce, and I take no pleasure in obscenities, blasphemies or the propaganda of the Soviets. And indeed, of this last there is not a word in the works of Mr. Joyce. There are obviously passages that, in the ordinary vernacular, would pass for obscenities and blasphemies . . . And the reader who prefers to ignore the existence of these things in the world has one very simple remedy, as far as *Ulysses* is concerned. He can refrain from reading the book. I am not asking him to do otherwise. . . .

141. Comment on Yeats's discovery of Joyce

1924

W. F. Trench, 'Correspondence: Dr. Yeats and Mr. Joyce', *Irish Statesman*, ii, No. 25 (30 August 1924), 790.

Dear Sir,—W. B. Yeats, the poet, has for long years made debtors and thralls of the lovers of beauty, by giving them to see life and the world made doubly beautiful by the light that never was on sea or land. J. Joyce rakes hell, and the sewers, for dirt to throw at the fair face of life, and for poison to make beauty shrivel and die. Now, the Dublin æsthete discovers Joyce, and Dr. Yeats undertakes that no citizen of Dublin shall fail to know his name. In season and out of season he has proclaimed him a genius. But be that so, Joyce is a genius. 'Tis true 'tis pity. But there have been geniuses who wallowed in the mire before, though whether any quite equally foul-minded, who shall say? . . .

142. Alec Waugh on Joyce's style

1924

Extract from 'The Neo-Georgians', *Fortnightly*, n.s. cxv (January 1924), 126–37.

. . . *Ulysses* has been described, not unwarrantably, as the greatest outrage that has been ever committed on the English language, but few writers have been possessed of a more clear, a more rhythmed style than James Joyce has at his disposal on those rare occasions when he chooses to employ it. . . . It was from the strictly technical point of view that *Ulysses* was, in the majority of cases, discussed; in its realism, in its crudity, in its obscenity it is perhaps the most startling document that has ever been presented as a serious piece of literature to a civilised community. But it aroused none of the controversy that is regarded as inseparable from such productions. People did not sit in circles and discuss James Joyce's message, or wonder whether men and women 'really were like that.' A new way of writing had been invented; the question to be decided was: was it a good way or was it not? Its notoriety is due undoubtedly in a large measure to its realism. But had there not been in *Ulysses* a single indecent phrase, or scene, or sentence, the extent and quality of its interest to those interested primarily in letters would not have been diminished. No sensational book ever owed less to its sensationalism. It is an exercise in a new technique; that is its value, that is its significance. It could not have achieved such a success in a period that was not passionately concerned with the carpentry of writing. . . .

143. Franklin Adams, comment on *Ulysses*

1924

Extract from *The Diary of Our Own Samuel Pepys*, Volume I (1935), p. 457.

A journal entry for 17 February 1924.

Read this afternoon in J. Joyce's *Ulysses*, with some great things in it, but I could not read more than three or four pages at a time. And a deal of it seems to me like a bad boy writing what he considers naughty words with chalk on a fence. . . .

144. Julien Green, comments on *Ulysses*

1924

'*Ulysses*, par James Joyce', *Philosophies*, No. 2 (15 May 1924), 218–22.

This thick book which probably did not deserve it has been persecuted. The latest edition, which is the fourth, carries an epigraph which contains a laconic account of its misfortunes.

[Publishing history of *Ulysses* follows here.]

[A brief discussion of the Homeric parallels as explained by Valéry Larbaud, No. 118.]

1924: *Ulysses*

. . . I will say here that the key to this work is perhaps less easy to find than Valéry Larbaud seems to think. Joyce's fame lies in hiding things. When a particular word is spoken, however, the book becomes lucid from one end to the other, and one sees that, in fact, it was simple and that it could not be otherwise.

I want to examine in another article what comprises the mystic and the symbolic in *Ulysses*: I borrow these terms from Valéry Larbaud. At present, I only want to concern myself with two points: the general aspect of the book, and an aspect of the principal character.

It is quite natural to link *Ulysses* with the category of gigantic works of which *Gargantua et Pantagruel* represents the type, and the name of Rabelais comes to the mind of the reader of *Ulysses* because he finds there the principal Rabelaisian characters: extreme abundance, obscenity, depth hidden under a comic mask. Sometime, and this again is in Rabelais, there are serious passages with a tone precisely more elevated than the usual tone of the book.

Ulysses resists a rapid examination; it demands a patient reflection. It is not read quickly because if one tries to read it quickly it is not understood, and not being understood, it is abandoned. At first glance it presents the aspect of a confused ensemble. It can happen that the bond which unites the parts is not grasped immediately, but the obscurity dissipates as one advances. The different sections of the book separate and become clear. They end by rising in some way and by dominating the subject. If the first pages are then re-read, they appear very clear. Two things are striking when this point is reached: the multiplicity and the unity of *Ulysses*.

Multiplicity. A profound sense of detail appeared from the very first words.

[quotes the first words]

The characters are numerous, and they speak a great deal, act a great deal. What results is a number of little tableaux and conversations which follow along in the same chapter and give it the aspect of a story independent of the rest of the book, allusions to some earlier or later chapters being, in short, rather rare.

Finally, there are no two chapters which reproduce similar situations. The setting itself changes constantly. The same characters reappear but always in different relationships. Thus there is a perpetual and infinite variety. To adapt itself to the description of these multiple scenes, the tone must be endlessly renewed. From there, several manners of writing result: sometimes a rigorous economy breaks the sentences of an entire chapter and reduces them to very succinct notations which gives vigor to the account and a sort of trepidation at the same time that it allows a prodigious accumulation of details. Sometimes, on the contrary, the style becomes heavy, as in the chapter on the visit of Bloom to the Maternity Hospital, a chapter which the author saw fit to write in the manner of the Middle Ages, in compact and interminable periods. Another chapter which concerns young, sentimental and excited girls in search of romance is written in a silly, foolish tone. Another, finally, which appears to translate the process of thought of one of the characters is written without punctuation; nothing separates the ideas one from another; they flow together without interruption except every now and then a rest at the end of a paragraph of four or five pages. It gives the impression of incoherence and of continuity. There are a great number of rhythms which correspond to different states of mind.

The unity of the novel is affirmed slowly but with power. A perspective is established as one advances into the book. Details are grouped and built upon, the great lines are accentuated, the scenes are arranged. A thousand little things which the author notes with care can seem minute (for example, the soap which Bloom buys before going to the funeral and which is spoken of several times thereafter), but there is a stratagem of great skillfulness, and it is with the most miniscule details that the author produces the strongest impressions; that is due, I believe, to the fact that he knew how marvelously where he ought to place them . . . One leaves the book with the impression of tumult, as after having passed through a crowd. But I only want to talk to you of a character around which the world of *Ulysses* accomplished its revolution. He is the unity of the book.

He is called Leopold Bloom, and he is a Jew of the common type. In Paris you meet him daily, and by dint of meeting him you no longer see him, but a sort of perversity which is the grace of the state of James Joyce makes him live in Dublin. It is necessary to believe that there are some Jews in Ireland, but this is a thing which is naturally not considered.

[A brief outline of Bloom's activities follows here.]

The universe finds in this Jew echoes of an indefatigable banality, but if the brain of Bloom only furnishes platitudes, these platitudes he lavishes with vigor at all moments and under all pretexts . . . It's the same, in some way, with his sensations: they are so primitive, they bring so few variations to the ordinary state of humanity that they become an aspect of ritual. There is in Bloom the elements of a great fatality.

[elaborates on this point and illustrates]

. . . I do not wish to suggest that having given you this episode [the funeral], I have given you the whole book, but it can, I believe, make you understand the general tone. There is, if you wish—but I do not like these comparisons—some Folantin in *Ulysses*; however, Bloom proceeds better than the dyspeptics of Huysmans; he is not at all sour; furthermore, he is Jewish. It suffices to follow him for several hours of his life to know all that he has ever been able to think, to guess the mechanism of all his little secret emotions. Ideas are born in him from the simplest sensations; they are linked by pure associations of words most of the time. As for his emotions, they have for a pivot point the cruel and vigorous desire of which I have spoken. Salacious and timid, credulous with starts of distrust, tormented with little unavowable ambitions, such is the man that Joyce pursues across hundreds of pages. He does not leave him in peace a single moment [Bloom's activities]. . . .

. . . Joyce has not invented new sins. Such as he is in his weaknesses, Bloom is universal, and the clay which formed him is not unlike our own. However, the Society for the Suppression of Vice wanted to outlaw him: it had been better, I believe, to take the renewed attitudes of Savonarola on the subject of the villainous words that one encounters in *Ulysses* and on the determined gestures which his characters make therein. But one cannot ask these people who want to make angles to penetrate the profound sense of this cryptic work; they would have been able, however, to suspect the presence of a mystery and to keep an easy silence.

145. Edmund Gosse to Louis Gillet

1924

Letter to Louis Gillet (7 June 1924), quoted in *Claybook for James Joyce*, by Louis Gillet. Translated by Georges Markow-Totevy (1958), pp. 31–2. Also in *James Joyce*, by Richard Ellmann (1959), p. 542 (exclusive of the last paragraph, which is taken from *Claybook*).

I should very much regret you paying Mr. J. Joyce the compliment of an article in the *Revue des Deux Mondes*. You could only expose the worthlessness and impudence of his writings, and surely it would be a mistake to give him this prominence. I have difficulty in describing to you, *in writing*, the character of Mr. Joyce's notoriety . . . It is partly political; it is partly a perfectly cynical appeal to sheer indecency. He is of course not entirely without talent, but he is a literary charlatan of the extremest order. His principal book, *Ulysses*, has not parallel that I know of in French. It is an anarchical production, infamous in taste, in style, in everything.

Mr. Joyce is unable to publish or sell his books in England, on account of their obscenity. He therefore issues a 'private' edition in Paris, and charges a huge price for each copy. He is a sort of Marquis de Sade, but does not write so well. He is the perfect type of the Irish *fumiste*, a hater of England, more than suspected of partiality for Germany, where he lived before the war (and at Zürich during the war).

There are no English critics of weight or judgement who consider Mr. Joyce an author of any importance. If, as you tell me, 'on fait grand bruit du nommé J. J. . . . à Paris,' it must be among persons whose knowledge of English literature and language is scanty. He is not, as I say, without talent, but he has prostituted it to the most vulgar uses. . . .

Do not think that I have any *personal* prejudice. I have never seen Mr. Joyce and before the war I contributed to his needs. I speak in an exclusively literary sense.

146. Louis Cazamian on Joyce and *Ulysses*

1924

'The Work of James Joyce', *Revue Anglo-Américaine*, ii, No. 2 (December 1924), 97–113. Also appeared in his *Essais en Deux Langues* (1938), pp. 47–63.

. . . One is not permitted to be unaware of Mr. Joyce whose *Ulysses* remains the most sensational book of recent years. One initiates himself then; and quickly a persuasion is imposed: whatever it is necessary to think of the work, its significance will preserve it from oblivion. A contemporary tendency achieves its extreme development there. In its title alone we can find rich material for analysis and reflection.

Never has the life of an author been more intimately involved in his work . . . His Irish nationality remains essential, and the complexities of his temperament specify it more than deny it. His attitude toward the revolt of his race is not simple. He seems to share profound motives; he is not kindly disposed toward the English, but before the religion of political freedom, the men who live it, and those who live on it, his criticism refuses to abdicate; no one has mixed more irreverence with sentiment.

His originality, a slender flower at first, only became by degrees the robust plant of today, thick with vigor. The poet of *Chamber Music* (1907) has delicate, slender inspirations; he sings in light cadences of a young gracious love, accorded to the changing tonalities of the seasons. These verses renew nothing, neither their measure nor their form are of one creator, but they flow from a fresh spring and their melodic fluidity has a fascinating charm. They are unworthy of invoking the simplicity of Verlaine. *Dubliners* (1914) is a collection of short stories, not less distinguished in its genre, and not far from opening a new road in art. Through the mixture of harsh realism and of pitiable humor, these short stories are related to the Maupassant tradition, which the Russian example mollified and made supple. *Exiles* (1918) is an attempt, a less fortunate one, at psychological drama. The capable personality of Mr. Joyce, his decisive talent, are revealed in two entirely different books, which are connected by a very precise artistic gradation: *The Portrait of the Artist as a Young Man* (1916) and *Ulysses* (1922).

The first of these works is what it says: a partial autobiography. It recounts the escape of the soul . . . This rich but rather frequently treated subject is renewed by the precision of setting, by a technique which is both sharp and supple, where the profound preferences of the artist are marked. To define this method would be superfluous; it outlines what *Ulysses* must push to its logical end. Under this initial form, the processes of Mr. Joyce have nothing which can alarm the most timid tastes; the average reader will accept them easily. . . .

[Stephen's artistic revolt is equated with 'all the revolts of modern immoralism'.]

His most certain originality, like that of Synge, is to have been able to blend into an intimate mixture crudeness and poetry; and this fusion is, without doubt, one of the formulas that the young Irish literary figures consider most important today.

Ulysses is the most remarkable illustration of it, if not the most perfect. This book, no less copious than enigmatic, is a thrilling problem. It seems that, solicited by the attraction of recent psychological research and under the influence of an ideal of rigorous truth, Mr. Joyce has left to swerve toward the realism of science an effort where art finds its reckoning, but was due to find it more so. This work, in certain respects, is ingenious but suffers from an internal lack of balance. Epic in its scope, it has extreme ambitions, eminent merits, and faults on the same scale. All things considered, its gravest vice is doubtless the dryness which sterilizes its intransigent objectivity. The poetry, this time too compressed or brutalized, evaporates like a subtle essence, and the powerful body which the labor of the writer has produced has lost with it the best of his life. Alone, some parts have divine animation, spark; others, in spite of their robustness, are languishing. But all concur with the esthetic meaning of the ensemble.

This is worth being studied for itself. To judge on form such a book is difficult, formidable. Passions are exploded around it, not without motives, through all the orthodoxies, forbidden in certain countries; it has been greeted by many good judges as a masterpiece, and in spite of its length and its price, has even experienced a bookstore success. Its admirers are not a little clique but independent minds, and of very different horizons; its detractors, on the other hand, are not all motivated by a hatred of newness. Without trying to decide between them, let's try to grasp and to interpret, be it at the cost of a laborious analysis, the intentions of a thought which imposes respect.

Merely to grasp these intentions would suffice for our purposes. They shroud themselves in the pleasure of many veils, of which the least are not those of symbolism. Many readers will close this book without being sure of having perceived the subject, nor understood the title. We believe we see—but our lights are uncertain—the echoes of the Greek epic and its heroes called forth by the breadth of the fresco and the variety of episodes; whereas the very modern and impertinently prosaic qualitv of these gives to the analogy the humoristic complement of contrast. Contemporary Ulysses is not a man but a philosophical idea, the scabrous adventure of the mind across existence; and the character of the ancient Ulysses, the wisdom tinted with trickery and skepticism, is not here concentrated in one character, but disengages itself from all the experience of life which is offered to us. To this experience vascillating limits are assigned. . . .

[The critic discusses the principal resource of art and thought in disorder and illustrates how this is not just the superficial form of *Ulysses* but organically and profoundly influential.]

To materially analyze such a work is without any doubt to do it harm. The essential is not here in the recounted things nor in their natural succession; the true drama is composed in us, in reading. But again it is necessary for the reader to record and assimilate a series of facts; and for those who do not know the text it is not superfluous to summarize—as much as possible—the economy of the narrative. . . .

[A lengthy summary follows here, pp. 101–2.]

As this summary across a complicated texture shows, *Ulysses* has nothing related to a novel, of an action constructed on the reciprocal influence of human personalities . . . Mr. Joyce wanted to give us his general view of things. Let us say, right away, that we are rather badly repaid for the pain that we are taking to penetrate so many symbols. It is in vain that we would seek here the robust intellectual framework which upholds even the fantasy of Goethe. . . .

What connects the pieces of the book least badly is a taste of mind, a temperament: the humor; and the more real genealogy of this strange work attaches it to the great master of English humorists, Sterne . . . The essential point is that Mr. Joyce manages these modes of expression with a mastery, with a spontaneity which seems perfect. In the history of forms, he is not in this regard an initiator, and that is all.

It is elsewhere that his personal originality bursts forth. The esthetic newness of *Ulysses* is to have pushed much farther a tendency already visible in *The Portrait of the Artist*, and a tendency which an entire movement of contemporary art encouraged. There is no longer a common measure here. Mr. Joyce still has numerous predecessors; one can say that he had numerous masters. But he surpasses them and carries their principles so much farther that he does the work of invention.

The principle that he develops is that of realism—and there would be no novelty there; but his is a realism deepened by a more exact notion of the sole reality which is as important to the artist as to the philosopher: the interior life. . . .

The only true realism, from this point of view, is that art reproduces the natural substance of life and reproduces it entirely. From this comes the special quality of the elements which Mr. Joyce assembles and also the form under which he presents them . . . For the first time among artists, Mr. Joyce tells us all, tranquilly. This is a shock to our habits and for our delicatenesses. But this is all perceived and formulated in the plan of the new psychology; and at once, the image of the reality and the style of the writer, more even than the conformity, are overthrown.

It is not only, then, that the psychoanalysis has passed through it. One would guess that Mr. Joyce has assimilated Freudianism, even if he does not make allusion to it. . . .

[discusses Joyce's literary antecedents in the use of psychological insight]

Mr. Joyce's art proposes with resolution to grasp and to reconstitute the intrigue of the mind; and he utilizes to this effect the conclusions of work accomplished by a half century of analysis. . . .

One could suggest then that his work follows the rules of which Mr. Joyce appears, unknowingly, to have been inspired. Consciousness is a language unto itself; thought, an interior word. What is this language? Not a series of propositions constructed and linked but a rumination which expresses itself incompletely, which jumps from one term to another, according to the law of least effort, and says only the indispensable. What are the elements of this expression? Rarely are they abstract words, in the normal man, in the normal occasions of life, but rather concrete words, reclothing concrete impressions—sensations, images—assembled according to a quiet intuition of the force by which they are animated, by their value, and by their interest for us, without these relations being defined or marked by the rhetoric of style, nor the categories of grammar. . . .

Ulysses conforms rigorously to these principles. The substance of the book is made up of a sort of continuous rumination of which the center is most often the conscience of the hero, but is also sometimes that of the author, and which displaces itself from one to the other with a sovereign indifference in regard to this accident which the individual is . . . In his effort to bring together the interior life with a simple series of terms, Mr. Joyce succeeds in confounding entirely the psychic language with the social language; or at least, does not take enough account of their difference. He thus suppresses entirely the quotation marks of his text, and this radical measure has only happy effects; it is harmful somewhat to the truth of the notations. By so doing, almost all the men sufficiently construct their purposes in order to distinguish them without possible confusion from their silent reveries. . . .

The countenance of a book so composed is rather particular in creating in the average reader a surprise which extends up to dizziness, and which even the familiarization cannot dissipate. The degree to which this first impression persists, or is destroyed, is integrated in the intelligence and in the delight of a complex art, measures the favorable or hostile reaction of the temperament of each. . . .

[A long example of Joyce's style follows here, with explanation, pp. 68–9.]

The interior world such as a precise observation perceives it is both discontinuous and homogeneous. The movement of conscience is made by a series of bonds; and nothing is more in contrast to the writing of Mr. Joyce. But, at the same time, nothing is more uniform than his vision of the world, and nothing is more uniform than his book. All the distinctions created by the intelligence and the analysis fade away; the intrigue of our internal impressions, and those of our universe, coincide; thoughts and emotions mix; finally, according to Mr. Joyce, we do not speak with others a language that is different from that which we speak to ourselves. . . .

From transition, from preparation, from explication, this art is not wanting in any way. *Ulysses* is the most abrupt succession of chapters, pieces, episodes; and what is true of the rapport of the parts is also true of the interior elements of each of them. The discontinuity thus passes from the style to the organization of the book; and the discontinuity serves the cause of a supreme preference for the esthetic and philosophical order, where the intellectual temperment of the author is expressed. At the bottom, this art is pantheistic. . . .

The malaise of the reader is not only of the intellectual order. This book, occupied entirely with human nature, lacks humanity . . . But *Ulysses* has the ambition to be a large and a total fresco; and this is what we can not accept. Let us add that the sexual obsession is uselessly persistent. To raise in the center of the book the bust of the god of gardens has its logical point; thus the vision of the moralist and the artist, once and for all is translated. But to suggest and to evoke this ceaseless image, under all guises, in all perspectives, is monotonous and tiring. . . .

It is difficult to foresee what will become of the career of Mr. Joyce after *Ulysses*. He has exhausted in a single blow his new formula; and that rightly reveals his weakness, this little fecundity. Certainly the future of an artist always remains open. But this book, far from showing the route to tomorrow . . . is the achievement of a school and a mode. . . . And, in the end, by his interior characters, his essential coldness, his radical curiosity, his taste for objectivity, the temperament of Mr. Joyce would find itself in easy accord with a literature of science and truth. But his notion of form, in order to be in unison, must singularly evolve.

1925

147. Ernest Boyd on Joyce

1925

'Concerning James Joyce', *The World* (New York) (25 January 1925), n.p.

. . . Apparently because the photographic realism, the sheer reporting, in *Ulysses* is such that it is absolutely impossible for any one who did not live in Dublin twenty years ago to understand its allusions, the book thereby becomes a work of cosmopolitan fame denied to any of Joyce's contemporaries. Having several times contested M. Larbaud's highly esoteric interpretation of *Ulysses*, which is merely one section of a prolonged autobiography, packed with realistic detail, and beginning with *Dubliners*, I will not rehearse the arguments again.

A new element in the controversy, which had its echoes here among the provincial cosmopolitans who take their cue from M. Larbaud, is supplied by this emphasis on 'Young Ireland,' meaning the Ireland of Sinn Fein, which is credited with a relationship to Joyce entirely unlike that of the writers of his own generation, Padraic Colum, James Stephens or Seumas O'Sullivan, or those of the older generation of Yeats, 'Æ,' Synge and Moore. It so happened that I was in Dublin during the very years when this now triumphant 'Young Ireland' was fighting the British Government, and I can assure M. Laubaud that never had Joyce a more hostile public than that. The indifference of most people, and the hostility of a few, were such that when *A Portrait of the Artist as a Young Man* appeared it was with great reluctance that the editor of the chief intellectual organ of the Sinn Fein regime allowed me to write in its praise, and the protests of indignant readers haunted him long afterward, as he had foreseen. In order to help the book I had to assume various disguises in different papers, which would otherwise have boycotted or slashed it. The people who really appreciated Joyce belonged precisely to that Ireland prior to 1914 which M. Larbaud dismisses as of secondary importance.

It was in Æ's Irish Homestead that some of Joyce's earliest stories got their first hearing, long before M. Larbaud's 'Young Ireland' was heard of. For the purposes of the myth, it is very convenient to isolate Joyce from the place and people with whom he was as inevitably associated as any other writer of his generation. Just as he compared Irish, a living language with a literature, to Old French, and on being challenged promises to modify his comparison to Breton—which is still wide of the actual truth—so M. Larbaud and all the devotees of the *Ulysses* cult will have to reconcile themselves to the inconvenient facts as to Joyce's evolution and the various signposts along the route of his fame. For instance, M. Larbaud cannot think of the *Little Review* without genuflecting before the editorial genius of Miss Margaret Anderson. As a reader of the *Little Review* since its first number in March, 1914, I am at a loss to reconcile these reverential allusions with the fact that in 1914 that review made no mention of *Dubliners*. It was supposed to maintain friendly relations with the London *Egoist*, but it made no mention of *A Portrait of the Artist*, which was running as a serial in the *Egoist* in 1915 and 1916. In fact, only when the irresistible perfume of obscenity floated on the air did the advanced thinkers suddenly discover what a great man Joyce was. Now they triumph by pointing out that the first edition of *Ireland's Literary Renaissance* did not mention those books by Joyce which appeared after it was written!

As a matter of plain, unaesthetic literary history, the first stories by Joyce to get recognition in America were those from *Dubliners* which I recommended to H. L. Mencken in 1914, who printed some of them in the *Smart Set*. For the rest, the credit for advancing the name of James Joyce is due to Ezra Pound. He got *A Portrait of the Artist* into the *Egoist*, and—I suspect from circumstantial evidence—it was through his offices that *Ulysses* came to the ears of the *Little Review*.

It is part of the process of making Joyce a coterie author to ignore the genuine pioneers on his behalf, who make no fantastic claims for him. As for M. Larbaud's 'Young Ireland,' it is so incensed by the praise accorded to Joyce at the Tailteann Games in Dublin last summer that, in a typical broadside, the whole tribe of Anglo-Irish writers has been excommunicated from holy Ireland. The anathema is reprinted from the Catholic Bulletin, the most widely circulated monthly in Ireland, in the local *Irish World* of Jan. 10. Yeats, Joyce, Lennox, Robinson and several of the young poets are declared to be bestial, filthy-minded and blasphemous. Æ is shown urging them on to grosser indecencies, and my complicity is proved by my having edited in New York an unexpurgated Maupassant which is, in some mysterious way, going to corrupt the well known purity of Irish life, of which we had, until lately, heard little since Synge defied the mob with his *Playboy*. M. Larbaud had better go to Ireland, to 'Young Ireland,' once more, and stay longer than two weeks. . . .

148. Edmund Wilson on Joyce as a poet

1925

'James Joyce as a Poet,' *New Republic*, xliv (November 1925), 279–80.

Mr. R. C. Trevelyan, the author of an interesting little book called *Thamyris*, or *Is There a Future for Poetry?* in the Today and Tomorrow Series seems troubled by the lack of seriousness and ambition in contemporary English poetry. His discussion of the future possibilities of comic, philosophic, satiric, didactic and narrative poetry only serves to call attention to the fact that there is nobody of any importance attempting any of them. Mr. Masefield's long narrative poems have fallen progressively further below the success of The Everlasting Mercy; and Mr. Yeats, without doubt a great poet, has seldom passed beyond his personal lyrics, to write anything but short plays which still remain lyric rather than dramatic. It might . . . be worth while, in connection with the apparently rather discouraging condition of English poetry, to consider a prose writer who is perhaps as closely related to the poets as to the writers of prose fiction.

Mr. James Joyce, whose first book was a volume of lyrics, has from the beginning shown himself possessed of some of the peculiar genius of the poet at the same time that he has evidently lacked some of the gifts of the novelist. This appears very plainly in his language: few novelists have brought the language of prose fiction so close to the language of verse—'her long fair hair was girlish: and girlish, and touched with the wonder of mortal beauty, her face.' 'Kind air defined the coigns of houses in Kildare street. No birds. Frail from the housetops two plumes of smoke ascended, pluming, and in a flaw of softness softly were blown.' But it is not merely in his language but in the whole effect at which he aims that Mr. Joyce is akin to the poets as much as to the novelists. Perhaps the most remarkable and characteristic of the pieces in his first book of fiction, *Dubliners*, is the long story called 'The Dead', which, however, performs none of the functions which we ordinarily expect of a story: it is scarcely an anecdote and not even a character study; if it represents a situation, it is a situation which does not come to anything. It is simply an exquisite and complex presentation of the sensations of a single person on a particular evening; and it thus sets the type of everything that Joyce is afterwards to do. *A Portrait of the Artist as a Young Man* is merely a succession of such presentations; and *Ulysses* the same thing again on a larger scale and with a greater degree of complexity. Less than any other novelist is Joyce interested in staging a drama or telling a story. When he has put before us a particular nexus of thoughts, emotions, perceptions and sensations as they are found in combination at a particular moment, he is satisfied. All his sweep is in the areas of society and of the human consciousness which he makes these moments imply. *Ulysses*, vast as it is, has no action and scarcely any movement: it ends with the character's falling asleep, as they do at the end of 'The Dead', after a day which, like most of the days which we know, takes no definite new direction from its predecessors. The parallel with the *Odyssey* does duty for a story and serves Joyce as a device for indicating the significance and relations of his characters, which his rigorously objective method makes it impossible for him to explain in his own person and which, as they do not realize them, they cannot of course reveal themselves.

Ulysses, therefore, has this in common with some of the greatest of long poems: that, though the effect is cumulative and the parts necessary to each other, we read it as a series of episodes rather than a story which carries us straight through. We appreciate it best indeed when we have already read it once and have found out what it is about, and return to it from time to time to read the sections separately. It is only then that we are able properly to realize what a satisfactory artistic unit each episode makes in itself and at the same time what it contributes to the whole. For this reason *Ulysses* has perhaps been more readily understood by people who are used to reading poetry, that is, poetry on the great scale, than by people who read principally novels. . . .

And there is a further particular reason why *Ulysses* is more likely to be understood by the reader of poetry than by the reader of fiction. Mr. Joyce has been preoccupied with a problem to which Virgil and Dante most anxiously applied themselves and which has obviously been one of the principal concerns of poets in all civilized ages but to which novelists, with the exception of Flaubert, have not paid very much attention—the problem of varying the style to fit the subject. . . . But one of the things which makes *Ulysses* formidable not merely to the modern novel but to the whole achievement of prose fiction is precisely its spectacular reintroduction of this problem and its appeal to standards which we long ago formed the habit of forgetting with the epic and dramatic poets who first set them—and whose race, like Mr. Trevelyan, we have come gradually no longer to count on. . . .

The poetic genius of Mr. Joyce appears particularly plainly in a part of the opening of his new novel which has been published in a French magazine, *Le Navire d'Argent* [*Work in Progress*]. This book is to begin, I am told, with a description of the river Liffey chattering over its stones—which are presently heard to speak with the voices of gossiping washwomen: they are babbling an indistinct rigmarole story, half unearthly, half vulgarly human, of some semi-legendary heroine; and Joyce's rendering of the voices of the river, light, rapid, half metrical but always changing, now running monotonously on one note, now for a moment syncopated, but bickering interminably on, is surely one of his most remarkable successes: . . .

[The article ends with a long quotation from the 'Anna Livia Plurabelle' portion of *Finnegans Wake*, pp. 196, 216.]

1925: ULYSSES

149. R. H. Pender on *Ulysses*

1925

'James Joyce', *Deutsche Rundschau*, cciii (June 1925), 285–6.

In spite of everything English literature has brought forth, Joyce is an author who has not submitted or bowed down before the controlling powers and who is in his own way just as radical as the most extreme German. It is characteristic in this respect that Joyce is no Englishman but instead an Irishman, and a Catholic Irishman to be sure.

The modern quality of Joyce is, however, different from that of the modern German. The dusk of humanity has two meanings: the sunrise and the sunset of humanity. Joyce represents the end of humanity, the individualistic epoch, just as Franz Werfel can be considered as the forerunner of the organized humanity. Joyce would like the barriers between individual and individual raised, wants to feel himself united with all others. The former never wants to lose the feeling of his individuality but instead wants it accented in all possible ways. He has formulated his life's motto himself: 'I will not serve that etc. . . .' This is the formula of a complete individualist, who is conscious of his weakness. The negativeness of this attitude which is especially emphasized in the choice of weapons, 'silence, exile, cunning'—all defense weapons—catches attention, Rembrandt would have said he would take shape or develop himself as far as was possible with paint and brush. And this feeling of weakness springs not from a collapse of ideals caused by the war, but instead it springs out of the continuous clash between his *Münschen* in all areas (social, material, spiritual) and the hard, victorious reality since his earliest youth developed and had almost reached a philosophical form. Joyce is, to that extent, the direct successor of Hardy. But with this consciousness of the weakness is joined, also through the slowly solidified development, an almost furious Will to dominate the external world. In this way and by this means, he succeeded in creating this weakness in *Ulysses*.

In his earlier novel, *The Portrait of the Artist as a Young Man*, he had delineated his entire development up to the break with the Church and to his proud individualistic acknowledgement. Until then he had always held his own against reality, against *his* reality—the environment of Dublin. Then, however, he had to yield to it; he chose for himself exile and silence. From there on the history of his development stops. In place of that we have in *Ulysses* a great effort to reach a complete mastery over reality, and especially over the reality before which he was yielding at that time and which constantly lived in his thoughts with extraordinary intensity. Whether he behaved according to his purpose in real life can not be asked, but he certainly realized this plan or purpose in *Ulysses*. There he refuses all, there he negates all which doesn't prove itself worthwhile from an individualistic viewpoint. And because he is weak, life seems to him as a great, colorless trivial, busy meaningless midweek lag, an unending accumulation of little happenings which altogether are worthwhile. Here is no strong personality which gives a beauty to life. Here, however, is a personality which has enough strength in order to give a deeply moving picture of the world as it appears to the modern, hyper-conscious weak individualist. The two main characters, Dedalus and Bloom, go, as it were, under in the excess of impressions which storm upon them. What is missing to them is a definite goal after which they with their entire body and unconsciously like a 100 meter speed runner strive for; all impressions which are not to their main interest useful are eliminated. The playing with philosophic myth, a too subtle power of reasoning in Dedalus, like the tired, weak, habitual sexual drive of Bloom, creates nothing valuable to them. Their entire will goes therein, not by the outside world suppressed.

Both are individualists, the one instinctive, the other conscious—both can believe in nothing higher than in the individual who consequently can not serve and who yearns for a drunken condition where the limitations of their personality and their fear of the feeling of weakness can be erased.

In the technical execution of the book we find the same tendency of expression. Everywhere the unity is diminished. At one time an entire life, occasionally several generations, was handled in a novel—here it is by a single day. Even so the psychological unity of life is diminished, often limited to an almost purely physical impression, and is reproduced with the help of imagistic and rhythmic techniques. But longer lasting moods, the emotional key-note of experience, are called forth through the use of a special style (a style of earlier periods, of journalism, parody, etc.). By this account, *Ulysses* is one of the greatest achievements of English literature. And in spite of the missing stylistic unity, this unity creates a strong personality. The book is, in fact, the tragedy of the late, weak individualist and it is the key to his art: he is not creative like his great models, and he must judge or criticize them after the unconscious criteria of their life and knowledge. He refuses all authority and convention, in life as in art; however, he doesn't have the skill or power to shape his personality to match convention and to impose his personality on the world.

150. Edwin Muir on the meaning of *Ulysses*

1925

'James Joyce: The Meaning of *Ulysses*', *Calendar of Modern Letters*, i, No. 5 (July 1925), 347–55. The same article appeared as 'James Joyce', *Nation*, cxxi, No. 3145 (14 October 1925), 421–3. The former version appeared in *transition* (1926), pp. 19–36. Added to it, in this appearance, was 'A Note on Ulysses', revised from the *New Republic*, xli, No. 523 (10 December 1924), 4–6. which became pages 36–45 in *transition*.

No other novelist who has written in English has had a greater mastery than Mr. Joyce of language as an instrument of literary expression, and no one else, probably, has striven so consciously to attain it. *Dubliners* was an ideal apprentice piece for an artist; in it Mr. Joyce set himself to describe accurately the things he saw, attempting at the beginning what most writers achieve towards the end. *The Portrait of the Artist as a Young Man*, marked a further stage. That book was as much a recreation of language as a record of experience. . . .

. . . In *The Portrait of the Artist as a Young Man* Mr. Joyce acquired the mastery of language, the knowledge of and reverence for its mysteries, which prepared him for *Ulysses*. He learnt, too, for the second time, the strict realism which, because it demands perfect exactitude in the rendering, is valuable as a discipline, makes an intensive demand on the artist's powers of expression, and by putting a strain on them enhances them . . . *The Portrait of the Artist as a Young Man* not only left Mr. Joyce with a greater command over English than any other novelist had possessed; it was as well a sort of self-inoculation against a sensibility grown burdensome. Without either of these *Ulysses* could never have been written. For in *Ulysses* the dual values of *The Portrait*, the values of life and art, of reality and imagination, are developed side by side until each attains its maximum of expression, and the discrepancy between them issues in a form of humour which through its intellectual profundity becomes universal. . . . Had Mr. Joyce not inoculated himself against sensibility by an overdose of realism he could never have attained this emancipating comic vision of the entire modern world. Had he not been so sensitive that he suffered monstrously from his sensibility his comedy would have had no driving power behind it. One feels again and again in *Ulysses* that the uproariousness of the farce, the recklessness of the blasphemy, is wildest where the suffering of the artist has been most intense. . . . *Dubliners* and *The Portrait* were a necessary preparation, an apprenticeship strengthening the artist against life. They were exercises working out a part of Mr. Joyce's problem; but in *Ulysses* the whole problem is faced and to the extent of Mr. Joyce's present powers resolved. . . . There is thus a necessary and an organic relation between him and his work, to create being, as Ibsen said, an act of emancipation. But when, as in *Ulysses*, the creation is encyclopædic, when it attempts to gain freedom not from one but all the bonds, all the suffering, of the artist's soul, the impulse from which it started becomes a part of the autobiography of the book as well as of the writer. What Mr. Joyce suffered from in writing *Ulysses* was obviously in its completeness the life he had known; our modern world in all its intellectual manifestations as well as in its full banality; . . . *Ulysses* is a complete course, a set banquet, of the modern consciousness. And being that no other unit could have served; the author could not have got into the record of a year what he has got into the record of a day.

But the banquet of the modern consciousness was to be a comic summing up as well as a banquet; it was to be not only abundant, but so burdensomely, absurdly abundant that all the courses would be made to appear ridiculous, as Rabelais made the courses of the medieval banquet ridiculous. And as Mr. Joyce's encyclopædic plan justified the time unit of his chronicle, so his comic intention justified the minuteness of his portrayal, his huge accumulation of imaginative material. His humour is on one side, like that of Rabelais, a piling up of one burden on the mind after another until the breaking point is reached—the breaking point of laughter. It operates by oppressing us consciously with all the things which oppress us unconsciously, and by exaggerating all this until it seems ridiculous that we should bear it, or more exactly that it should exist at all. . . . The more absurd and minute the description of physiological reactions, the greater obviously the effect. On the one hand an infinite immensity, on the other an infinitesimal smallness; the intellectual dreams and spiritual struggles of Stephen Dedalus in the one balance, the vagaries of Leopold Bloom's instincts in the other; . . . There is in Mr. Joyce's obscenity as in that of Rabelais an intellectual quality, as if in searching the recondite secrets of the natural processes of the body he were trying to penetrate to an unconscious humour of the cells, of those elementary principles of life which have built up not only the body but all this phantasmal structure which we call thought, religion and civilisation. His emphasis on the unseemly, on what, in other words, we have surpassed, depend upon, and wish to forget, is, at any rate, a necessary element in this kind of humor and an essential part of the plan of *Ulysses*. It is perverse, that is to say, intellectualised deliberately, but so it had to be to achieve its purpose.

The vision of the world whose mainspring is in this radical sense of contrast is one which, if it did not issue in humour, would be nightmare. In *Ulysses* it does not always issue in humour. The brothel scene is horrible partly because it is a mis-shapen birth, because, conceived as a grand example of the humour of horror, it attains, through its failure, an atmosphere of horror which because it is unintentional is strictly monstrous, and incapable of being resolved either into art or into human experience. . . . Had Mr. Joyce succeeded with this gigantic scene he would have produced something supreme in literature and not merely something supremely astounding and terrifying. It was obviously designed to be the climax of the work; in it the last resources of the theme were to be brought on the stage; the unconscious desires which up to now had been allowed only a chance or oblique expression were to come nakedly to the surface and attain freedom. They do not attain freedom. The brothel scene is not a release of all the oppressions and inhibitions of life in our time; it is rather a gigantic attempt to attain release.

But if we grant this crucial failure in the book, and a number of minor failures, there remains more comedy in the grand style than has appeared in our literature since the Elizabethan age. The last chapter has been much praised, but there are others only less admirable. . . .

[The critic discusses some of these scenes.]

What is it that through this use of contrast, this breaking of our resistances by accumulation, Mr. Joyce tries to set in the plane of low comedy? First of all, professional seriousness of all kinds, and secondly the objects about which people are serious in this way: religion, to which the comic reaction is blasphemy; patriotism, to which it is little less; literature, to which it is parody; the claims of science, to which it is an application of anti-climax; sex, to which it is obscenity. When comedy attempts to become universal it has perforce to include blasphemy and obseenity, for these are the two poles of this comedy just as the soul and the body are the two poles of human existence. To see religion with the eyes of comedy is not, of course, to laugh it out of existence, any more than to see sex comically is to destroy it. All that comedy can destroy is strictly the second-rate, everything that is not in its mode the best, everything less genuine than the genuine—a class of thoughts and emotions which make up the preponderating part of the experience of most people and of all ages, and is a permanent burden which at times may become unbearable . . . To destroy so completely as Mr. Joyce does in *Ulysses* is to make a new start. . . . But what is new in this sense in *Ulysses* it is hazardous to attempt to say yet; for the things which are most new in it have a breath of an antiquity which seems to antedate the antiquity of classical literature, and to come out of a folk rather than a literary inspiration. Mr. Joyce's prostitutes in the brothel scene exist neither in the world of literature, as that world has been conceived almost since its beginning, nor in the world of fact. They are rather figures in a folk-lore which mankind continually creates, or rather carries with it, creations and types in the dream in which sensual humanity lives, and which to humanity is the visible world. This folk-lore, which is the aesthetic utterance of the illiterate classes, and of the illiterate parts of our nature, which co-exists with literature, but in a separate world, is not inarticulate; but it expresses itself anonymously, and is such a constant attribute of human life that it rarely feels the need of the more permanent, the more specialised, expression of art. It attains its perfection from day to day by means which are as suited to its purposes as the means of literature are to the purposes of literature. Yet from it literature arose, for like literature, it is aesthetic, and has the freedom of perception which can only come when men are delivered from their utilitarian prejudices. And to it accordingly literature must periodically come back, as much to test as to renew itself. This is the world to which Mr. Joyce has in part returned, in part striven to return, in *Ulysses*. He has seen, as only a profound theorist on art could have seen, that the sources of art lie here, that here is the primary division in our consciousness from which flow on the one hand the laws of art, and on the other the laws of the practical world in which we live. . . . In *Ulysses* there are passages of unassimilated folk-lore which we feel do not belong to literature—diurnal phrases of Dublin talk which should not have survived the day, which, perfect in their time and place, get a false emphasis when set deliberately into the frame of a work of imagination. But where the attempt is successful, Mr. Joyce's imagination has a unique immediacy, a unique originality. In one glance we seem to see the life which he describes immediately before and immediately after he has set his seal upon it, and the transformation of reality into art takes place, as it were, under our eyes. Then we feel sometimes that in sweeping aside the aesthetic sense of three centuries, Mr. Joyce has penetrated to the aesthetic consciousness in itself, the aesthetic consciousness, that is to say, before it has become selective and exclusive, as the more it is developed and refined it tends to become, and still includes everything. It is, of course, obvious that the totality of the responses of that consciousness cannot be rendered in literature, of which selection is not merely a virtue, but also the condition. Yet in the history of literature, as has often been shown, the principle of selection sometimes becomes a conventional, an arbitrary one, and, indeed, continually tends to do so; and, therefore, it is at rare times necessary for the artist to put himself in a position where a fundamental act of selection becomes compulsory, and where he feels that every decision, whether to include or to reject, is significant not only on traditional grounds, but is made by his own unconditional volition and as if for the first time. *Ulysses* not only raises the problem of selection again; in part, it answers it by bringing into literature things banished from it, as we now see more clearly, on moral and conventional rather than essential grounds. In doing that, Mr. Joyce has both enriched literature and potentially widened its scope.

Ulysses showed the direction in which literature for ten years had been moving; it showed also the direction, or rather some of the directions, in which, perhaps for ten times ten, it will move. Into it various currents, Irish, cosmopolitan, personal, came together, and out of it they issued again clarified and transformed. Analysing *Ulysses* one could have drawn a chart of the future of literature, showing not only what would be attempted, but also what with good luck would be achieved; or rather one could have done so if among the various streams collected together in *Ulysses* there had not been one, and the most potent, which, mingling with the others, changed them, contributed to them something occult. This was Mr. Joyce's genius, over which nobody but himself had control. For the rest he not only hammered out a new grammar of literary art in *Ulysses*; he discovered a new field of æsthetic experience (a field on which others had labored without knowing what it was); and to describe it he invented a magic of speech unessayed for centuries, and never before essayed so consciously. It was because he went back so far to the fundamentals of art that his book had its enigmatic, primal atmosphere, and seemed, in spite of its modernity, hoary with years. One did not know whether to be astonished most by Mr. Joyce's systematic method or his discoveries, by his discoveries or his inventions. As a conscious practician of art he was not only accomplished, he was masterly; as a discoverer of hidden riches he was as mighty in his own field as Dostoyevsky was in his; in his evocation of the hidden magic of words he stood by himself. He renewed both the subject-matter of literature and the speech in which artists would for some time express it. . . Mr. Joyce went over the conscious life of men like a plough and showed the richness of the soil; and *Ulysses* gives us the sense of black magic which ploughed fields sometimes evoke. This feeling is probably a racial memory of times which saw the birth of magic, when the blackness of the upturned earth was an image to men of blasphemous violation and of inexplicable increase.

But everything in *Ulysses* has this mythical quality, and the humor, is like that of primitive peoples, the humor of size. Whatever validity there may be philosophically in Mr. Joyce's symbolical construction, in which each part of the book represents an organ of the human body, and the whole the human form divine, its humorous virtues are so clear that they leap out and strike the eye. . . . Mr. Joyce has pursued comedy down to its source, penetrating to the cells, to the dust out of which man rises. Through its minuteness his humor attains the cosmical, and gives one the feeling that not only men could feel warmed by it, but all the forms of that nature in which copulation and reproduction are so omnipotent. It is a humor entirely of the earth, as perhaps all humor is.

It is a humor, too, in which extravagance is reinstated after being banished for a long time as childish and contrary to mature taste. . . . Disregarding the fashion of centuries Mr. Joyce has recaptured the boundlessness of primitive humor and has set laughter back on its roots. He has not been ashamed to play the clown, to resurrect the mock-heroic, which everybody thought was safely buried, and to practise parody, which nobody considered a form worth the notice of an artist of serious purpose. And to all these he has given new significance, proving their possibilities, carrying them by that sheer courage which is intuition to a plane where they reach cosmic absurdity. The part of *Ulysses* where the thoughts of Gerty MacDowell are presented in the manner of a penny novelette is not only parody; it is a unique and poignant form of expression, a doubly indirect, a multiple utterance, in which almost everything is left to be implied and the triteness of the words conceals half-a-dozen meanings, some of them of an ethereal beauty. In handling subject-matter so trivial and so hackneyed as this Mr. Joyce shows most clearly the originality of his mind and the incisiveness of his art. His parodies of the daily newspapers do not merely amuse; they evoke a gigantic image of the fatuity of the mind. . . . He uses parody as a means of anatomising the mind, showing that it, too, has its absurdities, its gigantic humors, as unavoidable, in spite of its dignity, as those of the body; and by an extravagance calculated in its seeming excess he reaches the essential in a new way. And he has discovered anew the mystical power of extravagance in itself, scarcely recognized by anyone since Rabelais; and in the pub scene he has carried it to the length where nonsense has a meaning.

But as if in doing all these things he had not done enough he has described clearly for the first time the realm only half-glimpsed by writers such as Mr. D. H. Lawrence, Mr. Sherwood Anderson and Miss Dorothy Richardson. He has revealed the swarming world of sub-conscious and half-conscious thoughts which constitute three-fourths of our life, and he has shown that it has a magical and excessive beauty. In hardly any other work of modern times is there such an overpowering sense of the inexhaustibility of human life, a sense of richness which may well be too strong for the literati. Whether he has succeeded in articulating completely a new world in a new language one cannot yet say; one feels that here and there he has won only an approximate success; but that he has achieved so much is astonishing. . . . In *Ulysses* the total articulation of the sub-conscious body of man is obscured by the separate features, but by study if not by intuition they can be put together. The separate merits of the book we can apprehend immediately as we apprehend anything that in art is beautiful, but to appreciate its total beauty we have to draw upon reflection.

This fault *Ulysses* has; it has another which is more serious. For such a huge and multifarious work it is too continuously on one key. . . . Mr. Joyce is encyclopædic; he is learnedly minute; his book is, what Rabelais's works were not, firmly and severely constructed; but he is not satisfying for us, simply because one part of life he almost completetely ignores; and by its lack of relief *Ulysses* sometimes oppresses us: the complementary part of our nature is interdicted expression. Mr. Joyce's masterpiece has neither the breadth nor the sanity of supreme comic art; its richness is not quite that of nature: the atmosphere is overheated, and the horizon is too narrow for the objects which are crowded into it. In *Ulysses* life presses in too closely upon us on every side, too closely for us to see it clearly. That is as much as to say that Mr. Joyce has not won a complete artistic triumph over his subject-matter.

But his attempt is great, and his measure of success, considering the magnitude of the task, astonishing. No imaginative work of our time has in it so much of the occult and original quality of genius. In *Ulysses* the author has brought literary art back to its sources, and he has remained at them, drawing continuously from the fountainhead. The book has the quality which the Germans call ursprunglich; it is not a new mode of art, but rather a fundamental assertion of it. Consequently no work of our time has so completely the atmosphere and the authority of a scripture. It is the full utterance, enigmatic but not to be ignored, of one man. And like all scriptures it contains within it a principle of differentiation; many streams lead out from it, and it may well become the central point of a literature. The danger is not that it will remain unrecognized, but that in time it will overshadow every other potentiality of our age. Yet, though it may fetter the talents of a few artists, to the many it will give a clear road and their opportunity. On every side it is a beginning, and a beginning is what our generation has chiefly desired.

151. A French critique of Louis Gillet

1925

Georges Duplaix, 'Joyce à la "Revue des Deux Mondes"', *La Revue Nouvelle*, No. 10–11 (September-October 1925), 23–9.

A reply to Louis Gillet's article, 'Du coté de chez Joyce', *Revue des Deux Mondes*, xxviii (August 1925), 686–97.

The friends of James Joyce remain at ease no longer. The great seer of the century, the man with treasures, the Goethe of young Ireland, has just assisted at the deification of his own genius as the ultimate figure and the only one who matters in literary cathedrals by virtue of the incense of *La Revue des Deux Mondes*. Here is Mr. Louis Gillet disguised as a cherubin with wings of salmon-colored paper who strews rose petals and entones the *Gloria in excelcis*.

Everyone knows the importance of this venerable publication in matters of originality, the important place it has always consecrated to avant-garde literature and the numerous precursors of talent which its flair has discovered and pointed out to the public . . . But consider the celerity of this praise. James Joyce was born in 1882, his first work (a pamphlet on the Irish Literary Theatre) was published in 1901, and *Ulysses* in 1922; it is only twenty-four years after his first work and only three years after the publication of *Ulysses* and now Joyce is discovered by *La Revue des Deux Mondes*. . . .

Let one not imagine that the article concerned a paragraph of three lines . . . No, things have been done generously, and twelve large pages are dedicated to James Joyce. To Joyce? Not precisely, whatever the title may say, but to *Ulysses* rather. For the rest, two or three titles have been thrown into a note—while things like *Exiles*. . . a fine drama in three acts. . . are simply forgotten.

The ignorance of the erudite Mr. Gillet chagrins me a little. For him, Joyce wrote *Dedalus* and *Ulysses*: one point here: *Dubliners*? He does not know of it . . [Had he known more of Joyce's work] he would have learned that Joyce, who he says with great verbal audacity 'had broken nothing' until the publication of *Ulysses*, had, however, made tongues wag well before the *Portrait of the Artist*, and that from 1911 a faction had arisen against him which wanted to prevent the printing of *Dubliners*, in which the moral and political audacities, as well as the great realistic purity bewildered certain minds. . . .

[quotes extensively from Gillet's article for the purpose of rebuttal]

152. German comment on *Ulysses* by Bernhard Fehr

1925

'James Joyce's *Ulysses*', *Englische Studien*, lx (1925–6), 180–205.

James Joyce's novel *Ulysses*; it is a monstrous work. No English publisher would publish it. The New York *Little Review* printed fragments of it in 1919–1920 but was hindered in the continuation by the Society for the Suppression of Vice. Only in 1922 did Shakespeare and Company bring it out as a thick volume in quarto for 200 French francs. Should not this be a reason to examine the book more closely? Certainly not, because public opinion was right; its indignation was comprehensible. But doesn't one have to stop and think when the highest literary critique of France [the *Nouvelle Revue Française*] is seriously concerned about this book, when it elicits brilliant articles from well-known English poets and critics, when it causes enthusiastic reviews in America and a biography about Joyce, when Valéry Larbaud, in spite of all the opposition of the Irish literary-historian Ernest Boyd, thinks *Ulysses* is world literature? And are we supposed to be silent when we, after close examination, come to the conclusion, even when our character has to refuse the work a hundred times, that in spite of all it is an 'exceeding work of genius?' One thinks of the *Satyricon* by Petronius Arbiter. of

Laurence Sterne's half-conscious revelations of the unconscious, of Byron's *Don Juan*, of Flaubert, of Baudelaire, perhaps of Marcel Proust. And still *Ulysses* remains a giant statue in the fog beside all these, a sphinx in the desert, a weird comet in our contemporary sky. . . .

[A literary history follows here.]

Eighteen chapters in three parts on 732 quarto pages! Part I is the chronicle of Stephen Daedalus's life in the forenoon of June 16, 1904. Part II . . . describes the same forenoon in Leopold Bloom's consciousness and adds the impressions of the afternoon. Stephen's experience enters again into this contents of consciousness [*Bewusstseinsinhalt*] Part III is the description of the last two to three hours—after 2 o'clock in the morning—in Bloom's, Stephen's, and Mrs. Bloom's lives. On the whole a span of twenty hours.

[Here follows long quotations from Part I, ch. 1 ('Telemachus') and ch. 4 ('Calypso') with interpretative comment, pp. 183–7.]

At first glance, it seems as if Joyce breaks all that we feel is a unity into a disorder of atoms. But in the confusion of impressions which the work makes on us, three directions become clear to us. We realize: a new way of viewing things, a discarding of all former conventions so as to open up a view of the events of consciousness in its entirety, and a selection of new manners of style.

Henry James and Joseph Conrad had already left the simple plain, which is still kept by Arnold Bennett and his school, in expressing the individual relativity on many plains. Meredith and Galsworthy draw on the plain of appearances, but always in a way that we assume that scene into which Browning abruptly leads us. At first, Joyce walks the same paths as May Sinclair, Dorothy Richardson, Wyndham Lewis, only to leave them later far behind him. Like Marcel Proust, he spatializes time and memory. These two contemporaries are tortured by the same problem, which each of them solves in his own way, which probably points to the modern artist's new way of viewing things. But what does spatialization of time and memory mean?

[The critic uses the sentence 'A cloud began to cover the sun slowly, shadowing the bay in deeper green' from the Telemachus episode (p. 11, p. 9) and from the Calypso episode (p. 61, p. 61) to illustrate the spatialization of time.]

The sentence represented here is not a leitmotif. Its purpose is to fix the point of time in the only possible way, in space, by letting us draw two lines from the points registered in two plains of conviction; the point of intersection brings two beings into optical correlation. One involuntarily must think of descriptive geometry. We call this 'orientation' or 'geometrization.' The cloud is, of course, a sign of time beside its socially common aspect, a different value on the two plains of conviction, by virtue of the dying mother; here, associations while reading the newspaper.

The third kind of spatialization is offered to us by the above-sketched chapter of coexistences. Here we have the impression of many adjacently-flowing fields of visions, which we can watch regenerating from five minutes before three o'clock into the future. Only occasionally one field cuts through another in a certain moment on its way to the future. (Boylan sees the Heely's Poster-People going up the street; Miss Dunn sees them going down the street; Lenham and M'Coy see Bloom, who stopped in front of a bookcar of a street-merchant.) Usually, they run separately and only cross in unmentioned areas. But at the end we see the regeneration of an area which crosses all hitherto existing fields. The Viceroy of Ireland drives, with his body of attendants, through the streets and crosses the flowing field of vision of each character in the novel, just where he stands, . . . he crosses even the painted artists of the ad-signs. These are areas of conviction which are made visible and which rotate through space!

Related to this form is the fourth form. If one reads chapter sixteen and seventeen carefully, where Stephen's and Bloom's going home and their ways of thought in the kitchen are described, then one cannot get rid of the feeling that each of them looks into a room which belongs only to him, that these rooms sometimes come closer to each other, sometimes drift apart again; that means in the exterior and in the interior viewing. During these early morning hours, after their consciousness has grown shallow and has assimilated under the influence of alcohol, they seem almost to look into the same room. But the two rooms cannot come to a complete accord, since they experience as two divided and basically different beings these objects (contents of consciousness), one as a dreamer and thinker, the other as an animal practicus. That is why convergence and divergence change their perspectives. Joyce demonstrated this behaviour in the grotesque parody of the scientific style so that one could object; the attitude is being ridiculed here and is not allowed to be used by Joyce. In reality, only the troublesome way of describing elementary things is supposed to be struck upon.

[quotes two passages from the Eumaeus episode]

This is spatialization of perspectives. It is found not only in parodies, but throughout the book. Each figure looks into its own exterior and especially interior rooms, which are only imagined.

Interruptions in succession through insertion of pictures, geometrization, surface which flows into space, perspectives: they are all only pieces of threads in the ball of the problem of problems: space and time, the side-by-side and the succession (one after another), both in one, the side-by-side able to be experienced only in the succession. The succession is visible only in the side-by-side.

What kind of philosophy lies hidden behind this viewing? Let us not be deceived by thinking that we could find a philosophy which Joyce willingly advocates. Test-cases of this kind are seldom offered to the literary historian. In an artist's soul, philosophies of life, which contradict each other, often live closely together. But it is different with Joyce. The spatialization of the temporary, the geometrization is reminiscent of Bergson, but there is in it a necessary evil, to which the intellect, which is bound to space, has to reach for orientation. Joyce does not consider this an evil. The presentation of perspectives is similar to the mathematized philosophy of the new-realist Bertrand Russell, who gives a private space to each single being, in which space the being sees its perception, while on the other hand, the perspective, or public space is made up of all the individual spaces, is the location of the absolute bases for all things perceived from the standpoint of our private locale.

Everybody carries his space, his world around with him, but orientates himself to the fixed location. Russell stresses the continuation of space, time, matter, movement. A tower means the possibility to see an infinite continuity of tower perspectives, according to the infinite continuity of points of view, which any steadily marching observer could choose for himself. With Russell, geometry has its full rights.

But geometrization is not full experience; Joyce lets that objection pass; it is immaterial whether he received it (the objection) directly or through a side-channel from Bergson, or out of himself. We experience the absolute reality in qualitative, intensive states of conviction as true duration, as a growth which is superior to all categories and is always moving up to higher states of consciousness, while our intuition forms the time creatively. Now comes our intellect and dissects this, the only true, creative time into constant elements, which it (the intellect) lines up in space and measures up to what it calls time. But this time as only a time-phantom in space, only a line which runs through, only the face and hands on a clock, but not the movements of the hands, only that which Newton, overestimating its essence, called 'tempus absolutum, varum at mathematicum.' It is absolutely clear to Joyce that this practical time is only spatial transformation: Stephen Dedalus walks through the sand which sinks with each step. Over there, the cool room of the tower awaits him (44). 'Through the barbicans, the shafts of light are moving ever, slowly ever as my feet are sinking, creeping duskward over the dial floor.' Similar to a cosmic movement of continuity, the sun shines through the blastholes. Stephen has to fix them spatially according to the angles of the holes in the walls, the same as he sees the present walking westward geometrized on the surface of the earth, which turned, for him, into the face of his hand-feet (meaning hands of a clock). But before Joyce realizes it, the spatialization becomes a wonderful instrument of humor. He has fun seeing the different individual successions of conviction, which keep step with one another, in amusing opposition to each other, and he has fun drawing us up to his vantage point. . . .

States of Conviction: But the orientation is always illuminated and colored by Joyce's intuition. The bare orientation is seldom present and as such, mostly an abstraction of our critique. Impulses penetrate from outside into us as a sensorimotor presence to organize itself with our so-called 'useful remembrances' to an advancing action. But into the action intrudes the 'dream,' the direct experience which wakes into consciousness the 'useless' personal remembrances. And between action and dream, between intellectual-and intuition-activity lie innumerable middle-dispositions, on which our soul moves alternately and, according to the elevation of the plain, calls forth more banal, useful, or personal associations. The result for the artist is that our past lives in the present, either dark, hardly able to rise again, or as a living picture submerged in sleep, ready to obey the awakening call of perception, to walk into the 'dream', or waiting as a motorian remembrance, closely below the surface, till it can break through and further the action as a ministering angel (Cf. 392).

Joyce wants us to feel this system of turning on and off, according to which now the one, now the other succession of steps of memory-plains is flooded with light; this lightening and dimming here and there between the poles of action and dream, play and imagination. Into this system of alternating currents, as we see now, the space and time question is included. The wildest things happen in the Walpurgis-night, where reality and dream stand on the same level of actuality. The alternation is calmer than in the other chapters; It is orientation at the sensorimotor surface, which is spun around from lightly-going-upward, mostly only imagined but not executed actions, furthering associations, and receives its diversion from the steady stream of pictures, which come up from erotic depths and are never repressed by Bloom. Joyce allows the erotic powers which have been forced into the unconscious to have the intensity and originality which they possess in the human life, without subscribing to Freud's interpretation of dreams. He does not eliminate the erotic association if he wants to give us the entire human-being, and not only the human being who has been carefully cleaned and corrected by culture. But one cannot defend Joyce from the reproach that he gave too much to nature. Naturalnesses are easily thought to be superfluities which hardly further the view into the human soul, and which, when they sometimes in *Ulysses* degenerate into simple pornography, in reality are only untrue, paper animalities... The greatness of this book does not lie at all in these excrescences. He, who because of them reads *Ulysses*, is as little mature enough for this great book as is the moralist who takes them as an opportunity to ban and condemn the book as a whole.

It is more important to realize how Joyce handled the problem of the play of conviction on many plains, as a lingual artist.

The problem was difficult because the language had to be forced to express that which always has to break, according to its essence, the steadiness of conviction. Therefore, Joyce has to get the help of a special language, the parole intérieure, the rumination, which, by virtue of its effective, not yet stiffened order of intensity, still has something of the freshness of the stream of consciousness, in opposition to its sister, the correctly written and spoken language, which became quantity. Two-thirds of the entire book is communicated in this inner-language. The verbum finitum makes room for the infinitum; the syntactic relations are loosened; the commas become rare. In the last chapter, the ruminations of Mrs. Bloom—42 quarto pages—are done without a period.

To make it clear one would have to cite infinitely. The last chapter is an extreme case, because in a nightly monologue, the perceptions as a waker of associations are missing. Essential for Joyce's scheme is the information of Bloom's states of consciousness when he goes along the street after vising the editorial staff. A girl passes. Joyce lets Bloom ruminate.

[Numerous examples of Joyce's use of the interior monologue and interpretative comments follow, pp. 197–203.]

The humor swings the hammer to forge together, in boldest beats, the momentarily essential attributes into a unitary name. Sparkling bronze azure (225) he calls for a moment the waitress, Miss Douce (sparkling and bronze is her face, azure her eyes). These three words became a name as did the fusion Bronzedouce. In the same way, Blazes Boylan's name is suddenly Blazure. His indigo-blue dress and his reflection in the azure-blue eye of the waitress furnish the sound-elements for that name. When the voices of the two waitresses (the gold-haired and the bronze-colored) are united in laughter, the expression 'goldbronze voices' (249) slips instinctively from the poet. Leopold Bloom leaves the dining room as Lionellopold (276). Why? He wrote to Martha and listened at the same time to the Lionel-aria and is still delighted. Bloomusalem (457) is the name of the new realm (which he will find) in the Walpurgisnight. We can also see that the style, with its parodies and funny tricks, serves the same purpose as geometrization and intuition, action and dream, practical and personal remembrances and rumination. He tells, like they do, the great singular course of the wordly life, into which both the exterior and interior universe flow, but the entirety is seen from an intellect which finds pleasure not in directing its eye to the cosmic harmony, but rather in feasting its eyes on the grotesque connections which a quick joke creates between any simultaneities. In this way, *Ulysses* grows to be a gigantic joke-book of the world. Behind the fun lies something like a scale of values hidden by the fog. Its lowest points are in the darkest, lowest mud of animalism which has rarely been dug so freely as here; the darkness and the smells rise up high, but the scale is higher and stands finally on 'ethereal purity,' up there with the silent stars to which the spirit in this book sometimes soars. What is missing? The reader will have anticipated this for a long time: the will which creates acts, not actions. Stephen, as well as Bloom, is a mollusk which unresistingly surrendered to the play of consciousness. The only 'doer' is the drunk Tommy whc knocks Stephen out. The password of the book is retreat, defeat.

Why is it called *Ulysses*? It is the Odyssey of one day, an Odyssey under modern conditions.

COMMENT ON *Ulysses* BY BERNHARD FEHR 1925

[illustrates the parallels briefly]

But one should guard oneself from seeing the entire Odyssey parodied in *Ulysses.*

Finally, another question: To which class of novels does *Ulysses* belong? I maintain that *Ulysses* is a life-novel. It belongs to a long list of life-novels, which started about 1910! However, life is not described chronologically. Picture by picture is taken out of the soul in free-ideal sequence. The soul compromises everything, the substance of the world, the personal past, spread out according to values and qualities. What is the importance of the artificial striking of the hour? Glance into it for one moment, and you have the entirety. What is the life of a human being? So and so many minutes? No, it is the sum of these moments which became pictures determining his being. Thus, *Ulysses* is the great juxtaposition of life, biology, psychology, and cosmogeography in one.

153. René Lalou on Joyce's works

1926

Extract from *Panorama de la Littérature Anglaise Contemporaine* (1926), pp. 199–205.

James Joyce had . . . begun in the style of realism in fifteen short stories collected under the title of *Dubliners*, which bore witness to a rare mastery. There is no effort to establish an artificial unity between the diverse moments of the city, but what flexible variety in his evocations!

[summarizes the subjects of *Dubliners*]

. . . The form surrenders nothing to the richness of the content, Joyce evidently leaves realism to Maupassant; but very quickly he surpasses it to attain the fantastic and the symbolic, or higher still, the poignant candid emotion which makes his short story 'The Dead' a masterpiece of animation and of melancholy.

Thus, little by little, one sees James Joyce in *Dubliners*—the subtle imagist of *Chamber Music*, the vigorous dramatist of *Exiles*—abandoning the naturalist's attitude. . . . This evolution heralds the works of the second period. The narrative in *A Portrait* will obey the rhythms of the interior monologue, mixing the present and a past which his intensity renders actual, across conversations both garrulous and elliptical because we hear them only as they are relative to Stephen Dedalus: thus will we assist at the metamorphosis of the little obedient boy into the independent artist. By its extraordinary concrete richness, the work keeps a tyrannical power: it is a portrait, not at all a novel, of manners in spite of its national décor which Joyce pushes into the background. Because the supreme plan of the hero will be escape; he tells one of his scandalized companions: 'When a soul is born in this country, it finds itself caught in nets which prevent its flight. You speak to me of nationality, of language, of religion. I want to try to fly by those nets.'

From the material shackles of their nationality, Dedalus and Bloom of *Ulysses* escape rather easily. Triumph is more difficult in what concerns religion: more to the point, it will be less complete because it is desired less absolutely. . . . Stephen is nourished with the sensations of James Joyce. Well Joyce feels something with a terrible acuity, 'sometimes even to his extreme outward limit and sometimes to his interior center.' What he has felt with a new violence, he expresses integrally. From there, this poetry which the most troubled pages of his sensual and intellectual education conserve, the swamps that Stephen crosses will conduct him to a conquest of 'the enchantment of the heart and mind,' at the time when his apprenticeship as an artist will end. Then he will be able to break his chains, to take his flight into the light, to orient himself toward the double end which epitomizes all his effort: to seek 'beauty which has not yet appeared' and to translate into words 'the uncreated conscience of his race.'

Ulysses will not be, then, what has been said, the definitive statement of Joyce's art; this enormous book marks a stage in a conscient progression; it is, at the same time, an epic and a laboratory. In the eighteen chapters of this Odyssey, Larbaud has distinguished a rigorous composition: Telemachiad, episodes of voyage, and return. However, this long and complicated journey is accomplished in less than a day by a Dublin Jew, a modern Ulysses very similar to the ancient one, neither better nor worse than his brothers, but prodigiously fecund in trickery and in inquisitiveness. To depict him in his total humanity, Joyce has surpassed the audacities of psychoanalysts: more than the meditations of Bloom in the toilet, his erotic fancies on the beach unveil the eternal sexual instinct. The virtuosity of Joyce illustrates even to the interior monologue without punctuation the 'point of view' theory dear to Henry James. Direct or indirect narratives, dialogues, scenic indications, questionnaires, Joyce uses all the literary formula, including those of the catechism, with an incomparable flexibility. The universality of his technique and the cosmopolitanism of his thought, foster in *Ulysses* a teeming, swarming epic.

But the last word is not there. Since *Ulysses* Joyce has produced a fragment of the work that he is preparing, a vast symphony to the waves, by turn released and accelerated, which finish in liquid, nocturnal sonorities. Renewing the enterprises of a Rabelais at the time when French was not yet solidified, he treats the English language as plastic matter. He proceeds by shortenings and lengthenings, by deformations and solicitations, by ironic citations and nordic anticipations. While amplifying itself, the wave creates its own atmosphere and realism. This art of subtle transpositions, of exchanges between the sound and the sense appears difficult, but not abstruse; the thought and the technique sometimes impart their keys, witness all the names of rivers which are changed into verbs to ornament the dress of Anna Livia, river and woman. Having pursued farther than any other, the human soul and human word, having pushed to extreme limits the conscient desintegration, James Joyce has decided to give us the classic work which would summarize all these enrichments, where the artist would finally be free enough to impose on his creation the character of a divine necessity.

154. Pound on 'Work in Progress'

1926

Extract from a Letter to Joyce (15 November 1926), in *The Letters of Ezra Pound* (1950), ed. D. D. Paige, p. 202, and in Ellmann, ed., *Letters*, Volume III (1966), pp. 145–6.

. . . Ms [of *Finnegans Wake*, pp. 403–590] arrived this A.M. All I can do is to wish you every possible success.

I will have another go at it, but up to present I make nothing of it whatever. Nothing so far as I make out, nothing short of divine vision or a new cure for the clap can possibly be worth all the circumambient peripherization.

Doubtless there are patient souls, who will wade through anything for the sake of the possible joke . . . but . . . having no inkling whether the purpose of the author is to amuse or to instruct . . . in somma. . . .

Up to the present I have found diversion in the Tristan and Iseult paragraphs that you read years ago . . . mais apart ca. . . . And in any case I don't see what which has to do with where. . . .

POMES PENYEACH

July 1927

155. George Slocombe, review, *Daily Herald*

1927

'On the Left Bank', *Daily Herald* (14 July 1927), 4.

In a comment on the fourth number of *transition*, the critic comments on *Work in Progress* and reviews *Pomes Penyeach*.

. . . But the most notable feature in the review is the instalment of a long, unpublished, unfinished, and even unnamed work by another of the Paris intellectuals, James Joyce, measured with whose great stature all his imitators and disciples are but pigmies gesturing without speech.

The post that brought me the contemporary *transition* brought me also a small, thin, green, paper-bound volume of verses by James Joyce, his first collection since *Chamber Music* was published before the war.

The title of the book—*Pomes Penyeach*—shows that the author, in spite of his formidable gift of research and his giant labours, can still stoop to a modest jest at his own compositions in poetry. 'She Weeps Over Rahoon' is a heartbreaking little song for the dimly guessed author of *Ulysses*. But who since Milton has so spoken of himself in the poem called 'Prayer':

[quotes the first stanza]

There are thirteen of these poems. At a penny each, they are good baker's value for a shilling.

156. Æ, review, *Irish Statesman*

1927

Y.O. [George Russell, Æ], *Irish Statesman* (23 July 1927), 478.

It is many years now since James Joyce wrote the verses which were published as *Chamber Music*, verses which had a deliberate, carved, delicate beauty in which the most subtle critic could not have discovered one single phrase suggestive of the terrible realism of *Ulysses*. The lyrics were so restrained, so delicately fashioned, one felt that the poet would not trust his heart into his poetry. He seemed rather to wish to create images like the finest porcelain and two or three of the lyrics had a light carven beauty as if the transcience of some lovely motion had been stayed so that it might be enjoyed for ever. There is nothing in the new book quite so exquisite as the best lyrics in *Chamber Music*. The poet seems to have been aware that in his youth he had created something which perhaps became more beautiful in retrospect in his imagination because the full strength of his intellect had since been devoted to writing the most realistic novels of our generation, and his early verse may have littered in memory with the irridescence of a shell if a thought of it had come up when he was writing the meditations of Mrs. Bloom. Nobody likes losing a gift which once was theirs and Joyce seems every now and then to have tried whether he had lost the ancient art and the verses, all but one written between 1912 and 1924 are gathered up in this little volume. It is curious to find in this writer, the most resolute and unabashed explorer of the crypts and sewers of the soul a strain almost of sentimentality every now and then. This might have been written by almost any young versifying sentimentalist.

[quotes 'She Weeps Over Rahoon']

I quote this, not because it is the best, but because it has a psychological interest suggesting that somewhere in the realist a submerged sentimentalist was sighing and in other lyrics also there are traces of this submerged mentality. The strongest poems are those in which he is further from the old mood, poems like 'A Memory of the Players' or 'A Prayer', in which he seems to have deserted his old ideal of a carved, exquisite beauty and to have expressed a personal feeling or experience with passion and intensity. The book will have for many readers perhaps a greater psychological than poetic interest though I would be the last to deny the charm and precise beauty of some of the lyrics in *Pomes Penyeach*. They will be read by many who know Joyce only as the author of the *Portrait of the Artist* or of *Ulysses* with a surprise like that one feels discovering on a grey mountain height near the snows some tiny and exquisite flowers blossoming in some crevice amid the monstrous rocks.

157. Unsigned review, *Nation*

12 October 1927, cxxv, 403

The thirteen poems which James Joyce has put together cover a period extending from 1904 to 1924. It was in 1907 that *Chamber Music* appeared and in the years that followed the poet was immersed in his various prose volumes. Poetry, then, was no more than a passing phase with him, a brief flowering of sensitive youth into what was, for him, a sturdier growth and a profounder metier. The few lyric snatches that evolved from his consciousness were (and are) unimportant except in so far as they predicate a disposition enamored of delicate sound and fragile rhythms, for the prime value of Joyce's poetry is implicit in a fastidious arrangement of vocables. Of the thirteen short pieces in *Pomes Penyeach* not more than three are dated to any one year. They are manifestly casual impulses, brief sublimations. Three of them, 'She Weeps Over Rahoon', 'On the Beach at Fontana', and 'Alone', appeared in *Poetry: A Magazine of Verse* for November, 1917. 'She Weeps Over Rahoon', with its softly falling pattern, is the best piece in the little book. It is to be suspected that this tiny booklet is a cleaning-up of unconsidered trifles, that it marks the end of Joyce's appearance as a poet, that his poetry hereafter will be found (as most of it has been found in the past) imbedded in his prose.

158. Marcel Brion, review, *Les Nouvelles littéraires*

1927

'l'Actualité littéraire à l'Etranger, James Joyce, romancier et poète', *Les Nouvelles littéraires* (15 October 1927), 7.

If James Joyce did not have any luck with the publishers of his own country, he had, at least, the good fortune to find in Paris the most fervent and enthusiastic of editors. Under the sign of Shakespeare and Company, the Joycien cult was born, for indeed this is a true cult, ardent, exclusive, not without fanaticism, which now is organized into a witty fraternity of close or distant friends of the great Irish writer. From this shop . . . comes forth . . . a small volume of poems, clad in a delicate green, *Pomes Penyeach*. If I translate the title as 'poems for a penny,' I have said nothing because I have not been able to express the deformation which Joyce imposes on the spelling of his title so as to indicate current pronunciation . . . To make a counter-balance to these [Joyce's] novels—but such a balance would be rather subtle to note—here are these twelve poems. But we know that with Joyce all is intentional, premeditated, allegorical and—in the noble sense—calculated. We know that these little poems represent a parallel existence to that of the novelist who never ceases to be a poet but who in the rigor which he imposes upon himself, and which those who understand his work-methods are not unaware of, accords himself no neglect (*abandon*) . . . Twelve poems spread out over twenty years of the life of this man who ought to have fifty; twelve exquisite hours, formed with an attentive tenderness, with a background, perhaps of delicate irony, but whose value and contrast I feel better when I read the excellent passages [from 'Work in Progress'] in *transition* . . . this Cyclopean work where all the battles of history pass in a whirlwind of images and ideas . . .

[The critic here passes on to general comments on 'Work in Progress'.]

159. Edmund Wilson, review, *New Republic*

26 October 1927, lii, No. 673, 268

This little book, hardly four inches by five, contains thirteen new poems by James Joyce. Like the poems in *Chamber Music*, they are all brief lyrics, but they are much better than any but one or two in the earlier book. The pieces in *Chamber Music* aimed at the music, the lightness and the perfection of Elizabethan songs, and they derived somewhat, at the same time, from the contemporary Irish poetry of Æ and Yeats. . . .

These liquid snatches of song in two or three fleeting stanzas seem all that Joyce has ever cared to write in verse and, as a result, his range is not wide: he has only one or two notes. It is interesting to see that, among these late poems, there is one—'Watching the Needleboats at San Sabba'—which still seems unmistakably haunted by the lovely plaintive echo of Shelley's 'O World! O Life! O Time!' Joyce thus, however, attempts something which is difficult and rare and, if he publishes but little verse, it is because he knows that it is so. A success in this field, where the short lyric, with something of the completeness of epigram, must border on the vagueness of music and carry some poignant feeling, always has somewhat the air of a miracle. Only the Shelleys and the Yeatses can do it—and they not often. In these thirteen new poems, Joyce has outgrown the imitation of his early masters and caused the influences to contribute to a kind of lyric unmistakably original and with far more color and complexity than the songs in *Chamber Music*. There is not much of it, but it is real poetry—perhaps some of the purest of our time—and a single strain of its music is enough to strike dumb whole volumes which we may previously have pretended to take seriously.

[quotes 'She Weeps Over Rahoon']

160. Padraic Colum review, *New York World*

1928

Padraic Colum, *New York World* (15 January 1928), n.p. The same review appeared in *Dublin Magazine*, iii, No. 3 (July–September 1928), 68.

The poems in the little collection which James Joyce's publisher has just got out were written in different places in Europe—Dublin, Trieste, Zürich, Paris. They are by Ireland's most profound writer, and yet, with one exception, 'She Weeps Over Rahoon,' it would be hard to recognize any Irish element in them. The price of the booklet is a shilling, and they are *Pomes Penyeach*, and so one expects to find a dozen poems. There are actually thirteen, for Mr. Joyce remembers that certain purveyors in Dublin used to give something above measure which they called 'Tilly.' He puts his 'Tilly' as the first piece in the book. *Pomes Penyeach* are not, perhaps, representative of the James Joyce of to-day; they are more of a supplement to his first book, *Chamber Music*.

Curiously enough, they are nearly all night pieces; these thirteen poems, most of them only of twelve lines, have the faint colors of flowers of the night. And, like flowers of the night, they have a hushed, lonely, warning kind of beauty. They are poignant poems, and the singer and musician who is in James Joyce has moulded most of them. Two are in free verse, but the rest have a melody that is like that in old songs:

Rain on Rahoon falls softly, softly falling,
    Where my dark lover lies.
Sad is his voice that calls me, sadly calling,
    At grey moonrise.

The collection is small, the poems are as brief as poems may well be, but they all stay in the memory.

161. Robert Hillyer, comment, *New Adelphi*

March 1928, i, No. 3, 264

As lyrics merely, some of Mr. Joyce's *Pomes Penyeach* are among the most memorable of our collection [those being reviewed]. For instance:

[quotes 'Bahnhofstrasse']

The exquisite vowel sounds, the half-heard echo from the carol, and the music of the whole poem show an unconscious power that artistry alone can never achieve. And we wonder at these qualities until we notice that the poems were written some years ago, before Mr. Joyce had embarked on his Odyssey, before pedantry had conquered his talents. One critic in America, slavishly devoted to the cult of the later Joyce, praised these lyrics extravagantly, far, far beyond their actual merits which are, indeed, high enough. This is a curious inconsistency explained only by the fact that anything signed by Mr. Joyce is sacrosanct to some. The truth is that one cannot sincerely admire both these simple lyrics and *Ulysses*: they were written by two opposed personalities, one the sensitive youth who composed the poems, the other, the weary man who bestowed on them the title *Pomes Penyeach.*

1927

162. Yeats on Joyce in the Irish Senate

1927

William Butler Yeats in a speech before the Irish Senate, 4 May 1927. This extract is taken from the full text of the speech found in *The Senate Speeches of W. B. Yeats* (1960), ed. Donald R. Pearce, pp. 145–8.

Yeats is speaking in favour of a copyright protection bill, but against a bill before the Irish Senate which would not provide full copyright protection, and he has used Joyce's problems in getting *Dubliners* published as an illustration of the dangers of the bill without, in fact, mentioning Joyce's name.

. . . I do not like it to be supposed that I did not mention the name of James Joyce because the book [*Ulysses*, in this case] was a discredit to him. I did not mention the name, because it had nothing to do with the issue. Some 150 of the most eminent men in Europe signed the protest against the mutilation and piracy of James Joyce's book in America. Some of these men sincerely admired that book and thought it a very great book. Some of those who signed the protest did not admire it at all and signed it simply because of the copyright issue . . . I am not going to defend James Joyce. It is a very difficult question. Has the Senator ever looked into Rabelais? Rabelais is looked upon as one of the greatest masters of the past, and what is to be said of James Joyce may be said of Rabelais . . . I do not know whether Joyce's *Ulysses* is a great work of literature. I have puzzled a great deal over that question . . . All I will say is that it is the work of an heroic mind. . . .

1927: ULYSSES

163. Italo Svevo lecture on Joyce at Milan

1927

Extract from Italo Svevo (Ettore Schmitz), 'James Joyce', *Il Convegno*, xviii (January, 1938), 135–58. Originally a lecture delivered at Milan in 1927; a brief portion of this work appeared as 'Trieste, 1907' (translated Herbert Alexander), *Literary World*, No. 1 (May 1934), 2. The lecture was enlarged, and was translated by Stanislaus Joyce as *James Joyce* (1950) [90 pp.] (from which the present text is taken), reprinted 1967.

After reading *Ulysses* there can be no doubt that his nose is not very good, but his ear is that of a poet and musician. I know that when Joyce has written a page of prose he thinks that he has paralleled some page of music that he delights in. This feeling—I cannot say whether it accompanies his inspiration because I only know that it follows it—proves his desire. . . . [p. 9]

He is twice a rebel, against England and against Ireland. He hates England and would like to transform Ireland. Yet he belongs so much to England that like a great many of his Irish predecessors he will fill pages of English literary history and not the least splendid ones; and he is so Irish that the English have no love for him. They are out of sympathy with him, and there is no doubt that his success could never have been achieved in England if France and some literary Americans had not imposed it. . . . [pp. 15, 16]

A Portrait of the Artist as a Young Man could be inserted in *Ulysses* as one of the chapters if the manner in which the subject is presented did not characterize it as a thing apart. I consider it a kind of preface. Fate has assigned to it the place of a preface, a very notable preface, however, which has shown that it is able to live its own independent and glorious life. But the importance of *Ulysses* is now so great that in this first novel we see and hear chiefly those elements which are a preparation for the second and a commentary on it. Without knowing the whole story of the religious and artistic evolution of Dedalus one cannot thoroughly understand *Ulysses*. . . . [pp. 26–7]

If *Ulysses* did not exist it would be more difficult to discern how here in the *Portrait* Flaubert's limpid, impersonal narrative style is troubled by a new longing. Father Arnall's long sermon is probably the first attempt of Joyce as author to retire from the telling of the story after having introduced his character and entrusted him with the task. Nor, for other reasons, can one think of Flaubert when reading the love idyll in the *Portrait*. In its still unripe beauty and brevity it is the work of a poet who knows how to make a word do the work of a page and an image tell a story. . . . [pp. 35–6]

And now for *Ulysses*. One of those tiresome interviewers, the kind that thrives especially across the ocean, once asked Joyce, 'Why did you give your novel the title of an Homeric poem?' Joyce replied, 'It is my way of working.' Joyce loves to fetter his imagination with chains. Joyce the fantast and rebel is a past master of discipline, a fantastic and rebellious discipline. . . . [p. 37]

I am not a critic, and when I read these notes over again I doubt whether I have given a clear idea of this novel. It seems to me insufficient praise of it to say that it is the most significant novel that has appeared at the beginning of this century. It was not in my mind to settle what place in the world of letters should be assigned to Joyce's work nor trace the relationship with what has preceded it. Like any simple-minded reader, I have just tried to get you to share my admiration for it.

One critical observation I can make, and that is suggested by a good memory and not by any critical sense. It is this: that I can prove that Sigmund Freud's theories did not reach Joyce in time to guide him when he was planning his work. . . . [pp. 60–1]

Joyce's works, therefore, cannot be considered a triumph of psychoanalysis, but I am convinced that they can be the subject of its study. They are nothing but a piece of life, of great importance just because it has been brought to light not deformed by any pedantic science but vigorously hewn with quickening inspiration. And it is my hope that some thoroughly competent psychoanalyst may arise to give us a study of his books, which are life itself—a life rich and heartfelt, and recorded with the naturalness of one who has lived and suffered what he writes. . . . [pp. 63–4]

164. Armin Kesser on the German *Ulysses*

1927

'James Joyce', *Neue Schweizer Rundschau* (February 1941); also appeared in *In Memoriam James Joyce* (1941), ed. Carola Giedion-Welcker, pp. 28–31 [23–31].

The article begins with an account of Joyce's death and funeral.

From this place [the grave site in Zürich] my thoughts went back to the year 1927, the publication date of the German translation of *Ulysses.* The times were filled with an overwrought sense of crisis. . . . It was a time of feverish experimentation, of deep uneasiness about the old forms, and of a hidden longing for a new and obligatory meaning . . . So when *Ulysses* came out it was natural that it was considered to be a symptom of the crisis. The young socio-critical temperaments in Germany and in America scented in the new technique of *Ulysses* an addition to their compromising and socio-analytical methodology. They adopted the consecutive inner monologue, as Joyce had formed it, to show by way of contrast the mendacity of the controlled middle-class phraseology. . . . What definitely removes *Ulysses* from the neighborhood of contemporary efforts is the person of the author, his enormous mental powers, which portray the decay of a religious world and the crisis of the human being between two centuries, but with men which do not belong to the decay.

[analyses the lyrical-musical forms of the earlier works as precursors to the parodic character of the later sentences, the language-destruction and catechetic interrogation of reality in the early works]

It may be understood from these elements that the crisis which *Ulysses* represents had started long before. It is the crisis of a late-theological age. Stephen Dedalus, who wants to 'Hellenize' Ireland is joined in *Ulysses* by Leopold Bloom, the advertisement-canvasser. With this the commedia extends to the planetary; Bloom's common employment shows the interfering forces of our world; his figure enables the author to look out in all directions of the compass, but only the connection with Stephen shows the enigmatical duplicity of the work. Joyce saw the world with a mathematical and a mystical eye. *Ulysses* has been interpreted as a parody of Homer's epic, but I believe that it is at the same time an *agon*, a contest with the Greek poet. The divergency of the great form of the myth calls forth the parodic because the book has been written in a time in which the cherished beliefs of the old people turned into newspaper advertisements, and Apollo appears as a trade-mark for products of the cosmetic industry. Joyce has freed in a trial, which does not reach a verdict, the visible cosmos from the overformings of the ideologies, interests, and habits by making them visible to us. After the Walpurgis-night and the executions, one again and again finds places in which the parodic recedes and the original face of things comes forth. *Finnegans Wake*, the poet's last work, is an epos of the night. Here the language has left its system of rules and has become sound, but it is uncertain whether the sound is not the sinless state of the language.

165. Wyndham Lewis on time in Joyce

1927

Extract from 'The Revolutionary Simpleton', *The Enemy*, i, No. 1 (January 1927), 95–130; expanded as 'An Analysis of the Mind of James Joyce', in his *Time and Western Man* (1927), pp. 91–113; (1928), pp. 75–113 (from which the present text is taken).

This lengthy essay was attacked on many sides; one such attack was by Harry Levin in *James Joyce: A Critical Introduction* (1941, expanded, 1961). Lewis replied to Levin's attack on him in *Rude Assignment* (1950), pp. 55–8, an extract from which has been included to show the mature Lewis's evaluation of Joyce.

And that is what Joyce is above all things, essentially the craftsman. It is a thing more common, perhaps, in painting or the plastic arts than in literature. I do not mean by this that he works harder or more thoroughly than other people, but that he is not so much an inventive intelligence as an executant. He is certainly very 'shoppy,' and professional to a fault, though in the midst of the amateurism of the day it is a fault that can easily be forgiven.

What stimulates him is *ways of doing things*, and technical processes, and not *things to be done*. Between the various things to be done he shows a true craftsman's impartiality. . . .

The method that underlies *Ulysses* is known as the 'telling from the inside.' As that description denotes, it is psychological. Carried out in the particular manner used in *Ulysses*, it lands the reader inside an Aladdin's cave of incredible bric-à-brac in which a dense mass of dead stuff is collected, from 1901 toothpaste, a bar or two of 'Sweet Rosie O'Grady', to pre-nordic architecture. An immense *nature-morte* is the result. . . .

The amount of *stuff*—unorganized brute material—that the more active principle of drama has to wade through, under the circumstances, slows it down to the pace at which, inevitably, the sluggish tide of the author's bric-à-brac passes the observer, at the saluting post, or in this case, the reader. It is a suffocating, mœtoc expanse of objects, all of them lifeless, the sewage of a Past twenty years old, all neatly arranged in a meticulous sequence. . . .

At the end of a long reading of *Ulysses* you feel that it is the very nightmare of the naturalistic method that you have been experiencing. . . . The nineteenth-century naturalism of that obsessional, fanatical order is what you find on the one hand in *Ulysses*. On the other, you have a great variety of recent influences enabling Mr. Joyce to use it in the way that he did.

The effect of this rather fortunate confusion was highly stimulating to Joyce, who really got the maximum out of it, with an appetite that certainly will never be matched again for the actual *matter* revealed in his composition, or proved to have been lengthily secreted there. It is like a gigantic victorian quilt or antimacassar. Or it is the voluminous curtain that fell, belated (with the alarming momentum of a ton or two of personally organized rubbish), upon the victorian scene. So rich was its delivery, its pent-up outpouring so vehement, that it will remain, eternally cathartic, a monument like a record diarrhœa. No one who looks *at* it will ever want to look *behind* it. It is the sardonic catafalque of the victorian world.

Two opposite things were required for this result. Mr. Joyce could never have performed this particular feat if he had not been, in his make-up, extremely immobile; and yet, in contradiction to that, very open to new technical influences. It is the *craftsman* in Joyce that is progressive; but the *man* has not moved since his early days in Dublin. . . .

So he collected like a cistern in his youth the last stagnant pumpings of victorian anglo-irish life. This he held steadfastly intact for fifteen years or more—then when he was ripe, as it were, he discharged it, in a dense mass, to his eternal glory. That was *Ulysses*. Had the twenty-year-old Joyce of the *Dubliners* not remained almost miraculously intact, we should never have witnessed this peculiar spectacle. So though Joyce has written a time-book, he has done it, I believe, to some extent, by accident. . . .

I will now turn to the scandalous element in *Ulysses*, its supposed obscenity. Actually it appears to me that the mind of Joyce is more chaste than most. Once you admit the licence that, at the start, Joyce set out to profit by, it is surprising how very little 'sex' matter there is in his pages. What is there is largely either freudian echoes (they had to enter into it), or else it is horse-play of a schoolboy or public-house order. The motif of the house-drain is once and for all put in its place, and not mentioned again. It is the fault of the reader if that page or two dealing with it assume, in retrospect, proportions it has not, as a fact, in Joyce's pages. . . . There are several other things that have to be noted as characteristic of Joyce for a full understanding of a technique that has grown into a very complex, overcharged façade. The craftsman, pure and simple, is at the bottom of his work. I have already insisted upon that; and in that connection it almost appears, I have said, that he has practised sabotage where his intellect was concerned, in order to leave his craftsman's hand freer for its stylistic exercises. . . . In *Ulysses*, if you strip away the technical complexities that envelop it, the surprises of style and unconventional attitudes that prevail in it, the figures underneath are of a remarkable simplicity, and of the most orthodoxly comic outline. Indeed, it is not too much to say that they are, most of them, walking clichés. . . .

A susceptibility to verbal clichés is, however, not at all the same thing as a susceptibility to such a cliché as is represented by a stage Jew (Bloom), a stage Irishman (Mulligan), or a stage Anglo-Saxon (Haines). Clichés of that description thrive in the soil of *Ulysses*. This paradox is an effect of the craftsman-mind which has been described above; that is my reading of the riddle. . . . If you examine for a moment the figures presented to you in the opening of *Ulysses*, you will at once see what is meant by these remarks. The admirable writing will seduce you, perhaps, from attending too closely, at first, to the characterization. . . .

But if they are clichés, Stephan Dedalus is a worse or a far more glaring one. He is the really wooden figure. He is 'the poet' to an uncomfortable, a dismal, a ridiculous, even a pulverizing degree. . . .

It is unnecessary to quote any further; the reader by referring to the opening of *Ulysses*, can provide himself with as much more as he requires; these few extracts will enable anybody to get a more concrete idea of what is under discussion. It would be difficult, I think, to find a more lifeless, irritating, principal figure than the deplorable hero of the *Portrait of the Artist* and of *Ulysses*.

The method of the growth of these books may be partly responsible for it, the imperfect assimilation of the matter-of-fact naturalism of the *Dubliners* to the more complex *Ulysses*. . . .

What induced Joyce to place in the centre of his very large canvas this grotesque figure, Stephan Dedalus? Or having done so, to make it worse by contrasting it the whole time (as typifying 'the ideal') with the gross 'materialism' of the Jew, Bloom? Again, the answer to that, I believe, is that things *grew* in that way, quite outside of Joyce's control; and it is an effect, merely, of a confusion of method.

Joyce is fundamentally autobiographical, it must be recalled; not in the way that most writers to some extent are, but scrupulously and naturalistically so. Or at least that is how he started. . . .

The effort to show Stephan Dedalus in a favourable, heightened light throughout, destroys the naturalism, and at the same time certainly fails to achieve the heroic. Yet the temper of *Ulysses* is to some extent an heroical one. So you are left with a neat little naturalist 'hero,' of the sort that swarms humorously in Chekov, tiptoeing to play his part in the fluid canvas of an ambitious *Ulysses*, unexpectedly expanding beneath his feet; urged by his author to rise to the occasion and live up to the role of the incarnation of the immaterial, and so be top-dog to Poldy Bloom. . . .

In reality there is no Mr. Bloom at all, of course, except at certain moments. Usually the author, carelessly disguised beneath what other people have observed about Jews, or yet other people have believed that they have seen, is alone performing before us. There is no sign throughout the book that he has ever directly and intelligently observed any *individual* Jew. . . .

The radical conventionality of outlook implied throughout *Ulysses*, and exhibited in the treatment of the characters, isolated from their technical wrapping, has the following bearing upon what I have said elsewhere. This conventionality (which leaves, as it were, lay-figures underneath, upon which the technical trappings can be accumulated at leisure with complete disregard for the laws of life) is the sign that we are in the presence of a craftsman rather than a creator. That sort of effect is invariably the sign of the simple craftsman—an absence of meaning, an emptiness of philosophic content, a poverty of new and disturbing observation. . . .

In *Ulysses* you have a deliberate display, on the grand scale, of technical virtuosity and literary scholarship. What is underneath this overcharged surface, few people, so far, have seriously inquired. In reality it is rather an apological than a real landscape; and the two main characters, Bloom and Dedalus, are lay-figures (the latter a sadly ill-chosen one) on which such a mass of dead stuff is hung, that if ever they had any organic life of their own, it would speedily have been overwhelmed in this torrent of matter, of *nature-morte*.

This torrent of matter is the einsteinian flux. Or (equally well) it is the duration-flux of Bergson—that is its philosophic character, at all events. (How the specifically 'organic' and mental doctrine of the time-philosophy can result in a mechanism that is more mechanical than any other, I shall be considering later.) The method of doctrinaire naturalism, interpreted in that way, results in such a flux as you have in *Ulysses*, fatally. And into that flux it is you, the reader, that are plunged, or magnetically drawn by the attraction of so much matter as is represented by its thousand pages. That is also the strategy implied by its scale.

But the author, of course, plunges with you. He takes you inside his head, or, as it were, into a roomy diving-suit, and, once down in the middle of the stream, you remain the author, naturally, inside whose head you are, though you are sometimes supposed to be aware of one person, sometimes of another. . . . But the method of *Ulysses* imposes a softness, flabbiness and vagueness everywhere in its bergsonian fluidity. It was in the company of that old magician, Sigmund Freud, that Joyce learnt the way into the Aladdin's cave where he manufactured his *Ulysses*; and the philosophic flux-stream has its source, too, in that magical cavern. . . . *Ulysses* is a highly romantic self-portrait of the mature Joyce (disguised as a Jew) and of his adolescent self—of Bloom and Dedalus. Poldy Joyce, luckily for him, is a more genial fellow than Stephan Joyce—else the *Portrait of the Artist* stage would never have been passed by James.

Another thing that can be dismissed even more summarily is the claim that Bloom is a creation, a great *homme moyen sensuel* of fiction. That side of Bloom would never have existed had it not been for the Bouvard and Pécuchet of Flaubert, which very intense creation Joyce merely takes over, spins out, and translates into the relaxed medium of anglo-irish humour. Where Bloom is being Bouvard and Pécuchet, it is a translation, nothing more. . . .

The clowning and horseplay of english humour play a very important part in the later work of Joyce. In *Ulysses* Rabelais is also put under contribution to reinforce this vein, though it is the manner of Rabelais that is parodied, and the matter of that unusually profound writer is not very much disturbed. Since *Ulysses* (but still in the manner of that book) Mr. Joyce has written a certain amount—the gathering material of a new book, which, altogether almost, employs the manner of Nash—though again somewhat varied with echoes of Urquhart's translations. He has fallen almost entirely into a literary horseplay on the one side, and Steinesque child-play on the other. . . .

As to the Nash factor, when read in the original, the brilliant rattle of that Elizabethan's high-spirited ingenuity can in time grow tiresome, and is of a stupefying monotony. What Nash says, from start to finish, is nothing. . . .

The close similarity in every way of those characteristic passages that

I have quoted will be evident. In the first of the extracts from Joyce, curiously enough, he reveals one of the main preoccupations of the hero of *Ulysses*, namely, that arising from the ravages of the gentleman-complex—the Is he or isn't he a gentleman?—the phantom index-finger of the old shabby-genteel typical query pursuing the author. In this instance, as he is not writing about himself, we are given to understand that the figure in question is *not*. His gargantuan villain-of-the-piece is not even allowed to be very closely connected with the noble *de Trop Bloggs*. But the implicit theme of the entire piece, what moves Joyce to churn up the english tongue in a mock-elizabethan frenzy, is the burning question still of his shabby-genteel boyhood, namely, To be a 'toff,' or not to be a 'toff.' . . .

Into *Ulysses* a great many things have been mixed, however. You will find many traces in it of the influence of T. S. Eliot and of Pound's classical, romance, and anglo-saxon scholarly enthusiasms, not to be met with in earlier books. *The Enemy of the Stars*, a play written and published by me in 1914, obliterated by the War, turned up, I suspect, in Zürich, and was responsible for the manner here and there of Joyce's book. Then the viennese school of psychology made Molly Bloom mutter, 'What are they always rooting about up there for, to see where they come from, I wonder?' or words to that effect. No Irish Molly—however much of an 'eternal feminine' abstraction—would ever have soliloquized in that manner but for Sigmund Freud. Miss Stein can only be used—owing to the restrictions imposed by the naturalist method—when a character is half asleep, day-dreaming, its mind wandering, or, in short, in such circumstances as justify, naturalistically, the use of Miss Stein's technique. . . .

So we arrive at the concrete illustrations of that strange fact already noted—that an intense preoccupation with *time* or 'duration' (the psychological aspect of time, that is) is wedded to the theory of 'timelessness.' It is, as it were, in its innate confusion in the heart of the reality, the substance and original of that peculiar paradox—that so long as *time* is the capital truth of your world it matters very little if you deny truth of your world it matters very little if you deny time's existence, like the einsteinian, or say there is nothing else at all, like Bergson; or whether space-time (with the accent on the *time*) is your god, like Alexander. . . .

Rude Assignment (ch. X, pp. 55–8)

. . . My book, *Time and Western Man*, contains an elaborate analysis of the writings of James Joyce, and more especially *Ulysses*. As to *Time and Western Man*, it will be sufficient to say that in my view, at the period at which I wrote it, the philosophy in the ascendant was destructive, and that it should be combated. In its pages—and it is a book of considerable length—I provide a very detailed answer to that disintegrating metaphysic. . . .

My critical appraisal of the work of Joyce was, however, unambiguously partisan. It derived from a set of principles which were clearly enunciated. Its validity depended upon the validity of those principles. If you did not agree with the philosophical premises you would not agree with the criticism, and could disregard it entirely. . . .

It was because my position was defined so circumstantially and with such unmistakable plainness that I did not regard what I said as in any way personally offensive to Joyce: nor did I anywhere imply that he was not worthy of the greatest attention and respect—the space I allotted to him is evidence of that; or that his work was other than *of its kind* a masterpiece. It was the *kind* I did not like so much as some other kinds. . . .

So all Joyce had to say was: 'I like and follow Vico, and Bergson, and Freud. My friend Mr. Lewis does *not*. He has a perfect right to his opinion: and naturally, with his views upon those masters and teachers by whom I have been guided, he would not like what I do as much as otherwise he might. As it takes all sorts to make a world, there is room for Mr. Lewis and those of his predilection: and for me, and those who think as I do.'—But he did not say that. He was a man who heard criticism with difficulty. On my side, I feel I should have been more circumspect: I warmed to my subject. I was perhaps too forcible. At that time I was about the only writer in English-speaking countries who gave utterance to such opinions, and I had to insist in order to be heard. . . .

We were talking once, I remember, when I first got to know him about the cathedral at Rouen; its heavily encumbered façade. I had said I did not like it, rather as Indian or Indonesian sacred buildings are a fussy multiplication of accents, demonstrating a belief in the virtue of *quantity*, I said. All such quantitative expression I have at all times found boring, I pointed out. I continued to talk against Gothic altogether, and its 'scholasticism in stone': the dissolving of the solid shell—the spatial intemperance, the nervous multiplication of detail. Joyce listened and then remarked that he, on the contrary, liked this multiplication of detail, adding that he himself, as a matter of fact, in words, did something of that sort. . . .

166. Herbert Gorman on Joyce's form

1927

Extract from 'Joyce Today and Tomorrow', *New Republic*, No. 1 (April 1927), 197–9.

Now that five sections of James Joyce's new novel, a work not definitively titled as yet, have been published in various periodicals, it is possible to make some tentative remarks upon the probable evolution of Joyce's form. It is obvious, first of all, that the form of the work in hand is not the same as that of *Ulysses*, although it is equally obvious that it is a natural growth from that gargantuan achievement. It will stand in relation to *Ulysses* as *Ulysses* stood in relation to *A Portrait of the Artist as a Young Man*. The creative faculties of Joyce rise from work to work, as from plane to plane, with a consequently increasing density of symbolical phenomena. . . . As a pure artist, Joyce naturally does not scaffold his work with an explanatory concordance. He completes the structure and leaves the door open—in the case of *Ulysses*, the title itself —and it is through that entrance that the reader who would understand him must enter. . . . As a matter of fact, James Joyce is incessantly preoccupied with form and, in *Ulysses*, had subdued his material to a form both elaborate and rigorous. His scheme, the setting of modern realities in relation to an ancient myth, required a new technique; and such a new technique he invented, unconstrained by the prejudices of an audience unable to forget its preconceived notions of what a novel should be. It would, of course, be a mere supposition, offered as a conviction, to assert that Joyce's new novel will be as perfect in form as *Ulysses* (for five scattered segments from a large scheme do not give us enough to go on); but no one who is familiar with his painful self-discipline, his extraordinary industry, his ceaseless rumination and his meticulous exactitude, will doubt his determination to make it so. . . .

The charge of formlessness and incoherence has so often been brought against *Ulysses*—even the Homeric analogies have been questioned—that it may be of interest to go into this matter. The settlement of such a question is certain also to illuminate Joyce's new work, to throw into relief its ground scheme and to impress upon the reader the degree of reasoned coordination to be expected in it. The theme, then, of Leopold Bloom's day in Dublin was first conceived as a short story as far back as the period of *Dubliners*, but it was afterwards put aside until a large quantity of material had been assembled. Then, after the completion of *A Portrait of the Artist as a Young Man*, it was taken up and formulated in Joyce's mind as a realistic epic with a spiritual skeleton of myth. The organization of so much material called for an enormous systematic scheme. Already, in Joyce's work, the myth had made its symbolic appearance in the Dedalus (Diadalos) of *A Portrait of the Artist as a Young Man*. And, for *Ulysses*, Joyce elaborated, not merely a whole set of Homeric correspondences, paralleling the entire *Odyssey*, but also a whole zodiac of deliberately planted symbols which served each as a nucleus around which different sections of his material should cluster. Of these parallels and these symbols Mr. Joyce has drawn up an exact and complicated diagram; and it is from an acquaintance with this diagram that the present writer speaks. . . .

[describes the structure of *Ulysses*, and devotes an entire page to the scheme of the Hades episode]

Joyce is a very great grammarian and there is reason for everything that he does. He is not smashing things to pieces, but rather is he refashioning them into a new order upon a new plane. In this next book, therefore, we may look for the treatment of a myth embracing the Irish spirit, a myth through which monstrous figures move, change their shapes and identities and melt into one another, a myth filled with a colossal humor and driven by Vico's hinted sense of an historical philosophy, a myth offered in a language suited to it, a language compact of coined words, phrases and sentence structures, starred with reiterated word-associations and rhythmical sound approximations that will suggest the flow and suck of river water or the differing degrees of the mind at sleep in the night. Abstractions move as beings, and beings are translated into abstractions. It is, after all, the natural evolution of Joyce, and those readers who expected another *Ulysses* must make up their minds that they will never have it. They must adventure beyond *Ulysses*, if they are to continue reading Joyce. . . .

167. Yvan Goll on *Ulysses*

1927

Extract from 'The Homer of our Time', *Die Literarische Welt* (17 June 1927), 396–400. Also reprinted in *Living Age*, cccxxxiii (1927), 316–20 (from which the present text is taken), and in 'Der Homer unserer Zeit: Uber James Joyce', in *Leitgemasses aus der Literarischen Welt von 1925–1932* (1963), ed. Willy Haas, pp. 98–101.

[The article begins with biographical observations and general comments on the plot and characterization of *Ulysses*.]

Ulysses is the most formidable parody anyone has ever written on the universe of God and man. It owes its force to the fact that it arises from a deep ethical conviction and a sense of comic despair such as only a true poet can feel. In Irish humor the face remains as impassive as a kettle full of boiling water—until it bursts. Joyce is no longer reverent. I believe that he enjoys parodying God most of all. But how unimportant all this must be to one who can depict accurately the daily middle-class routine without twitching an eyelash. He describes his hero's activities in the bathroom with the same indifference and objectivity that he describes him purchasing a cake of soap. He is no more shocked by the shamefully concealed sexual immorality of the middle classes than by a debate in Parliament. Everything that the hero thinks, feels, and dreams is written down coldly and fully in this book. The author rises above it all. . . .

Joyce's eye is a microscope, but his realism is quite different from the realism of Flaubert. There is nothing to which *Ulysses* can be compared. Joyce sees every millimetre of a man's nose and then describes it in such a way that it seems as big and important as a pyramid. This is no ordinary realism; in referring to Joyce's work we must use another word and call it superrealism.

Joyce has given everyone the impression that he has fashioned a new language. He has. Many English critics have united on this point, and claim that for the ordinary reader *Ulysses* must be translated into modern English, for it is written in the dialect of the year 2000. Skeptics may shrug their shoulders, but what can they say to the fact that Joyce has mastered all the English dialects and forms of speech from the time of the Middle Ages to the present? And that he has written in all these styles, one after another, in a single chapter of *Ulysses*, moving on and on until he ends with the modern journalistic and movie prose? . . .

Apart from all these virtuosities and eccentricities of speech, Joyce has introduced to the technique of fiction a new element of the greatest importance to all European literature—the inner dialogue. Here the author lets the character think and speak for himself. Everything that whirls through this character's head is written down, often in half-words, sometimes only in syllables, absolutely mechanical, always following closely the actual experience of the person in question. A color, an intonation, a recollection, suddenly lifts us from our chair and carries us off to some distant countryside of dreams, of childhood, or of the future. The unknown and the unconscious spring to the surface from slimy depths, and the author presents them to us raw.

The closing chapter of *Ulysses* is a quivering masterpiece such as no one will ever be able to give us again. Here we follow the half-waking dreams of Marion Tweedy Bloom, full of bodily warmth and gross fancies, as she lies in bed beside her husband, recalling her different lovers, one after another. There is not a single punctuation mark or capital in this whole chapter of forty-two pages, and thus it achieves the desired effect of scattered, illogical thoughts.

In the same way each chapter and each subject is treated in its own appropriate style. There are no misprints here; not a word, not a comma, is out of place, and there are no errors in the conversation or in the grammar. A single powerful will has dominated it all. *Ulysses* is the most unbridled piece of literature in the world, yet it is also the most carefully planned. Although one is constantly running into unfinished sentences and isolated words, the prose is built up with as much art as Homer's hexameters or Petrarch's sonnets. The apparent obscurities and inconsistencies are intentional.

Joyce is a great student of language, and a great manipulator of it, too. He is almost as finished and intense a lyric poet as Mallarmé. He has carried poetry to its uttermost limits. Some people damn Joyce completely. Others can only compare him to Rabelais, Shakespeare, Swift, Flaubert, or Dante. But no one's work approaches his in magnitude and novelty. James Joyce is our great poet. . . .

168. Another Goll comment on *Ulysses*

1927

Extract from Yvan Goll, '*Ulysses*: Sub Specie Aeternitatis', *Die Weltbuhne* (27 December 1927), 960–3.

. . . *Ulysses* by James Joyce is no novel, but rather a poem written in prose. The novel would have been written in hexameters in antiquity, in terza rima in the thirteenth century, in octa-rima in 1800 (meanwhile, today, an epic poem written in hexameters is low-grade decadence in literature).

About the quality, the fineness, the rhythm of this prose—a little later. First, the peculiar title must be explained. Why *Ulysses*? Joyce wanted to write a version of our *Odyssey*, that is the peregrinations or wanderings of a man like you and me from the everyday world, names Leopold Bloom, a Dublin citizen, of Jewish beliefs, an advertiser with a large newspaper, of an average education, sensual, lazy, without particular talent.

This layman's *Odyssey* lasts only eighteen hours of one day—exactly: on the sixteenth of June, 1904—and the author needs 1585 pages in order to represent all exterior and interior events of this Dublin Day.

Well, why then *Ulysses*? Because Joyce studied for sixteen years at a Jesuit school and his brain was unprecedently formally dulled. He wanted to create a modern Odysseus, nothing lay nearer than the sketched out plan of the eternal poem for a basis. And, therefore, Joyce's *Ulysses* likewise is divided into three great divisions: the beginning or opening is the Teleachie, the actual wandering and the homecoming.

This epic consists of eighteen cantos, or rather eighteen chapters. Each of these chapters is self-contained (or comes to a conclusion), and each stands in correspondence with the cantos of the *Odyssey*. Each chapter is unified or conducted in a different rhythm, in a different language form. Each stands under the sign of a particular symbol of its own prose form corresponding to a different organ in man, and to a different artistic consort or mate, and each has a special color (as in the Catholic liturgy) and signifies a distinct hour and day.

James Joyce has for his own use set up a chart or table which appears to be far more developed than the tables of a medical handbook.

An example will offer light on his method: the fourth chapter of the main part comes under the sign of Aeolus and occurs at noon in a great newspaper office which is compared with the sound of the winds. The doors are always slamming and the windows are always open. The symbolic figure is the editor-in-chief. The appropriate organ in the human body is the lungs. The chosen art form is rhetoric. And the author has (in the original text) employed and placed together 120 forms of discourse in a way that no other scientifically grammatical work has yet achieved. Journalism is characterized as incest, and one remembers that Aeolus had six sons and six daughters who married one another.

In order to bring about or make possible the complete and full accomplishment of his plan, James Joyce has read for eight years of uninterrupted work more than a thousand philosophical, astrological, medical, theological and grammatical books, from which an extract is often put down in a sentence. Therefore, Joyce had to dispose of a phenomenal amount of thought. Also his knowledge of language is startling. He, who at the beginning of his career had studied medicine, then on account of his incomparable voice had wanted to become an operatic singer and finally for the last ten years has been a language lecturer in Trieste, commands Latin, Hebrew, Greek, French, Italian, German, Spanish, Gaelic and all of the low dialects of England since the twelfth century. And in a single chapter, one finds in the most compressed form, all of the shades and dialectical variations of today's spoken English: Scotch, Irish, Chinese, Indian, and Negro-English.

But for all of this, the poet has created for himself his own language —the Joyce language. For this reason, *Ulysses* is very difficult for the average Englishman to read, and many a part is incomprehensible. How much better then for the German reader who reads the translation in which all has been made suitable. In the English language there are, however, several commentaries and guides to the better understanding of *Ulysses*. . . .

And now I hear Protest from all sides: this is all not proof on behalf of its being an ingenious work.

Certainly not. All of the above is only the theoretical explanation of the book and the work which it has involved. Now one must read it, however, in order to get the soul of the book.

Ulysses is comparable to no existing book in World Literature. It is singular and entirely new. Such prose is the language and the rhythm of the present poetry. A logical and grammatical architecture. The vibrations do not originate in the external rhythm of a meter but instead on the internal vigor and essence of the words—the grammar. The soul doesn't float in ingenious clouds but instead shines out of carved stone. A construction planted with method and written with glowing imagination, erected with the squared-stone of logic but exposed to the light by the sun of poesie.

And what is there, condensed to over-life-size; the vision is no fantastic story, no history, no myth; but instead only the present reality, the reality of your life and mine.

As God created Eve out of Adam's rib, so has the poet out of the real, earthly being of humanity created the companion—poesie. . . .

1927: WORK IN PROGRESS

169. Mary Colum on the enigma of 'Work in Progress'

1927

New York Herald Tribune (24 April 1927), n.p. A review of *transition* (April 1927).

. . . *Transition* proudly opens with thirty pages from a new work by James Joyce. In *Ulysses*, that triumph of genius and psychology, Joyce created a character, Leopold Bloom, with a completeness, a perfection of detail, which had not really happened in literature before. The book was largely comprehensible to an intelligent reader of modern literature—largely is used advisedly, for *Ulysses* cannot be entirely comprehensible to anybody not Irish because of the subtly national, local and linguistic allusions and references, some of the most obscure of which are used as an aid in the revelation of character. His new work, judging from such selections as I have seen, is likely to prove all but entirely incomprehensible to anybody. I copy out for my readers the following characteristic passage from his contribution to *Transition*: . . .

[quotes from p. 7]

If the curious reader will read this aloud to himself he will perhaps find that it reproduces the sound of a flowing river. And if such a one should happen to know about Dublin, its topography and history, he will perhaps gather an undercurrent of allusion to the story of Tristan and Iseult as it exists vague and muddled in the subconsciousness of a native of the place in which Iseult's story had its beginning. But no literary critic could possibly admit that a work, of which any considerable portion was written like this, could belong to the domain of literature. Now, I solemnly ask the editors of *Transition* did they know what this contribution was about? Did they not publish it entirely on the reputation of Mr. Joyce or their admiration of his genius, without knowing what it meant? Has not Mr. Joyce presented them with something for publication which, detached from the work of which it is an integral part, means almost nothing? . . .

170. Henry Seidel Canby, reaction to 'Work in Progress'

1927

Extract from 'Gyring and Gimbling; or Lewis Carroll in Paris', *Saturday Review of Literature*, iii, No. 40 (30 April 1927), 777, 782–3. Later appeared in *American Estimates* (1939), pp. 170–1.

The giants in the old fables were often lacking in a sense of proportion, sometimes in a sense of humor, and so are those Titans of English-speaking Paris, the half mythical James Joyce and that lesser mistress of experimental prose, the prophetic Gertrude Stein. Joyce we have been able to estimate as a figure of more than common size by his vigorous *Portrait of the Artist as a Young Man* and the powerful technique of *Ulysses*, a Gothic cathedral of a book rich in portraits, gargoyles, and grotesques. The conception of *Ulysses* was clearly giant-like, the execution subject to controversy. Its details were praised by some of the discriminating, but by more who delight in art in proportion to its obscurity, and detest the very name of common sense. . . .

Ulysses, we are told [in the latest issue of *transition*], was a night book, the new work is a day book and the rivers of Ireland are its heroes. Apparently it, too, is to have scope and plan, not to be judged from the brief extracts so far published. Therefore without prejudice to the scheme of the whole, which may be as impressive as that of *Ulysses*, we can study the expression by which this giant of our days proposes to erect his second cathedral. It is not English, although there is vigor in the sound of it; it is not indeed language by any known tests; nor is it sound merely, since some of it is unsoundable except by Gargantuan lungs. . . .

[quotes from pp. 1–2]

In between is of a like intelligibility. The man has a design, that is certain, for Joyce is a giant, even though myopic, he can write, one feels that, but what has he written? What (students of 'Ask me Another?') does it mean? Here at last is the consummation of Browning's 'Francis that broke through language and escaped!'. . .

171. 'Affable Hawk' dissatisfaction with 'Work in Progress'

1927

Extract from 'Affable Hawk' (Desmond McCarthy), 'Current Literature', *New Statesman*, xxix (14 May 1927), 151.

'Here say figurines billycoose arming and mounting. Mounting and arming bellicose figurines see here. Futhorc, this liffle effingee is for a firefling called flintforfall. Face at the eased! O I fay! Face at the waist! Ho, you fie! Upwap and dump em, Ⅎace to Ⅎace. When a part so ptee does duty for the holos we soon grow to use of an allforabit.'

In the case of the above passage, however, we need not feel any sympathetic pain; for the writer, so far from being an aphasiac, is a man remarkable for a command of words. It is a passage from Mr. James Joyce's new work now in progress; and so far from standing out from the first thirty pages printed in the April number of *Transition*, published by the Shakespeare Co., it is characteristic of their texture. But though every deformation of word and sentence in this passage is intentional and deliberate, it should no more provoke laughter than the attempt of the unfortunate sick man to state that he took his dog out in the morning. It should disgust. The taste which inspired it is taste for cretinism of speech, akin to finding exhilaration in the slobberings and mouthings of an idiot. It is always possible that a dash of the Thersites mood may contribute to a work of art, to which mood, so deep its envious loathing of all that is human, gibberish and worse may become sympathetic. But although only a fragment of the work in question is before us, it is clear that this element will be out of all proportion. How poor, too, the sense of fun, if fun it can be called, which sustains the author through the labour of composing page after page of distorted rubbish! No low-water-mark comedian of the halls, smirking and strutting before the indifferent audience, ever sank lower in search of fun than to pronounce 'little,' 'liffle,' or exclaim 'O, I fay!' 'Ho, you, fie!' One of Mr. Joyce's muses, too, is that dreary lady Mrs. Malaprop. The eye, of course, cannot follow for more than a line or two this manufactured language. When will it strike Mr. Joyce that to write what it is a *physical* impossibility to read is possibly even sillier than to write what is mentally impossible to follow?

172. William Carlos Williams on Joyce's style

1927

Extract from 'A Note on the Recent Work of James Joyce', *transition*, No. 8 (November 1927), 149–54. Also appeared in *Selected Essays* (1954), pp. 75–9.

Two statements made early in this article establish Williams' context for his remarks on Joyce's style: 'Style is the substance of writing which gives it its worth as literature' and 'Styles can no longer be described as beautiful. . .'

The beauty that clings to any really new work is beauty only in the minds of those who do not fully realize the significance. Thus tentatively, Joyce's style may be described, I think, as truth through the breakup of beautiful words.

If to achieve truth we work with words purely, as a writer must, and all the words are dead or beautiful, how then shall we succeed any better than might a philosopher with dead abstractions or their configurations? One may sense something of the difficulties by reading a page of Gertrude Stein where none of the words is beautiful. There must be something new done with the words. Leave beauty out, or, conceivably, one might begin again, one might break them up to let the staleness out of them as Joyce, I think, has done. This is, of course, not all that he does nor even a major part of what he does, but it is nevertheless important.

In Joyce it began not without malice I imagine. And continued, no doubt with a private end in view, as might be the case with any of us. Joyce, the catholic Irishman, began with english, a full-dressed english which it must have been his delight to unenglish until it should be humanely catholic, never at least sentimental. . .

We are confronted not by reasons for its occurrence in Joyce's writings but by his style. Not by its accidental or sentimental reasons but its truth. What does it signify? Has he gone backward since *Ulysses*? Hish-hash all of it?

To my taste Joyce has not gone back but forward since *Ulysses*. I find his style richer, more able in its function of unabridged commentary upon human soul, the function surely of all styles. But within this function what we are after will be that certain bent which is peculiar to Joyce and which gives him his value. It is not that the world is round nor even flat, but that it might well today be catholic; and as a corollary, that Joyce himself is today the ablest protagonist before the intelligence of that way of thinking. Such to my mind is the truth of his style. It is a priestly style and Joyce is himself a priest. If this be true to find out just what a priest of best intelligence intends would be what Joyce by his style intends. Joyce is obviously a catholic Irishman writing english, his style shows it and that is, less obviously, its virtue . . .

[Here follows a comparison of the similar styles of Joyce and Rabelais.]

Joyce is to be discovered a catholic in his style then in something because of its divine humanity. Down, down it goes from priesthood into the slime as the church goes. The Catholic Church has always been unclean in its fingers and aloof in the head. Joyce's style consonant with this has nowhere the inhumanity of the scientific or protestant or pagan essayist. There is nowhere the coldly dressed formal language, the correct collar of such gentlemen seeking perhaps an english reputation.

Joyce discloses the X-Ray eyes of the confessional, we see among the clothes, witnessing the stripped back and loins, the naked soul. Thoughtfully the priest under the constant eyes of God looks in. He, jowl to jowl with the sinner, is seen by God in all his ways. This is Joyce. To please God it is that he must look through the clothes. And therefore the privacy of the confessional; he must, so to speak, cover the ache and the sores from the world's desecrating eye with a kindly bandage. Yet he must tell the truth before God.

Joyce has carried his writing this far: he has compared up his reader with God. He has laid it out clean for us, the filth, the diseased parts as a priest might do before the Maker. I am speaking of his style. I am referring to his broken words, the universality of his growing language which is no longer english. His language, much like parts of Rabelais, has no faculties of place. Joyce uses German, French, Italian, Latin, Irish, anything. Time and space do not exist, it is all one in the eyes of God—and man . . .

To sum up, to me the writings of James Joyce, the new work appearing in *transition* ('Work in Progress'), are perfectly clear and full of great interest in form and content. It even seems odd to me now that anyone used to seeing men and women dressed on the street and in rooms as we all do should find his style anything but obvious. If there is a difficulty it is this: whether he is writing to give us (of men and women) the aspect we are most used to or whether he is stripping from them the 'military and civil dress' to give them to us in their unholy (or holy) and disreputable skins. I am inclined to think he leans more to the humaner way. . . .

173. Eugène Jolas *et al.* answer Wyndham Lewis

1927

Extract from Eugène Jolas, Eliot Paul, and Robert Sage, 'First Aid to the Enemy', *transition*, No. 9 (December 1927), 169–74 [161–76]. An answer to Lewis's *Time and Western Man* (No. 165); see the Introduction, pp. 24, 26, for a discussion of this controversy.

. . . The 'Analysis' reveals nothing at all about Joyce and little of importance about Lewis.

Because Joyce is skillful enough to vary his style according to subject matter and to use certain landmarks in literature as reference points, Mr. Lewis accuses him of unorganized susceptibility to influences. Because certain parts of *Ulysses* have the texture of every-day life in Dublin, Mr. Lewis shares Mr. Ernest Boyd's error in taking the great epic to be merely another *Dubliners* on a large scale. In accusing Joyce of 'taking his material from the Past,' he forgets that the book was started in 1914. Only a public stenographer could be more up to date. As a matter of fact, Mr. Lewis is farther behind *Ulysses* (Feb. 1922) than *Ulysses* is behind the Dublin of today.

He misses Joyce's sense of the tragic, even to the point of stating that Joyce is not Dostoevski . . . throws in a page or two on sex and Y.M.C.A.'s the high spot of which is the original and startling observation that the 'savage with a loin cloth is chaste'; and after deploring Joyce's naturalism winds up with a confession that he 'prefers the chaste wisdom of the Chinese or the Greek' to the 'fanatacism' coming from the Ancient East 'and that he is for the physical world.'

Now if Mr. Lewis had really had the courage to attempt an analysis of Joyce, he would have included the new work, an entire book of which is now available, and which is freer from both *local color* and *local time* than anything heretofore written in any language. . . . His remarks on Joyce are rehashed from the pronunciamentos of various critics concerning *Ulysses*, findings of which the original authors are almost invariably ashamed today. . . .

. . . Thus, heroically brandishing his lathe sword, he charges Mr. Joyce, Miss Stein, *transition*, Surrealism, Communism and other alleged danger spots in the structure of the Western World. . . .

Anyone who had intelligently *read* one or two numbers of *transition* would have discerned the obvious facts that Mr. Joyce and Miss Stein are at opposite poles of thought and expression, that neither of them has anything in common with the Dada or Surrealist movements. . . .

174. Gertrude Stein and T. S. Eliot on Joyce

1927

Bravig Imbs, *Confessions of Another Young Man*, (1936), p. 154.

To talk about James Joyce in Gertrude Stein's salon was rushing in where angels feared to tread, but that was exactly what Eliot was doing, and I realized then what great affection both Gertrude and Alice must have for him, for if anyone else had dared praise Joyce to their faces they would have read the Riot Act forthwith. Eliot was blissfully unconscious of the fact that he was being more than impertinent, and went on and on talking about this wonderful 'Work in Progress', and how happy he was that Joyce had joined their forces.

Finally Gertrude said magnanimously, 'Joyce and I are at opposite poles, but our work comes to the same thing, the creation of something new. . . .'

175. Eugène Jolas, memoir of Joyce

1927

Extract from 'My Friend James Joyce', *James Joyce: Two Decades of Criticism* (1948, 1963), ed. Sean Givens, pp. 3–18. Also appeared in the *Partisan Review*, viii (March-April 1941), 82–93, and in *Partisan Reader* (1946), pp. 457–68.

The length of Jolas's personal reminiscences made during a fourteen-year association—during, that is, the writing of 'Work in Progress' or *Finnegans Wake*—necessitates considerable extracting.

On a Sunday afternoon, in the winter of 1927, Joyce invited Mlle Adrienne Monnier, Miss Sylvia Beach, my wife, Elliot Paul, and myself to his home in the Square Robiac to listen to his reading of the manuscript ('Work in Progress') in question. We listened to the Waterloo scene, which subsequently appeared in the first issue of the review [*transition*, which Jolas edited with Eliot Paul]. His voice was resonantly musical, and at times a smile went over his face, as he read a particularly exhilarating passage. After he had finished, he said: 'What do you think of it? Did you like it?' We were all stirred by his verbal fantasy, excited, even, but puzzled. It was not easy to reply with conventional phrases. There was no precedent in literature for judging this fragment with its structure of multiple planes and its novelty of a poly-synthetic language. Some weeks later, he let me read the entire manuscript. It was not more than 120 pages long, and had been written, he said, within a few weeks during a stay on the Rivera in 1922. Yet it was already complete in itself, organically compressed, containing the outline of the entire saga. Even the title had been chosen, he indicated, but only he and Mrs. Joyce knew it. It was still a primitive version, to which he had already begin to add numberless paragraphs, phrases, words. In a moment of confidence he told me something about the genesis of the idea. His admirer, Miss Harriet Weaver—who, some years before, like a Maecenas of other days, made it possible for the struggling writer to be freed of financial worry—had asked him what book he was planning to write after *Ulysses*. He replied that now that *Ulysses* was done he considered himself as a man without a job. 'I am like a tailor who would like to try his hand at making a new-style suit,' he continued. 'Will you order one?' Miss Weaver handed him a pamphlet written by a village priest in England and giving a description of a giant's grave found in the parish lot. 'Why not try the story of this giant?' she asked jokingly. The giant's narrative became the story of Finn McCool, or *Finnegans Wake*.

The first issues of *transition* containing instalments from what was then known as 'Work in Progress'—Joyce told me that this provisional title was the invention of Ford Madox Ford who had previously published a fragment in his *transatlantic review*—brought forth a fanfare of sensational outbursts. The confused critics in France, England and America snorted, for the most part, their violent disapproval. Miss Weaver herself regretfully wrote Miss Beach she feared Joyce was wasting his genius; an opinion which disturbea Joyce profoundly, for, after all, it was for her that the 'tailor' was working. His friend Largaud said he regarded the work as a *divertissement philologique* and of no great importance in Joyce's creative evolution. H. G. Wells wrote him that he still had a number of books to write and could not give the time to attempt to decipher Joyce's experiment. Ezra Pound attacked it in a letter and urged him to put it in the 'family album,' together with his poems. Only Edmund Wilson was intelligently sympathetic. After a while the reactions became more and more vehement, even personal, and on the whole journalistically stereotyped. Joyce continued working at his vision. . . All his friends collaborated then in the preparations of the fragments destined for *transition:* Stuart Gilbert, Padraic Colum, Elliot Paul, Robert Sage, Helen and Giorgio Joyce, and others. He worked with painstaking care, almost with pedantry. He had invented an intricate system of symbols permitting him to pick out the new words and paragraphs he had been writing down for years, and which referred to the multiple characters in his creation. He would work for weeks, often late at night, with the help of one or the other of his friends. It seemed almost a collective composition in the end, for he let his friends participate in his inventive zeal, as they searched through numberless notebooks with mysterious reference points to be inserted in the text. When finished, the proof looked as if a coal-heaver's sooty hands had touched it . . . Sometimes he would bring with him [to dinner at his favourite restaurant, the *Trianons*] a page he had written and hand it round the table with a gesture of polite modesty. He never explained his work, save through indirection. . . .

After a while I started making preparations for a new issue of *transition*, and this stimulated him to work. He attacked the problem with savage energy. 'How difficult it is to put pen to paper again,' he said, one evening. 'Those first sentences have cost me a great deal of pain.' But gradually the task was in hand. It was to be known later as *The Mime of Mick, Nick and the Maggies*. He wrote steadily on this fragment during those frenetic months [Autumn 1931], constantly interrupted by moments of anxiety about the health of his daughter, and his own resultant nervousness. At his hotel, where we would work in the afternoon, he gave me a densely written foolscap sheet beginning with the words: 'Every evening at lighting up o'clock sharp sharp and until further notice . . .' which I typed for him. After a few pages had thus been transcribed, we began to look through the note-books—which he lugged around on all his travels —and the additions, set down years before for a still unwritten text he had merely outlined in his mind, became more and more numerous. The manuscript grew into thirty pages and was not yet finished. He never changed a single word. There was always a certain inevitability, an almost volcanic affirmativeness about his primal choice of words. To me, his deformations seemed to grow more daring. He added, ceaselessly, like a worker in mosaic, enriching his original pattern with ever new inventions.

'There really is no coincidence in this book,' he said during one of our walks. 'I might easily have written this story in the traditional manner. . . . Every novelist knows the recipe. . . . It is not very difficult to follow a simple, chronological scheme which the critics will understand. . . . But I, after all, am trying to tell the story of this Chapelizod family in a new way. . . . Time and the river and the mountain are the real heroes of my book. . . . Yet the elements are exactly what every novelist might use: man and woman, birth, childhood, night, sleep, marriage, prayer, death. . . . There is nothing paradoxical about this. . . . Only I am trying to build many planes of narrative with a single esthetic purpose. . . . Did you ever read Laurence Sterne . . . ?'

We read Goethe's *Farbenlehre*, but he finally said he could use nothing from it. He was interested in a comic version of the theodicy, and he asked me to get one of the Jesuits nearby to give me an Augustinian text . . . He discussed Vico's theory of the origin of language. The conception of the cyclical evolution of civilizations born from each other like the phoenix from the ashes haunted him. He began to speculate on the new physics, and the theory of the expanding universe. And while walking with him, I always had the impression that he was not really in an Austrian frontier town, but in Dublin, and that everything he thought and wrote was about his native land. . . .

A British clipping came saying that Joyce was trying to revive Swift's *little language* to Stella. 'Not at all,' said Joyce to me. 'I am using a *Big Language*.' He said one evening: 'I have discovered that I can do anything with language I want.' His linguistic memory was extraordinary. He seemed constantly *à l'affut*, always to be listening rather than talking. 'Really, it is not I who am writing this crazy book,' he said in his whimsical way one evening. 'It is you, and you, and you, and that man over there, and that girl at the next table.' . . . His knowledge of French, German, modern Greek and especially Italian stood him in good stead, and he added constantly to that stock of information by studying Hebrew, Russian, Japanese, Chinese, Finnish and other tongues. At the bottom of his vocabulary was also an immense command of Anglo-Irish words that only seem like neologisms to us today, because they have, for the most part, become obsolete. His revival of these will some day interest the philologists. Language to him was a social as well as a subjective process. He was deeply interested in the experiments of the French Jesuit, Jousse, and the English philologist, Paget, and *Finnegans Wake* is full of strange applications of their gesture theory. He often talked with a derisive smile of the auxiliary languages, among them Esperanto and Ido.

Back in Paris he became more and more absorbed by meditations on the imaginative creation. He read Coleridge and was interested in the distinction he made between imagination and fancy. He wondered if he himself had imagination. . . In those days I remember reading to him a German translation from a speech by Radek in which the Russian attacked *Ulysses*, at the Congress of Kharkov, as being without a social conscience. 'Well,' said Joyce, 'all the characters in my books belong to the lower middle classes, and even the working class; and they are all quite poor.' He began to read *Wuthering Heights*. 'This woman had pure imagination,' he said. 'Kipling had it too, and certainly Yeats.' His admiration for the Irish poet was very great. A recent commentator, asserting that Joyce lacked reverence for the logos in poetry, inferred that he had little regard for Yeats. I can assure the gentleman that this was not true. Joyce often recited Yeats' poems to us from memory. 'No surrealist poet can equal this for imagination,' he said. Once when Yeats spoke over the radio, he invited us to listen in with him. I read *The Vision* to him, and he was deeply absorbed by the colossal conception, only regretting that 'Yeats did not put all this into a creative work.' At Yeats' death he sent a wreath to his grave at Antibes, and his emotion, on hearing of the poet's passing, was moving to witness. He always denied too that he had said to Yeats that he was too old to be influenced by him.

Joyce had a passion for the irrational manifestations of life. Yet there was nothing in common between his attitude and that of the surrealists and psychoanalysts. Nor did his experiments have anything to do with those of the German romantics who explored the mysticism of the individual world. Joyce was an intensely conscious observer of the unconscious drama. During walks in Paris, we often talked about dreams. Sometimes I related to him my own dreams which, during the pre-war years began to take on a strangely fantastic, almost apocalyptic silhouette. He was always eager to discuss them, because they interested him as images of the nocturnal universe. He himself, he said, dreamed relatively little, but when he did, his dreams were usually related to ideas, personal and mythic, with which he was occupied in his waking hours. He was very much attracted by Dunn's theory of *serialism*, and I read to him that author's brilliant *A Theory with Time* which Joyce regarded highly. . . .

The reception given this labour of seventeen years was to be a disappointing one. Among the few whose analysis struck him as being comprehensive and conscientious were, in rough order of his appreciation, William Troy's essay in *Partisan Review*, Harry Levin's article in *New Directions*, Edmund Wilson's essays in the *New Republic*, Alfred Kazin's review in the *New York Herald-Tribune*, and Padraic Colum's piece in the *New York Times*, as well as one or two from England and Scotland. From Ireland there was little reaction, and the reception in France, on which he had counted so much, was lamentable. This state of affairs was a source of deep depression during the last year of his life, and was responsible, more than anything else, for the fact that he was completely indifferent to any suggestion for a future work. . . .

For Product Safety Concerns and Information please contact our EU representative GPSR@taylorandfrancis.com
Taylor & Francis Verlag GmbH, Kaufingerstraße 24, 80331 München, Germany

www.ingramcontent.com/pod-product-compliance
Lightning Source LLC
Chambersburg PA
CBHW071143100726
47908CB00002B/235

* 9 7 8 0 4 1 5 4 8 7 5 0 4 *